Creatures of Habit

Creatures of Habit

a novel by

Julie Baumgold

Alfred A. Knopf
New York
1993

THIS IS A BORZOI BOOK
PUBLISHED BY ALFRED A. KNOPF, INC.

This is a work of fiction. Names, characters,
places and events are the product of the author's imagination
or are used fictitiously and are not intended
to represent actual people, places, or events.

Library of Congress Cataloging-in-Publication Data
Baumgold, Julie.
Creatures of habit : a novel / by Julie Baumgold.—
1st American ed.
p. cm.
ISBN 0-679-41805-9
I. Title.
PS3552.A8453C74 1993
813'.54—dc20 92-54801 CIP

Manufactured in the United States of America
First Edition

To
Norma Baumgold and Joseph Baumgold (1907–1976)
for one life,
William Meredith and J.H.P. (1943–1985)
for the other

Creatures of Habit

Eyes

From the beginning, they called me "Little Shit." My father was "Whitey"; my mother was "Cigarette." They went to Cuba. They were social—big ball gowns and cigars going past my crib. Drivers waiting downstairs at all hours.

I was born in the Park Avenue building that my grandfather built—the one with the green marble arc above the doorway and no Jews, except us. We were full of old money, ripe to be ruined. We were all so careless. My mother threw big pieces of jewelry down on a desk at dawn, her heavy satin skirts swaying as she rumbaed down our long, long hall, dropping ashes. We slept behind masks, forgetting, trusting the lawyers and people around us to protect and save us and never let the bad life in through the door.

Finally a man walked in on Italian driving shoes with little rubber nipples and took us all. His nose, his clothes, his name were new. He slid his eyes around doorways, stared and studied, and only Cigarette knew what he was as he listened with his pinned-back ears. He said he was one of us, a distant Alexander. At first, we were even richer. Then it was all gone.

"You've got to make me whole," my father kept saying into

the telephone. He carried a small brown suitcase from room to room in the house, unfolding and refolding the papers, calculating his mistake in his head with the numbers that never betrayed him. The papers cracked and the suitcase cracked and I stood at the window holding back the silk as the Frank E. Campbell men put him, now light as a child, into the black station wagon.

We lost it all. Houses, cars, all the stuff. And, still careless, we rushed out and left the rest behind—the Chinese silk pasted to the walls, the Russian chandeliers hanging from the ceiling, the marble fireplaces stained with pale circles where the glasses had stood.

"Little Shit," my father said in Spanish the first time he used my nickname, when I was three. "You kicked that nurse in the face," he said, leaning over me in his captain's hat. The blue cigar smoke floated up over my canopy bed to where the cherubs were painted and caught in the drapery of clouds. In the middle of the night, my doctor had wrapped me in a blanket and driven me to the hospital, where they removed my appendix. The nurse spilled yellow powder meant for my scar, it got inside me and burned, so I kicked her in the face. No one ever understood.

"Mierdita, you kicked her in the face," my father said, and he seemed proud. I was Libby Alexander, his Little Shit. I was bad, always in fights, turning my back and whirling off in a roomful of enemies. Always making scenes and sending round notes of apology, like my mother, a woman who still seemed to be smoking years after she put out her last cigarette.

In the hospital, they discovered I was deaf in one ear and had unusually acute hearing in the other, and my eyes were slightly crooked. "You have special ears, Libby," Dr. Larry told me a month before he killed himself in the men's room of the planetarium, across from his office.

He was right. I can hear a conversation four tables away in a restaurant and can lip-read what I can't hear, which helps my work. So that was me—crooked eyes, freak ears, divided down the middle, meant for duplicity, meant to be the one off to the side with the notepad, the watcher, the spy. The one causing silences, interrupting the merriment as I pass. The one looking up into skies for the hurtling doomsday rock, listening with one good ear for the whoosh of disaster.

I became the Pimpernel. I wrote about the new versions of the friends who had lounged around our house. I went to small dinners where certain guests studied the air above my head all night and raised their shoulders when I went past. I went to many others where people skated across the ballrooms to me like they had marbles under their feet. I went to places where the klieg lights split the night skies and the corridor of photographers out front flanked the doors like a gantlet at a medieval tourney. "Stop where the lights are," I always say to the taxis, "stop where all the people are," where things are opening and the night is just beginning.

I married two men and both tried to choke me. Only my dogs were fooled and, curled in half-sleep, looked up at me with blind love through the white slits of their eyes. The people who worked for me caught on right away. After a week in my house, those Kansas summer girls imported to take care of Josephine would come to me with red eyes and ask for the town church. They waited for me to ask what was wrong. I never did. They put on skirts and sleeveless mall sweaters and spent their Sunday mornings, heads bent, in pews striped with sunlight, praying to be delivered from me. I didn't care. I waited outside the church and drove them back to the house.

Then, in the middle of my life, I decided to have Dr. Melville March even up my crooked eyes, to correct the wild, rather sexy falling lid on one.

"Has your eye always drooped like that?" my first husband asked me, waiting until after dinner the night we met. He pulled out the pocket flashlight he carried along with the fat trachea needle in its plastic sleeve in case anyone was going to choke at Côte Basque that night and the small tool he would run along his patients' dead feet. "It's ptosis," he said, shining the light into my tunneling pupil. "But it could be a brain tumor," and I knew I would marry this one so he could keep watch.

Dr. March cut into the skin fold, sewing up the torn muscle. My left eye, always hooded, popped right open. It looked like a glass eye. The light fell on the eyeball in a little square and made a gleaming window above the iris. Then—for the eyes work on a seesaw effect (according to the second surgeon I saw)—my right lid lowered. It fell right down and took on a dead, exhausted look. I was the mirror image of what I had been. The pain was shocking. I never took off the sunglasses I had made on Madison Avenue.

"Don't say anything, but Little Shit has been disfigured," my mother told the family. My brother said she became so excited that she lit one of her guest cigarettes, crushed the orange-rimmed butt into a plate, then wiped at it with her sleeve.

"I'm a freak," I said to Dr. March, who was afraid of the Pimpernel. He had taught his face to remain just this still at unwrappings. "I have to get up three times a night and put wet handkerchiefs on my eyes. My eyeballs are frying and I'm using the Hypotears. I use the Lacrilube."

Dr. March wiped back his hair, which had been yellow for nearly sixty years, and said nothing. His face, which he had stopped at forty-five, did not move. The surgical nurse stood at his side, on guard for overreaction.

I put my face right up to my mirror. I drew back. I tugged at the lid of the high eye without stop like the second doctor said to do. Whatever had made my eyes beautiful was gone. My vision had changed, too. I saw through a film. Every night I glued shut the eye that would not close with grease, and still the tears wet my cheeks under my sleep mask.

One night when the pain had pricked me awake, I picked up the six-volume boxed catalogue of the worldly goods and property of Lee and George Solomon. Before the IRS, the SEC, and assorted government agencies could get at him, George had disappeared. It was one of those Wall Street trader fortunes backed by family money and taken into junk. The banks had moved right in and seized everything they could, which included the apartment at 670 Park and the art. The auction house, determined to make the most it could from the forced sale, decided, once it had won the rights from its competitor, to sell everything in three days "on site" to give it the heft of accumulation of the great English estate sales. They had never done it this way before, inviting the known bidders to the site and relegating the spillover crowd to closed circuit TV in the auction house. The catalogues had come to my door by messenger, but I hadn't been in the mood to look at them before.

I picked up *Painting and Sculpture,* Volume I, and a heavy card fell out. It was a note from George Solomon asking me to go to the sales and tell him which of his friends were buying his things, or, as he put it, "pawing through my disgrace." "You should know, dear friend, I am completely innocent and will be back to prove it." I wondered how many people he had sent that note to.

Before the catalogue took the rooms apart, each "Highly Important" piece by its "Extremely Rare" counterpart, it showed the Solomon rooms assembled, full of flowers, caught in the moment when the fruit and flower fairies had tripped out and the crowd was about to burst in on waves of dinner laughter. The Solomons were fast and still rather young, and there was always the scent of danger, possible and present, around them. Their rooms pulsed. Here they sat, and here they danced at their Bal Masqué in the Style of Inigo Jones, their Evening in the Old South, their Highland Fling, all documented in hysterical detail by Diana McBride, Sally Kirk, and, I regret to say, me. George always stayed on the side, watching his wife dancing by, his eyes on his pictures, as the businessmen bent over him, talking into their hands.

And then it had stopped. Lee Solomon shut her doors to us and became private, as though she anticipated the injury to come. She was said to have taken on the tan and sandy look of old money, as if she had spent the last forty summers barefoot on Fishers Island. Gradually the brown had reentered her hair.

I missed George, the way he would cup me to him and lead me and a conga line of billionaires along the halls, telling us the same stories full of titles suffering to possess and horrid deaths that dealers, drawing velvet curtains in back rooms of galleries all over Europe, had once told him. He loved to cruise with the other rich guys in tow and make their jaws drop—which was hard, because each had imagination when it came to spending. Midway through the tour George would always stop at one tiny bathroom and crack open the door on his *Dante's Dream.* "Have you ever seen anything like this?" he'd say, laying a large buffed nail on either side of the frame and bringing his face to it, and in the rich hum of approval he'd smile out at me.

As I turned the thick pages and thought of the fugitive Solomons, I began to feel sleepy.

In the morning, Carter called and said he expected me back for the Solomon auction. The Pimpernel was to jump from its usual position on page 10 and fill an inside page with pictures. I went to my evening closet as though it still mattered what I wore. I decided to go out for an eye patch and stop at the new coffee bean place.

"Which is the closest to French coffee?" I asked the young man polishing the perfect glass jars.

"What do you mean by 'French' coffee?" he said, as though the word 'French' hurt his tongue, and he continued polishing, pumping up and down on his toes, still not turning to look at me. It was going to be one of those encounters. I felt the rage hormones starting to mount and focused on the price chart as a mantra to calm myself. I could either answer or leave. La Minita Costa Rica, Arabian Mocha Mattari, Ethiopia Longberry Harrar, Apricot Decaf. Yes, I could breathe again.

As I bought half a pound of the Beowulf Blend, a Bentley with smoked windows pulled up and the driver ran in. "Please, I'm in a big hurry. Where's the Jamaica Blue Mountain?" he said, staring at the empty glass jar in the Rarities section. It was sold out at $24.99 a pound. "I have to have it. Don't you have some in the back? They must have their coffee."

Just then, I saw a short gray-flannel leg emerge from the car, and, in the space between one polished loafer and the cashmere calf, an electronic ankle cuff, the kind the feds use to keep track for house arrest. I saw a flapping vicuna coat and felt the breeze from the door.

"Is there a problem, Harry?" George Solomon said. "Oh, Libby. Well, there you are."

"I got your note with the—"

"The catalogues came out well, didn't they? I hope you're going for me. No, don't worry, it will all be straightened out. Lee's in the car. Why don't you come say hello? We're going away."

"But can you?" I looked down, but George pretended not to understand.

Lee sat there hugging a small case in her lap, dressed all in gray.

"I can't believe you did this, George, for some coffee. I mean, the Pimpernel! What next?"

"Don't worry. I won't write anything. I wish you both luck."

"Now, listen, if that Blue Mountain comes in, we're at The Greenbrier under the name 'Ezra Sheets.' Send us ten pounds," and George put his finger to his lips and Lee blew me a tiny sour kiss and fluffed her thick hair as the car slid from the curb into the traffic of Lexington Avenue. I wondered how he could disconnect himself, the radius of his anklet. The Greenbrier was the perfect place for them to hide in their ruin—one of those old white resorts that swallow their guests and revive and celebrate a vanished way of life.

At home, I tried the eye patch, then lighter dark glasses. Disobeying Dr. March, I put on mascara, though every lash hurt to the root.

"Libby, you must go to another doctor," a friend told me on the phone from Texas. "I will find you a name. We're flying in for the auction." I was ashamed to tell her I had already seen another doctor. I said I would see her there.

II

The Study of Dinosaurs

It was a warm night, so I decided to walk down Park Avenue. Ahead of me people I knew kept popping from buildings, hugging their catalogues and walking in the same direction, rushing, a bit hectic, to celebrate the new downfall.

I saw the Dells coming out of 790 followed by their personal specter. For a moment Jimmy looked undecided, as though he had not yet forgiven me, but then he cocked his finger and blew me away, pursing his sensual little bud mouth, and I knew that was the end of that episode.

"We haven't seen you in so long," Blanca said. She paused, and the bodyguard paused, shifted his shoulders, and hovered over us all like an umbrella.

"You're a bad girl," Jimmy said.

"We're just back from Telluride. Jim bought the Lodge. We'll fly you out whenever you want," Blanca said, and they were off past me, having imparted their news bit, their long legs flashing out in stride, their eyes ahead on the clot of photographers who were already rushing back to them.

In front of 670, drivers were opening the doors to so many station wagons, Jeeps, and Range Rovers, it looked like a night-

club in the Veldt. The photographers were bobbing desperately on the street, and a quiet neighborhood crowd watched
the arrivals as they scampered in like the new downtown crimi-
nals, uneasy now because buying was just beginning to be considered a sin. The women's heads were bowed into the long
flings that marked the change in season; the men moved off to
the side, heads lowered and bent, as if they were scarcely attached to their wives. But certain women stopped and held in
place. They assumed an attitude, an expression and shiny animation that lit their bodies before the strobes could. Sometimes, I must say, the sight of me had exactly that same effect.
The photographers began clicking and whirring—that sound
of fifty shutters tripping which was so much a part of my life
that, after a while, as if they were crickets in the country, I
ceased to see or hear them.

Behind my glasses, sunk in my new dimmed universe, I felt
almost invisible. Without explanation of my absence, I had
gotten down Park Avenue with only a few waves. The auction
had drawn people back into town from the West and from
Europe, wherever they had gone to hide now that things had
really changed. Among the photographers I saw my friend Sal.
I knew he had to be upstairs to photograph the clothes. I went
over to him and he raised his camera, then put it down.

"They won't let me up," he said.

"Did you tell them who you were with?" I took him to the
women at a desk set up in the lobby and went to the oldest one.

"If Mr. Taglio doesn't get in, you can tell them upstairs the
Pimpernel is going home right now." She was already picking up
the phone.

Chica Starck was in the elevator. "I hear they put Lee's jewels
in cases in the kitchen. Why didn't she just take them?" she said
into the air, and then, looking right into my glasses, she began,
"Mierdita! What happened to you?" and her peppy voice,
which always sounded like she was eating something delicious,
fell. She had one of those accents that grew stronger with each
year spent outside her native country, and the silvery look of

those dark women who make themselves very blond and thereby, somewhat jarringly, keep the characteristics of each.

"John said he saw you up at your school," I said quickly. "He says the kids love you."

"Well, they really do. It's my Spanish. Sam drives me up Bruckner Boulevard every other week now," she said, stroking above her eyelid. "What's wrong with your eyes?"

I could feel the general shifting of bodies as everyone in the mahogany box studied my glasses. Escalators are wonderful social mechanisms, because you can see people or miss them if you choose; but here I was trapped in an elevator of physically corrected people with my mistake. Behind me gleamed the shaved down teeth in their sleeves of porcelain; the high, motionless hair of impossible colors. The faces were devoid of age but not young, like wet beige kid gloves someone has blown into; the body folds were sucked away, strictured and hidden by rich clothes; the odors were cloaked in crushed flowers. I was surrounded by all the replaced parts of bionic New York in their black night clothes.

"Who did it, then?" Chica whispered, finally, as the elevator slowed. It was very quiet, with that special anticipatory elevator silence.

"I have pinkeye," I said. "I really shouldn't be here, it's so contagious—goes right through the air," and everyone started moving back and away, hoisting their catalogues as shields.

In the entrance hall right above the little desk a notice said, "WARNING: U.S. GOVERNMENT SEIZURE. This property has been seized for nonpayment of Internal Revenue taxes due from Saul G. Solomon by virtue of levy issued by the District Director of the Internal Revenue Service," and I knew that of all the things in it, George would probably be most injured by the retrieval of his long lost first name.

"Paddles! Really, what fun!" said a woman I didn't know.

"You're Mrs. Alexander. Well, we don't need any identification from you," said the auction girl. "We're sorry you couldn't come to the viewings with our curators." She handed me a guest list, just like this was a party.

"But I reserved from Tokyo," said a deep voice behind me.

The doors to the apartment were open: first the ornamental iron gate, then the vault door coated by overlapping faux finishes of marble-framed onyx and fake burled wood. I patted one of George's stone sphinxes alongside the registration table.

I usually like to come early when the rooms are cold and watch them fill, but already there was a rush of happy noise, clinking silver trays of champagne. Almost everything in the drawing room, the sitting room, and the libraries had been left as it was, as though Lee and George had just rushed from the room to greet a new guest, except that everything was tagged with fresh yellow, red, and green Day-Glo circles, and the dining room and ballroom were filled with chairs and auction boards and those wired holes where the more important paintings had been taken down. Everyone was walking and cruising, nodding and picking things up, looking at the colored tags and turning them over and fanning, fanning with their red plastic paddles as the guards watched. I looked around and saw people the Solomons had invited to their children's parties, friends who had copied Lee's tablescapes with their forests of silver, those who had hopped the world on George's plane.

I looked from floor to ceiling. The Solomons had spent their money trying to imitate one of those European apartments where when you hit the tapestries clouds of dust rise into the dense air, where the silks on the chairs have rotted to threads so that you can weave your fingers in and out in moments of boredom, where young girls in high heels trip on the Aubusson, which is thin as a piece of linen. The eyes of the ancestors on the wall are full of rebuke, and everyone who works for you knows too much about you and your family.

In the main hall, Sylvia Mendes stood staring in rapture, chin raised before a small picture of a floating Ophelia from George's pre-Raphaelite collection. "Where have you been? There's no paper without the Pimpernel," she said.

Long ago, Sylvia had been my great-uncle Simon's teacher at the Arthur Murray Dance Studio. Then, for years, she was his dancing partner. They had danced through the big white-restricted mountain ballrooms—two forbidden exotics, the Jew and the light lady of color—while my elegant aunt, who looked like Ava Gardner but danced like a stick, sat holding their mambo trophies. Who knows how they got in. Sylvia has forgotten those days, so no one can ask.

"I remember Lee walking me through here years ago. Then she stopped inviting me. I'm going to buy the boule chest there," she said, pointing, as Olivia and John Pinza came in, still with their photographers' smiles on their faces. "I can't think why *they're* here. He hasn't paid his maintenance in six months. He has to take down his own garbage. They're squatters."

Gayle Pope was in the room. Sylvia and others watched as she walked. The objects she studied were noticed, for she was famous for her restraint. I drifted along behind her and Bill. Their entrance was marked by a slight pulling back as they moved in the distancing vapor of power. They still had not seen me, and I held back to watch them, for they behaved differently when they knew I was there. It was always a wary circling: we were partly friends, partly each other's prey. I was not quite safe, nor were they, and we both knew it.

Gayle saw her friend Olivia, who imitated all she did. They were both dark and finely drawn, only Olivia was tiny—she looked like Gayle seen at the end of a long hall. They kissed and pulled back, still holding hands with their arms outstretched in a seesaw of admiration in front of George's Venetian secretary, which had drawn its own crowd. Chica joined them with Blanca Dell, and for a moment we all stopped, we breathed in and digested. It was so rich, even for New York. Then everyone shook themselves and seemed to recover. They rushed at each other with flutters and cries, as if their own magnificence had given them energy. The photographers closed in, snapping. I saw Gayle and Blanca, taller than the others, preening and swaying.

They were like the showgirls I remembered from my child-hood in Paris and Vegas. It was always the showgirls versus the dancers. The showgirls were the really tall ones who used to come out last, making their entrances after the quick-bare danc-ers had finished, and each girl was fabulous in a different way—tiers of tulle and feathers and flowers and rigged ships on their heads, and each was made to loom even larger with a headdress or panniers—and they would parade around so stiffly, with their arms out like penguins, with such remote expressions you would almost not notice they were bare-breasted.

"Blanca, honeychile, looking good," said Don Stock, crouched and shooting her from every angle.

No one missing but the Solomons, I thought, looking over at the Pinzas, the Popes, and now the Dells standing around George's high-Italian micro-mosaic table, all looking down and almost joined as though it were a seance. Seen through my green glasses the women were like Nereids; their ballerina arms, each with a tiny popping muscle, waved in a chain. They bent forward to stare down into the pietra dura and whisper. They often grouped themselves thus, especially when there were photogra-phers around. At about their ears stood their husbands, talking business, no longer quite so caught up in their new lives of eating risotto till two a.m. at a table of smoking ballet dancers, wearily smoothing their new hair as they picked up the check.

I saw an old actress moving forward, blindly seeking the television lights, like a sea turtle crawling to deposit its eggs in the hot sand. Her red hair curved in two lacquered wisps over her wig. A quasi security man supported the pink brocade of her elbow, piloting her around so that everyone would rush over to or away from her, the young ones pretending she had not seen or would not know them. Without looking, she pushed me aside, shoving forward into the heat of the exploding glare.

It was an unusual division. In this large front room were all my people swiveling and halting to be photographed. And then in the dining room, over a threshold as thick as it was invisible, was a quiet roomful of the others, tall people unknown to me and those in the front rooms. I thought of them as trees in a forest I could never enter—these people of the Zoo, Presbyterian Hospital, the old Museum, and settlement houses, who lived in back apartments on Park Avenue with kitchens and bathrooms that had never been changed in forty years and small dim squares of inherited landscapes on the walls so nondescript that it was hard to imagine that anyone ever loved them enough to buy them. They hired waitresses in black uniforms to pass trays of crackers with a square of cheese, emerging from pantries thickly repainted peach. They stood straight and not young in their own cloaked circles, radiating disapproval in their wacky academic versions of dressing up, looking out at the others being photographed, their small eyes blinking behind thin rims at the foreign display. They did not know the Solomons. They were from the Victorian Society and had come for the pre-Raphaelites. It was their time now; their values, like stinginess, had won. Among them were the curators and museum trustees, who watched over those with the old treasures but crossed the threshold to charm the money in the front room.

The only one I knew was Ames Reed, who, of course, was holding a drink. As his wife once told me, "Ames needs a drink to walk into a room. *Any* room—the bathroom, a closet." When he traveled, his "roadie" went with him, sloshing away on the floor of the car. At least it made him pleasant. Ames saw me and came out and chose to ignore my glasses.

"George always liked these very dark and violent pictures," he said. "Couldn't get enough of those arrows piercing the flesh and suffering women. All the good stuff is what his parents bought in the fifties. It's a schizophrenic collection."

I bent over a small table and, as I wrote this down, stared into the dark, furious face of George Solomon resting on a ski pole inside a Fabergé frame. Next to it were tall sheaves of simple field wheat perfectly lined up, the stalks tightly tied with austere raffia knots, as though a monk with lots of time had bound them. They had replaced the usual tangle of forced roses and lushly exploding peonies angrily jammed into silver bowls where, smashed against each other, they quickly and expensively died.

I saw Sandy Fisher coming towards me. We looked at each other critically as old friends do.

"Take them off. You look blind," he said.

"All right—come in here." I pulled him into a bathroom by his wet hands. "That was *Dante's Dream,*" I said, pointing to a nail, and raised my glasses and watched his face.

"I see. All right, put them back on."

It was warm in there, and Sandy is a very large fellow. He began opening the cabinets above the sink.

"Look, everything English. Penhaglion, Floris . . . she's replaced every single thing with an English equivalent. That's Lee—no Crest for her. And by the way, don't you think," he said, sitting down on the top of the toilet, "it's too festive here—like running into Sotheby's to look at pictures on a rainy weekend? Am I taking you home?"

Sandy takes me places and returns me home, though he usually goes back if the party is good. He reports to me. He sees and hears almost as well as I do. Sandy believes that things are more likely to go wrong at the last moment, with no explanation, and that it always pays to have rich friends. He has a high, strange laugh, bordering on hysteria, which makes people turn around angrily at movie screenings. I first heard it at Joe Allen's in Los Angeles the summer when my father and his mother were dying, and we each ran away, met, and immediately appreciated the other's weakness of character. That summer we had brandy contests, though he was three times my weight. However, a fellow named Campbell, who had nothing imminent to forget, always outdrank us both.

Outside the door we heard laughter, the kind that still makes me open the door. A woman in a black suit passed and looked at me. I had listed her name once. She had her little toot of fame. She was mine.

I began to see people imprinted with donuts of vermilion lip gloss, which meant they had been kissed by Diana McBride. Now I was nervous. If Diana was here, Sally Kirk was, too. And there they were—Sally and her seeing-eye, Baron Gray, who stared at my glasses as though he could see through them.

"Who's that?" said Sally, looking behind me and tugging his sleeve. Sally never knows, because she can't see. But people go right up to Sally, within inches. Down, down they bend. She puts out a thin, dry hand and touches their clothing, which is why her column is full of descriptions like "nubby tweed." Sally was a red until about ten years ago, when suddenly she appeared at a party in evening clothes. She writes above the table with a small, thin pen. Diana is a lap writer. I know I have to pay attention whenever I see her across the room, head bent, curls bobbing. No one sits down to dinner till Diana arrives.

Diana, Sally, and me. We're the three Furies stirring the broth. We pass the all-seeing eye among us. We know the secrets. We are the chroniclers, the creators. These people don't exist in the public mind till we quote them, write their names, make them characters, and bring them on our stage as players in our regular casts. We raise them. We drop them. We make them interesting. But they have a way of sneaking around corners and working things out for themselves, of re-entering the play in new designs and configurations, of making their own deals. They are our creatures, but they are often sneaky.

We deal with a very small group, in the low hundreds. The rooms that open to us are those of the people who want to be written about. Sometimes they have no pasts at all. They come to us sucked clean of previous life, as if they had just been pulled from an autoclave, with all living tissue and marrow drawn from them, and only their sudden money left.

For me now it's like studying dinosaurs. No one cares. Why start an education learning the names of creatures who are dead and not coming back? They are over—*finito,* gone from the earth. But that's what I do—pry up these old bones and classify them. I know their territory, their enemies, where they go when the sun sets, and just which ones among them will survive when the earth moves and swallows them, too. It will be soon.

I know the habits of these little tyrant kings and their big, thin women, careening together, still buying more clothes and more art, tearing up their houses and ripping out forests and hills, rising and falling and bobbing back from places with storms of butterflies and elephants on the road and peasants squatting and looking up at them as though they mean something. We give them that, too—Diana, Sally, and I. We validate them.

I know that we are living in the last days, that it's all ending, and that we, their scribes, are also becoming extinct. Diana has already begun to write about movie stars and the royals. With no more displays, there is no one for the Pimpernel to scold. I have written myself out of their rooms, out of existence. Now everyone is disappearing, imitating the old tired Christians, hiding and selling their pictures to the new blood. They die out and I track their jewels, first in the catalogues, and then at a party on someone brand-new, for there are still, even now, a few new fools to leap out and dance with the others.

Here's this woman, it's the second time I've seen her. Chanel suit, good shoes, nice jewels. I don't ask her name.

"I read every word you write," she whispers.

They all do, and they call when their placement drops on my list. They call Carter, my editor. They send their thick cards, flowers, and more if I allow them. They whisper other people's secrets to me in raspy voices at eight in the morning. They get in great flaps and walk by me looking at the wall. They pretend to love me, to lay out their lives on the dinner table like a rich rug, but mostly they put themselves in front of me and smile and try to think of something to say that I can quote. They linger and wait for the splendor of themselves to occur. Sometimes, even after twenty years, it still does. Sometimes I have nights when the candidate analyzes his campaign, the comedian tells stories, the anchor leaves early to do the news he has just told us, the actor arrives late after his play, the writer writes into the note card in his palm as the harpist and flutist play and we stare into a van Gogh, its fields streaked with blood. The hands of the host hover over his Sumerian artifacts, showing them to a man who has walked on the moon, so that I wake at three a.m. with all this clashing and replaying in my brain as one rich conversation . . . and that is why I do what I do, to be there for the rare nights like that—and, of course, for the money.

In the days of my greatest power, before Carter moved me back to page 10, they analyzed me and parsed the text. They knew my methods—how I would lead up to things by mentioning an old incident two days before revealing a new scandal. The more I insulted them, the more they ran after me, because at least I had included them. It was hard then to have a life outside that power. But I tired; then Carter tired. The Pimpernel grew old, suffered, understood, and grew kind. I began not writing things. I was moved to page 10. The picture at the top of my column had frozen years ago, as had the headshots we used, which pleased my people because they all looked ten years younger. I had lived through two groups aging into the old guard, two social generations, and was now faced with their heirs, movie star children, and people so very junior I had no idea who they were. There were always new people coming from elsewhere whose houses did not fit them yet. When they spoke to one another, it was often with pauses, considering their words. At least most of the titles, the "vons" and "zus," had left, and I no longer had to hear *"Aspetta,* Libby" when I wanted to go home. All the princes had gone.

"The whole thing is so sad," said a voice behind me and I turned to see Holly Whitney, former head of the Victorian Society, the one woman in New York for whose arrival any hostess would hippety-hop over double-quick. "Lee brought so much to our board. I don't know why I let Ames bring me tonight. No, just wait," she said, waving him back. "I find this very, very sad," she said in a voice that had spent many years breathing silvery air.

"They're starting the auction now, Mrs. Whitney," said a maid, for all the older society servants, of course, knew her.

"I know they are all right," I whispered, bending to her.

"People take such pleasure in these things," she said, and her light eyes, still shocking in their effect, filled and dimmed.

Boots Simpson was cruising the hall, wrapped in some kind of a flapping Chinese robe. "I hope you're coming to my dinner," she said, and I nodded, now remembering a strange call about Tibet from her secretary a month before.

Against the wall, bracketing the Chanel woman, were a thin, watery-gray couple who did public relations and always managed to be at impossible places like this. Adele and Arthur Buttenwisen were ignored, seated vilely, and yet always around, palely loitering, clinging to the walls, whipping smartly forth with their damp hands outstretched whenever they saw a byline. "Libby, I'd like you to meet Barbara—" but I pretended not to hear and sailed on.

"You must come Tuesday. We placed you with . . ." a man said, interrupting what I was saying to Sandy. But of course I was a nonperson, a worker approachable by all, expected to stop talking when they parked their tall bodies in front of me. It was almost like being famous, the way they felt they could claim me at any time.

"That woman is the Pimpernel," someone said, as I nodded to Dr. March.

"They don't have to be *so* dark," he whispered.

Now there was a great movement through the rooms and depositing of glasses. The chateau floors creaked and groaned with age. Mixed with his parents' Impressionists were George's own knights with spurting wounds and women with their white hands bound or pressed to waxen foreheads in fairytale despair.

I saw a young boy with a blond crew cut slithering around the corner, talking into a microcassette and writing in a black notebook. He was quite tall, and his clothes showed effort and calculation. I felt some sense of money strain about him, as though all his funds had gone into this one costume—the shoes too new, the blazer buttons replaced on an old jacket, the shirt on its first wearing. He walked on the balls of his feet with his back very stiff, the notebook raised, and his ass arched out as though he were being observed from the rear. As we passed Lee's bedroom, I saw Blanca and Gayle sitting on Lee's convent-worked sheets, whispering. They waved, but vaguely, as though they were not quite there participating. They wiggled their fingers, but none would break the circle to come over as they would have done just a few months ago.

"Mr. Yatsuro, this is the famous Mrs. Alexander," said a man I had seen somewhere before.

"Ah, the Scarlet Pimpernel," Yatsuro said, moving his group forward like a centipede. "They seek her here, they seek her there . . ."

We passed the kitchen and I stopped in. Here, for the first time, I felt the true dismantling of the great house. In the triple pantry, the cabinets had been left open. Dishes from the top shelves had been put out on the counters in stacks. Every surface was covered and heaped and tagged. And I saw in them all the parties that had been and never would be again, that whole era of flying in chefs and salsa groups. The amounts were shocking even for the typical abundance of the great house: whole services for fifty, glasses that pinged forlornly to the touch; immense stacks of folded linen, from handkerchief-thin lunch napkins to dinner sets trimmed with lace; a row of mahogany dining carts. The silver vault stood open, filled with huge chests and shelves of unwrapped plate, all numbered; six antique silver grape shears imprinted with grapes; silver bowls and trays and serving pieces—a compulsive overstocking that could be seen as luxury or as terrible insecurity. In one corner I saw Saul's burled wood humidor and looked up the estimate.

"Did he die of natural causes?" the woman behind us said.

"If you consider putting a lawn chair in your garage and leaving the motor running 'natural causes,'" said the man. I started to laugh. The woman thought I was laughing at her and looked even more tentative.

"They're starting. I saved seats," Sandy said, hurrying along, as waiters passed, each carrying a ballroom chair like a token sacrifice to the auction god. I looked around, and as far as I could see, Holly Whitney was not there.

The Red Rush

The art dealer was leaning against a pillar in the ballroom, studying the TV press pool. They had just been let in and were dragging their cables and cameras, hooking their metal boom boxes to wires now falling from Lee's silver ceiling. We watched as a camera box hit the wall and a chunk of yellow glaze went flying.

"Intrusive bastards," he said. "Always there like little doggies. Er . . . not you, Libby—not you, of course." But we were all hoping that this evening's sale would bring, if not the most expensive painting ever sold at auction, at least some glimmer of the ebullience of the last decade, which had been so good for his business and for mine. The dealer was probably the last of the long-necked, heather-haired English picture peddlers still fluting and barking all over the city.

"Some dreadful stuff," he said, jabbing his long finger into his catalogue. "We wait for the big one." He meant Renoir's *Au Moulin de la Cocotte,* which had its own special catalogue and was expected to break records. "Little doggies," he said again. The dealer had those beach-club eyes. They flicked up and studied the intruders. I knew he was always especially friendly to those he held in contempt and would hate if he had the energy.

A woman in crimson was instructing the crews not to turn their cameras on anybody who was bidding in the audience. She wagged her finger at them.

"Libby, how about giving up your seat, babe?" one of the TV guys called. "Come back here and help us with some of the names."

As I started back, a number of Japanese men came down the center aisle. Their wives wore modest silk dresses with puffs at the shoulders and carried the rope handles of the shiny shopping bags favored along Madison Avenue. Many of them held catalogues, including the special hardcover one entirely devoted to Lot 23, the *Moulin.*

A conversion board had been hung from the ceiling and showed the time, and now the room began to fill with men with that combed-back, gelled hair ending in wings of defiant curls on the nape and colored silk pocket squares foaming from their blazers. Every once in a while they would pit-pat smooth, smooth their shiny hair and look over at their blondes whose throats were circled with white, marble-sized pearls that failed to turn them into ladies. The auction columnist for the *Times* asked one of the Japanese men where he was going to sit and placed him herself, where she could watch him during the bidding.

"Good evening, ladies and gentlemen," said Ronald Marsden, introducing himself. "We are pleased to offer for your competition this evening the collection of Mr. and Mrs. S. George Solomon, Lots 1 to 34, the terms of purchase of which are subject to the rules. I call your attention to the buyer's premium. Since this is a forced sale, we are acting as the receiver for the courts," he said, in that hollow voice which gave immediate importance to everything he said.

A small Courbet of a laughing peasant woman leaning on her elbow was hoisted onto the easel. "I have three hundred and fifty thousand," said Marsden, "in the rear . . . The bid's up front at five hundred thousand. Five twenty-five way on the left . . ." and the bids went bouncing from here to the telephone to the dining room. Half the first row was roped off, but there was no place like the confessional booths upstairs at Sotheby's to hide the high bidders. There was silence, and all had entered that worshipful pose, heads tilted back, nostrils up. A girl stood guard over the rope, twisting in on one ankle as she whispered into a portable phone.

A few more Japanese men came in and she lowered the rope, for there was this new social presence. Perhaps the time had come for me to know them. Now they stood apart, though still near each other, almost inviting our approach. They were here, swinging their little black shoes out of long dark cars on Fifth Avenue, sitting downstairs at the Metropolitan Club awaiting our attempts. I thought of going over, but what could I say? Where could I begin, and where would it lead? And so, as usual, I sat and watched as they bobbed and bowed to each other, standing in pools of silence, until the business cards were passed.

Facing us was a lineup of society blondes in black lace, the otherwise unemployable daughters with art degrees whose fathers had picked up the phone to get them these jobs. They stood, each attached to a phone, into which they were murmuring numbers. Among them were the bid spotters, the old black men who had been with the house since the forties and could detect a bid in the faintest twitch, but now were being replaced by these blondes on the phone. Since this was such a big night, there was also a long second-row lineup of the curators in black tie.

Hands, many holding pens as if they were talismans, were shooting up.

"Seven hundred fifty thousand," said Marsden into the hush, "right front."

A man snapped his raised fingers to get attention, and made the flat hand signal to cut his bid in half. All was quiet except for the sound of the thick pages turning and the snicking of the numbers on the conversion board, clicking into yen and deutschemarks and francs and lire. There was a Vlaminck, a Utrillo, a Degas that began at two million and went to four and a half in a minute. I think the Popes got the Lautrec right from the wall.

"There's still plenty of money around," said John Pinza to Howard Goldenson, the bankruptcy lawyer, one of the recent fortunes built on this new industry of ruin. Now it was time for the *Moulin*.

"Well, I guess I'll be off," said Ames, and everyone laughed, and now there was a rustling tension in the press part and a hoisting of equipment, all of which seemed pointed right at the forbidden audience.

"Lot Number 23, *Au Moulin de la Cocotte,*" said Marsden, and it was the first time that night he had given the painting's title. "Five million to start . . . six, seven, eight . . . I have twenty-five—twenty-six—twenty-seven—twenty-eight—thirty on the phone. Thirty-one million dollars." Marsden only says "dollars" when he wants to show real respect for the sum. One of the dinner jackets who was on the phone raised his hand at forty million. Then it went to one of the blond girls on Marsden's left. It was a war between the blond man and the blond girl, each with his telephone socked to his ear as though it were sewn.

There was a stir in the back of the room and a shifting as two giant men in dark suits rushed the room. They locked arms as though peril were imminent, until they finally deposited the bodies they propelled in the front row. As their arms parted and the wedge broke open, I could see in the center the tops of two heads, one large, the other the fire color a blond gets in a setting tropical sun. It was like a twister zipping through a field; everything bent back and stopped, and then there was a rustling and shaking and craning that began as everyone said, "Who's that?"

"Who is it?" I asked John Pinza, who had stood up to see as the two figures were sitting down. None of us had ever seen a power rush in a private home, though guards were the new family retainers—functioning as nannies, teachers, hired friends, and a guarantee there would always be someone to talk to. Still, the Dells had left their man in the lobby; the ex-secretary's man stood by the door, a hired reminder of his past.

"Do I hear forty-three?" said Marsden, who seemed annoyed at having to repeat himself.

"No idea," said Pinza.

As soon as the man sat down he must have gestured, for now Marsden, looking right at him and smiling, said, "Forty-four million."

At forty-five million applause broke out. Then the hush descended. "Forty-five—say six," said Marsden. The blond man on the phone nodded. He raised his hand at forty-eight. Fifty-one. The cameras were focusing, ready for a record bid. There was a long pause as the girl had it. "Will you say sixty-six?" said Marsden in that charming way he has. At seventy-one million, the man on the phone waved his hand to signal "no more." I could not see the man up front. The girl on the phone was very young, with a barrette in her streaked pageboy and the small, old pinky-yellow pearls her father had given to her as a young girl, and I wondered if her life would be changed by bidding for the second-most-expensive painting ever sold at auction.

"Seventy-one million, down it goes" said Marsden, waiting for the man in the front, and then it was sold to the telephone and the buzz started. Disappointed, a contender, in some way a failure. Before they took it down, I looked at the figures dancing in the garden of a neighborhood dance hall on a summer evening with lanterns in the trees and straw hats, red drinks on the tables, red ribbons in the hair, the gaunt, pretty men and the Renoir girls so alike.

The joy of the party night made me think of the old times of this room, once mirrored and silvery with stars on the ceiling, as I had seen it in a history of great New York rooms, when it belonged to the Rysdales, before the Merdills and then the Solomons, who had covered it in canary damask with huge "tears-of-the-Irish" stones around the edge, which Lee copied from a duke's house. Here were other dancers, the whirling silvery ghosts of past nights, a stamping cajun band for Midnight in New Orleans, their last ball. But the only ghosts were from the far-distant past, for all of George's friends were here, their hearts starting to rev ten lots before the number they were chasing. Auctions were the perfect competitive sport for them. To bid against another rich man and win was better than standing around in hip waders in Alaskan water. A whole climate had been created where no one wrote his final price in the margins anymore but went with the unstoppable need, so that Brancusi's *The Kiss,* a cracked rotted egg locked in a glass dome because of its vile smell, went for over $38,000 last year. Here the bidder had only to shrug or scratch a nose or merely look at one of those old men and the number would surge from his eyes. He'd gotten it! It was his. It used to be one of the seven Rembrandts in a Havemeyer dining room, and now it was his!

"Libby, I think I *do* know that man," John Pinza said to me. "I think it's Jack Kahn."

"No it's not," the man next to him said. "I know him well."

"Who's Kahn?" I asked John.

"He's from Canada. He started Conogenex, just sold it. He was George's partner on some kind of deal."

"I never saw him here."

"He's not Kahn," said the other man.

The guards had moved to one side but were still scanning. I signaled to one of the phone girls and asked who the man up front was.

"We're—I—can't say," she stammered, as the mother-superior type who had lectured the press before beckoned, and she vanished back into her telephone.

"He's buying," someone said. If Kahn or whoever he was wanted to become instantly known in New York, he had only to appear like this and nod a few times. Next to him the woman had turned to study the crowd that was watching her, but I could not quite see her yet.

Again there was stretching and even a bit of laughter, for they had just put up on the easel one of the smallest paintings I had ever seen. After the huge Landseer horse, it was like a joke, and a few more people laughed, but I didn't.

"That's our Renoir!" I said out loud, though I didn't mean to. The Pinzas turned around. Sandy nudged me. But it was. There, inside the same four-inch-thick frame, was the six-by-six-inch picture of a little house and two weeping willow trees. Even across the room it glowed—the willows all pink and green, with flames of orange fire and the tiny luminous house and path. I knew the oversized "R" in the corner. It was our painting, which my great-aunt Harriet had stolen years ago, supposedly to sell in her gallery in Paris. She told Cigarette she had sold it for $25,000, but the check had bounced. Cigarette still called her every few months and hissed at her about family. When had the Solomons gotten it? And why?—for it was much too unimportant for them.

"Say something," Sandy said, but the bidding had started, and I was actually shy. "I have an opening bid of fifty thousand," Marsden said. "Sixty, seventy, eighty thousand." I raised my hand.

"What are you doing? Oh, God, you don't get in at the beginning!"

"One hundred thousand . . . in the rear . . . one hundred and ten . . . one twenty. . . . Do I hear one thirty?" Marsden said, smiling at me.

"One fifty," said a man's voice.

"One hundred sixty thousand." I nodded.

"Two hundred," said Marsden finally. "Fair warning," and he picked up his little ivory hammer.

I saw a blur of faces looking. Everyone knew I had no money. It was one of the things assumed about me, in the way everyone assumed the Pinzas would follow the Popes. It upset their expectations to see me be a participant, even on so tiny a scale. I raised my hand high.

"Two ten in the rear." My heart was hurting and banging. Sandy told me later how pale I had grown. I nodded. Marsden and I were dancing, whirling through the room alone, pressed together. A kind of red rush had taken over, and I saw and heard only the numbers, which meant nothing. I felt a cold heat, something like a killer rage or the flight-alarm response of a baby about to be dropped. It was the unstoppable panic of one foot over the edge of an empty elevator shaft.

"Two hundred and twenty five." I nodded. "Fair warning," said Marsden to the man.

"All done," Marsden said, banging the gavel.

It was not the first time I had leaped off the edge, as my apartment testified. I had Truman Capote's snake, Diana Vreeland's chandelier, and Marlene Dietrich's chair from the movie *A Foreign Affair*—made with its legs cut down to display hers.

"You got it!" Sandy said, and when I hugged myself my hands were wet and cold. I felt none of the joy that begins with lust for the thing that is beautiful or underpriced. I felt only dread. I knew I was trying to buy back my lost life. But it was all confused. This was no revenge. I only knew I had to get it. It felt like my last chance.

"Didn't you tell me once it was a fake?" said Sandy, who always saw and said the worst.

"Not at all," I said, as Eddie, one of the spotters, brought the paper for me to sign.

"Congratulations," said the Pinzas.

"It's good to see you, Miss Libby—after so long," Eddie said, and I knew he thought I was rich again.

"Can you hold it steadier?" I said to him, but it was my own knee banging up against the clipboard. Eddie had known me since Cigarette wheeled the giant Silver Cross into Parke Bernet in the days when a minor Degas was six thousand dollars. Cigarette rocked me with one hand and kept raising the other. Often she forgot and just left her finger in the air as she finished whispering to a friend. "Once you have it, you always forget what something cost," she told me one night, wiping off her makeup with a wet towel and flinging it on the floor. That was one of her lies, like "Buy it—you will always find a place for it."

She would look at a wall, hurl herself at it, hammer a nail into the eighteenth-century paneling, decide it was wrong, and try again . . . and then I'd find her at midnight hammering with the heel of her evening slipper and trying to fix the holes with a brown eyebrow pencil. Cigarette never believed in measuring or planning, and all the wrecks were left behind, the damage, and the forty-year-old children with Band-Aids still on their fingernails.

Now one of the old men was pointing to the Rossetti on the wall: *Veronica Veronese,* estimated at two to three million—a girl in a reverie in a green velvet dress. It was the last painting George had shown me.

"This is a beauty," said Sandy, but I was still dazed. I'd have to sell all my jewelry.

"Danny Gates is here! On the staircase, on a phone. He's here himself. I thought he always sent Chris."

A few other people had spotted Gates and were watching. Some looked because he was the only handsome man in these rooms who wasn't carrying a tray, some because he was with two beauties. Others, who knew who he was, studied him as the ultimate rarity, the almost-never-seen famous face, the absent presence. For a while I think Gates had known how his elusiveness worked for him, and then he forgot about it, because by that time he was truly hard to find. He sat on the steps between his two models, his knees up, the phone against his dark face, and I felt the same pain I had when I bought the painting. He was one of the few here who didn't care if I noticed him or wrote his name on any list. He would never make any attempt to pass before me and have his presence recorded. He had built his whole empire on pretension, and yet he had none himself. I looked and he saw me looking, and my bad heart flopped right across the room to him and sat at his feet with the models as he bid into the phone.

"He asked me to get him all the Rossetti books last week," Sandy said, which I knew meant he had asked an assistant to tell Fisher to buy him the books.

"Do I hear three?" said Marsden, looking down.

"I don't think a Rossetti has ever gone this high," said Fisher. "Look—he's got it up front, Kahn or whoever."

Gates got up, and so did the models as if they were attached. He liked the kind of girls who go to the bathroom four times during dinner and come back wiping their noses and stand over the table squeaking and creaking in their leather, drawing all the stares in a room. He was somewhere far in his forties, and still raiding bodies from other eras to forget, lonely for the years he would never see again.

"You stay," I said, waving Fisher back. "You can tell me the rest." Near the dining room was a large pantry, with two phones on the floor and a cheap wastebasket, and crouched on the floor near a sign saying "Client Services" was an old Japanese man with his catalogue open to a Picasso drawing, *Etude des mains.* He seemed to be repeating prices into the phone as I passed. I picked up the documents that told me I had just spent two hundred and twenty-five thousand dollars plus premium and tax on Renoir's *L'Arbre d'Or,* my own stolen, possibly fake painting. I took a last look in Kahn's direction, and just as I did, the woman with him turned around.

I had seen her that very afternoon on Madison Avenue from my taxi stopped at a light. She was coming from the jeweler Boris Le Beau holding one of their shopping bags. She wore a short navy suit with a white tank top and gave the impression of sun and someplace else. She had a wide, square face innocent of age and innocent of expression—a face that waited for things to happen because of it. Her hair was not particularly thick, but it curled at her face and then hung down her back and it was that red-gold color of women leaning out of ancient towers waiting to be rescued. She left the store and then seemed to catch sight of another piece in the window, for I saw her turn almost in a dance and start to go back in. I had found that such an unusual and extravagant thing to do that I had wondered who she was and why I had never seen her before. But, of course, she was new. While she performed that pantomime, I had found it impossible to look away. There was a nervous quality to her beauty, her movements all self-conscious, as though she knew she was being watched. At that instant she had whirled, and her blue glasses seemed to look into my green ones through the window of the taxi.

Gates was walking towards me. I looked at him as the two girls melted back and began whispering.

"You bought something?" he said, as though he had seen me recently.

"The little Renoir. It used to belong to us."

"I gave up on the Rossetti. I let the man up front get it. Something just came over me."

"They say he's Jack Kahn. I'm not sure."

"Oh, well, then," he said, though I was sure he had not heard of him, "I'm sure if I'd sent Chris he would have gotten excited and bought it. But I wanted to come here myself. I wanted to see how this apartment looks at night. I've seen it, but never with people in it, and yesterday I almost bought it."

Moonwalk

Gates did not want to speak in the elevator, which was unusual since most people here behave as if their elevator men, waiters, and drivers are deaf. He crooked his finger above his lip and we stared into the birthmark on the back of the elevator man's neck.

"I'd be safe here," Gates said as we passed the monitors, the doorman, and the armed guard, which only 620 and a few other buildings employed. As at many buildings, the stonework was being repaired and scaffolding had been put up, but here there was coiled barbed wire on the top and the scaffolding had been cut out to conform to the branches of the trees. The whole building had been cocooned in white net, giving it a ghostly air and making it seem more precious than its neighbors. Spotlights focused up into the dark blue sky. Inside the security booth the monitors showed the half-washed stone streaked with white light.

"We're going to walk," Gates told his driver, and waved him away with that flip of the hand that says "follow and wait," and the navy Wagoneer slid away from the other cars.

"Is there anything like Madison at night?" he said, and the hands that he stretched out shook slightly. I knew that the store and its expansion over the last few years had strained him. Though his divisions were supposed to be well run, still all the decisions were carried to him.

"Can you feel how it's all ending? I knew it tonight for the first time when I put down my hand. I just looked around and stopped wanting—even the apartment. I'm not going to buy it."

"You would never move anyway."

"No, it's more. I feel it. Why are you wearing the glasses?" he said.

"Why are you?"

"I have to hide my red eyes or else they start all kinds of rumors. Let me see," he said, walking closer, but I backed quickly away.

"Well, come along then," he said, no longer interested. "You have beautiful eyes. No wonder people tell you things."

As he said this, my left eye began to burn, which meant it was drying out. I tried to squeeze it shut, but I needed my Hypo-tears. It was just like those horror movies where the victim of some body-altering chemical has to duck into an alley and goes through dreadful changes, hair and fangs sprouting and bursting out; but there are no real alleys on Madison.

"I have to put in some eye drops," I said.

"Are you going to the right doctor?"

"This whole thing takes time. My daughter can't understand any of this." He looked startled, and then I realized he knew nothing of Josie or my second marriage, or if he had known, he had forgotten. We were standing in front of a store where a set of sheets cost in the thousands and a towel was $115 on sale.

"We're making sheets, but nothing like these," he said. "Western sheets like Montana, white and fresh and flapping on a line."

He stopped again to study the photographs of some jewelry in a window, and I thought of the jewelry I would have to sell and all that Cigarette and I had lost, and how we went down the generations marked by a trail of lost stones: my mother's star ruby; the yellow diamond ring removed during a card game on a holiday, wadded into a Kleenex, and flushed into Biscayne Bay; the diamond earrings left on the bathroom counter of a plane; the pins and rings strewn like pebbles.

"How are you going to pay for the Renoir?" Gates said suddenly. "I want to help you. If you hadn't written that first story right after—" and he waved west, because I knew he could never bring himself to say "Hollywood"—"none of this would have happened. Let me buy it for you. You can pay me back," and he signaled to the driver, who stopped, and got something from the glove compartment.

"Take it," he said, just signing a check. "It's good luck. Well, then, this is the second time you've said no." He said it as a warning.

Then I knew he remembered, and it had meant something when he threw his arm over the back of the banquette at the Polo Lounge fifteen years ago and asked me to stay another week and then, as a punishment before the contemplated sin, Cigarette called and I fled home to watch my father die. I took that tidbit of glamour—the stares coming at us from the dark, the short flare of desire—back with me and kept it through all the trouble that followed. Again and again I would go back to the dark of the Polo Lounge when he had asked me to stay another week and returned to me all my stillborn illusions.

"Look, you can just see the top of the store from here. I did this walk so many times with Nancy. You know, she was the one who left me. She couldn't stand never going out—but whenever I go to something like tonight, I know why I stay home," and he made this little snicking sound he makes, almost a snort, which actually was quite annoying. He put his arms around me right under my breast and stood pressing into me.

"Why don't you come home with me, Libby? Let's get in the car."

"Aren't the girls waiting?"

I looked back. The girls had not gone home. I could see them stumbling along a few blocks behind us in their tiny slip dresses and high heels. Whenever we looked back, they would whisper to each other and collapse in giggles behind their hands, leaning against another foreign store that had gone out of business.

"I'll send them away." He was already walking. "I want to see the new windows." He stopped and studied every store from the saddler Knoud to the last florist, passing the doorways with cardboard houses where the sick slept with their unimaginable dreams. At an Italian shoe store, he told me he had sold thirty thousand pairs of his Gators last month. This seemed to reassure him. There was nothing in any of these stores he would have to pause before buying. I knew he used to love presenting himself, astonishing the clerks, buying in every color, though he knew it a cheap triumph. If it ever got too close or unpleasant, there was always his driver following in the car and he could spring back into his own world. Still, his pleasure made me happy, and though no one was around, I was ridiculously proud to be with him.

"Seventeen stores gone," he said suddenly, staring into a window where a "For Rent" sign was propped and where the metal letters had been pried from the stone. "Can you feel how it's all ending? You don't have to trip over three of these guys every block to know."

As we walked, he kept nudging me to the left. He had a strange way of moving, weaving from side to side, as if he were not fully conscious of the act. He walked with tiny rapid steps, as though his feet in the tight velvet shoes were not quite part of him, and yet I knew that when he was alone and not turning to charm anyone, he was extremely aware of all that was around him. When I had known him years ago in his actor days, he would weave through the studio lots with the same ineptitude, bumping into the sound-stages, almost unconscious of his effect. The way he drove, without signals or regard to lanes, his eyes on the person next to him, the car slowing ominously as he spoke, was even more frightening, as though he thought the machine would somehow take over and save him. He had made himself incapable of most ordinary life functions and was rather proud of his princely needs. He rose from a restaurant table and a bill was sent to his office, the tip added on as though a generous specter had passed through. He always went back to the same places where he was known, staying with them long after their lights had gone down. Surrounded by his retinue, his screens, he hadn't answered his own phone or opened his mail in twenty years. He kept looking for what he called "magic," which was really nothing more than his memory of his past. Even after he first returned here and was between fortunes, there were still people around to filter out the other world for him.

Thus we stood and he stared at the fruit and the boxes of soap at the only food market on Madison as though they might hold some wisdom that had eluded him. It had been years since he'd been in a grocery store. Caught in the grand gesture and in some impossible Hollywood vision of himself that he had adopted early, he had really forgotten how to live an ordinary life.

"You know, we didn't see you when the store opened, and all those people you write about were there. They still come back. This is what makes me furious," he said, frowning into the Stetsons and the tooled leather boots at Aspen Skip's. "Skip thinks he owns the whole West."

"And you own England, Maine, what else?"

"No, it's different. Now look at that," he motioned to his driver and leaned in the door of the Wagoneer, which had been slinking along behind us. He got out a piece of paper and wrote something down.

"Want to go lose a little of my money? There's a house up the street where we can play."

I told him I had to go home to write my column. As we passed, a man aimed his finger, made shooting sounds, and did a little dance of anger behind us in his socks.

"Next week he'll get himself a real gun. At least let's stop at the store. I'm there so much they put in a bed for me on the top floor." A policeman crossing the street looked over at us but then was distracted by the model girls. As he talked into his walkie-talkie and looked away, I saw Gates empty his pocket, and a bit of powder drifted up into the air. At the next corner he stuffed something in between two bricks, though there was no sign of the cop.

We were there. I saw stacks of white crew sweaters, and gleaming engraved silver cups, a single rusty crimson oar from the Harvard crew.

"We brought some fruit over from England to do 'rowing' right. He calls it 'the frozen moment.' "

Everything was exactly right—too right, in fact, the way it was all massed and flung together as though some spoiled blonde had just tossed it there, a jumble of white socks and sleeveless tennis vests, the hard mottled browns of tortoiseshell and alligator and the photographs of old teams. No one saw the work and the money it took to get this perfection. No one but Sandy and his crews saw the long cars filled with art directors and stylists biting their cuticles, the photographers and models going crazy inside, violating the roads of Vermont. No one saw the crates pried open on the loading docks and the guys standing around laughing as they pulled little plaid Victorian boxes from their raffia shells.

"I look at this and to me it says a rich, peaceful place. It feels good. It calms me down."

Gates had told me how he grew up in a place where everything was ugly. It was a small apartment, but everyone yelled from room to room. His family always expected the worst. They got into rages, thought everyone was cheating them, went through life boiling and fuming. They would slam the doors of the few taxis they took, and start to argue with the driver. They were always crowding Gates, bending over, pulling at him. His mother, convinced that he was anemic, ordered special cuts of meat and followed him around with tablespoons of bloody juices. She'd tear off hunks of bread for sops, and even at four he found those large, pinky-gray bread mountains unattractive. Gates wanted a distant, private place of low voices and good smells, harmonious extended families, and whispering green beeches to hide under. Things were simple and effortless there. People said "Thank you" and "How nice" for the least little thing and waited, their right hands folded in their laps like they were bound, till everyone was served. They wore good old clothes and had cocktails in the evenings on the large, cool porches of old white summer houses across the street from clubs full of blond children and men who put on ties on Sunday morning and women with white arms and flat bosoms roaming long lawns, trailing imaginary racquets. Of course he didn't say all this, now or then. He'd see a picture of the Duke and Duchess of Windsor playing shuffleboard and say to his crew, "I want that," or he'd mumble something like "Shooting birds in Millbrook," and his people would all pile into the long cars and go scurrying to make his worlds.

"Jesus, look at that!" He looked stricken.

I looked at the window and I looked again, but I couldn't see anything wrong.

"Behind the trophy. She left a duster—Windex and a pink plastic duster! Fuck." He charged at his car, picked up the phone, and began calling the night watchman. "I've forgotten my keys, Peter, and I'm getting a busy signal. It must be broken again. Go get the keys from the trunk. They'll be walking up from the auction. I want to fix this myself," and he was almost dancing in the most absurd way.

I asked him why he didn't just let it go, but of course I was talking to a man who had divorced his last wife, whatever he said, because her voice was wrong.

"It spoils everything," he said, and put down his jacket on the steps for us to sit on. "It matters." It was part of the world he opened up—those calls from men with distinguished voices asking him to hire their daughters, the awards and honorary degrees, the waiting planes, the shifting when he walked into any room. Because he knew what it should be, it mattered.

We could see the first of the Solomon crew approaching down the street: a huge, surging mass coming through the evening mist like a medieval riding household—first the great lords and ladies cloaked and wrapped and carrying their catalogues like heraldic shields to identify them. They were walking forward as the few photographers who had waited behind for the "after" shot were leaping backward, crouched and snapping; and behind them all followed a long line of cars with fur coats curled in the rear seats like little sleeping creatures. Each of the ladies had her court and retainers, her walkers, jesters and fools and the lesser ladies— miniaturized, diminished versions, attached to them lower down on committee lists—the younger brothers and their wives. It was a great, festive rush. The few people still out on the streets stepped aside in astonishment and watched as New York soci- ety, in one of those grand clumps that happen only one or two times a season, made its way up Madison.

"Peter, see if you can get us in without setting off the alarms," Gates said. We pushed in and Gates turned on the special lights. He explained how the bulbs had been shellacked a tawny yellow so an amber glow would settle on and shiver off the deep red-brown woods, the silver-framed brides, the jewels sold in desperation, and the pasts of other lives in the glass cases. Old library tables were heaped with piles of cashmere, and each had its own tablescape, as though some fabulous moment had been abandoned, suddenly uninhabited by the people who lived it, and only these things remained behind as relics.

Gates unlocked the doors to the window case and reached in. "I can't quite make it—I'm going in."

He had to crawl to get behind the scrim, his slippers hanging out into the store. I saw him bump his chin on the oarlocks and upset a crocodile-framed picture of a laughing rower.

I was writing the Pimpernel's first paragraph when I heard a huge sound like a cannon or a crash and then felt a shiver from the ground, heard a thud, and clunks I later knew to be manhole covers dropping down. I dove under a table. In front of me hung a curtain of silk rep ties with little fishing flies, stripes, stirrups, horses arrested in impossible moments of dressage—were these the images I would die with? For no reason, I looked at the clock and saw it was 11:19. I thought someone had blasted into the store. I didn't move.

"I need help," Gates called. "I don't know what that was, but I'm pinned here."

I was afraid to answer, afraid to raise my head in case some creep with a business suit and ski mask was standing over me.

"Are you all right, Libby?"

"I'm okay. What was it?"

"Don't know, but get me out."

I crawled over to the window. The giant crewing oar, its white and crimson paint peeling, had pinned his leg. A stack of heavy, leather-bound old rowing journals had fallen on him, too. His hair was streaked with sweat. I climbed in. Just then the startled faces of Adele and Arthur Buttenwisen appeared at the window. Behind them Madison Avenue was filling with water from a huge gash. The car was still there, but Peter was gone. A wisp of white smoke came from the pit. I lifted the books off Gates.

"You need help?" Arthur Buttenwisen mouthed through the window.

"Tell them to find Peter and call the police from the car," Gates said to me. Even in extremis Gates never talked to people he did not know. "See if they can find out what happened."

Arthur, whose early years as a reporter had taught him to read lips, said through the window that the water main had broken. People all over Sixty-ninth Street were hanging from their windows. An old man holding a brandy glass was leaning out dangerously far. The street was wetter now. Suddenly Peter's head came bobbing up from the floor of the car.

I got the books off Gates but could not move the oar. "You know those movies where the mine shaft collapses and someone gets pinned?" I said.

"What can we do now?" said Arthur, and I told him to have Peter let him in. I put my hand on Gates and pulled and again felt the strength of his arm. Arthur was climbing in, and soon we were all piled and tangled with each other as we tried to lift the oar from the soft piles of tumbled crew sweaters and the megaphone used to call the strokes, all of it very old because old was better.

"Adele has gone for assistance," Arthur said, perfectly happily, for he had turned into a central figure and was close to the glamorous Gates.

"I thought someone had blasted in," Gates said to me as all the store lights went out.

"Danny Gates, this is Arthur Buttenwisen," I said.

"Oh, the p.r. guy," Gates said, and now they could talk. It was very dark, for the streetlights were also out.

"In the shoe department on the wall there are some sconces with candles," said Gates, and Arthur went trotting off. Gates climbed out of the window and pulled me to him. "Think about coming home."

"Oh, so sorry," said Arthur. "The candles . . . um . . . I'm afraid they are fake."

"There's no such thing as fake candles," said Gates as we heard the first sirens. "Here, take this." He reached into a stack of cashmere sweaters and gave one to Arthur. "You take one, too," he said to me, and he wrapped one around himself. We began to grope our way forward, but we kept bumping and tripping and falling over chairs and tables, umbrella stands full of knobbed walking sticks, and glass cases, until finally we made it to the street.

"Here they come," said Adele, looking not at the convoy of police and fire and emergency rescue trucks lined up across Madison but at the fringe of overdressed people moving down the street, the first of the Solomon crowd. Even in the deep blackness around us, they were unmistakable, with their barks and brays of rich night laughter. The water, now a small river of silt, was rushing back towards them.

Much later, Veronica Kahn told me that on the sixteenth floor of 17 East Sixty-ninth Street, Jack Kahn, having one of his long white nights, had heard the explosion and pushed the button next to his bed so that the emergency generator whirred on, making theirs the only apartment on this part of Sixty-ninth Street with power. Veronica heard her daughter, Aurora, calling her nanny. Kahn was at the window, not having bothered to check the generator, for he just assumed when a job was done for him it was done right. For an instant, he must have had no idea whether he was seeing a bomb or a crime. In the bluish light the men were merely the forces to repair disaster there to serve him.

Three police cars, parked horizontally, sealed off the street from all northbound traffic. Jackhammers were already pounding the pavement open, and from the cracks trickled thin blue threads of smoke. Large trucks backed up with beeping sounds. From somewhere in the center of the hole a thin, frail geyser shot water and small pieces of rust and pipe. Then, from deep in the crack three little geysers erupted, as though in imitation. Water on the tarmac made it flash in the gleam of the streetlights, and then they too went out, and it was dark except for the emergency lanterns. Still the gusher rose from deep inside the core and danced like an evil specter taking his glee. Glass had burst from the windows, and some had shattered inward. Hundred-pound manhole covers had popped twenty feet up—like "flying pizzas," as one fireman said. Gates and I and the Buttenweisers saw all this from the street. I could just make out Olivia and John and the Dells and the Popes, all still holding their catalogues, being turned away at the barricade. The water lapped at my shoes and the cuffs of Gates's trousers. Adele's tight face shone, acid-washed by the red and blue emergency lights.

I happened to be facing 17 when the Kahn woman came out, a purple shearling coat thrown over white satin pajamas and flat white kid slippers on her long feet. Her hair was pulled back into a long ponytail, the kind I had always wanted.

"Hey, Danny, we could all use a pair of your Gators!" Bill Pope called.

Gates looked back, and when he turned around, I saw him see her. She was talking to a fireman, who looked down, very tense and braced, as she tilted her face up to him, her features etched by the lights against the night. She appeared in the white steam; little mad flicks from the light reflected in the water were popping and snapping off her.

"I'm serious," said Pope, but Gates did not even answer.

The water must have seeped into her slippers, for she raised one foot, then the other.

"So that's where she landed," said Gates, still looking.

The Pit

As I was writing a weak column on the auction I heard a shout. It was one of those random night cries that come in between the car alarms and the sounds of smashing metal. I waited for it to continue but it was swallowed by the night. After I had finished and made the late edition I could not sleep. At six I decided to walk my dog over to the hole. After a year here, the city still terrified her, for she was a country dog, a stray from the woods I had found dying by the side of a road. She still shivered in the street, turned her back on the traffic at the corners. She sunk to a deep combat crouch and slunk through the streets, tail tucked under to her belly, eyes darting, ears flat to her skull, blowing her coat in fear like a soldier creeping forward under full attack.

"I hope you are going to show him," said a man passing us under the scaffolding that had shadowed my building for five years. I was often stopped for my dog. In this purebred neighborhood, she was the rarity. People pretended to take her for an exotic breed, though she was one of the commonest mutt types, all black with white paws, an embarrassingly thick, plumy tail, and unmistakable cur eyes that mistrusted everyone but me. Perhaps they were being polite.

She tried to hop into the bit of green surrounding a tiny starved tree, but this tree was framed by metal fencing inside which was a wooden picket fence. Often, ivy was planted as a psychological deterrent, though it never stopped her from thrashing around. Other times, the whole tree surround would be cross-hatched with thin, sharp wire in a lethal grid. She scurried along, diving under the parked cars, scrambling, her toenails scraping on the pavement, cringing at the grinding garbage trucks, the tire screeches, and shattering glass I no longer heard. We passed the "ghost car" the police had begun parking on my block at night and one of the many cars whose steering wheel was locked with a red Club and whose windows said "No Radio," like an identification sticker in the club of fear. "No Radio, No Valuables, No Nothing." Only the buildings, rimmed by scaffolding as their masonry was repaired, were protected. It was still so early, the light bulbs glowed in their yellow cages of wire mesh, without which they would be smashed every night by hordes of night boys with sticks. I looked up at the windows. There was always someone watching, and always someone watching the watcher.

We got to the hole, which was surrounded by the usual paraphernalia of emergency, curled snakes of cables and hoses, workmen in black rubber raincoats diving into the steam. There were maybe fifty men working, and a few looked up silently. The pit must have been drilled open after I left, and I saw the main pipe inside, four feet in diameter. What kind of rats and bugs were down there, feeding on the dripping waste? I wanted to ask, but I just stared as I stood on the splinters of glass and saw the flames from the manholes and the smoke now shooting up and spreading out like gray fingers into the sky. A long line of firemen supporting heavy snakes of cable was still blasting chemicals into the hole, where I half expected to see tormented souls walking the circles of the pit among the flaring flames. A fog hung over the street, raining random dust on the silt like volcanic ash, and now there was a small chemical soup underfoot. Sparks from a cracked cable had ignited the trapped sewage gases, and the stench was impossible.

In my cramped and squeezed world, where all the faces repeated and the same bodies pressed smiling against each other summer and winter, the disasters were all the horrible abuse or vengeance one furious human could wreak on another. There were no natural disasters. The beak of a stone gargoyle was more likely to fall on someone walking by than a tree. Here, lightning could not crack the fortress, nor could the earth be shaken. Perhaps a tidal wave or a flood could send us clinging to spires and penthouse terraces, but otherwise we were impenetrable, untouched by all but our own villainy. Neglected by nature, the citizens avenged themselves by acting as badly as they could.

Of course there was rot. We were eaten from within as the city turned on itself, its immune system collapsed. The hundred-year-old pipes were always bursting. Greedily raised buildings with cracks in their girders could cave in. All around were failing systems, waiting to fall down, and it was always hard to fit the new parts into the ancient structures; only in the tropics could they give in to decay and make a virtue of it. I looked up. Coming from 17 was a man in a tan chesterfield with a brown velvet collar, shoes with no socks, and chino pants like only the Little Noses can get away with. He ducked his head into his collar when he saw me, and allowed himself to be yanked forward by a small white ratter—Caroline's "Bucky," in fact. Even at this hour there was someone to avoid, someone with an injury or grudge. But then he seemed to change his mind. He raised his head and walked up to me; after all, Chip Streeter was an aristocrat.

"Good morning," he said, just as though I had not ruined his life.

"I'm sorry about what happened."

"I don't suppose you know where they are or anything?"

"If they were back, they would have been at the Solomon auction last night, and they weren't. I'm as shocked as you are, Chip."

"It's really all your fault. Otherwise we never would have brought him over. Who needs burled door lintels and marbleized chair rails, and who needs an English lord in his overalls to do them?"

I couldn't say anything.

"I walked in the evening he showed up and he was sitting on the steps in his damn tweed jacket with a cocktail talking about moving walls."

Chip walked over to one of the workmen, as though the disaster had just occurred to him. "Just what happened here?" he said, and the man told him about the water main break.

"Same thing happened ten months ago. Why didn't you fellows fix it up then?" And he looked down at his wet shoes.

"We're fixing it now, asshole," the man said, and walked off, his boots marking the fine tan silt that now covered all of Madison and Sixty-ninth. Cloudy water ran in rivulets that rolled where the street sloped down. The traffic was still sealed off in all directions by roadblocks. I took a small bottle of Tears Naturale and, turning my back, squirted my sore eye.

"Chip, there are new people in your building—Jack Kahn supposedly. Who are they—"

"Just don't find them an English lord to stipple their walls," he said, and walked towards Fifth. I watched him and rewrote the first paragraphs of the Solomon auction. Now I got it right, remembering things people had said that I had forgotten. Chip returned carrying the Style section of the *Washington Post* with the little turds inside far from his body.

"Our board is very scrupulous," he said, passing me.

I was awakened at eleven by the phone. "Libby, I have a blind item for you," said a thick voice I instantly recognized as Olivia Pinza talking through a scarf. "It's all around town that Gayle Pope is sneaking out to meet Count Farnaut in the afternoons."

"How do you know?"

"Ask the clerk at the Surrey. Ask anyone."

"What made you think I would run this? I don't do blind items anymore."

"Why? Isn't she important?" said Olivia, letting the scarf drop a bit.

"I always thought she was your friend." The phone disconnected.

I decided to let the next call go, but when I heard the lurid drawl of Hugo Salm leaving a message, I picked up. "Didja hear about the explosion? The flood. It's a total disastah. Someone was just moving into 17 and had all his furniture in the basement, and all the tables warped. . . ."

I could see him sitting on the edge of his mother's green silk chaise, the legs of his pants spread out like sausages, the black phone with numbers of varying degrees of unlisted privacy that connected him to his women and ten or twelve truly frightening men in various inbred but far-flung sets. Every morning from eight to ten he called and was called. It was a little like one of those call-in radio shows, but Hugo attracted his own craziness. He was the golden phone, like the message-center desk at a hip L.A. hotel where everyone's business is known. All because he still dragged his old bones everywhere that everyone else was too tired to go.

". . . in the maisonette," he was saying. Hugo and his aging band of elbow cradlers all had a bit of money carefully preserved. They were the village elders who, unable to breed, at least preserved the oral history of their tribes. They passed the old society stories down to their successors, always with improvements. They knew lifetimes of lovers, generations of secrets, and when they were gone, the stories would end. They would end together, these women and their bachelors. They read and saw just enough to make themselves amusing in short spurts, and each had his convenient women, though there were often jealous overlaps. In their eyes alone these women never changed, but were ever frozen somewhere in their snappy midforties, even as the flesh of the upper arms they held grew looser as they helped the women into their cars, leaving them at their doors and returning home to put down the night's favor-crammed shopping bag from the thousand-dollar dinner. They all had enough Estée Lauder for Men to exceed the most optimistic estimates of their life spans.

As Hugo spoke, I looked through my invitations, putting aside the stiffies. I was invited to everything that cost money, but my invitations always came with the price crossed out and stamped "Complimentary," and the chairwoman always called to get me for her table. I was invited to dinners at home, too, though fewer now. The large calendar on my bulletin board was emptier, and on any night, where there used to be six or seven events, mostly walkabouts, now there were only two or three from which to choose. Of course, there was an endless flow of new books and movies and restaurants awaiting my opinion. And actors. And events with check-in desks manned by long-haired girls in suits enjoying their first jobs. Whenever I went to a screening in one of the large Broadway theaters they still quickly ripped the tape from the reserved area, and they snapped down those ropes whenever I went downtown late, but this was rare now. The Pimpernel ran three times a week. I flipped most of the charity stuff into the basket. The time had passed when rains of glitter and circles of confetti fell out of envelopes, when drivers hand-delivered the tubes and stiffies with a rose or a ribbon. Now many came on brownish recycled paper and even burlap bags with pictures of plate-lipped tribes of the Eastern Arc and endangered species. Often the secretaries faxed ghost invitations, or called, as Boots's had again yesterday. I put aside the admission card for Anne Macfarlane's memorial. We were in the doldrums, things were shutting down. The ballrooms were filled with those who, according to their most recent quotes, never went out. I knew I had only to mention Jack Kahn to Hugo and he would have told me everything he knew, but he also would have told Sally Kirk that I asked.

"What do you know about Jack Kahn?" I said finally.

"Oh, something bad happened in Canada, but I can't remember what. Why'dja want to know?"

"Nothing, really," I said, deciding to call Tom at the paper's morgue, which I did on hanging up.

"He's weighted with prizes. Every scientific honor—then one of those accidents that make a fortune. Conogenex. He invented some drug that cured high blood pressure as a side effect. Sold the company. Sally just called to ask," he said right away. "I didn't give her any good stuff. I'll fax the rest. He is a cell biologist, too."

Tom told me that he had become the sixth-richest man in Canada—an estimate I later learned was wrong, because Jack's business mentor had told him, "Real wealth is what you don't show." He said there was a picture of the first wife and the house outside Toronto so big it had to be photographed from the air, surrounded by miles of split rails like white dotted border lines. There were lists of his inventions with their dates. All his top research men stayed with Conogenex. No clips for the second wedding.

"I like the way you made him just appear on the scene last night. It was a pretty good column."

It wasn't, but I was finished for the week, and I was going to take Josephine to the Carlyle for the Englishwoman. Twice a year we put ourselves through this ritual, and I had a feeling it was coming to an end. Sandy met us downstairs and we got into an elevator full of the smells of other places that live only in hotel elevators. The Englishwoman opened the door and tried her best to smile, for it was getting harder to sell the English Royal look every day. Now even the dimmest and most ambitious mothers knew where all those nanny clothes led. The royals had let Miss Holm down. She was even more bitter this year.

"Mrs. Alexander!" she said, as though I had not made an appointment and my presence was a slight surprise. She looked at Josephine as she slouched in, a child raised on hors d'oeuvres, a prisoner of her "sissy clothes." Then she studied Fisher, large and damp in his authentic but misplaced tweeds.

I was trying not to let my eyes wander to the beds, which were filled with the usual irrelevant tiny sweaters and hats, lisle socks, underwear of the purest cotton, all so dowdy and well-behaved-looking, folded and fetishistic. Against the walls stood racks of smocked dresses with ducks and bunnies hand-embroidered on, and stiff wool coats with velvet collars and scalloped edges that used to come with matching zippered leggings, the kind our Irish maids had sweated to remove, kneeling at my feet, as my hands and face burned on winter afternoons. The tables and the desk were covered with pram shoes and Derby lace shoes with stubby toes and button closings, the same kind I had stamped at my mother in years of fits.

Donna Ashland, an old friend of mine, was there with her son Trevor, which showed just what Miss Holm thought of me, to have doubled up on my appointment.

"What do you have in shirts? My ties never came," the boy was saying, very imperious, not only accepting this whole vanished-empire thing but enjoying it, thumbing through the swatches of tweed and velvet in the drawer like a good little soldier.

Josie shot up her eyebrows and shrugged her thin shoulders to convey the proper attitude. She yawned and sat right down on a carefully folded yellow sweater circled with tiny orange chicks. She was beaming her contempt, sharing it with Trevor, and he shut the drawer. Then they both managed to register that they were here just to indulge their moms, hopelessly besotted by England. We had begun all this years ago with the large navy carriages that passed in the park wheeled by large white women in nurse's shoes. Inside the carriages were our totems, even then moving into Little Noddy dreamland. For we were the White Jews, running far from the great-grandfathers with accents who supported these lives.

"I like this and this for the collar," I told Miss Holm. "I think Josie's too old for the hat."

"Many of our nine-year-olds are still wearing bonnets," she said.

"Never," said Josie, as Miss Holm crouched down on her knees without seeming to be on her knees. It never diminished her at all to be crawling around taking the measurements of some wild and squirming young Tyler or Topper.

"How long would you like her to wear it?" said Miss Holm.

"At least two years," I said, and then I realized she meant the length. And Donna looked at Trevor and her mouth curled, as did his.

As usual, I was shamed by my own pretension into spending more than I had planned, but I knew the Eatons of Bond Street would let the bill ride a good year or so before the formal letter, which was always a reminder, never a threat: "One white rabbit smock. Sent with compliments."

I was worn out as we left the suite, but Miss Holm was almost smiling. Sandy looked sorry for me. That same blond boy I had seen at the auction was coming out of the dining room with Gayle Pope, but they were too busy talking to notice me; he looked very happy in his poor clothes with the notebook tucked in his pocket.

As we got off the elevator, I saw the Kahn woman. She was wearing a jeans jacket and skirt and flat shoes and had some kind of a satchel slung from her shoulder, so that from a distance she might have been one of those rock-star girls temporarily trapped in the grandeur of the lobby. She walked with the stride of someone pacing the borders and looked very young. As I saw her, she saw me and seemed to know me, and so we both stopped.

"Veronica Kahn," she said, as Sandy gave a fat little breath. "Someone pointed you out to me at the auction. I've been reading you for years," and out of my last few columns she picked the best one and praised it. "I have a little girl, too," she said to Josephine, who studied the wall, though instructed to receive each word delivered to her by any grown-up as though it were the most fascinating piece of new information, to shoot out her hand, lock eyes, and answer.

"Such a beautiful girl," she said over Josie's head, and she touched my arm. I hate people to touch me. Sometimes at a party they come over when I am talking and kind of pull at my sleeve. I always ignore them as long as possible. Her hand was very warm and slightly wet. I could tell she was one of those people who have an excess of body heat, a slightly flushed complexion, a perpetually moist palm, a need for air conditioning. They go around always hot—a *candela*—opening windows, pulling at their clothes, underdressed for the weather but somehow drawn to the tropics where their inner heat is neutralized by the climate.

Her voice was rough, with one of those Australian accents that slap each word around a bit and go all crude at the ends of the sentences. She wore her young clothes unselfconsciously with all the security of beauty. She was filled with sun, a kind of gold color of skin melting into the red-gold streaks in her hair. She stood as though it was an effort to keep still, like one of those people trapped between just going off and getting back, compelling you to pay attention now that they have poised in their flight.

She had eyes of the palest green, with dark brows above and dark lashes around them like stars. Her nose was rather flat and slightly flared, but that imperfection, suggesting passion, made her more compelling. She had a small scar as thin as a line written in white pencil above her upper lip. It looked like the kind of thing that might easily have been removed but hadn't been. She wore almost no makeup, so that the dark under her eyes, a pale mauve, became the slight exhaustion of youth. Her face had many mistakes, but all of them worked to her advantage. She was dangling a small cushion from one hand, and I asked how she liked it here, not listening as much to her answer as to the way she spoke.

"I really don't know yet. All our furniture is floating in the basement—we lost the lot. I keep going back to Toronto and the island"—she raised the cushion to explain—"so I'm only partly here."

A bit nervous and ready to tell all, I judged; and so I asked her to join me and Hugo at Lampwick after Anne MacFarlane's memorial service. She agreed but, as she waved and walked out to her car, a black Range Rover, not new, I saw her frown, which meant she had not been invited.

"I hope I'm included," said Sandy, and he was breathing hard. "You'll have her first, ahead of Diana and Sally. I could keep Hugo busy while you talk."

I scarcely heard him, for I was planning to tell Gates about the lunch. He had told me Veronica had been at his house in California one night—"a long strange night with a strange girl," as he had put it—and had said no more but had looked hard again at the place where she had stood. He had not crossed the street for her, and I wondered if he would go to Lampwick. I knew he liked intrigue if it was all in his favor and he could control it.

It was good for the Pimpernel to find a new person now that so many of the others had bunkered in and become reluctant, refusing interviews to the magazines that had created them and celebrated their fictions—though, of course, their secretaries gave out lists of friends willing to talk about their good works. Now they all came attached to their conscience quenchers, dragging them along like anchors. They'd drop their causes—the ballet, AIDS, Tibet, the rain forests, French hospitals, English trust houses, Save Venice, Veritas—and *boom! boom!* safe harbor! I thought of those dim waves at the Solomon auction, the wary bodies sunk deep in their cars behind smoked windows. They had all pulled back out of range and were using p.r. flacks, guys like Arthur Buttenwisen, to keep us away. Lee Solomon had been the first in the retreat of the dinosaurs creeping back into the jungle.

"The important thing is that she wants the Pimpernel, other-wise she would have walked right by you," said Sandy. As we walked home, we passed the hole again. There was no looting, for the streets were closed off and the storefronts were already sealed by all the guard services. Each had a different uniform, and it was like several private armies had assembled.

"How do you like your new coat?" I asked Josie.

"Big woop," she said, putting a finger down her throat. "Just don't expect me to wear it."

Lunch with the Wave Dancers

Anne's mourners mounted the wet steps of St. Jude's slowly, their drivers holding umbrellas overhead. Those of her age stood studying the steps as though deciding whether Anne was worth it, smiling with the simple joy in outliving anyone. The rich ones leaned on men with many social engagements, who slowed their pace accordingly as they brought their old brides in past the supplicating saints.

Claudio Tavola was rooted at the head of the center aisle. He looked out over the crowd, plucking his favorites from among them like choice produce from his early days at the markets. I watched him washing his hands with joy just the way he would before shaving extra white truffles on my fettucine at Lampwick. Not every memorial service had its own maitre d', but Anne MacFarlane's did, and half an hour before the service the entire cathedral was filled and heaving with anticipation. Only last year I had seen Claudio standing just like this at the ramp of Anne's jet, handing out the Lampwick picnic hampers for her annual birthday shoot in Scotland. Claudio saw me, and that host smile which had made Lampwick the restaurant it was came flooding out. Claudio bent down and whispered to the usher who would march Hugo and me and his other chums up front at a stately pace to the special section under the photographers, for the entire left balcony had been given over to the press. But I refused to go and ducked under the ropes, tugging Hugo along.

"See you later for lunch," I said to Claudio. It was considered bad planning to go to an eleven o'clock memorial service without having made a reservation nearby for that big thank-heaven-we're-still-here hooting lunch that always follows. Very few lingered to see the family, who, after all, and especially in Anne's case, were quite beside the point. I was joining Hugo and Veronica. I had also told Gates that Veronica would be there, knowing how torn he would be between his desire not to go and his interest.

Of course, this wasn't a funeral with some awful metal casket squeaking by on rusty wheels; this was a celebration, a thanksgiving, the usual bodyless New York death. Any grief had been muted; the famous of the world had been given time to assemble. Programs were printed. Outside St. Jude's, traffic had been stopped and had to be rerouted, and the sidewalk was clotted with a mass of black umbrellas just like the English country funeral Anne would really have loved. The mourners walked in, eyes down, trying to look sad, though she was widely detested. Instead, most looked slightly abashed until they saw their friends, and then there was the usual uncontrollable waving across the pews and blowing of kisses, motioning to cross the church, squirming for recognition, the hopeful patting of empty seats. They might have all been here to celebrate Anne's life. I, at least, knew I was here to celebrate her death. She was gone, removed from my landscape, and I was free of her bad tongue. Unpleasant klieg lights beamed from both balconies onto the altar, picking the gold from within the mosaic, where it gleamed, bouncing off the marble columns. One spot was aimed out at the audience, so that I kept having to shelter my eyes.

I whispered to Hugo, but I could tell he was restless as his friends all marched past us, for the ushers insisted that everyone parade to the front, then circle round to fill the sides. As they passed, he kept bobbing up, trying to catch their eye.

"There's someone up there I must go see," he said finally when he could no longer bear it. He switched up his scarf and ducked under the maroon ribbon which they had put across our aisle and was off.

"Could everyone make room for two more?" an usher said, and he was winking and smiling. I watched as a couple who had just been seated in the rear, way on the side, were moved up to better seats.

Blanca and Jimmy Dell came down the aisle, and the photographers began whirring, bending over the railing, their long lenses pointing and vibrating. "Look, now they are moving up. They are bumping the chiefs back," someone said, as the entire brass of the city (Anne had been married to ex-mayor Taylor White) rose and shifted for the Dells. Now I could see the couple plucked from the back. It was Howard Goldenson, the bankruptcy lawyer, and his girlfriend, Laurie Holt, dressed in dark green love-puppy leather.

"We welcome you to this service of celebration for our beloved friend Anne MacFarlane," said the Reverend Russell Greene.

I saw an usher approach the Popes, but Bill waved him away and they kept their seats on the side. Gayle nodded to me as the hymns began. Diana McBride, head bent, was already writing. I had stopped paying attention when a blast of horns brought me back. "Leave it to Anne," I thought, as I saw the four members of La Trompe de Chasse, their horns slung against their chests.

"There is death in life and life in death," the reverend was saying. "It comes to all alike," and here he stretched out his white angel sleeves and splayed his fingers to include the Popes and the car baron; the chiefs and the former mayors; the scribes; the talk show host who was trying to talk over the girlfriend to Howard Goldenson. There were the ghost of Anne's autobiography; the ex-President and his son-in-law, the doorknob king whose wife could have been bought at the Jockey Club for five hundred dollars a night ten years ago; the newspaper distributor who was wearing a gun on his ankle; the head of the Bank of

New York, the richest man in the country; a woman who ruined her marriage by falling for her personal trainer; two media barons who were already making their move on MacFarlane's company. There, too, were an old man who owned hotels and a man from Newport who had courted his wife when she was seventeen, following her on horseback with his car and driver, and a woman who, when she discovered her husband's affair, bought herself a diamond the size of a golf ball and rolled it down the hall to him when he came home. Athena Rossos, the anthropologist, was whispering to a woman who spent her first marriage crawling through her *Schloss* on a leash, skinning her knees. Anne's old chum, who was next to me, was frowning as I took notes on the usual assortment of gentlefolk, nitwits, liars, elbow cradlers, billionaire third wives who put *y*'s into their first names when they were sixteen in anticipation of position, distant family, and curious fools, the restructured but unrepentant, indicted but still invited.

"Yes, death stands in the garden waiting to pick his ripe fruit. Death is the watcher in the garden. Death shakes the trees, and all the high livers and spenders, the gallivanters and dancers on the rim, and good people, too, are going to be his. We will all be his, returned to the bosom of our gentle Lord Jesus. Now let us pray."

I saw Donna Ashland, once a fellow student at Miss Viola Wolff's dancing classes for young Jewish gentry, cross herself and hurl forward to kneel on the leather prie-dieu. Next to her was the blond man again, this time nodding to me. I must remember to ask who he was. He had been standing in the back of the chapel trying to negotiate his way in. He smiled at me as I stared at his notebook, now out.

"We are living in an age of retribution when the guilty shall be punished and the greedy shall give back."

"Where is this in the text?" said the old lady next to me.

"Those who have lived in sin shall stand in the glare of exposure, those who are mighty and stiff-neck-ed shall bow and fall. Those who have been liars in the sight of God . . ."

"I can't find it."

"I think he's just going on. It's not written here," I told her.

". . . And men shall be shown for themselves. They shall stand naked. Those who have danced with Satan shall be pulled down by the ankles. The wicked shall be burned with their own words. Those who walked past the poor with their noses in the air shall themselves stretch out beggar's cups."

"What *are* you writing?" she said.

The last thunderclap must have reached right to the gastric juices, for many in front of me cocked their watches and looked ready for lunch.

"In fifty years of memories, we all have different ones. It's difficult to know where to begin," said the former Defense secretary, as I sighed. "I want to talk about Anne as a friend. She was a woman of paradoxes, hugely enjoying her wealth, all her appetites . . . her faithful Joyce, who, when we were traveling, carried all her suitcases stuffed with Hungarian salami . . . the airplane menus she devised . . ." and on he went about how impervious she was to the many appeals to intervene in the news—a terrible lie, as I well knew.

Behind one flower arrangement, I saw the black eye of a television camera moving and tracking, and as I looked from it to the votive candles, the vaulted ceiling, the mosaics and pieced colored marble, I was carried back to the Byzantine Emanu-El and all the holidays when I had counted the pillars or chosen my favorite stained glass window or read the Bible until, as my anger faded with age, I began to listen. I sat there with my grandparents in my English dresses and then with my parents, when my grandfather forgot himself and talked out loud and prayed in Hebrew, bowing slightly. The accents around me changed as one by one people died and rose to stand as ghosts behind the new faces filling their seats. All those years, until, without trying, I found that I knew the prayer for the dead by heart.

". . . And when she was sick at the end and I visited, she would always say, 'Tell me something amusing.' I knew that meant gossip. I'd always tell her about the time we were in

Tangiers, a late night, when she fell down the steps, hitting her head on every stone step, and I wrapped her head in a towel and we got on her plane with her head bandaged at two a.m. and flew to Paris. Of course this story was her reassurance of her own indestructibility."

Suddenly there was a series of loud barks and squeals and electronic squawks on the PA system, which somehow had gotten connected with one of the security or cop walkie-talkies.

"They're here on the West Side," said a cop voice.

"Out through the rear with the shitheads!" said another, and then another series of mournful squawks and squeaks, and tittering from the rows, and the Defense Secretary was shrugging as more sounds came through.

Then came Anne's children, their grief having been vetted, typed out, and edited by the massive MacFarlane public-relations machine. Each, now worth a hundred million or so, had recovered enough to memorize his speech. It was here at last; the wild, addicted sons came home to the tribe, earringed, their hair tied back, in suits that did not fit, for they did not wear suits in the kinds of places they lived hiding from the injuries of their pasts. But they were healed today, full of amusing anecdotes about Mum, this sunny, quirky, almost Disney character that none of us knew. I thought of Anne with her little raisin eyes sunk in a suet of a face and the way she had of saying the most wounding things. I saw her against a sky in Virginia with her rifle cocked. Her motto was "If it flies, it dies," and her whole essence was involved in feathers moist with blood, drooping necks, tiny beaks. I saw her draining her flask as the dogs went to cradle the little birds in their mouths.

". . . arranging the pencils on her desk like a Zen archer," said Bo, who lived as close as he could to Hazelden.

"Life was a banquet for her, and she was never sated," said James.

"As a child, she seemed like a goddess to me, especially in the way I saw others react to her," said Susan.

"She could have washed her hair," said a voice from behind.

"When I found the rest of the world was not like my home . . ." said Whit, and there were a few more electronic squawks, as though Anne herself was protesting from the grave this inclusion of her very weakest son. "Farewell, dear Mum, from Skipper," he said, finishing, as they all had, with a direct address to her that caught at his throat, filled his eyes, and ended with a sob. It was the unfortunate sibling competition replayed to see who could leave you with a gasp, a catch in the throat, that little part at the end when you breathe out at the past glory and present deadness.

All these well-crafted remembrances were delivered in the late-twentieth-century cocked-hip style introduced to New York by Rosamond Bernier in her lectures at the Metropolitan Museum and stolen by Athena Rossos and others. The method was simply to walk out on the stage or into the pulpit and, without any modest phumphering or nose wiping or gracious rambling, without any coy gesture to death or nervousness at all, simply begin, "As Picasso told me at lunch in his garden," and sail forth in the scarcely spontaneous but seemingly effortless English mode.

"And so the portrait has been painted," said the Reverend.

"Dust to dust, ashes to auction," a voice whispered behind me.

"Hush," said a woman as the choir sang "Speed, Bonny Boat" and a lone huntsman from La Trompe stepped forward to play "O Jerusalem," the title of which was the closest Anne Heymann MacFarlane came to her roots in life or death. A High Church burial—arrows of desire, chariots of fire—it was the ultimate White Jewish dream.

"A very plaid memorial service," someone said as we filed out.

"That was some story about falling down the stairs," said the ex-President. I was right behind him as he made his way to St. Jude's side door, which was hidden behind shelves filled with neatly folded old sweaters and with boots for the poor.

"Out the other door," said a cop, showing no recognition of

the large head or the famous loud voice. "We are holding this exit." They were, in fact, actually holding it for Diana McBride, who swept past with her scarves flowing out, and she paused to let the ex-President through, but he bowed to her, and they did this shady little dance of you-first-no-you, sidling all the way out into the street. As if a valve had been released, they streamed out into the rain and the arms of their drivers, who held umbrellas, bobbing them down as they climbed into the black cars.

A navy Lincoln cut through the Park Avenue traffic and pulled in perpendicular to the curb. "Now that's showing off," someone said. The driver rushed over to the old man who owned hotels and detached him from the lamppost where he was leaning. He gently pried apart his fingers as a man in a business suit, his fetcher, appeared and the two handed him into the car, where I could see a flash of skeletal ankle that I knew was Holly Whitney.

It was a pin rain. The tiny needles were blown side to side by the wind as I walked up Madison. The men had left the hole and waited in tents. Yellow rubber blankets covered the pipes. Outside on the steps of a church the homeless had drawn their cardboard boxes stamped "Fragile" and "Rush" in close to them. The gutters ran with bits of city life, the dark juice from the hole, silt and red clay and pieces of the crust, tarmac and mica. Finally, I felt just too wet and put out my hand.

The driver had one of those names where you can't tell what is the first name and what is the last, and sat against a cushion of wooden beads. He had a laminated list of instructions, one of which said, "It's nice to be important, but it's more important to be nice."

Today again Lampwick would be in full thrust, though the restaurant business had slowed and Claudio had quietly removed two tables from the window wall up front. This wall, glazed shrimp pink, was hung with sketches of the most visible women in New York—the caricatures so faint as to be flattering. It was a simple gimmick, but it had launched Lampwick ten years ago. Space on the old ego wall was limited. Women had their secretaries call to suggest when they would be available to pose in their offices. Husbands tried to work deals, offered to back Claudio in Aspen and L.A. My picture had been one of the first, though I hated Lampwick. It was like being trapped in a heaving rose. Hugo Salm was the only man on the wall. Claudio had hung his picture in the center, and the artist, Diego, had given him a forked tongue.

Recently no one had wanted to be seen at Lampwick. "I haven't had lunch at Lampwick in a year," was a frequent remark to show seriousness of purpose, but this was a wet day after death. Claudio had left the service early to get ready to receive his mourners, and I could imagine him at the door, almost on tiptoe, tilted forward for the early arrivals, standing in front of the ice-bedded fish, the flowers of vegetables that would never grow to maturity, the baskets of black and white truffles big as bull's balls—all the riches of the world's markets, flown in for us, for this moment. It was especially wondrous on a day like today, when Lampwick would briefly encompass all the gleaming dreams of food, shelter, and acceptance in Claudio's improved smile.

I stood in the small hall between the inner and outer doors— for some the wings before they were on stage, for others the very rim of the viper pit. The hall, flanked by mirrors on both sides, was lit, if possible, even more dimly than the restaurant.

Sylvia Mendes was there, lifting the little dimples the rain had made in her helmet of hair. "Some rain dance," she said. I agreed, though I could never really understand anything she said. Long ago, Sylvia must have danced the brains right out of her head, for since then she has made no sense at all, though this has not hurt her socially. When her sentences trail off into the clouds, people don't notice, or if they do, they mistake it for charm and think she is making an effort.

"Well, the old witch is dead," Athena Rossos said, shouldering past. "I hope St. Jude's does as well for my wedding."

Just as I entered, I saw Veronica with Claudio. Claudio bent forward and studied her, enjoying his temporarily refreshed power.

"She's with me, Claudio—my friend from Canada, Veronica Kahn."

I heard a commotion behind me and the whine that could only be the entrance of Hugo Salm. "Pretty color," Hugo said to Veronica. It was a red dress, the color of first blood, and with her hair it was like a flame tearing through the dim pink rose. Perhaps it was deliberate, for she knew people would be coming from the memorial in their dark clothes.

A woman followed us down the row nodding.

"A great beauty, still," said Sylvia.

"No money left," said Hugo.

Often conversations at Lampwick went on like this. Topics or names mentioned at one table were taken up at the neighboring tables of the window wall and traveled down the row to start a conversation at the next table, like a child's whispering game. Everyone knew this wind-tunnel effect, this wall of sound, and accepted it as part of lunch at Lampwick.

I looked around. Baron Gray and Sally Kirk were watching the ex-President build a White House out of sugar cubes. Lampwick was the kind of place you see your whole life flashing by if you have lived a certain kind of life. The women belled out at me through the icy sweat on my glass, all those I had invented, scolded, and abandoned. They moved from table to table below their taller, younger, thinner selves with the gaiety and lightness of water spirits dancing over the waves. Their clothes were new, the walls freshly glazed. At each table, the flowers were full and forced, bursting in their moment of ripeness, still wildly and crazily lavish; there was no bound wheat at Lampwick. The climate caught the last hot moment of terminal joy before rot sets in. A warmth came over the room, like a flush, and I felt a feeling of belonging to this world, being known and knowing, which was very dangerous.

"Who's that with the sunglasses?" I heard Veronica ask

Hugo. "Sitting with the one with the ribbon and the one with two sweaters tied."

"Oh, that's Donna Ashland. A very happy girl. I knew her when she was a little Jewish"—he pronounced it "Jush," like it had nothing to do with him—"girl at The Breakers. A very wild little child always into the bushes with anyone—the cabana boy, the lifeguards. One year they found her during the Easter Sunday egg hunt. Now she's got just what she wanted—Dudley Ashland."

They were getting on very well. He was explaining the whole room to her, or at least those on the window wall. She had watched him quietly for a while, and then she seemed almost to relax into the role of his student. She asked him questions and let him lecture her—even when he told her things I guessed she knew, she pretended interest—and when he questioned her, she told him nothing but her travels, however he picked at her.

I saw the Dells coming in (strange, he never had lunch with her, and they never went here), and they took the table next to us. Blanca came over to kiss Hugo and me. I saw Jimmy Dell look at Veronica. His snake eyes were contradicted by his full kewpie mouth, the kind the old stars painted on to look innocent.

"Drop your bag," Jimmy hissed to Blanca.

Sam Chalk was coming down the aisle, waving his way along the corridor of stares, mesmerized by his infamy. Now I saw Athena, whom he had opposed, representing her husband, in her first divorce, half rising from her seat to look at him, turning so that the folds of her neck were strained and corded.

"Very sick," said Hugo. Chalk's bone-white skull popped in patches from his crew cut.

"Drop your bag *now*," Jimmy said.

While Blanca fumbled on the rug for her alligator clutch, Sam stopped. "Sam," said Jimmy, sticking out his hand, which was hard for him because of his problem with physical contact—a major impediment in his pursuit of fame and sex.

"Oh, Sam!" said Blanca, very flushed from scraping up the

little gold components of her purse so she would not have to kiss him.

"Well, don't I get to sit down?" he said. "We have a divorce to discuss." And now Jimmy Dell understood why there was a third chair at the table and why Blanca was smiling in that way. And this before he could get to say even the first of his planned words about beginning new lives!

Hugo and I grew very silent, listening.

"Do you think we could sit over there?" Sam said to Claudio, motioning to the rear of the restaurant, shunned by all but Holly Whitney. It was common to have these first discussions in public with witnesses. Chica's husband had asked for a divorce as she was being made up to give a party for six hundred.

"Terms," said Chalk, and got out his notepad. Soon Jimmy Dell got up. I did not dare say anything to Hugo, but after a moment I went to the phone to call in the story, and on the way back I stopped to say something to Blanca, who had put on dark glasses.

"Did what I think just happen?" I said to Chalk, though I was sure.

Then I saw Danny Gates. A woman I did not know came up to him. I read her lips as she said, "Are you sure you want to go in? The place is full of journalists."

"Please take my call at three," I said to Sam. "I don't want any mistakes."

"Danny Gates is here," I said to Veronica as I returned. But she had seen him.

"I can't imagine why he's here. I've never seen him here before. I'll have the sole," Hugo said to the waiter.

But of course I knew why Gates was here, having summoned him to his vision on the night of the flood. He had seen her and remembered her, but not enough to wet his feet to find her. It would have gone no further were it not for me. People find their way to the inevitable, but sometimes only with a little help. Most men just will not follow after a face—it's too much trouble, and there is always another around the corner. Often since, I have examined why I did it. Perhaps because I thought I was safe. He liked young girls, after all. I really had forgotten that the other thing he liked was his own past. Sometimes I like to aid people in their desires, but often I am just as happy to obstruct them. I might have gone the other way here, and made sure he never saw her again. I like being a go-between. I enjoy trouble from a distance. I am completely suited to listening to opposite sides and seeing the point in each, to holding the hand of the one on the left while smiling into the face on the right. Is this a character defect? You could call me a pander, a troublemaker, a director, a pimp, they are all accurate.

"Hmm," said Veronica, looking up and smiling, for Gates was looking at her, and then I was sorry I had rolled this boulder up the hill and pushed it over. "I'll have some brown rice and vegetables—steamed, not grilled. What kind of water do you have?" and she stared at the waiter in such a way that he could not say "But madame" as she flicked her hair back and opened her face to him and to Gates, who was watching. And now they had fallen into a performance for each other, each aware the other would be watching the little gestures, like the courtship fluffings of birds. She pulled at her blouse and fanned herself with the large menu. A *candela*, flushed now, burning.

Gates looked away, but he kept looking back. And in my heart I said no, this is a mistake, I did not quite mean this, and went chasing after the rock, which was pounding down the hill. Now out of my control, my mistake was scraping down the mountain, growing to monstrous size, ready to crush the town below. "Stop!" I said, but it was too late.

"And who is that fat little man over there?" said Veronica, pointing near Gates in such a way that her long fingers were displayed, and I was surprised, for she had gardener's fingers.

The brim of Athena's sable hat had hidden the corner table from Hugo, and he had been too busy telling stories to have checked as he usually did. Hugo never felt comfortable until he knew everyone was ranked in place, according to his view of this universe. Now, as he leaned forward almost to the exploding flowers, I saw him start, as though a coldness had shot down his left arm. He put down his fork. He looked again, and I imagined what he saw. He saw the young body in swim trunks and the bland face, sketched and framed and photographed as I had seen it among his obelisks and tiny Greek torsos. Always the same face. Everyone knew it, but no one ever said it, and that was the way it was for the bachelors, as they still called themselves, of his generation. Sometimes they were invited to the same dinner, but they were always with a woman, and they never arrived or left together. They never even went to a play together. I knew Hugo saw all those summers when each might leave his particular house party and they would meet for a week in whatever country was no longer fashionable that year. Around them things had completely changed, but it made no difference. It was never said. They never kept shaving kits at each other's houses. They never, except during that summer week, had breakfast at the same table. For almost fifty years one or the other, or so it was said, would call up around midnight and talk over the parties and sometimes go to the living room till he heard the knock on the door, for they never even had each other's keys and wouldn't until the health of the other worsened. That would be the first and final intimacy. I saw Hugo look at Veronica as though she were everything ugly, for that fat little man was Baron Gray, and Hugo had loved him, and no one else, since he was twenty-four.

"That is Baron Gray," he said, controlling himself, though his eyes had filled. "A great gentleman to know."

Since it was the only kind thing he said all through lunch, Veronica should have paid attention, forgotten about picking the shells off the glazed grapes, and looked at Hugo's horrible eyes.

"I'll sign now," Hugo said.

Gates was moving along the row. I knew I had to do the Dell story for page 2 and then the memorial as the Pimpernel. Gates kept moving as we rose. The three of us were still in the outer hall in a small damp clump of umbrellas and coats when he caught up. Hugo was half out the door, but he backed in again. "A photographer," he said.

Gates frowned. He had a black cashmere coat over his shoulders, dark suit, white shirt, and plain dark silk tie. A piece of his hair fell over the rim of his tinted glasses, and yet there was nothing random in the way he looked. He and Veronica were the same size. I saw her look at him again before Hugo, fussing, pushed open the outer door.

Sal began taking pictures. I stepped back so that the group was the two of them with Hugo in the center looking annoyed. Gates turned his head, and Veronica smiled in the most animated way I had yet seen. Both their drivers stood by their car doors waiting, and Sal was hopping back to photograph Veronica as Hugo popped up his umbrella.

"Can I drive you?" Gates said to me, though looking at Veronica, who gestured back at her car, behind which Sam Chalk had double-parked his Bentley with all the police stickers.

"That's enough," Gates said to Sal, and pushed us into his car, which was first in line. He closed the door in Hugo's face. "I'll take you home," he said to Veronica. "I know where you live."

"Where's Hugo?"

"Let's go," Gates said, as Veronica turned and waved to her driver to follow. "I saw you the night of the flood," he added, but Veronica was looking back at Hugo.

"You insulted his friend—the fat man," I said. "They've been friends for forty years. Baron used to be very handsome."

Now Gates and Veronica turned to each other and each took a good look, for it was like looking into a mirror and seeing a male or female version of oneself. They both smiled, satisfied with the way their beauty had aged. It was silent for an uncomfortable time. Then Danny looked down, as if he had failed. I was in the center, my feet on the hump of the car, more aware of her leg than of his because of its unusual warmth.

"Poor Hugo," I said, and we started to laugh. We all knew something was continuing. I could see them: on the porch of the tennis club or the large corner table of the downtown place; the summers in Italy in espadrilles, their arms wrapped around each other, their pants flapping around their thin thighs; the East Hampton house with the pair of black Lancias in the driveway. Veronica, the woman with the best figure in her exercise class, eating a plate of tomatoes, her eyes looking over a dune; flying to some island, flying back, with the expensive leather bags and tiny trunks being carried to and from their plane. I saw, too, the affairs each would have; the unexplained trips; calls from a phone booth; and always the workmen in their houses, preparing them for the life they would never quite get around to living together. Always there would be service trucks in the driveway; tradesmen passing through the kitchen filled with the summer abundance of the great house; the cars roaring past each other over the white gravel; the drivers waiting at the airport to pick up borrowed people to distract them; and finally the real estate agent walking the next rich couple through the empty house with the catalogues and bills from the clubs still on the table.

The rain pounded large heavy drops, steaming the windows as we rode through our own white mist. They were talking like strangers, Danny answering questions about the store and where he got his ideas and who did his ads—I noticed he did not mention Fisher or Oliver—when he leaned across me, causing my umbrella to drop. He put his hand above Veronica's lip and traced her scar with his nail. I bent to pick up the umbrella, and when I looked up something had happened in the car. It was different, though they were only talking about horses.

"I have a house in Connecticut," Gates said. "They have very good riding up there if you need a place." He laughed at the idea. "Are your feet wet? Peter, hand the lap robe back."

Why don't they just dump my body into the street? I thought, as Veronica slipped her shoes off her long, narrow feet and Gates threw a gray squirrel-lined blanket over us.

"You can let me out here," I said to the driver.

"You're not coming with us to the store?" Gates asked.

"I really can't. The Dells are getting divorced," I said, crawling over him; but this fact, which would soon set everyone going feverishly for weeks, caused no reaction.

As I walked home, I felt myself catching cold with every step.

"You must have been beautiful when you was young," said one of the street guys, looking up from his cardboard doorway.

The Branch in Between

That Veronica Kahn called. I think she is having all of us in for a look at the apartment," Angelo said. *"Order more,"* I heard him say to his assistant. *"Joan, where is that guy? Too much aggravation."* He had cupped his hand over the receiver. *"Unless they're out of them. Very slow to pay. Save them for me."* I heard hammering. *"The credit is due right away.* I don't really have the time, but I said I'd go."

Talking to Angelo was always like this, with infuriating multiple hook-ups, interrupted connections, and the perpetual uncertainty of just who you were talking to. Tradesmen were always hanging on the line, so that often I spoke to his painters and carpenters as well as his clients. Unless it was a weekend and he was very lonely, Angelo never called one person at a time. I knew he sat trapped in a corner of one of his immense rooms, the rest impassable, stacked floor to ceiling with dangerously deranged towers, chairs on top of chests and priceless pier tables, folded squares of sixty-thousand-dollar drapes, with tole lamps and spindly legs sticking out, monkey sculptures and blackamoor arms reaching from the pathological clutter which I always feared would make him truly the victim of his possessions and kill him one night as he fought through fire, battering down the

walls of his furniture, trampling the Staffordshire dogs and obelisks, whipping aside the bare wire hangers that hung from the
chandelier arms and held the few jackets in which he always
looked immaculate.

"Why don't you call her and see what's going on? *Unless
they're out of them.* You could walk over with me tomorrow. *Put
it there. Careful! That's a very fragile textile on the floor. What are
you giving me? I don't want to upset my body chemistry! Sometimes
you give me two niacin and I turn all red."*

I did not know what I wanted to do about this. A universal
reluctance had fallen over my people, a sudden shyness, as
though the Dells had made so much fuss that everyone else had
backed from the spotlight, scared by their former flamboyance.
In the past they had allowed themselves to be written about with
childish delight again and again, unaware they were showing off,
for it wasn't just money they were displaying, it was all they had
learned. Since the Solomon auction and the memorial, I had not
been invited to any more massings. Perhaps what I feared had
happened and I had become the enemy.

I forced myself to call Veronica. I needed a new person to
write about.

"I'm right in the middle of seeing decorators. I've booked
them every hour, and I'm just setting up my greenhouse—that's
what I do, a bit of bonsai—but if you want to come with Angelo,
come along. You can stay on—he's the last of the morning. But
please don't write anything. Come as a friend," she said, just as
I knew she would.

"Maybe it's easier if I come later, after Angelo leaves," I said,
and she paused before she agreed.

At that moment I heard that "da-da-da-*da*" knock at the
door, always so falsely cheerful and always so full of threat, which
meant Cigarette was here. She had finally come to see the
painting. Of course, even when I don't open the door myself, I
know when my mother is in the house by the click of her heels,
the strict rustling frictions of her stockings, the disturbance in
the particles of air as they swirl around her form, dressed as

expensively as is now possible, toe to unmoving hair. First the heavy tread, then the half-furious face, always ready to be betrayed or disappointed in me, ready to revive fault, for she is the repository of ancient grievances, the storehouse of permanent hurts that I have long forgotten but she has written down. For years, she has been waiting for a sitdown with me, a terminal venting of grievances—a situation I have done and will do anything to avoid, for myself and for her, fearing that her bad heart will burst before the catalogue is recited, my final crime. I sit hovering between truth and the need for heart-patient calm, with calm always the loser.

As usual, she walks in as though something is wrong here and stands fixed to her spot in the safe zone near the door, ready to depart. Her eyes tour the room, regretting her generosity, for most of the furniture here is hers, and come to rest on me— undergroomed as usual. She is punishing me for her own unsolicited dutifulness when I was a child, as though anything had required her to buy me eight dresses and then return the six I didn't like.

"Mother," I say, drawing back so I don't have to kiss the perfumed cheek, so strangely, frighteningly soft. She notices.

"Of all the paintings in the world, why did you have to buy mine?" she says, her eyes flaming on the tree immediately. "There's no light here. You can't see it. This is not an apartment for art."

"Didn't you want it back? Now we can straighten the whole situation out with Harriet. Maybe I won't have to pay as much for it."

"*You* won't have to pay! You know it's mine." There was one of those pauses during which we used to watch her disregard the long, growing ash, eyed by everyone else as it arced its descent to the carpet; but now there was no ash. "When are you going to return it?"

"I just made the first payment. They are letting me work it out."

"But you can't possibly think it is *yours!*" Voice rising: "Harriet stole it. I never was paid. And where did you get the money?"

This was the beginning of a big row, the kind that would lead to her storming out, a week of silence. In fact, she rarely leaves calm. After about half an hour, the collective failings of Josie and I usually so oppress her that her straight back bends to a premature dowager's hump, the metaphorical repository, the very backpack, of her griefs. And yet there are no real yelling rages. She simply blows away in silent fury, leaving the fires burning, the trouble stirred up.

I've always thought of Cigarette as beautiful and tall. But she is actually quite short, and only recently, as I look down at the top of her head, have I been able to see her as short. It's the long face with the strong chin. Cab drivers, bullied by her voice, always used to study her in their rearview mirrors, thinking she was Lauren Bacall, though she is half the size.

When I was a child, she always had bed trays brought to her in the morning, her crumpled ball gown and print satin shoes with rosebud toes thrown on the chair; but I cannot remember her other than fully dressed, girdled into her narrow skirts, her flesh compressed, her toes so squeezed by her expensive shoes that long ago they became deformed—everything tight, cinched-in, shiny, always in black and red, storm and volcanic fire, with her green eyes shining through.

One by one, my childhood friends used to ask why my mother did not like them. "It's just her expression," I would say, meaning her sense of self, a mysterious drawn-up grandeur that came from a lifetime of being loved. Were she an empress, Cigarette could not have more self-regard. She would rather go home from downtown midway in her shopping than be seen carrying a package. Now that she can no longer buy things, which was the whole point of her taste, she is somewhat lost and spends her time having the remaining things reglued, repaired, and repolished.

"Let's let it go for now, Mother. It's back. You can borrow it whenever you like. I'll leave it to you in my will." We were now in the familiar and dangerous territory of property (which means *her* property). Property—lost, remaining, future—hangs over us all now that we are in a state of ruin, for, of course, there is her will. A few years ago Cigarette went to a stationery store and bought packs of colored stick-on tags, which she began to affix to the undersurfaces of much of her remaining furniture and objects. Immediately, we all broke the color code, and very few holidays have passed since without one or two descendants deliberately dropping napkins to see on just whose table we are eating. Rare ashtrays and plates are also inspected, and we are always watching each other's Band-Aided hands for pickups, each other's bodies for sudden crouches. Of course, the fuchsia neon tags are mine. She has told me.

She had taken a few steps from the door to study the painting, as though trying to read in it evidence of my betrayal succeeding Harriet's. She too was lost for a moment in the colors of the past. For, if I had lost things, how much more had she lost! By coincidence, her three closest friends had killed themselves (though one was a double suicide and the other perhaps a mistake), leaving Cigarette the burden of their mysteries and the idea of suicide as a sensible middle-class alternative. I knew she would rather die than depend on me. I also knew she would rather die tomorrow on Fifth Avenue than ten years from now on Third. Already she had made each of her children vow to disconnect the tubes. But from me she was looking for something further. From me she was looking for deliverance. I was the one nominated to put the pills down her throat and then go to prison. So why, I asked myself, did she walk briskly around the reservoir, flapping her arms, as she passed my group, the laggardly Peabrains? Why did she join a class of thirty-year-olds at her club and fill her refrigerator with nonfat foods? Double-jointed, double-faced, born the day before me, like me, under the sign of the two-faced twins.

"It's Lucy," I said, handing her the phone. "She's tracked you down. Weren't you supposed to have lunch?"

That exercise class at the club had supplied Cigarette with a team of surrogate daughters who did not disappoint, a whole tribe of eager, nonworking Fifth Avenue girls rich enough to take her instruction in extravagance. As she held the phone, I studied her long jaw and thought of how she always overdid things: too much oil or mustard or salt, too long in the oven, the pots untended when the cook was off; the long ash growing, growing before the final fall.

"I'll be right there," Cigarette said.

"I have to go too, Mother. I'll go down with you."

She picked up the little package she had left by the door to drop off for a friend who had been knocked down by two men carrying an antique carpet.

Veronica stood holding her front door open with one foot as Sally Adams's assistant stuffed a sheaf of fabrics into a Clarence House bag. Little swatches kept falling out, and Veronica's foot in its alligator loafer began to tap, which seemed to make the woman even more nervous. Veronica was wearing jeans with a white shirt and her large emerald set in a man's gold ring on her pinky. She had long ago passed the stage of dressing up for anyone; she no longer bothered to play any roles. And yet it was all planned. Beside the door was a small mound of open canvas bags, the kind the driver hands to the pilot before the plane takes off. I heard music—one of the groups I didn't know anymore—that changed the tone of the place, reducing its grandeur.

"Is she any good?" Veronica asked Sandy as soon as the elevator doors had closed, for I had relented and brought him along. "I didn't like any of her things."

"They're happiest with fourteen rooms in Greenwich," he said to her in the drawl he'd developed on the train out of Long Beach. They "got" each other right away as some people do, especially two completed self-creations.

Off to the right was the main staircase, still with the wrought iron and old velvet railings. The good southern light lay before us, pooled on the floor like the trompe l'oeil circles one hostess had stenciled on her floors. Half of the living room had just been painted a pale yellow, and some of the walls still showed the sheets of linen preparation. It was empty except for two gilt chair frames placed in front of the fireplace.

"An ancestor?" Sandy asked, looking at a portrait of a very dark woman with an infanta ruff that had been built into the boiserie.

"Isn't she ugly? She's going," Veronica said, and we headed for a small parlor, where she sank into a chair so plump the down sighed under her. In front of us was a bench filled with boxes and shells and the kind of objects people who travel a lot pick up in places like Bali and the Galápagos.

The air conditioners were on, but the sulfur smell from the pit seeped in through the double glass and the silk puddled on the floors. The stench had lingered for days and many gagged. People burned their Rigaud candles but could not buy new ones because some had exploded and all the green ones had been recalled. Outside, the few lunatics who had always walked the streets in surgical masks were thought to be prescient.

"Today, we had no water and no phones. Jack had people over with special lines, but they don't work," she said. I knew the basements now were wading pools. The logs that some buildings provided for their tenants were floating along, loosed from their bins. Strange vibrations were felt even as high as the upper floors, and since many elevators weren't running, the men stood around, their white gloves clasped behind their backs, out of habit still listening for buzzes as they argued the next race.

"When we first moved in, the Stillman children had spray-painted on the walls 'You win, Grandma!' I suppose that's some story." She looked up.

Standing in the doorway was a miniature man in a dark blue suit. He was perfectly formed, from his child's feet in narrow cordovan shoes to the thick hair combed straight back and the eyebrows which arched up in wings of perpetual surprise at the failures in taste and scale that always surrounded him. His shirt was the most brilliant of whites, his handkerchief folded like origami, and his skin shone with a recent tan. He moved like a dancer, and was across the room before any of us could move, soundless on his tiny, shiny shoes. His eyes remained locked on Veronica, but they had seen the whole room. He waved and cruised by the air at my neck.

Banished in the last decade, Jean-Pierre Fournier and his minimalism were now back in favor. His rooms were simplified to the point of poverty. What Angelo added to rooms, he subtracted. In fact, he was known as the Subtractor. They were stripped, denuded, pared down to puffy white sofas on shiny dark brown. They were daringly boring and unobtrusive: lumpy floors, rocks, bones, neo-poor old bathtubs, and crucifixes. That was his trademark—an ancient cross in every room. He told all his clients his favorite room was a hut in Haiti and watched their faces.

"I don't think I'm quite the boy for this job," he said.

"Oh, but this is not what I had in mind," Veronica said. "I don't want it to stay like this. It's too old fart. I want to rip it open and let it breathe."

"But I think, Mrs.—" he paused and looked down at a paper—"Kahn, that you want your young friends to gasp and take tours, and that just is not the way I work at all," he said, and he swiveled on his feet with a slight pained smile and held out a tiny brownish hand.

"Do you think that?" she said. "Do you really? Is that your *assumption?*"

"Why don't you at least have a look around, Jean-Pierre."

"But you see, Libby, I *know* the apartment. I did the apartment when Poppy Stillman had it. I know every floorboard, and the grandchildren, and that is why . . ." He looked down at his shiny shoes and lined them up on the shiny floor.

"I was so interested in having someone who understands simplicity." said Veronica.

"This is such a hard season for me. I don't think . . . But I will take a walk around with you—for Libby." And so we moved through the rooms.

"I'd fir out that wall, lower the ceiling—I'd move the doors to line up. I wanted to do it before, but the Stillmans . . ." He cradled his elbow with his other hand.

"His eighty-thousand-dollar doors," I whispered to Fisher.

"This is my orangerie, where I work on my trees," Veronica said, coming to a greenhouse. "Of course, most are in dormancy now, like the miniature evergreens—the azaleas and boxwood."

"I never could understand the appeal . . ." said Jean-Pierre, pretending to look at a dwarf juniper but checking his enormous old watch.

"Each tree is a little bit of nature, but all concentrated, and no two are the same. This one is perfect," she said, bending over. "Three branches—one toward heaven, one toward earth, and one in between—that is man." She put her hand on his sleeve. "The clipping table here." There were racks of tiny scissors, rolls of wire, and stacks of bonsai books, which, as I picked one up, looked read, with pink semicircles on the pages where her nails had skated.

"This is what you never see, what makes them small—it's not only cutting them back, it's these," and she lifted a tiny tree, the trunk bound, trained to "weep," and pried it with her nails from the earth and showed us the roots, wrapped in cheesecloth tightly bound with coiled wire into a ball dripping nuggets of earth.

"When the roots come through, you cut them off. You see the beauty on top," she said, and held it up near her face, "and then the bound roots, the screaming roots."

"Why do they all have a rock?" Sandy asked, not hearing.

"Good lord, I must fly," said Jean-Pierre suddenly, "my plane to . . . I'm so sorry." He glided to the door, but he looked back. Veronica had whirled around, and it was as if she gathered force from the motion, for it swarmed around her and came roaring at him down the hall. It was like a buzz in the air as she spun him in and took him over.

"I must never finish," she whispered as she walked to him and stood very, very close.

"With me, you never will," he said, and gave her his small leathery hand.

"I'm surprised Fournier even came," Sandy said to me. "He almost never accepts a job anymore."

At this moment we heard, from the rear of the apartment, sounds of many languages, raised Asian voices, a muted shriek, the thump of perhaps a chair turning over, and the unmistakable sounds of mad little shoes flip-flopping across the marble floors. A child with a wet, bunched-up face flung open the door and hurled herself into the room.

"This is Aurora," said Veronica, as if she couldn't help it. "You must tell me," she said, and now she put her face right next to the girl's, almost as a disclaimer of connection.

"Nordis says I can't wear my flipflops to school."

"Well, you can't."

Behind Veronica a tall blond Swede in eight inches of skirt and twelve inches of pointy boot stood full of attitude. "She wants to wear the shoes for the beach to the school."

The child flung herself down and began to sob and roll along the dark, shiny floor. Veronica looked far into the middle distance at a piece of silk taped onto the wall as the Swede picked her up and, keeping out of the way of her fists, carried her off.

"I guess you know what that's like. Her new school, Park Episcopal, is so stuffy, and this year we apply her for kindergarten."

Aurora was certainly the right name for that school. I could see it hanging in the hall with the autumn leaves pressed with shaved crayons ironed on wax paper, printed above the coat pegs with all the last-name first names and those rooted in the ancients of Greece and Britain.

"Sometimes I feel overwhelmed—all the houses and things— but when it's too much I just leave and book another trip," Veronica said, as we made our way to their bedroom. There was a small pyramid of shiny silver weights by the door and a rolled-up lavender mat. An electronic memo pad, a small icon with a black Jesus, and two stacks of books, one topped by *Living in the Light,* were on her side of the bed. She showed us half of a double-edged crystal—Aurora had the other half—to keep her spirit close to the child when she was away. She was holistic, and rather far along the path, curing things I had never heard of, full of happier past lives; but she was not peaceful.

"Maybe I could help," Sandy said. Already they were planning and laughing, and I saw Sandy, more than slightly dazzled, fall in and become part of her household.

Just then a man's step crossed the bare floor above.

"He's always here now. You know someone has to leave the house in the morning, so I do. I travel. Always have." Veronica told us then how she had left home in New Zealand when she was fifteen. She had gone to live with her brother, who did not like her and wouldn't even lend her an alarm clock the night before her first modeling job. She had left on a Turkish ship and was put in a cheap cabin until the captain saw her and then a cabin was found on the top deck. She had been upgraded ever since, given things and flown all over the world. Wherever she was, the doors of the great houses opened to her and all the models who were friends of the sons of the house. She had walked through unsafe places and done daring things and danced at Castel's till four and climbed into low cars for gear-grinding rides through Paris streets, and one of her men called her "Legs" because her legs were so long. She quit modeling when she had to pose with a twelve-year-old, and wound up in California, where she started on the "path"; and then there was a hiatus and her past dropped away.

We could hear a fax in the next room, and Veronica went in to call her travel agent, who was answering her about the Pyramids. At Lampwick, Hugo had told her they might be closing, and she would have to go there right away if it was true.

"I can't stay anyplace more than a few weeks," she told me over her shoulder as she pulled the paper from the machine.

I was totaling up the years of her story to get her age when a large man appeared at the door and waited until she went over.

"Jack wants to meet you now," she told me. "Lazarus can take you up."

Jack Kahn had been waiting. He looked like he had just gotten up from a slab, revived by a jolt of current, and positioned himself alongside his computer, half turned to the door. His eyes were socketed deep in a head too large, and when he walked forward to take my hand, it was as though the head were too heavy causing him to rock forward and back like a nodding doll. He had stubble on his face and colored smudges on his cheeks and hands as though he had been doing pastels or something with the child.

"I have read you, Miss Alexander. I feel I know your mind, though, of course, who can know anyone's mind? When I knew it was you bidding on the little Renoir tree the other night, I let you have it, though I wanted it because of Veronica's trees," he said, and waved to a chair and stood over me nodding agreement at his own words, his hands clenching at his sides, his nails bitten. He wore one of those belts with the big silver buckles and the end that loops over it to make it look as if the person is too cool to fasten it and just casually knots it instead, but the belt lost its war with his intense face. He had yellow socks and ostrich shoes but he did not seem to belong to any of this, for it was the costume of someone who loves himself. I imagined that Veronica had started to dress him a few years ago but had lost interest, leaving him unfortunately stalled in the late eighties.

"I really didn't know what I was doing that night. My family used to own that painting."

"I know," he said, meaning he had investigated me. "Perhaps you would like to see what I have been doing here," he said, waving some computer sheets. "Updating a chronicle of infidelity, a history of my wife's betrayal. Logic tells me that this has a finite life. I love her. I love her guts. I still love her like crazy. But something is wrong."

Two men in blue shirts came in the open door and handed

Kahn some papers, and he looked and said "Yes" or "No." The men watched every nod but seemed to have no reaction to how he looked.

"Individuality is unavoidable; categorization is fundamental and adaptive; and memory is recategorization with decoration. All perception is an act of creation, and all memory is an imaginative act," he said. I was still sorting this through while staring at his belt loop when he continued.

"We are trapped in a weird tragedy of communication, you see," he said, before the men were quite out of the room. "She is terribly afraid to be found out, so she drives me into the wall. She punishes me. She has become totally heedless. We need interpreters. We have always had our interpreters. You," he said.

It was not a question or an invitation. I have accepted that often strangers seem to know my face and talk to me like this. They make assumptions. I have always drawn the sudden confessions of mad people veering to me in the street and the ramblings of tormented chairmen at dinner. They tell their secrets to the one person whose job it is to tell. But now I wanted to get out of this room filled with a stranger's emotion.

"Of course you know Veronica is an hysteric," he said, moving from one piece of furniture to another, standing by each and holding on to its back, seeking anchor there. "Like one of my professors once defined it—when an hysteric walks into the room, you get an erection. They project their emotions. It's the way they move their heads, their little gestures.

"Lying is an act, a motive. Act is motive and breeds more . . ." I could not hear him here, for he was adrift, from one puffy armchair to the next upholstered buoy far across the large room. "The lie can be an act, but also a source of motivation and thus information. Something is off the track here. Proust wrote about how an unanticipated coldness can accomplish more than cosmetics and a beautiful dinner dress."

I had retreated to study the Rossetti of the woman in the

green dress. A canary perched on the open door of its cage. At times like this I still think about my hand wrapped around a glass, the cozy rattle of the circling ice, the heat poured over the cold combining in my throat, and the relief.

"Something is happening across the street." And Kahn waved down at the hole, now buttressed with wood, with twin mountains of copper sand beside it, so that I thought for a second he meant down in the pit.

"We were in that store across the street and a man bumped into her, touched her on the elbow. He said, 'I'm awfully sorry. I'm terribly sorry,' and he put his arm around her. She stood looking into space, rigid, her face still. I know that look. Three times he came over to apologize with this phony accent. With Veronica I have had to keep close track of these things. I have since found out that man was Daniel Gates. She knew him before."

"It doesn't sound like—"

"Maybe it's because she has nothing to do. She has never been a mother—I accept that. She is not a first-rate intellect."

"Well, who is?"

"In science Crick, not Watson. In business and science, some think I am." He was serious. "You must understand our values are not the same. Her life is externals. It was too late when I began to love her to fix it, and so I allow her to run. I've given her her own money. I never understood her, till I saw her walking through the village of our island and having all those people know her. You have to do that here—make this her village. She has to fit someplace."

I could get her started here socially, make her known. He wanted the Pimpernel to root her here and somehow that would distract her from Gates. He came over to where I stood staring as though the listless girl in the green room might get up, take my hands and pull me away. He waited beside me, arms folded, caught in the kind of love that was heading towards a crime.

"She wants to be important. Did you ever hear that perfect love means loving those through whom one became unhappy."

Kahn was one of those word thieves. It was hard to tell where his words ended and someone else's began.

As Lazarus brought me down to Veronica, I heard loud German, which seemed to be answered by Spanish. Veronica did not move, but her eyes narrowed, and then, more than conscious of her own drama, she walked to the double doors and pulled them shut. I asked her a few questions and began writing and we went to look for a picture of her, which was not difficult, since she had kept her portfolios. We found a good one of her in the wind of a long Australian jetty. None of her pictures had the scar above her lip, and none were as interesting as the face I was looking at.

The doorman was out of uniform—his expression of the crisis, I guessed. While I was upstairs, Con Ed had raised orange smokestacks and tents and a telephone van had stationed itself at the corner.

I had promised to go to Boots's party that night. Mercifully it was to be at home, for how many nights of my life was I expected to sit down to dinner in the Temple of Dendur with a drunk on one side and a troubled investment banker on the other as the Hank Lane Orchestra played "Jeremiah was a bullfrog" into my ear?

The next day the Pimpernel discovered the Kahns in their bare apartment above the pit. It was hung with doomed lovers and drowned maidens, as their furniture floated through the basement among the logs. I left all the unhappiness out and wrote a small matching fairy tale. I think it was the first lie I have ever written, and it scared me. *Home* magazine called immediately to ask if I would fly to their house in Toronto, but I refused, for I knew that one day before they could run the story Veronica would call—"Oh, by the way, darling, have you heard the news?"—and it would be all over. Or she might not call, if she thought she could get away with it.

At ten, Veronica's driver brought a tiny, ancient tree, gnarled and wizened in its pot. He handed it over with some embarrassment. With it was a note on a postcard from the Tate and a sheet of instructions for its care. I had to drown it and wire it and clip it—on and on she went. I studied her writing, which was full of large looping and swooping capitals with dramatic curling tails. Another illiterate in town, but at least she cared for something.

"You're on your own," I said to the tree.

VIII

Boots Gets Serious

There was a burning smell in Boots Simpson's hall rather like patchouli incense and, inside the door, a long bench on which books and periodicals were lined up in stacks: *News Tibet; The Suppression of People: Accounts of Torture and Imprisonment in Tibet;* an old embargoed press release dated December 1, 1989, from the Physicians for Human Rights. Instead of Boots's usual coat minion there stood an industrial-looking rack with wire coat hangers sagging with the weight of anoraks and exhausted trench coats, under which was a pile of worn briefcases and backpacks with Greenpeace stickers. It was ominously silent for such a crush of coats.

I walked into the living room and saw Ames Reed by the door. "What's all this?" I said, and immediately a circle of serious faces turned around, and a few said "Hush."

What *was* this? When I accepted Boots's invitation I expected the last Europeans and shrieks of amusement from the corners of the rooms and a dark back room with a loud band and people slumped and the periodical tinkle of broken glass and stray margravines and old Harvard Wasps and drunken counts and young girls who flicked their hair in tight black dresses to go home with them. That was the old Boots, who would have run over hooting to press at the air around my head while she looked over my shoulder at the door. Could I have misread the invitation? And then I remembered her secretary had phoned and said something about Tibet, which I took to mean just another excuse to have a party. No, now I was remembering it, my explaining to the secretary how of course as a journalist I never give money and her saying something about oh no, it wasn't like that at all.

I sat down quickly, which wasn't hard. The whole room was filled with bamboo ballroom chairs, most in a huge circle. For Tibet and accounts of torture Boots couldn't have her usual little gilt chairs with the tie-on velvet cushions that roared Old Fart dinner. These chairs said, "We are serious students of life—pull up your socks, pay attention."

Where was Tibet? I wasn't quite sure. I thought it was somewhere near India. All those eighth-grade geography tests I cheated on! Yes, of course Asia, but where? And what was the problem? Who was torturing them? I remembered all those *Lost Horizon* people stumbling over the pass and collapsing in the snow and the woman's face starting to age and wrinkle hideously and collapse into bone. That's all I knew.

I noticed the wife of the publisher of my paper, who suddenly was wearing glasses. In the front row a Tibetan man was picking his ear.

"When I was in China this spring . . ." said a woman in a cheongsam whom I recognized as Dorothy Porter, the only socially visible Chinese woman in the city. But somehow I could not hear; her soft little voice grew dimmer and dimmer.

"Perrier or soda?" the waiter whispered, bending over me. "I mean club soda—they've been recalled."

I had dressed all wrong with my black sequined suit. The man in front of me tugged up his gray sock to meet his corduroy pants. I looked for Boots and found her in a sort of robelike thing with huge amber beads twisted all over and the same expression of rapt devotion on her face I had last seen at a lecture on the furniture of Versailles. She too was wearing glasses. A humbled quiet, almost a pall, filled the room.

On the table in front of me was a basket of Brie and water biscuits and a few bunches of grapes starting to pucker. There was also—and my eye lit on it—what appeared to be a typed guest list, one of those documents the secretary had to make for tax purposes (if you can deduct Tibet), with the affiliations and the acceptances and refusals and the After Dinner and Cocktails Only people. Casually I put my copy of *A Human Approach to World Peace* by the Dalai Lama on top of it, then looked around to see if anyone was watching. No one was, so I picked it up. I began to study the names and titles. This must be the honky list, for there were no Tibetans, only one prince. A very serious crowd—all world-affairs writers, professors, intellectuals, the hitherto socially despised. No wonder I knew almost no one. I could not understand why I was here. I began to count the number of people wearing glasses in the room, then the dirty shoes. Every few minutes a pair of shoulders would jerk as one of the audience started awake. I could not hear, except when the senator spoke in that voice of his, all swoops and emphases. But still I understood very little.

"Do you think I could have a Coke?" I said to the waiter, who was one of the old school, before actors picked up trays.

How this room, which once had looked like the perfect set for *Blithe Spirit,* had changed! The windows overlooking the park and the zoo were bare and clean, with only a few double sheets of Skyline Thermopane between us and the night. Giant bamboo trees grew all over the room, their spores combining with the dandruff on the professors' shoulders, and there were at least six Buddhas cradling votive lights, fruit, and flowers on their ample laps. Between the two windows that faced downtown was a twelve-foot Buddha, and there, against his fat robed knee, sat Boots in her spectacles, looking dangerously ready to loll. Everywhere were low tables inset with silver and ivory and crammed with baskets and worked silver boxes, strewn with hangings and cloths and artifacts.

"Could we get the senator to speak to the problem?" said a man who sounded annoyed. Next to him, a man kept lifting a strand of his long hair and twirling it round his finger. I tried not to look, but I could not stop. Then I tried to concentrate, but I kept thinking back to Gates and Veronica and if it would happen and if I should stop it or maybe even help it for a while. I began to see the faces across the room. One or two of the old crowd were there after all. I saw Chip Streeter, who knew Boots's husband from Harvard, and Chase Porter who wrote about American history. I knew Chase came from a house where the library was hung with Constables floor to ceiling and there were Bonnards going all the way up the staircase and, in the dining room, on the rotting silk walls, actually a painting of Manet by Monet. I heard a floor man had been sent to Europe to buy the special wooden floors, and when they were sent over, he installed them and Chase's mother had said, "No, no, Franco"—or some name like that—"I want them to look like watery sunlight on a rainy day." It was that kind of family. The last time I had seen Chase he was walking up Madison Avenue at two-thirty in the afternoon in maroon velvet pants talking to the flat of his hand.

There was a stir at the back of the room, and Cherry Frontsmann swooped in and hovered like a hawk cruising the skies for morsels. A giant, blond, thin woman, she perched on the edge of the bamboo chair and searched the room until she saw me and frowned. I'm sure Cherry knew all about Tibet, for, as much as I had turned from the rest of the world, she had given herself to it. She was actually a pioneer of the new serious mood, for her dinners had always been filled with foreign-affairs types and members of the Council on Foreign Relations. Of course she had totally stopped inviting me.

As I spread a film of Brie on a cracker, it came to me. I was supposed to reveal this new horn-rimmed Boots—quiet, studious, devoted to abused foreign peoples, sitting high up here on lower Fifth surrounded by professors and chairs from Columbia, spies and American heirs, all of whom could identify with the exiled and abused. But this was more. I felt myself on the very brink of the mood of the new decade. Here was the new seriousness, the retreat from the vulgarians. Gold beaten into bamboo. Horn rims misting with sincerity instead of taffeta poufs. Water to drink. It was a full retreat from that viciously fast flowering of cash and display and showing off and racing around buying things and stapling fabric and the morning arrivals of Old World workmen who would sit sewing on tassels where the fringe turned a corner.

I remembered a party from the week before in a designer's apartment. His wife had photographed a book in India, and there she was, bent over the designer's English center table in a very strict author jumpsuit with a belt from India, her long black hair dribbling onto the stack of books she was signing.

In front of me, Chip Smullion raised his hand. In the deep quiet of a library I could hear the breaths rise and fall, while behind the hostess the blue night of Fifth Avenue gleamed and twinkled.

"Let me just, if I could, read this passage from Yoeden Choedak's account of her interrogation," said a man, and he raised his pamphlet. "That should answer your question. 'Then I was taken to Drapchi Prison, where Chinese policemen tried to strip me again. I cried as my clothes were being ripped off . . . Then I was beaten all over my body with the electric stick, many times on my breasts, mouth, and head. . . . Ever since I have difficulty remembering things and learning new words. I think this is from the electric sticks.' "

"What are you doing here?" Cherry said. She'd moved back to stand over me. "Shhhhh," said someone else.

I began to feel guilty. I decided to be nicer to Angelina. I hadn't been very nice to the Indonesian dwarf who came before her. The more I thought of Angelina, the more I was reminded that she had been very glum of late. There had been many sidelong glances, many lowering, reproachful looks. Now, as we passed in the hall or stood next to each other in the kitchen—I sticking my fingers into the pyramids of raw vegetables she had

so meticulously slivered—I saw that darkening of the counte-
nance almost as though the pigment of her face had deepened,
and her brow lowered, and a certain sadness came into her eyes.
At the same time her nose seemed to widen and thicken, her
nostrils to flare, like a scared horse. Now, come to think of it,
her smiles were very rare. There had not been those impromptu
rice cakes or offers to make my favorite tempura in a long time.
I felt a sort of scurrying sideways movement around the house
as she narrowed her body to slide past the white devil in the hall.
And those absences, those prolonged trips for bread and carrots? She was out looking for another job. Having seen this
many times before, I promised myself to call Mario Casaba, the
employment man, in the morning, just in case.

I could not live without my Angelina. I knew the disruption,
the psychic pain, the grim procession of the dignified souls to be
interviewed, and I knew how bad my judgment was in these
domestic interviews. In the six months before Angelina, I had
hired a religious maniac who arrived in a man's suit carrying a
briefcase and asked for more money the first day; the dwarf, who
even after a week needed a map to go to the cleaners; and a
Brazilian who could not cook or iron but was sweet, and had a
mustache of sweat on her upper lip from trying so hard.

"Who is that woman you wrote about today?" said Boots,
coming up to me, beads banging, Tibet forgotten. "Doesn't she
do anything?"

"Actually, she does bonsai."

"I hate bonsai. Do you know Jay Lightfoot? He is doing a
book on Tibet, maybe."

"I've seen you before," I said to the young blond man.

"I really admire your writing. I wrote my master's at Berkeley
on you."

"On me?"

"Yes—to me your work has always indicated a precise ther-
mometer of where we are now."

"Come have some dinner," Boots said. "It's all vegetarian."
And so it was, those tasteless heaps I remembered from the

sixties wherein the only excitement was the stray crunch of a few pignoli nuts.

"I really love eating food like this," Boots said. "I think it's so pure. How do you like the apartment now?" she whispered behind the back of the editor of *Tibet News*. "And my new group?" She got up and named all her guests as though those on the Tibet brigade could conceivably not know each other, but I think she did it for me, not knowing I had filched her list. The man on my right averted his head from my black sequins the entire night, and so I turned to the tweed shoulder on my left. I always try to pay attention, for the man who bores you at dinner tonight might be the scandal of tomorrow. I began, and he answered "yes" and "no." I looked into my tomato juice and thought fondly of its paling and puddling at the edges to that nice watery vodka pink. I looked across the tables at Chip, who also no longer drank. Those of us who no longer drank knew each other and understood, could feel the vibrations of each other's agony across the long dinners across the long rooms.

Finally, Boots began to read from *The Status of Tibet*, her hands clasped in front of her as if she were praying into her beads. For the moment I was saved from conversation, and behind my green glasses could squeeze my eyes shut.

"No calls," said Mrs. Lazarheit as I came in the door, "but Angelina left you this." I recognized one of my Tiffany envelopes, now all strangely swollen and clanky. My keys, and wrapped around them, a tiny neat note I could not bear to read.

"She's gone!" I said to Mrs. Lazarheit. And like a bolt I heard the Latin voice of Chica Starck: "Never, never pay them on the Friday. Arrange to pay them on the Monday or they never come back."

"Maybe I can help a bit," said Mrs. Lazarheit, but I knew better than to open the sacred compartments that separated baby-sitter from housekeeper.

"I'll have to call the man in the agency in the morning. He'll know someone."

It had to be right away, for the whole system of motherhood functioned only because of the Angelinas, who took the children to birthday parties and bought their classmates presents and sat in the orthodontist's and doctor's waiting rooms and school assemblies. The only times the actual mothers were ever seen were for a few very rare, very social birthday parties when they were curious about the apartment, though sometimes they did appear in those bright orange ponchos for after-school safety patrols. In pairs, they walked past stores with their SAFE HAVEN stickers, appearing to their stunned offspring like large alien creatures, the absent mommies from space.

No Angelina! I couldn't work without the calm of a well-run house. Mario's Filipino girls had spoiled me. I was used to the ironed sheets and washed lettuce sweating inside plastic bags and peeled carrots in ice water always ready, the decapitated strawberries and the gentle creaking of the iron over the board as the stacks of folded sheets rose higher. They did these things without being asked, as though the same fussy mistress had taught them all. It was like being cared for by the silent and invisible hands at an enchanted castle. Many women had "backup girls" for weekends so they were always completely "covered" and could dance out the door.

"This is the way mister like his shorts," the mistress would say, showing a mysterious and never to be repeated facility with the iron and the starch, and then she would disappear out of the kitchen, out of the land of machines in the back of the house. She would drift away like Gloria Guinness, who once, according to some article I read, took a guest right to the very door of the kitchen in her Acapulco home and said, *"You* may enter. I have never been in the kitchen. I'll wait for you here."

Mario worked from a little office in New Jersey where the women came to sit like shadows against the wall. I remembered without enthusiasm those Mario calls. "Hello, good afternoon," he'd say at any hour, always dead calm because he had been a diplomatic attaché. "We have an applicant named Mona, thirty-two, a college grad-u-ate . . ." and meanwhile all the women—high-strung was a charitable description—would be sitting tapping their pencils to their cheeks, dangling their high heels from their insteps and studying their inner knees or looking up and deciding to have their ceilings reglazed. Sometimes they only thought it; sometimes they would actually say it, because they somehow said unspeakable things to Mario: "I don't want someone to *talk* to, I want someone to clean my toilets."

And still the calls came in, and still he sent them out—the Segundas and Mindas and Zanys. Still that calm voice of Mario in the morning. He had a woman, a college graduate, and there was another . . . he would find me someone.

Traffic was tied up because of the hole, and now I settled into my weekend—Sandy Fisher was taking me on a photo shoot for Gates.

IX

Trophies

I'm worn out," I told Sandy as he closed me into his Jeep. "It's the Dell divorce. Jimmy or Sam Chalk call every hour. Blanca's other lawyers are faxing me, and I have to write almost every day now."

I leaned back. The sun glinted on the little round horn rims perched on his fortunate nose as we headed to the Lincoln Tunnel.

He had the usual dollar in his change well, not for the tolls, but as a blood money tithe, to hand to the guys who would fall on his windshield at all the exits and entrances. The car next to us was running its wipers to keep them away.

"I saw Sylvia Mendes rushing to the Society Library yesterday to get last Wednesday's paper. She couldn't miss an episode."

"Everywhere I go that's all people ask me about. I'm a prisoner of their divorce."

I knew how my readers loved pain and any nasty news, how they called back and forth with each detail and rushed for the afternoon tabloids which they said they never read and always were nudging me for more, fretting over blind items, feeding on the bones. "Have you seen . . . ? Call when you've read it," they would say to each other as I raced with Diana and Sally on my story and took the late angry calls from Jimmy Dell. They needed the Dells as they had once needed the Solomons, to live outside their own lost lives. It was one of those stories that made everyone nervous—everyone had at least seen them around and felt they knew them, for the Dells had opened all their doors.

It was as though an angry god stood at the base of our little world rattling the boughs. Each frippery that once had been celebrated, encouraged in every possible way, was now impossible to contemplate. Dirty! Dirty deeds! It had gotten worse since the night of the explosion, as though the opening of the pit had released a swarm of evil imps, leaping from the geyser in the blast of rot from the underground. The feds marched into the downtown offices; old firms collapsed; the business stars were fired, their beach houses foreclosed. They were divorcing their third wives, hiring grave dancers and the new specialists in restructuring. The angry little god stamped his foot and shook the trees and the coconuts fell one by one to the sidewalk where people sagged on gratings behind the signs that explained their lives, silently jiggling Styrofoam cups.

In between came the calls from Mario ("Hello, good afternoon") and the procession of crushed souls with scarcely spirit enough to lie as the details of the Dell megadivorce and its millions were being beeped to me from the next room. Jack Kahn's voice came, too, whispering plots over my machine as I stood by my dryer hugging the warm towels to my chest.

"I'm glad we are going," I said to Sandy.

"Well, Oliver isn't too happy."

"I don't care. What's the theme of the shoot?"

"It was supposed to be Katharine Hepburn Connecticut, but it's gotten to be a hunt in Far Hills. It's not really *where* it is; it's *what* it is. These were the only Polaroids Danny approved, so Oliver had to go along. I wanted the Legover Hunt Club. That was the real thing. Seventy-five years of Protestant squalor—two hundred sets of filthy golf clubs with turds of turf falling off and that smell of clubhouse furniture paste and old books. Dust puffs blowing under the chairs. And on the walls pictures of

'Colonel A. H. Montgomery Aboard Flipper,' written in this spidery, alcoholic hand. I don't know why, but it just didn't Polaroid."

I knew Sandy could go on like this forever. His scouting trips for Gates brought him deep into the forbidden lands of the Little Noses, where his affected drawl, his large English suits and Docksiders fooled no one.

"What *more* could he want? We were trying not to squeal. All these helmets saying 'LHC,' and the saddles. It was colder in the clubhouse than outside. Just imagine a yellow building, black shutters, black trim, in the middle of one thousand acres, and the men's locker room in the barn, with the clubs and the dirty lockers filled with unwashed underwear, and peeling paint and this sea of cracked leather armchairs. I met this great old boy, one of the trustees of the reservations. They have seventy-three tracts in Massachusetts of Cabots and Lodges and Pingrees. There's this one man who brings his refrigerator from Boston each summer with the food still in it, and then he brings it back. We had lunch at some inn and he said, 'I'll have the pork.' Ooooo! Then he asked me what I did for Gates. I told him that I interpret Protestant fantasies for Jews. Believe me, he got it perfectly."

Just then his phone rang.

"They sent me hounds that *don't match*. I don't believe this. Put me on with the trainer—I'll wait. What do you mean, 'nervous about his nose'? It's not a huge beak. Okay, it's big, but the old guy is not Jewish, he's Italian, Oliver. Maybe they don't *have* to match. If two are okay, bag the others, forget the trainer. You can get François or Alex to put a little powder on the nose."

"I'm so hungry," I said.

"We have six cars with their tailgates down stuffed with food."

"Isn't all that stuff sprayed?"

"Yeah, but we had the caterers in. We auditioned caterers for six hours last week."

The phone rang again.

"I don't know if the manes should be pleated or not. Ask Janie Childs. If they want to wear shad bellies and meltons, let them. They know the right thing.

"You should have seen all these people jumping in limousines and driving around and going into the houses so beautiful I couldn't speak, and they'd say, 'Can't stand the chintz in the bedroom, we need new chintz,' and spend hours interviewing caterers for themselves."

When we got to "the property," as Sandy called the Childs estate, neither the horses nor the real blonds had arrived, and Oliver was raging and François was washing his makeup brushes in Evian.

"Well, I'm not sitting around for two hours—let's all go shopping," said a woman called Andy who was someone important with Gates's team. "We'll go to that bookstore you mentioned."

"I don't think he's open," said Sandy, ducking his head as he does whenever he lies.

"We'll get him to open," said Andy. "Just give me the directions."

We piled into two long silver cars with uniformed drivers, cars that had never been seen in this part of New Jersey, even when someone had to be driven to the airport. There was Andy in her jodhpurs with riding shoes with fitted uppers and gaiters and a hand-knit cardigan and a Chanel quilted parka, and Chris, the store art director, with his thinning blond hair in a ponytail halfway down his back and a wisp of a beard and a long cognac canvas duster, and someone called Martin who was wearing golf collection clothes, and the grandfather model they had decided not to use this time, all dressed "country," Gates country.

Like bullets piercing the landscape, the long silver cars sped past the horse farms, bouncing over flattened balls of fur and feathers.

"Bookstore first, then, if we have time, the golf trophies from the Hedge Club," Andy instructed.

"This can't be it!" she shrieked as we pulled up to a tiny

used-book store with dusty ducks in the window and a painting of a deer alert with fear. It was closed, but Andy began to bang and call, and the man in the cognac duster joined her, until a wispy-looking old man with a fringe of white hair and glasses up on his forehead came to the door and opened it a crack on what surely must have been one of the worst sights of his ancient life. At that moment the other car pulled up and the rest of the Gates team ran crunching over the gravel like it was some kind of race.

"I'll give you fifty bucks if you open for us," Andy said, and the man just looked at her and stood aside and they all fell in. He couldn't seem to unlock his eyes from the cognac duster (was it an apparition? was it an angel? some wild prince?) as they raced past the old Underwood typewriter where he had obviously been typing postcards on the desk next to one of those 1950s rotary phones.

"Look at that!"

"Did you catch the typewriter?"

"I'll take all the pillows!"

"Not those—I want all *those!*"

"It looks like marble!"

"I want that lamp! I'm dying! Those shades are great!"

"Oh, look—art books!"

"Marty, get those pillows!"

Now, as the dust was rising, they put their scarves up to their mouths and kept on as though they were being pursued by another band of maniac collectors right down the road.

"We came for books," Andy said suddenly, and they began measuring the books on the shelves.

"What do you think we need—three feet? Four feet?"

"What are we up to so far?"

"You could all get out of my shop," said the old man suddenly, but weakly, in one of those voices the Little Noses take centuries to breed, and he was talking now, not to Andy but to the "grandfather."

The barking continued from the back of the shop, those New York voices. "What are we up to so far? Two thousand dollars?

Do you think we should just take them all? Have we got six feet of books yet?"

"Can we put the rugs on hold?" Andy said, coming up to the old man.

"Those are not for sale," he said.

"I hope you've arranged the discount?" someone called out to Andy, and everyone froze.

"That's Camilla's job," she said, and indeed Danny had hired a forbidding Englishwoman just to bargain in situations like these.

"Yes, but she's in Providence."

"Well, I'm not going to do it," Andy said. "We'll pay retail."

"How much we got so far?" someone called.

"Shit is all I got so far. What are five stacks? About fourteen hundred?"

Then Andy began trying to explain to the old man how these were for Danny Gates.

"Who?" said the old man, so that Andy couldn't go on. "You could all get out of my shop," he said again, but even more faintly.

"No, no," said Andy. "It's too great."

"We need him to itemize them for us, then we can send the truck for them."

"Maybe I can speak to him," I said finally, and they all looked at me. "These people are from New York," I said. "They are used to buying things like this. You can charge them whatever you want—just write out a bill. You've been awfully kind to open for us." I saw him nod as we all left.

"How about the Hedge Club on the way back—to get the golf trophies for the store window?"

"Let's do it."

The long entrance to the club, marked by tidy matching whitewashed rocks, the signs saying "Private," the greens where only a few old men looked up startled as we approached, had suddenly dampened everyone.

"I think we'll wait in the cars—it looks kind of stuffy," Andy said. "You go, Marty," she said to the man in the golf collection clothes. "And take Walter," she said, nodding at a fat man with a shaved head and pointed black beard, in black pants and black leather-trimmed sweater. We were all rather silent as we waited and waited.

They came back with big smiles.

"How did it go?" I asked.

"You should see how really nice the barman was," said Marty. "He let us Polaroid everything."

"Andy, you should see the lockers—they're *so great!* I wanted to buy them. We're going to copy them. We got really close, too. We saw the president of the club. He was *so* nice. He said they would never consider it, but he was really nice."

It was now after twelve, and we headed back. A long table with a floral cloth and flowers from the Childs' gardens had been set up, and everybody was eating lobster salad.

"How did it go?" Sandy said.

"Amazing," I said, "but no trophies."

As we were eating, little streaky-blond Childs girls with their hard hats came riding by.

"Each blond is getting five hundred dollars a day," said Sandy. "I've never seen so much blond in one group."

"No, you can't eat in makeup," someone said to one of the models.

"She's in the family," Sandy said to me. "We use the family in every ad. See, it has to be a family, but a family no one can quite figure out. No mother, three sisters, the brothers, the grandchildren, now the nose."

"He looks like my father, but my father is living with two bodybuilders in Mexico," said Mary Childs.

"We have to get rid of all the fat ones," someone said, nodding in the direction of the riders. "Blond or not, they're too fat."

Sandy hoisted me onto a split-rail fence. It was so beautiful. I was overlooking five hundred acres along with all the fat Childses in their pinks who had been weeded out. Sandy waved his white handkerchief and the entire fake hunt with matching dogs and all came galloping over the hill. Everyone gasped.

"This is the most wonderful moment ever!" Andy said to Fisher and she wiped her eyes. And it was: all the Protestants watching all the Jews watching all the horses.

"I had no idea you'd be here," Gates said close to me. He must have come up the hill during the charge. Everyone whirled at once and almost fell off the fence.

"Mrs. Childs would love to meet you," Sandy said to Gates. "All this," he said, waving his hand around, "is hers."

"Looks great, but I'm on my way to the country. I just stopped to take a look."

"But Mrs.—" said Sandy, and put his hand to his mouth as if to hush himself, for he had vowed never to beg Gates for things like all the others.

"If you want to come," Gates said to me, "I can have you driven back tonight."

"Yes," I said quickly, because Mrs. Childs had spotted Gates and was moving towards us. We ran past the hams and the wheels of cheeses, the sausages sizzling perpetually in silver chafing dishes. We ran like guilty children, afraid to look back, to his car, where Peter hadn't even shut off the motor.

Over my shoulder, I saw Mrs. Childs in her breeches waving and the fat girls on the fence swinging their boots, a lineup of disappointment. Gates was already bent over his papers, and I studied the changing trees as we passed. I was again just another body in the car.

"Kesselman, what's up?" Gates said into the phone, and he listened a long time to the answer before he said, "It's that bad?" The papers on his lap were heavily marked. He read some figures to his business partner from a black looseleaf and then shook his head and made changes in ink in the margins, ignoring me, as though he knew I was happy enough to be here studying his profile.

"This is my road," he said finally, sweeping the papers back into his case as if they didn't matter at all.

We stopped in front of a small white house I took for the caretaker's cottage until I saw the garden and the rare trees, everything transplanted, as he explained, but looking quite as if it had always belonged, which was precisely the genius of Gates.

He walked me past a rock pool filled by a waterfall now switched off and showed me an arbor and his barn across the road. The land was fenced in, and the fences descended the meadows for miles. Inside the thick-walled house the silence was interrupted only by the violent swirl of the leaves. We sat in front of the stone fireplace, where a perfectly laid fire had been set, awaiting only a single match to burst into its choreographed tower of flame.

"I've never had it photographed here," he said, as though that were the ultimate tribute, and explained everything about the place.

"Are you in trouble?" I asked, thinking back to the car and the papers.

"Yes," he said, and, knowing that I have a face that receives troubles, suspecting I might know something he did not, he told me. When he had started his business, Robert Kesselman of Castle Industries had set him up, taking a one-third interest and handling the financial side. Over the years, he had traded Kesselman more and more of his share for the money to live as he wanted. He had lost his majority interest long ago. Now, with the recession, his business had turned. People wanted cheap things.

Gates spoke slowly, as though he were rehearsing his part, trying to justify it and see how it would play. I was shocked but did not show it. He was another man full of luxuries standing on the rim of the pit. I was remembering what Sandy had told me long ago about how Gates's people all took advantage of him. Gates did not know that he paid for Oliver's town house and Andy's taking the Concorde and being met by a Rolls. "He's just not a businessman in that way. He counts on Kesselman," Sandy had said. Sandy told me they all thought Kesselman was after Gates in some way because he was jealous of Gates living the life he wanted with the girls and the gambling. They all knew Kesselman sneaked his men in when Gates was away, gave them gifts and bonuses, and had them report to him. I had asked why no one had told Gates, and Sandy said no one wanted to start trouble. I was about to tell him this when Gates spoke.

"You think I went to Cuba when I was seventeen?"

"I know. We checked when I wrote it, as much as we could, though Cuba is not very checkable."

"That's why I chose it. I never went there. I was a kept boy." He studied the stones and then looked up. "Oh, no—a woman." Outside, the trees rained their leaves and the wind blew them past in lazy leaf storms.

"Broadway and Seventy-ninth Street. A woman drove up in a Cadillac and I got in. I had nothing better to do. She'd be about sixty now if I could find her. I've tried, but she's gone. The store, the way it looks here—all that is from her. It wasn't any dream, like I told you. It was just the way she used to live, even in Florida, with old things, stacks of books. This is her, too.

"First there was a time in New York, and then we had a long time in Florida. My missing years. I went out there"—he waved west—"without her, but she had sent me." He was silent as the leaves fell, and I asked her name.

"Nadia, and a few more in between and after. We tore around a lot. She had a house at the end of a street on Biscayne Bay. The Cubans went there every night to fish with lights in their nets. That's when we used to go out all night to all the clubs. We slept all day. Then she'd read to me in the coffee shops. Do you know that book *Dead Souls,* and the Chinese poets? It was like a singer singing just to you.

"I never understood why she stayed in Florida. They didn't understand her at all there—except the bad guys, the connected guys in the coffee shop at the Fountainbleau. She was like a little showgirl."

Elements were not working here. The Cadillac . . . connected guys . . . Russian writers. But he could not invent Gogol. I saw them by a pool. She was wearing one of those two-piece Jantzen suits with the bottom like underpants and a turban and those little plastic eye-cup things like Cigarette wore in the fifties with the chains and the little weights falling down behind the ears. A pair of those Miami high-heel slappers. And he was wearing a black nylon European bathing suit, the kind I would have called disgusting when I was ten and might have looked idly across the Fontainebleau pool in one of those long waits to swim after lunch and seen them. It was a displeasing image. What was Gates hiding?

"She sounds like my mother. That whole Latin chica-boom thing. Only my mother is not Latin."

"Neither was Nadia. Her money was a mystery. It came by check from some bank in Massachusetts. I never could figure it out, and eventually it spoiled everything. She gave me thirty thousand dollars in a brown alligator wallet with a ticket to California. She made a few phone calls to the guys who knew the guys in the coffee shop. I want to find her. I want to pay her back. I owe her like I owe you, Libby. I've had agencies looking for years. I still have a man out."

I heard Peter returning and the crackle of paper bags in the kitchen.

"Maybe I should go home now," I said, waiting for him to disagree.

"All that stuff Andy and Oliver do is wrong—much too exaggerated. I know better. Nadia showed me the difference."

We had dinner and Peter drove me home very late that night.

X

The Rapid Beating
of Little Wings

I stood on the windy corner of Eightieth Street and Fifth Avenue, leaning against a mailbox. Boots and Chica were late, as usual, and I was beginning to think that our walking group might have to disband or walk on without me. I had called us The Peabrains, a name I once muttered and Chica instantly had printed on hot-pink sweatshirts which none of us ever wore. The Peabrains were not quite as grand as Gayle and Blanca (who both had personal trainers and would never get this close to me, especially in the morning without makeup), but they loved to learn about and inform on the others, and thus we walked, I needing exercise as they needed exposure. I learned things, but I had to be careful, for they planted lies with me all the time. There had been a sudden decline in the tone of our group since Athena left to plan for her wedding, and there were many days when I felt myself the only reason for their being there. If it's true that we look for characteristics in our friends that are extremes of what we see in ourselves—that the nervous are drawn to the very nervous, and the thin beauties have even thinner friends—I had chosen an appropriate name.

Far down Fifth I could see Boots's purple exercise suit, and

I saw Chica in her spandex coming up with another woman who was swinging her arms. That must be this Barbara that Chica was trying to get us to take on. Even from a block away I could see that all her clothes were new.

"Donna will meet us at the entrance. You know Barbara, of course," Chica said. Barbara was wearing a yellow nylon Gates "Grapevine" exercise suit. "Libby knows Danny Gates," Chica said, following my look. "Where were you last night, the tent or Sylvia's?"

"Party," I said, huffing a bit, for we had come to the hill by the Metropolitan Museum leading up to the reservoir. It was a famous fact of Sylvia's dinners that you were even more uncomfortable after five minutes in the room than when you first arrived. As each new guest stepped in, Sylvia approached, wringing her hands, provoking a flutter of ill ease. Her eyes patrolled the borders, assessing the groups, hoping for a repetition of that night when the playwright bit off the drama critic's earlobe. "Not bad," I said. "She had Gayle and Bill and Howard Goldenson and the girl."

"I hear Sylvia had her eyes done again. Are they any good?"

"They're okay. At least they both seem to close, but they still are very red underneath."

"Well, you don't have to worry anymore. Yours are so much better. I can see through the glasses."

"I did not have my eyes done. I had my ptosis corrected. There's a difference."

"Are you writing Sylvia's?"

At this everyone slowed and looked at me. Boots bent over her knee. We paused on the old iron bridge, hoisted our legs, and bent over them, supposedly stretching the tendons.

"Who did the food? Was it Clark again, or did she get herself another chef?"

"It was too good," I said, feeling the hard little bulge at my stomach. "How's Tibet, Boots?"

"The Dalai Lama is doing better. They are almost saved. I'm

giving a party for the rain forests in December. I'm doing all kinds of other stuff. You're all invited to everything."

"What were you wearing? What did everyone wear?" said Donna.

By this time we had fallen into groups on the cinder path, but everyone slowed to hear what I would say. This was work. I hated talking about something before it was written.

"I'd rather hear about you, Barbara," I said.

"I'm not doing much this year except applying Celia to school." I was immediately aware of her voice, which in some way, whether accent or musicality, had been trained—either that or a master control was exerted. I've never trusted a singing voice. It reminded me of the murmuring lobby mothers at Josie's old school. Even the bums who stumbled into the church house were awed by the low, harmonious hum and waited, quietly slumped, to be helped. I learned then what lies and trickery, spoken by those whispery voices, bloomed in the dimness under the watch of the dark early rectors.

"My older girl is at Birchley, but still, we're going through the whole thing. I took her there yesterday for the interview. Jack Kahn's wife showed up."

At this we all stopped totally, as we usually did only when describing facial surgery, and a pair of serious runners dipped off the path and ran around us, giving us bad looks and spraying us with cinders. The Peabrains were definitely an impediment on the path, but such a familiar one that most of the runners just ran around and ignored us.

"She's making a big move. She's all over the place. Libby made her," Chica said rather resentfully. "But I began the whole thing. I told her how to find you at the Carlyle. She went after you."

"I saw her at Mimi's sample sale, trying on stacks of clothes. She must be very busy. Your friend Fisher was there with her."

"They put her in the front row now at the shows."

"I'm thinking of asking her to chair Veritas," said Chica.

"How did you know her?" I finally asked Chica.

"Julio knew her. She had quite a large court around her. A big hippie house in California with playboys and professors hanging from the trees."

"What happened at school?" I said finally.

"I was wearing my Birchley clothes," said Barbara. "I always keep three things I only wear there, my skirt down to midcalf and some ugly sweaters I got at Brooks Brothers. They stuck me in a room, and they were having an admissions meeting next door—already! It made me nervous that I might be late in this whole thing. I mean, there's no guarantee for siblings anymore, but Celia has good scores. I never heard anything like this. Some man from the board and Mrs. Harris—the one who never washes her hair—and another one I did not know. They were screaming with laughter. It gave me chills."

"Did you hear any names?"

"Well, they got to the Dell girl, or at least I think it was her. I heard Mrs. Harris say, 'I don't think we want any more of *them,*' and then they started reading out scores and her letters, which said things like 'a clear and burning intellect'—and 'an enriching presence'—that gave them another hoot."

"Well, we've all written letters like that," I said. "We've all done those things."

"The man kept saying, 'How was the performance score?' I mean, really, it was all numbers! That's all they kept saying— 'What's the address? What are the scores?' "

"I never thought letters did any good," Donna said.

"The thicker the applicant, the thicker the file," I said.

"Finally I just couldn't take it anymore," Barbara continued, "and I went over to the window and I saw that Veronica Kahn getting out of her car. She really is amazingly beautiful, but the child—"

"She had her car?" said Chica. "No one dares to take the car, especially now."

"She didn't even have the sense to open the door herself. She waits for her driver to come round. That's how you know she was not born with money," Barbara said, looking round at our group, none of whom were born with money but Donna and me.

"All those gestures, like people are watching. First the legs went out, then she stood up—leather dress—smoothed it down, then she bent like this." She stopped to demonstrate, pressing the palm of her hand on the small of her back, and we all stopped, causing another pile-up and mutterings from the runners. "Then she stood up and sailed in, just assumes the little girl is following, which she wasn't, so she had to go back. At this point they all came out of the admissions room, wiping their eyes. They'd had some jolly time. I'd just introduced Celia, though they all knew her from Stella, when in she came. This is ten minutes late now, and the child immediately falls down."

"What do you mean?"

"I mean she tripped and fell flat, the poor thing," Barbara said. " 'Well, that's an unfortunate beginning,' Mrs. Harris said to her. Veronica didn't seem to notice. She was looking around at all the little girls in their uniforms and the 'marms,' as I call them, and she says right out loud, 'Oooh, I love it here,' as though it were her choice, as though she does not know anything and no one had prepared her. Doesn't Park Episcopal do that anymore?"

"She probably missed the meetings," I said.

"Well, that school is *so perverse.* Mrs. Harris was ravished, gave her a big hot smile. Forgot that her skirt is up to her thigh, forgot the high heels, forgot the fact that there was no husband along, the *leather,* and *beams* at her. The more rules she violated, the more she showed she didn't care, the more they lapped it up. Harris took us around herself, and I assure you it wasn't to impress me. They just could not have loved her more if she was black, because that's their dream—the Haitian in the navy Mercedes with the seventeen-room apartment and great scores. When Mrs. Harris said something to me about one of our letters, she said, 'Oh, do you need *letters?* My husband can help me with that'—just right out like that.

"So we had the tour and the speech about how in a girls' school the girls can, of course, hold all the elected offices, and something about boys' brains being slower because of oxygen intake. Mrs. Harris looks just like one of those women from the Soviet consulate—really heavy, with those pudgy toes pushing out of her shoes. We all had questions, but she kept saying 'I will answer that *upstairs*,' which meant the gym. We all stood on one side in a semicircle, holding our coats, and she was about fifty feet away. They try to make it as uncomfortable as possible. I would have been nervous myself if Stella wasn't in.

"We walked through the library and the labs—Veronica is stumbling down the stairs in her high heels and keeps looking at her watch. Then we have our talk with the head, Miss Raidy. Veronica asks for a catalogue. Miss Raidy says, 'We always send one ahead,' and frowns. I asked my question about the Latin curriculum; then she turns to Veronica and asks, 'Do you have any questions?' She says, 'Aurora's nanny is out in the car. Could she come in and wait, and take Aurora home? I have to leave.'

"All I can say is that the child is in—except for that drawing she did. I mean, all the girls filled their pages and she came in with this tiny, tiny rainbow way over in one corner and her pinwheel cutout all wrong. By then the Swedish girl was in the room in her spandex. They love you to thumb their nose at them," Barbara said wistfully. More White Jews running from the truth, I thought. It had taken me two weeks just to write the letters to the people who were writing letters for me. In my day I had failed admission to Birchley, disqualified when I let my coat fall from my shoulders and walked right past it, a gesture which Josie had inherited in toto.

"I forgot the strangest thing of all. Guess who came to pick her up? Stella saw him at the corner and recognized him."

I knew before she said it.

"What are *they* doing together?" Everyone looked at me.

"Too much talking, not enough walking, Chica."

"Well, I'm off anyway," said Chica at Ninety-sixth Street. "Are you coming, Boots?" Then she ran down the steps, her little sneakers making plopping sounds (for someone so thin, she had a very heavy tread), and Donna ran after them to where the Mercedes and driver were waiting next to the man with a cup and the sign that said, "Will Work For Food."

"Wait up," Barbara said, and then she too was gone, and I walked on alone, crunching through the cinders.

It was lucky they had left me, for as I rounded the curve where the path arcs west around the reservoir, I saw Jack Kahn against a tree. Again he looked as though he had posed himself for this ambush, as though he had tried different positions to achieve this one effect, straining to be casual, but it was all wrong. He did not belong in the park in the middle of the morning. He did not fit the tree. It was a waste, and it meant he had had me followed. He was not exactly leaning, but rather propped there, as though without the trunk he might slump into the ground to be lost.

"I knew you would be here," he said as though there had been no interruption in his last monologue. "I've been taking seven-hour walks and playing Bach partitas to hold it at bay." He walked slowly alongside me, and only then did I notice the dog, a large brown spaniel. Kahn's face was pale and moist, and he looked fat. He carried a heavy lined suede jacket over his arm, though the day was warm. His guards had disappeared long ago.

"You know about the camel whose balls were crushed between two rocks? One Arab said to the other, 'Didn't it hurt?' The other said, 'Only when your thumbs get in the way.' I've been an obtuse fool. Athena told me to protect myself."

"So you've been talking to Athena."

"It's best not to crowd Veronica, as you told me. I see it all clinically—depression, obsession, spasms of sexual jealousy."

He told me how he had met Veronica at a museum party in California and how she had liked him because he looked like a country doctor. She liked his thighs, he said, and he looked down then as though to check they were still there. One of his researchers brought him along to her home. A lot of men hung around then, and they all had ideas, and he was just one of the group staring down at her, half hearing the talk and waiting for her to tire of whoever was paying for the house. He had taken her away from the house, but for a month afterwards people still went there and stood talking under the trees and the house went on without her.

"She was seraphic," he said, and he stopped again as he had been stopping every few steps, facing me and standing way too close, while the dog hung his head, then eventually plopped down. A running girl passed us, her hair whipping out like a torn flag. There would be an interlude, fifteen or twenty minutes, as he set out his theories of her betrayal, backing up and encircling old scenes and injuries, presenting Veronica's actions as he once might have explained his work to a visitor in his lab, standing in his white coat, drawing diagrams with a grease pencil on the large Lucite wallboard. Rationally, he went through these perfectly irrational facts and details, swelling them into proof.

He mentioned someone called Rafe and I asked who he was. "Oh, he was the fellow who brought her to the party where we met. He had been keeping her for years. All that time she was also taking enormous sums from Gregory, who was some kind of Rothschild, you know."

I was way behind, though by now I had heard stories of their beginnings, how each, because of the complicated nature of the passion, had required advisers. Over the years the number of participants had grown; the panders and spies, the helpers and consolers were scattered from here north in an ever-expanding network of listeners, divided into sides. I was new, one of the temporary ones brought in just for this rough patch, but I could imagine life for the consultants of those early days, putting aside their lives to pick up the phone and live in their borrowed passion, friends who, even as they sided with one or the other and drove the two apart, must have envied them. They were like two trapped birds flying around a room beating hard at the air till they found each other and their way out. Jack made his discoveries, won his prizes then—his brain had enough energy for it all, as though the torment, the sneaking around fueled him.

"I'm empty except for her need," he said. "If only we could have a common base, do something together. If she could see what good there is in it," and again he was facing me and too close.

Knowing that the child was no answer for either of them, I suggested perhaps he should buy her another house, something that needed a lot of work so she could go back and forth with her cushions and her electronic notebook filled.

It was late now, long past lunch. We were sitting on a bench, the dog stretched at his feet, paws twitching. It had been more than three hours.

His driver was waiting for him at the Eighty-fifth Street entrance to the park. Jack handed him the dog and we got into the car. As we drove down Fifth Avenue we passed 946, where a doorman in white gloves was bent over a long black car, handing out a woman in tight jeans and a studded leather jacket. Half the apartments on Park and Fifth were filled with maids in uniforms bringing Evian bottles to their mistresses who were waiting in spandex unitards for their trainers to arrive. Whole staffs were still uniformed, ready for the kind of lives that no longer took place, except perhaps in the fantasies of both servant and master.

I saw another building wrapped in gauze the way the Solomons' had been. "Look at that," Jack said.

I didn't tell him my grandfather had built it, because I knew it would not have mattered.

XI

Inner Mansions

Ever since I carried it home in a small wooden crate, holding tight with both hands, I had been obsessed with my *L'Arbre d'Or*. I had propped it against the mantelpiece, gotten up in the middle of the night to stare at it as though it were an oracle to explain to me the mistakes and confusion of my past and lead me into my future. I would stand in front of my painting, looking at the weeping tree, the path that led by the house to some place I would never reach. The tree was on fire in the late-afternoon sun. It was burning on the path. I pulled a chair right in front of it and studied the way the tree made a ball like a child's tree does. I tried to explain to Josie what I saw in a tree, a bit of a house, and a pale fire. I was glad it was mine again.

There was still trouble with my stormy mother, who continued to think the painting was hers. I would never tell her what I had paid, but she had finally agreed to lend me some money. My jewelry was going up in the next unimportant jewelry sale. I sat there and stared and thought until my weak eye started to tear. It was time for Chica's committee lunch, but I could not move. I was annoyed at myself for having accepted. I had long ago made it a rule never to go to women's lunches, even for

Veritas, but Chica had begged and had sent over our committee list, which showed that both Veronica and Blanca Dell were coming. Though I doubted Blanca would show up, I had questions to ask her.

I went, but, as a gesture of disapproval, I did not "dress." I knew this would make the women uncomfortable, but then, anyone without money made them uneasy unless they were helping them out. I was early, as Chica had requested. I refused to play that game of who could be last, as though arrival were in order of importance. As the maid opened the door, I saw Jean-Pierre clutching a green velvet pillow to his chest, trying to glide out of sight. I was the first. The fires were about to be lit; the huge drawing room was still cold for the flowers—too many for a lunch, she must have had a dinner the night before.

Chica came wobbling in with her funny little walk, her feet splayed out like a dancer's, her hips but a handspan in a yellow lunch dress.

"Galanos," she said immediately. "I got it out of Lee Solomon's boxes for my thrift shop. God, I miss Lee—she was so generous."

"What's new here?" I asked, looking around, for it was impossible to tell. The apartment absorbed so much. Whenever I arrived at Chica's there were always two little craftsmen with impenetrable accents and ancient cracked fingernails crouched by the chairs measuring and sewing on fringe. This apartment was her only work of art; not an inch was unornamented, and she had run out of rooms, then houses before making this her profession. She saw me looking around. In Chica's house eyes bounced and were expected to, or she was disappointed.

"I never give a lunch until everything is perfect. You can write this one." She smiled, and her lips drew up, revealing her healthy pink gums.

"Did you tell everyone?"

"No, but go ahead, have fun, and it's good for Veritas."

I saw Jean-Pierre kind of slithering and squirming in the corner, his dignity disrupted. He was wheeling one of the maids' shopping carts around, removing things. It was filled with braided candlesticks and rare boxes, all the detritus of the last decade. I guessed Chica had become nervous and summoned him for this last-minute exorcism of her excess. He looked all muddled as he hugged a needlepoint pillow to his chest before tossing it into the cart. He went around tweaking and punching at the pillows, and then he drifted from the room, tossing a few "ciaos" into the air.

"You out at lunch—this must be important," said Gayle Pope, arriving with Olivia Pinza.

"You look beautiful," said Olivia, as they each went through the ceremony of kisses and lowering themselves onto a chair with a small squirm, depositing their bags at their feet like offerings to the couch god.

One by one the women entered in their lavish lunch suits, a rope of gold to cover the necks, and big buttons of pearl and gold at the ears, their faces so much younger than their hands. I had seen them all at Athena's shower two months ago, a rush of suits with this same rustle of purpose. Then, just as the gifts were being torn open, Hugo Salm had appeared like the bad fairy, carrying his little Asprey bag. Gayle, Olivia, Donna, Athena, Cherry, Boots all flew at each other with the swoops and cries of birds descending on the ocean. They touched each other with little stroking movements and settled themselves gently like birds on the waves until soon the large room was filled with the particular chirping of thirty women. Despite the size of the room and the three back-to-back sofas, everyone scraped chairs across the carpet and sat bunched in one large circle. It was like the giant hive I had shown Josie at the Museum of Natural History—"The Nest of the Social Weaver"—each bird flying in with her grass and twigs until the whole massive but fragile throbbing structure was achieved.

"Forgive me for being so late," said Veronica, and I looked behind her to where Diana McBride stood framed in the doorway with Nancy Noyes, a poisonous enemy of mine. To punish me for once accurately describing one of her dinners, Nancy had become Diana's main source. We had been marching past each other for years with the fast-beating hearts of hatred. Since I had the pen, I tweaked her whenever I could, always left her name off lists, even my "Others present included. . . ." I looked furiously at Chica and gave Diana a big smile and listened to the voices around me.

"He's not the tutor. We have to *go* to the tutor. But the homework man comes to us every night at five," Donna was saying.

"Who do you use?" Veronica asked. She was right in there now, all trace of defiance gone from her clothes. She had that polished professional look, everything very new and rehearsed, and was wearing her sunglasses as a headband.

I noticed that, as usual, Chica had been careful to include a few of what the Peabrains, copying the English royals, with whom they had much in common, called "Wrinklies," those women of another generation who had no need to hurl clothes and addresses at each other and were so much calmer and further along. Some of the women went back fifty or sixty years into pasts that were now happily vague. They were the surviving major beauties of their age who had found their style years ago and thus never seemed to age. Some of the pasts were wild and sexy, as anyone could tell, for they all still had their good bosoms and legs and voices acquired so long ago they had become the real thing. Athena was sitting among them and making herself charming.

"The strangest thing happened to me this morning," Nancy said. "I live across the street from a hair place. I've been looking at it for years. It's called Rows of Corn. I've been meaning to try it since Kenneth's burned up, and today I needed a shampoo, so I just walked in, didn't even make an appointment. It was a *black* place. There was no way to tell from the name. 'Rows of Corn'—it sounds blond if anything, cornsilk, you know. You can bet they all looked up when I walked in, but I was not going to just back out."

"What did you do?" asked Chica.

"I would've died," said Laurie Holt, Howard Goldenson's girlfriend, whom he had forced on the committee.

"I mean, you'd think they'd call it Hair of Color, or Black something-or-other, just to let you know. The woman said, 'How can we help you?'—very nice—so I actually stayed. After all, I really needed a shampoo," she said, patting her light hair, and everyone laughed.

"Where's Blanca? It's getting awfully late. *Some* of us have to go back to work," Chessie Bell said in her loud, rapid television voice. She had gotten Carpel Tunnel Syndrome from jabbing the buttons on her portable phone and was wearing a cast from her hand to her elbow.

"Did they use black products?" said Olivia suddenly, turning her small ring.

"This little Jew—I mean Jewish fellow, who usually does my hair is away," said Nancy.

"They are digging up a black man buried in Brooklyn that they think is a saint. He used to do all the white people's hair. He was very famous for it."

"That reminds me—I think we should do our meeting now, because all we really have to do is elect someone to chair the party. We're the committee," said Boots.

"Well, I can't," said Gayle.

"We're going to be in Vail all winter," someone said.

"I'd love to do it," Veronica said then, as everyone turned to look at her.

"Any objections?" said Boots. "We will all give you our secretaries and our lists."

All the women had now taken out their hard cards, Asprey cases, and little gold pens, but no one had put on glasses. Diana McBride was taking notes, still looking around wildly at the ceiling and the floor, as Chica watched her pen, enraptured. I had been on the Veritas board since the mid-eighties, when it met on the top floor of St. John's in front of a blackboard, when women in penny loafers argued politely over two-thousand-dollar expenses with the faint presences of old scared New York.

Now, of course, we were Wall Street and a long granite table in one of Howard Goldenson's Park Avenue conference rooms, where guilt flowed in rivers down both sides of the table on which the investment bankers and traders rested their expensive elbows.

"We want to do something different this year. No big party with fifteen-thousand-dollar tables filled with Wall Street. We should sell two-hundred-and-fifty-dollar tickets."

"That sounds so junior. We made eight hundred thousand dollars last year. We can't afford to lose our base."

"I think it should be a lecture," said Boots. "Nobody could criticize us for that, and people would learn something for a change."

"We could charge a thousand a seat if we get someone good."

Someone suggested a poetry reading; there were groans. Two of the women wanted a lecture on gardens. Someone else wanted novelists reading from their works in progress.

"I might be able to get you the Dalai Lama," Boots said. "It's the year of Tibet."

"Since Veritas is about education, we should focus on that."

"He won the Nobel Prize," said Boots, injured. "It must be serious or nobody is going to dare come, especially now, for a thousand dollars."

"I've been reading this book, *Loins and Lions*. Helen Kasmanian," said Gayle.

"I've heard of that," said Olivia.

"Who?" said Chica.

There was a small discussion of the book and whether they could get Helen, during which I waited a beat longer than I should have.

"I know Helen," I said. "We were in school together. She's very difficult, but I think she will do it and be exciting."

I could have said a lot more, like how Helen never, in four years, used a bedsheet but slept between two duvets, long before anyone else had heard of duvets, or how once, when she was bored in chapel, she had crawled out under all the seats from her place way up front, or how when I won the Smyser Prize and she did not, she had turned me in for keeping my Volvo P-1800 on campus.

"I like the lecture idea. No expense. Why don't you see if we can get her? But can we charge a thousand dollars?" said Chica.

"Oh, Jack will underwrite it anyway and pay her," said Veronica.

"*We* always underwrite it," said Gayle. "With the Dells."

"No Dells this year. Let's get Wanda Kent."

"How about no press—or maybe just a few, like Diana and Libby?" said that new Barbara woman.

"Let's have lunch. Why should we wait for Blanca? She's always late."

"I have to go," said Diana, rising and looking at Nancy Noyes, who would supply her with the rest of lunch.

"My driver had the most terrible accident," Ann Sullivan said, sweeping in on the gusts of the departing Diana and flinging open her shawl so that it struck Olivia, who said nothing. "Poor man, we were hit on Park Avenue. We had to get out—they bumped right into us. I was afraid it was a robbery."

"Gayle, I read somewhere they took your car at the opera."

"It was the Pimpernel."

"A gun to the driver's head."

"It must have been a Mercedes. Our detective told us they can have them on the boat for Buenos Aires in six hours. They especially like Mercedes and BMWs. Was it a Mercedes?"

"A BMW—the big one."

"Well, they got *us* at the museum. They call them 'car pirates' now. They tap you in back. If you stop, they pull you out. The police told us if a car hits you from behind and it's just a tap, not even to stop."

"It doesn't happen when you leave your guards in the car," said Gayle.

"You have guards now?"

"Just one. But he's martial-arts-trained and an ex-convict, and now we've gotten him a gun, too, so that's like two."

"You should never do that. They'll just kill him."

"Look at these favors, Chica," Olivia said, examining a shell box bound in gold. "What's in them? Can we eat them?"

"Is this Chinese food? Who does it for you?"

"My Ching," Chica said.

"Your *chink,* did you say? Really, that's so racist!" said Boots.

"I said my *Ching,*" said Chica. "You better watch what you say—the Pimpernel is here."

"That was unnecessary," I said.

The few who did not know me looked at me.

"Tell us, Libby, what is your column for Wednesday? Who are you attacking now? You've gotten so grumpy and socialistic since your eyes," Chica said to the silent table.

"I never like to tell," I said into the void. "But you can relax, I'm not working today." Now everyone was looking at me in my forty-dollar black sweater from the defunct Fiorucci. I realized it had happened. I was of an age and reputation so that now when I spoke at a table these women hushed up and expected something clever to come out. But I was not at all like the Pimpernel, especially in a large group of women. At this point I half saw one of the waiters pouring me a glass of wine, but I was too distracted to wave him off.

"Do you ever see your friends, those Solomon people, those terrible crooks who ran away?" Nancy Noyes said suddenly into the silence.

"Quiet, Nancy, that's sacred territory," Olivia whispered, but I heard.

"I'd love to know what's become of them. Michael is so glad we never got in with them," said Nancy.

"Libby *has* heard from them. Tell about it," said Chica.

"Yes, tell," said Chessie. "Do you know how I could reach them?"

"I can't," I said, glaring at Chica. "I think Chica made a mistake. I've heard absolutely nothing."

"In trouble like her father . . . all stick together," I heard Nancy Noyes saying from the other end.

"*Who* all sticks together?" I said loudly.

"I didn't mean . . ." said Nancy.

"Yes you did. I, and every other Jew here, knows exactly what you meant."

"Calm down," said Athena. "Please."

"Don't let it get to you," said Veronica, putting her arm on my shoulder.

"Always *very* emotional," someone whispered. "Known for scenes."

"I don't think I can stay here anymore," I said, standing and walking, heart pounding, to Chica's end of the table, near Nancy.

"Oh, don't go," said Chica. "She didn't mean . . ." but I was already on my way over to Nancy. I bent right over her, so close I could smell the sweet noon breath of the real drinker. Her little eyes, without makeup, were sunk into puffed dumplings of red flesh. There were deltas of broken veins on her powdery cheeks, which were wet with a few tears. For a minute I pulled back.

"Why would you say a thing like that?" I said, bending over her.

"I didn't mean . . ."

I walked away to the door, and then I returned quietly to my seat. I was shaking, and I swallowed so I would not cry, but my chest was heaving. I felt my hand reaching for the wine.

"Oh, *don't!*" Boots hissed. "She's not worth it. It's been so long."

I drank the whole glass and looked down at Nancy as my headache immediately began. The table was still mostly silent, just a few seconds away from breaking into pockets of whispers. I took Boots's glass and poured it into mine.

"That old bitch," someone said.

"She's awful," said Boots.

"Don't pay any attention . . . old drunk," someone else was saying. "Everyone hates her."

I don't know whether it was the wine, but suddenly I felt warm and almost happy. I was no longer the tolerated intruder who might either betray them or lead them to glory. I was a friend. They had been waiting for so long to pity me for something more significant than being "poor," and I had just given it to them. They were, after all these years, taking me in. But this was so dangerous. I thought of Sally Kirk in her evening dress with her evening pen and notebook. I wanted to leave, but I could not move. I felt a throbbing in the socket of my eyes, but I couldn't reach for my drops. I could not leave. I wanted a Scotch, a big Scotch, and I wanted it right now.

I had to force myself to stay after lunch, because I knew if I was the first to leave they would all start talking about me and my outburst; already I sensed an urge to discuss me beginning around the room. But just then Blanca Dell walked in, and she was with a man.

"This is my new life," she said, holding on to his arm. "This is Philip Ives." He was a perfect mannequin, his hair, seemingly wet, rising in wings at the nape of his thick neck, a straight face with a straight little nose, a white T-shirt, khaki pants, and a white raw silk jacket. He was shining and gleaming and quietly at ease in this nest of women.

"He sings," Blanca said. "Philip, play something for us! I met him in the lounge bar of the Ritz in Paris. He writes all his own songs. I just sat there every night till he came over," she whispered to Chica and Boots. "He's from Vermont, a very old family."

"Are you related to Robert Ives?" said one of the women.

"He's my father."

"I didn't know there were any Iveses in New York."

"I live in California," Philip said.

"Do you think he's a fag?" someone whispered.

"I know he's not," said Blanca.

"I'd love to hear him," I said, and truly meant it.

"Oh yes!"

"Do 'Long Island Madness,' " Blanca said, and put her hand on his knee.

" 'It's a Long Island kind of madness, wires overhead . . .' " he sang, his black patent Belgian shoes thumping on the pedals. He wasn't wearing any socks. " '. . . And then I hear her knocking on my door,' " he sang out, and, as I knew he would, he knocked three times on the side of the piano, making Chica's flowers bounce. He had a strange, smoky voice full of vibrato, kind of like Johnnie Ray or Chris Montez. Chica's mouth hung open a little. Blanca rubbed her hands. I did not dare look at Nancy, who was getting up to go at last with a few Wrinklies. Veronica seemed restless and flicked her nails. Caught in the beat and thump and the quivers of his voice—which really was not very good—I finally calmed down.

Veronica came over to me and suggested we walk home together. "Let's go to the Carlyle and have tea," she said.

On the way over she began complaining. She felt beset and exhausted by what some would consider the glories of the position I had made for her. Having a photograph taken now felt like a day's work to her. I walked along nodding, for we must at least pretend to believe those we call our friends, and then I told her that Jack had talked to me. I don't know why I told her. I just was so shaken that it came out. She was not a bit surprised.

"Jack always goes to my friends. It's an old pattern. He gets desperate, and he tells everything, but this latest is very sad. He barely knows you."

"He's very upset about what happened in the store when Danny bumped into you. He's turned that into a whole affair."

"That's so like him. To focus on one tiny particle and to choose wrong! That bumping thing wasn't Danny at all. It was some twenty-eight-year-old English boy. What else did he say?"

"I promised him I wouldn't tell."

"Don't you see, he *wants* you to tell! I must, I see, start to explain this to you. It was so peculiar. This young English boy bumped into my breast. I know English men are educated to think that sort of thing is very serious, and so he kept apologizing. I didn't know him at all. But Jack has decided it was Danny. Afterwards, he called me a whore because I said goodbye to the boy as we left. You don't know this side of him. He said, 'Who is that man? He seemed to know you,' and I told him I had never seen him before, only we were both rather tall and fair and foreign. He said, 'He was in the same vicinity for an excruciating amount of time.' And then he just decided it was Danny. I think I really have discovered Jack going around the bend here."

"When you tell it, it really sounds like Jack—"

"Jack's afraid that if he gets help, his genius will disappear. That's his excuse. But he might well go back into why he used to pee into his sister's toy box. Jack loses sight of his conspiracies. I can't remember after so many stings. The thought chills me. He is too solemn, too preoccupied, too punishing and accusing. I spent three years with him just totally damaging to all of us, even his wife. Are you sure you still want the brandy? Maybe we should have some tea instead."

"Tea with brandy," I said to the waiter, and perhaps because she had seen me out of control, Veronica kept talking, all the while shifting and turning, rearranging her legs or hands, pushing back her hair. This was perhaps the second time she had really spoken—other times she had rushed away on the verge of some confession.

She would always be bolting off somewhere, her cellular phone pressed to her face like armor, making excuses to the appointment waiting for her at the other end, and yet what did she do? Unless in the middle of a seduction, both she and Gates were always only half present. No one could ever have all their attention; and the intrusions, the frustrations were part of their appeal. They were never there at the appointed time, were always running off. When I picked up on a call placed by one of their secretaries, there was usually a long silence before they picked up. But now she spoke.

"You know, it's been like this all the time," she said, and told me how once before they were married she had left Jack and gone off on her old Greek boyfriend's yacht. She had seen him all hoary with age, with gray chest hairs popping from his sheer white shirt, appearing out of the mist on the dock in Corsica, and they had stared at each other. There had been a week of parties with Greek beauties in diamonds, and he had satisfied all her urges for luxury, but he was "awfully rude." She was lying next to him in her bikini on the deck and saw a fly crawling along his leg and she knew he had fallen asleep. She looked at me as though I must understand this. "I never knew how tortured I could be by a relic, some shrapnel," she said. And when she came back home kicked out by the Greek, as I guessed—Jack stood in front of her house looking up until the doorman called her to report and she came down.

"He doesn't know who I am. I gave up on the idea he would see me any other way. In all this time, I had never even seen his wife," Veronica said, and then, one day, she followed her.

"She was so calm," said Veronica, who described how the wife had waited in the lobby of a Toronto hotel one afternoon as Jack paid Veronica to have an abortion, making her sign a document saying that the child was not his. "And all I could see that day was that she was wearing the same embroidered boots he had bought for me."

In all her stories I saw the maniacal pursuit of drama and discovery characteristic of illicit love. Veronica had a talent for all this. It was almost a profession. There were hotel rooms and messages left at airport gates and code names and bribed clerks. First, Jack's wife to trick, and now Jack; her love always had its parallel victim.

"Maybe you don't understand, Libby. This social stuff is for him. He stands in my dressing room and tells me what to wear. He watches. When I have Carlos in for my hair and makeup, he has them take it down or pile it up. He has no Conogenex anymore, so he works on me. That's his job now, rebuilding companies in ruins, taking failures apart, breaking them up until they look like successes—and me.

"He loves his new life and the fact that people look at me;

they think they know me from my photographs. He likes it more than I do. He's always been after me. He keeps talking about the tone of my body, my arms, the color of my nails. Once, before I married him, he went into my kitchen. I had this big blue kitchen, and he began to take out all the spice bottles, and I could see he was getting angrier and angrier because they were all brown. I never cooked—people brought me food, and the spices were old and they had all discolored.

"He loves these people—Bill Pope, Jimmy Dell—even though he's smarter than all of them. He loves being in a restaurant with them and having people turn around to look at our group."

Finally, I asked her what had happened that day in the rain after lunch. She paused and I studied the combinations and small failures in her face that made her a beauty—and not a dull one, either. I wondered if after a while it would be possible to forget her beauty or if each time I saw her I would re-examine her, looking for signs of decline. When did she know she was beautiful? How had she grown up with it and used it? Was she one of those who never felt herself beautiful and was always, without enthusiasm, demurring, mentioning this or that flaw?

"After you left us that day, Danny took me to the store and showed me all around. Those girls were there, kind of hanging back, but available. We even went downstairs to see all the bags of stuff in the basement that were ruined in the flood. He kept asking if I liked things. Everyone was trying so hard not to look at us or hang around, but a few customers stopped him. He took me to his offices upstairs, which were all being redone—major money spent. No one was there—it was like they had been suddenly cleared out, because all the phones were still ringing. He kissed me. You see, it went back years.

"When we left, he took my arm and pulled me along through the main floor. Jack should have seen *that,* instead of some stupid Englishman. They were shutting up, but there was one girl just standing there, waiting with all these shopping bags. She looked like she would have waited for him all night. She followed us out. The hole was so big then—so much steam. 'She'll go with you,' he told me. 'These are some of the things you liked.' Outside, all the men were staring and lowering the new pipe. One of the men I talked to the night of the explosion saw me and the girl and he called out, 'Been doing some shopping?' It couldn't have been more public. I threw the bags in the back of Rory's closet and took a very long nap. We were going to the ballet that night. Before we left, I looked, and the light was still on in Danny's office, and when we got back and Jack was sleeping, I snuck into Aurora's room. Such beautiful, extravagant things, and some I know I didn't choose, so he must have chosen them for me ahead of time."

She had thought about Gates all that first weekend, remembering everything he had said to her and finding it clever. When she said that, I understood that she was gone, for unless he was selling something, Gates could barely speak. She no longer had a choice. She would leave everything for time with him. She was in a very bad mood until they met in the Bemelmans Bar on Monday, for all this had collected inside her. She bent down and had him feel the way her heart was pounding, and then she could not hear anything he said. She looked at his mouth and wanted only to kiss it right then. But they were trapped in a place where she was known. Gates stood up and threw some money on the table in such a hurry that the bills fell to the floor and the waiter started after them until he saw the money lying there. Because he had a girl at his house, they went to The Mark, a block away but there were no rooms. Gates led her around the corner to a dark row of private houses. One of them was abandoned, and there was a large tree off to the side. It was quite dark by now, and Gates put his vicuna coat on the ground and pushed her down. She put her coat over them, so they were for a time indistinguishable from all the human bundles slumped in doorways. Later they went to the Surrey.

Veronica said that when she came rushing home after ten, Aurora, who resisted all discipline, was still awake and asked why her legs were shaking. "I went into the bathroom and cried.

I was so happy, and Jack never came out of his office until I was asleep. I really don't know what I'm going to do about him," she said. She did not sound unhappy.

I rubbed my eyes and dragged my left eyelid down to my cheek until the red dome of my eyelid pulsed. When I looked up, Hugo Salm was standing there.

"Well, how was lunch?" he said, ignoring Veronica. "Who was there? Did Blanca come? What was everyone wearing?"

"We were just going. I'll call you from home," I said.

"Yes, I have to pick up Aurora," Veronica said, and just then I understood. By telling me all this, she hoped to win me back from Jack's side, re-engage me in the drama, perhaps even have me tell. For some of these women, it wasn't a fact until it was announced. How could they believe in a marriage or a divorce, how could they believe in their own love until it was a blind item? She was telling me and not telling me, perhaps to keep me from focusing on something else. I might never know what, for she was entirely complete in herself, as she dusted her hands across the front of her suit, shook out her hair, and thought she had fooled me.

XII

On Her Right

Once at a party, a man from Hollywood told me that a woman never leaves a man until she has the next man to go to. It was too hot a night to argue. The floor of the room was filled with overheated bodies sprawled on cushions, for this was the end of the sixties. Our hostess had made a mistake with the votive candles, and every few minutes a limp hand reached up to fan a familiar face or burn itself on the hot glass as it tried to pinch out another flame until the room had grown quite dark. Everyone knew each other too well to bother talking much. There were no new impressions to be made, and the heat healed the various rifts that had already occurred. Those who were doing things quietly fed information to those who wrote about them; those who had once done things drank and watched, waiting to catch the next chance rill of energy—too many of this last group, but even they were subdued by the heat. The air was dead and dank. The man from Hollywood was leaning against the bare fireplace, his black silk shirt open—this wasn't his group at all.

"So you don't really agree," he said. I knew his wife had just left him for her costar.

"Only if she's over thirty," I said, and, then, thirty seemed very far away. Of course, I might have said there's the woman who leaves a man so she will not kill him, but that was another story.

The man from Hollywood must have sensed a movie in my lack of response, since he took my arm and led me into the den. Because I liked him and was very young, I told him this other story, then, in a form he would understand—a flat, one-page treatment of the facts.

"But what's the impediment?" he kept saying, as though I were selling him a plot. "Couldn't you have her doing something?" He was already converting it, and I could tell he thought it wouldn't play. The public would not accept a girl like mine, though he could understand the man. I think most of the men at that party had tried to be versions of the man.

"I only told you to give you one exception," I said.

"That kind of story would work much better if she left him just as he was going to make the big deal of his career. She should be a model or something, maybe with a boyfriend she supports, who beats her up. . . ." And he was off, writing his own story, which is the story everyone out there wants to tell.

I remembered that night now as I looked across the tables at Veronica, who had seated herself at this, her first large dinner party, with Danny Gates on her right. They were laughing, as the architect on her left pretended to listen across the table.

Veronica had consulted me on certain details of this evening but had been unusually reticent about her guests and seating. "Let me keep some surprises," she kept saying as she read me the menus, careful now because food had to be poor and hearty, and there was a whole list of banished substances, like caviar and truffles. Her voice was again light and rushed, as though she were just about to dash out of the house to more important things. Whenever I tried to talk about myself, however briefly, she'd begin to "ummm-hmmm" every few seconds, and so I stopped. She felt she could invade my life at will, call at any time, and I would never lose my temper, never print anything to betray her. Apple brown betty? Stroganoff with noodles? But never whether it was all right to seat your lover on your right at your first New York dinner.

Why should I have been surprised? If I had learned anything by now, it was that hiding inside these most ordinary lives, ruled by routine and enslaved to habit, were people ready for murder, suicide, daring rescues and escapes, riding the white water, the taking over of a plane or its resistance, unimaginable acts of bravery and mad risky love. They could all be heroes or villains at any time. Even the ones who could see ahead to the hours in lawyers' offices, the boxes and packing crates, the crying children, the upset in routine—all the real foes of passion—would leap happily into the turbulence and disruption.

I was placed at what must have been Jack's table, but Jack was not yet there, and Boots Simpson was talking across his chair to Hilary Reed.

"Have you spoken to Olivia recently? She's working like a dog at *Fences*—like a dog because she *has* to. They sold their apartment and moved to a high-rise on Fifty-fifth Street, a modern one, because they had to," Boots said as I leaned over.

"I heard the marriage was bad, too," said Hilary.

"No, the marriage is all right, just no money at all. He lost it."

First Lee Solomon, then Olivia had to learn again what it was to be without things—to acquire them, love them, and lose them. They drew in closer to their families and tried to protect them from the tongues. There were honorable losses—with money paid back—and dishonorable ones which amounted to thievery; but little distinction was being made.

I cut into something I realized must be crab cakes just as Jack walked into the room. He seemed remarkably calm and happy, and I realized, since he never even looked at Veronica, that he had no idea Gates was here. He must still think that Gates was the man in the store who touched or didn't touch her breast that day. Just then Danny looked past me to Jack, approaching his face as if trying to understand him. Jack now was combing his hair back without a part, and it ended in a thin torrent of downtown curls, much at psychic odds with his large, lined face. Gates turned away.

"Quite a feat to get Danny Gates out of his house," I heard Boots saying to Jack, and once again I blessed my freak hearing, but Jack had not heard.

"What *is* this?" Hilary whispered.

"Goulash," I answered, reading off the porcelain menu card in the center of the table, which was almost lost in the forests of silver and groves of Veronica's bonsai that replaced the usual collection of antique snuff and cigarette boxes. Obviously, Veronica had taken my advice to keep the food simple, with some resemblance to the plant or creature from which it sprang, for we had long ago passed the day when people hollowed out their vegetables to receive other vegetables, or their fruits for other cleverer fruits.

Now I saw Jack turning to Boots, but still he had not heard.

"What do you think the chances are for war with Iraq?" I said quickly, as a tall old man bent over to straighten my knife, and for a second I registered the large amount of old Irish live-in-type servants now stationed around like silver sentinels, their light eyes bearing down on the beaming fork-lifters. Whatever Jack said was interrupted now by Lazarus, who leaned over and whispered to Jack. I think that Jack, who was rich enough to do what he wanted, had arranged to signal Lazarus so he could leave the table whenever he was bored.

"I must take this call."

"I can't understand what he's doing," Bill Pope said. "All the markets have closed."

"How really rude!" said Hilary. "Just what does he do now? He sold his company, didn't he?"

"He can't do any research now, so he invests, and he buys companies in distress. That's why the grave dancer is here," Pope said, gesturing to Howard Goldenson.

"I don't know why I accepted tonight," said Blanca. "Except I wanted to bring Philip out and Veronica's been so nice. At least she looks happy, and they have gotten Danny Gates."

"Remember Audie Miller, that girl from Ford in the seventies?" Bill Pope said, leaning back. "Gates was after her for a while. Me, too, before Gayle. She told me Gates met her at the Plaza one afternoon for a drink. It was just once, but when he was out on the Coast he used to call her every day. It went on for months. She was very bright and she had a great smoky voice. Finally it was all arranged. He was going to fly her out to Palm Springs for the weekend. He was driving from Hollywood. He met her at the plane, and she told me how they had a very romantic drive—they were all over each other—to the Racquet Club. Then, when they got to the bungalow, Gates suddenly decided to play tennis. It was about ninety degrees, full noon, and she couldn't understand it, but she went out to watch. He served one serve and pulled something in his back. Audie told me she never saw anyone in such pain. And that was the weekend. Gates got himself a doctor and she flew back to New York.

"Audie Miller—I really *liked* that girl. Now I never will feel young flesh in my hands again," he said, and looked over at Gayle, challenging her to hear.

"What?" I said.

"Never will feel young flesh," he said, as though he was doomed with his thirty-seven-year-old wife. I knew Pope liked leaning across his dinner partners and saying impossible things as Gayle watched across the table. He needed to betray, to live on the rim, which was why he climbed mountains and kept Astrid Payne. The Popes were always returning from doing dangerous things in distant places where they went wrapped in their usual luxury.

Howard Goldenson was studying his hand. I could see him peering down, and I knew he was looking under the table at the piece of paper he always carried with a list of things to talk about.

I looked at Veronica. "It's an art form," I saw her saying to the architect, "from China, not Japan . . . two thousand years old." Her hand separated the branches of one of the miniature camellia trees. "One to the left, one to the right, and here, to the rear, for depth."

She was wearing one of those eve-of-destruction floaty things the women wore this season as they sat around, money shoulder to shoulder with money, at home where it was safe and no one was poor and they could say the unmentionable out loud. Veronica was free now. I watched as her careful room fell away; her guests disappeared; Jack, and the child in her butterfly pajamas. She had begun her next life, and I knew she would do anything to keep it. Across the table from her, Donna, having a rough time with Howard Goldenson, was trying to glimpse herself in the mirror over the former Solomon breakfront as Howard picked a crab membrane from his mouth.

"Audie Miller—I still hear that voice. I should have married her. How 'bout a hand job under the table?" Bill Pope said to Boots.

"Edgehill—any day now," Boots said to me. "They're going to have to do that intervention thing with him."

"What could I say I just bought that would impress you?" Pope said.

"He's under a lot of pressure," said Hilary in such a way that I guessed Astrid Payne would soon be back at her agency.

"What are we all working for, killing ourselves for? To leave a stain on the rug," said Pope.

"What?" we all said.

"Oh, I don't know—think of it all as a big rug. I just want to leave a little stain to show I was there in the room." He broke into a noodle mound, and a muddy river flooded his beef.

I began to eat then, for the food was really very good, and the room, nude of fringe and disturbing excess, was dull and restful. Everything was a watery monotone, pale green and subdued, barely lit and whispery, toned down till it was scarcely there, and against this the good old woods and the agonized Christ glowed.

Jack did not return until they had served the ovals of white lemon curd in a raspberry puree puddle. He was holding a computer printout.

"It must be a joke," Boots whispered, waiting.

Jack did not sit down, but, rather, tapped on his glass with his knife, and as he did, the computer sheets unwound almost down to his knees, and he began.

"Veronica and I are very fortunate to have found such friends here. We welcome you all in these perilous times."

He was actually naming his guests, in that awful way as though congratulating himself. ". . . Howard Goldenson, the lawyer we don't want to see come into our offices but welcome to our table; and you, Blanca, who took time out in this difficult moment in your life to introduce us to your friend—uh—"

"Philip Ives," she said.

"And Chip, who got us into this building; and Gigi Farnaut— we just read about his new house in London . . . Libby, the much-feared, much-loved Pimpernel, our first real friend in this complicated town. We're so glad, Libby, that you have finally taken off those glasses and we can see your green eyes. . . ." And on it went, the vile march around the tables, the usual celebration of the guests he was introducing only to himself and congratulating for their friendship with Jack and Veronica Kahn. He was pleased, he was richly pleased. His face was younger, almost rested in the light of the candles. I noticed how carefully he was dressed and groomed, the smoothness of his skin, the cleanliness of his hands, though the nails were still bitten. Veronica sat posed with her dutiful wide pink smile. Finally, I believed this was for Jack. He enjoyed these men who were as rich and richer than himself, these men with the same code, who protected each other's dishonesty. It was a world as jealous as science and as cruel, but perhaps not as lonely.

"We have a tradition—" he continued.

"Since when?" Boots whispered.

"—that each guest stands and says something—a few words. You begin, Libby." But I declined. "Bill, maybe you can tell us about what's happening in the publishing world."

Everyone actually added their verbal thank-you notes, mentioning "the beauty of the surroundings" and such; and then Jack said, "You may have noticed the quality of the meal here tonight. We managed to steal Corey Gallagher from Lampwick. Lazarus, would you get him, please—make him come out?"

Corey came out flushed, embarrassed, wiping his fat hands on his apron as sweat dropped down from his forehead.

"Tell us about what we ate, Corey."

"Did you write this for him, Libby?" Boots said.

"You forgot to mention Danny Gates," Boots said to Jack after Corey had spoken. "That's your real triumph tonight—getting that recluse out of his house. We've all eaten Corey's food, but none of us have ever been to a dinner with Danny Gates."

Jack was just raising his forkful of curd, and he held it up so that the raspberry dribbled down in thin filaments.

"It's very important to have someone really famous at a dinner, like Claudette Colbert or Jerry Robbins—one of those living-legend types," said Boots. "It keeps everyone alert, perks up the mood. I mean, you keep thinking about *It Happened One Night* and how she stood on the road raising the hem of her skirt so the cars would stop, and those pajamas, and the 'walls of Jericho.' Of course, no one ever dares say anything—it's like mentioning a book to a writer. . . ." And on she went.

Kahn had looked around and now was staring at Gates, his face startled but held still, and I thought of the little trees on the table, so calm and perfect above the soil, and the roots bound into their wire cages below.

"I mean, Claudette doesn't have to talk even, which she does, and quite well, with that buttery voice—being in her presence is enough for me, just looking at her and beginning a sentence 'Claudette . . .' Don't you agree, Libby, you need someone that famous around—or someone in a scandal or just out of jail? I love all the men who can tell about minimum security."

In fact I did agree. It always helped to have a freak at dinner.

"Boots—" he spoke the name with some effort—"what is so special about Mr. Gates, if he *is* here?"

She looked startled. "Of course he's here—next to Veronica. He never goes out. No one can get him. I've just about given up, though after tonight I might try him again for the rain forest. Did you know he used to be a movie star? *The Angelfish Club* and something else. Big hit, then he quit."

"I must tell you all about my tour of the UN," I said into the immediate silence. "I took my daughter, because I think it's important again now." I saw Veronica raising a spoonful of dessert to Gates's mouth. Some of it must have dropped, and she went fumbling in his lap, swabbing with her napkin. Was I the only person watching this? "They have some artifacts from Hiroshima." Jack was watching. "Melted teacups and blue jeans that have disintegrated to shreds from the heat. But the most amazing"—now they had both risen, and she was pantomiming about just going to help him get cleaned up, and Jack had half gotten up—"thing is this statue of St. Agnes that was in front of a church that was totally destroyed. She fell on her nose. The front of it is kind of randomly blackened in patches." Jack sat back down but was still looking at the door. "But the back—you have to walk around to see the other side—is completely flat and pitted in craters, just sheared off where the robe would normally go out. The guide said there are now three tons of TNT for every human being on earth."

Jack began to stroke the back of his head, then picked up one of his new nape curls and began twisting it savagely around his finger. He kept half-rising from his seat.

"Jack, perhaps you could tell me, and maybe Boots wants to know too, about the chance of a war." I stopped because he was not listening, and turned to Bill Pope, just as Veronica and Gates returned, followed by a woman wheeling a harp, whom Veronica introduced as Angelica Leung from Juilliard, and since she was introduced there was a reverent silence—otherwise she would have played the same pieces in the same way but would have been ignored as just dinner music.

Danny and I were almost back to back, everyone having

switched places for coffee, and as the girl began to play, he shifted his chair closer.

"Why are you here?" I asked him.

"Well, it's convenient," he said. "No more dark glasses, I notice."

"It is foolish and dangerous." I felt Jack watching. "I hope you know what you've started. You look terrible."

"Bad time for the business."

Veronica frowned at us. I was afraid to look at Jack. I heard the clink of his fork on the glass.

"How could I have forgotten Veronica?" he said into the murmuring, which then became silence. "She has never been more beautiful, more radiant. She must be in love. Happy birthday to my darling girl."

As everyone turned to congratulate her—Kahn's first words swallowed by the instant reaction, carried over from childhood, that everyone has to birthdays—he went over and bent to kiss her, looking as he did at Gates. Veronica was laughing, protesting, and I knew why, since her birthday was near mine and had taken place six months ago.

Next morning when I called to thank Veronica, she was not there, and Lazarus told me they had gone to the country with Sandy Fisher to look at houses. Sandy had told me that on one of his scouting trips for Gates he'd found a house for them in Connecticut. I wondered about the scene that must have taken place last night, why Veronica had provoked Jack that way. At least it was settled that the man in the store was not Gates. The party had ended early, chilled by the harp and by the absence of Jack, who left again during the music and did not return. If there had been a fight that night, the presence of Sandy in the morning would act as a buffer, though no one bothered to put on any shows for him.

Sandy called as soon as they all returned very late that night and told me the whole day from the beginning, with every detail given equal weight—the same annoying style of narration that Cigarette always chose. The crispness of the day, the quality of the lunch in the garden, and the degree of visible pain in the car were all given equal prominence, and I gripped the phone with impatience.

In the car ride out Jack and Veronica had not spoken to each other. Veronica said that Jack's sleep machine had broken—he had one of those things that make white sound—and he was tired.

"Do you know how hard it is to ride an hour in silence trying to make conversation with two people who do not want to speak? Finally, I gave up and pretended to sleep."

Then he told me all about the house, how they got to see it because he knew one of the sisters who owned it, the one who was forcing the sale. It was five hundred acres, once all owned by her father, from one of the old German families. He had built each of his three daughters a house placed as far from the others as possible in the corners of the property. But the daughters could not get along, and finally they decided to sell the whole thing.

The old man had built himself a house, too, a very strange house, all white marble and only ten rooms, but each room was vast. In 1920, an era when great American men were building, he had no desire to compete with his neighbors who transplanted castles stone by stone. His was ostentatious but privately so, with dressing-room walls of peeled birch bark and a solarium in the Egyptian style with lotus motifs frescoed into the walls. The library was Circassian walnut with pillars. Vertès had painted the murals in his wife's bedroom. In the center was a spiral stairway with alabaster banisters and no visible means of support. It was a house for their paintings and a house to die in—very much the kind of house you build at the end of a life, like a rehearsal for a tomb. They had built it on what was believed to be the highest point that was not a mountain in

Connecticut. Jack and Veronica both liked that, and the fact they were said to have filmed *The Swimmer* from there.

They walked through the white house and all over the land. The whole place was wild, with huge, ancient trees and paths carved into the forests. It was full of hidden coves, sudden clearings, and ravines. The only shaping hand was seen in the even row of pines that flanked the entrance and a formal garden behind one house. It was both very grand and unpretentious, in the way that crowd did things—no name on the road, only two old stone pillars and a number, nothing to signal it was an estate.

Jack had wanted to fly up in the helicopter, but Fisher told him it wasn't that kind of place at all. They drove over the brown pine needles right up to the white house, which had been abandoned for years. Half of the windows were out, with paint chips clicking down onto the ormolu. The sisters' children had used it as a place to hide, and the pine needles had blown in thick piles across the white marble floors. Fisher felt like he could still hear the children playing Red Rover, hiding in the empty rooms. He told Jack and Veronica of the paintings that once hung there.

Jack wanted it right away. At the end of the day they walked through the woods to a clearing where the light came piercing in, all purple and green turning to white like lost moonlight. As it grew late, they had called for the helicopter to come up. Veronica sat in the back tapping into her electronic notebook as Fisher, the real estate agent who flew back with them, and Jack all looked at her.

I knew it was the old man's house she wanted, the idea, the high white place, another escape.

XIII

Proof Through the Night

I looked at my bulletin board, though I knew I would find the same dangerous void. In fact, the only thing on my calendar that Tuesday was one of Josie's dance classes. Outside, the traffic crashed over the temporary steel plates they put up covering a deep hole. At least they had abandoned the construction site across the way. I no longer heard the pneumatic drills and the steel joists dropping, though the car alarms still went off with the random madness of victims. The garbage truck had passed from its two a.m. cycle, but now as I watched, a cement mixer drove into the site. They were back. Whenever one part of the city had healed, a new incision was opened up.

"Hello, Elizabeth, this is Mitch," said a voice on the phone. I recognized the deep, eager voice of desperate young Wall Street.

"What is this in reference to?"

"I'm with the Royce Investment Group."

"Hey, Mitch, I just inherited a lot of money and was thinking of contacting the Royce Group when I got it all together," I said, then I hung up.

A man across the street was barefoot, sewing in the air.

Another boy had just been killed for his eight-ball leather jacket, and women with large asses were being jabbed in the backside in Penn Station. Today both the *News* and the *Herald* had some skinhead gay-bashing story on the front page. Then I looked again at the *Herald*. It was a professional photo of that blond boy I had seen going around. He was dressed in dark clothes, posed on a chaise, with his handsome, pouty face propped on one hand and his eyes beckoning everyone forward to take a chance with him. "Writer near death . . . savage bat attack . . . blood pools on the snow . . . dog crouched by the body, leash dragging in the blood . . . notebook found . . . severe internal injuries . . . facial lacerations." He was half barefoot; they had taken one of his sneakers. His name was Jay Lightfoot, as I now remembered. I wanted to know more, but I did not have time. I knew I would have to take Josie to dancing class, because there was no longer any Segunda. Last Friday I had had the conversation.

"This is not working out, Segunda. I'm afraid I will have to start looking for someone else. You're welcome to stay until I find someone."

She looked down. As she moved into my office to change her clothes, I felt a great desire to have her out of the house now, forever, to end the whole sad battle between her intelligence and mine. And with that decision I felt a jolt of joy and fear. I did not trust her. Josie was in the house. I put a paring knife in my pocket. I lay a large carving knife out on the counter. It was taking her very long in the bathroom. I pushed the knife half under the bread box to cover it and pretended to be doctoring her doomed yellow beef stew as she came out.

"I think maybe you better leave the key." Here I held the knife in my pocket. "I'll call if I want you to come in on Monday."

She put down the big brass key ring in the shape of a prize-fight ticket commemorating the Tyson/Spinks fight that Donald Trump had given me. Too many Filipino hands had held this key since Angelina. I tried to name them as I threw out the stew.

Perhaps the Pimpernel should go to the Haversham Classes.

It was low, but I had nothing else to write about, and I had long since exhausted my emergency columns. Often now as I circled the rooms deserted by all but the most shameless publicity seekers, I'd hear the loud piping of Josie's voice, pure and cruel, judging me. Why are you here? What are you doing? Come home. Diana had taken over the British *and* Monegasque royals—a good idea, because you could say anything about them and invent it all, whereas movie stars went crazy. Sally Kirk was doing fashion and writing about her own parties. I was left with the publicity-crazed grandparents.

By the time we arrived at the side wing of the Abigail Adams Smith Museum, to the right of the tiny door that said "Colonial Dames of America," I was worn out from the coat fight, which involved dragging Josie by the hair. Teardrops pocked the front of her black velvet dress and polka-dotted her shoes.

Donna Ashland sat down next to me. "We just got two cases of Mountain Valley water. We're making all the ice cubes out of it. Tomorrow I'm telling Trevor to brush his teeth with it—in case they poison our water, you know." She whispered this last, shrugging off her shocking-pink parka, having made the same observation that I did, that all the Jews wore Chanel, while all the Christians wore sneakers and parkas flagged with lift tickets. She flipped back her bright blond hair and looked a bit lonely in this room without a convenient mirror.

"That's a little beauty," Donna said as a tall girl with straight blond hair and the tiniest upturned nose passed by, tugging on her white gloves as though she had been doing just this for her nine years. Her hair bounced, and her small, confident blue eyes squinted at the room. She was wearing no socks. It was December. But they never wore socks, and sometimes those noses never grew, so they would be sixty-year-old women or men walking through winter with little child noses and no socks on their feet.

"My granddaughter," said a gentle voice.

"Aren't you Mrs. Russell?" Donna said, drawing in her

breath as she suddenly noticed the old woman in the blue down coat with the blue knitted cap that matched her eyes.

"Why, yes—how did you know me?" She had a high, flutey voice, the lovely voice of the real ones.

"Johnny, my ex-husband, knew your son. We were walking one day and he pointed you out. How is Jay?"

"I really don't know. He hasn't spoken to me in twenty-five years."

"Johnny was at his wedding."

"Yes, that was quite a do," she said, smiling with her deep yellow teeth. "Are you English?"

"No," said Donna, caught.

"You sound English. I lived in England once. The King of Jordan bought my house. I had five American bathrooms brought over. I think he liked them. I guess I must leave now—I'm working next door," she said, meaning the Colonial Dames headquarters. "I just came in to see Kate," and she waved at the bare-legged girl. "I must sneak in to see her, because Jay won't let me be with her since Mummy's funeral and the will." And she told us this long, intimate story of her mother's secretary and her mother's will and how her son blamed her and wouldn't talk to her at the funeral. "How could Jay think an old Radcliffe girl—I'm going to be eighty next month—would do something like that?" she said, and stood up slowly.

She looked like one of those women I used to follow through the Kips Bay showhouse, hearing them drawl on and narrow their light eyes at each other until finally I figured out what they were doing. They certainly weren't there for decorating tips. They were never going to put cork on their walls or marbelize their wood floors or stencil sayings from Lewis Carroll in their halls. They were there to see which of their things were valuable, and they left ruddy with happiness to know that Romia's éta-gères were worth fifteen thousand dollars. Mrs. Russell was one of those old babes with impossibly thin ankles I'd see tripping into the Colony Club in a loden coat leaning on some tall old boy in a fawn chesterfield. They had their original faces and they let their hair go yellowy gray and they were related of course, somehow cousins or half-brothers and -sisters or step-whatevers, connected in the great gentile web which they all memorized. They were part of that world of people who never left their lights on in the day, who distrusted waiters giving "specials" and always ordered from the written menu, who kept their toilet paper rolls on top of the tanks, wore their espadrilles into November, and fought over the wills and codicils that transported their property through the generations. They were the only people who knew exactly who they were and liked it— those masses of slightly tarnished silver-framed family for ancestor worship, those anxious eyes seeking others of their kind in resorts—which is why they kept better track of their generations and seemed to dwell so much less in turmoil.

"Step together. Step turn," said Frederic Marshall, who ran the Haversham Classes, pushing Susan Marshall forward, the two of them gliding by on the balls of their feet. His white hair was streaked with traces of the old blond and combed back militarily, razored at the nape. He had that faked voice of someone who doesn't really enjoy children, a tiny red pug nose in a pallbearer face. Something army here, and the crooner voice "Step together, step turn" floating through the drafts of the Abigail Adams Smith Museum. Muted, ancient, insisting on proper dress, no rubber soles, crossed ankles for the nymphets. At this stage in the year the girls had already been taught to introduce themselves to their partners and been through the rudiments of such extinct dances as the cha-cha and the Charleston, dances meant for the lost world of places where guys with ruffled cuffs shook maracas and women with bare midriffs swayed across shiny floors.

I saw poor Barbara, who had been conscripted to dress up to be hostess that day, and the old fierce urge to misbehave came over me.

"Look at that dress," said Donna, who had acquired the fairly loud, authoritative voice that makes people flinch. She had piloted her blond boat through many marriages, maintaining the same look she had chosen when she was twenty-eight under the early tutelage of her first Christian husband, a look that suggested she had just dismounted and thrown the reins to a groom. Her favorite movie was Nick Ray's version of *King of Kings*. The sight of Jesus stumbling through the stations of the cross always made her cry.

Once I had taken Josie to Doubles for one of Trevor's birthdays. Donna wore a large gold cross around her neck on a heavy chain that swung forward into her grandmother's face every time she bent over to introduce her, slurring the name just a bit. I watched Mrs. Samuel's scared eyes on that rocking cross, mesmerized, as her mother kept trying to get Donna to tuck it in. Donna had hired the most esoteric eighty-year-old puppeteer, who had hand-stitched all the superheroes but now was trying to do this lovely little play about Easter bunnies and moon fairies, and Donna kept interrupting in her loud social voice— "Let's have the superheroes *now! . . .* Let's move it *along!"*—and the old girl was getting more and more nervous, until finally the strings tangled just as she was weaving in the Hulk theme. I gave Donna a rest for a few years after that. And now here we were, back on the ballroom chairs, just as we had been at Viola Wolff's.

"Alex got a turtle," said one of the little boys to his partner. I looked at Donna and thought, "So rich, so rich, maybe she will give me a million dollars," which is exactly what everyone thought when they were with Donna, holding themselves in check, keeping her hours and putting up with her worst.

"Did you know his grandmother was Jewish? That makes him a quarter," said Donna, at once more comfortable with and more condemning of the child.

"How many boys made sure their partner was right next to them when they went to sit down?" said Mr. Marshall. "How many boys made sure they stood in front of the chair and made sure the girl sat down first? How many boys made sure when they did sit down, their partner was to their right? How many started a conversation with their partner?"

"Your daughter keeps scratching her neck," said Donna.

The boys were swinging their legs back and forth on the chairs. One, in a crested blazer, had his khakis turned up and a wand in his breast pocket like a cigar.

"Girls, go to the center, please. Boys, be thinking about what you should be doing when the girl comes back."

"Side together step, side together step," said Marshall as the pianist played "Blue Moon." Some of these pairs could walk off the floor now and go through an entire first marriage together not unhappily. Already you could tell the beauties, the smooth ones, the uncertain, the hopeless bouncers and step counters.

Josie *was* scratching her neck. Two tall men in suits, the dance police, circled as the children bounced and stomped their way through "Moon over Miami," tapping those who needed correction on the shoulder and helping them out.

"There are two silver dollars in my hand. The next time the music stops you must decide if they are both in my left hand or if neither one is there," Marshall said into his microphone as he made the two coins disappear. The pianist played "Moonglow" and the children shuffled off, Josie making a face and biting the tips of her gloves. Three times Marshall had them divide into groups and guess, until the crowd was whittled down. Each time they won, the girls squealed and jumped in the air, their little legs flashing up.

"Look at your daughter. There must be *something* on her neck. You should check," Donna said, and a few of the mothers and babysitters turned around.

"Now guess the year of the silver dollar," Marshall asked the last two couples as "Fly Me to the Moon" was played.

"Remember I talked to you about the steps in the cha-cha. Step-step, one-two-three—back, back, drop the hand, one-two-three."

Donna waved to Dudley, her English husband, who had just

come in, and was standing in the back. We all called him A.D. for Available Dudley, for he always showed up to wheel the baby carriages up and down Madison, mix the cocktails, and take her abuse. He too never disagreed with Donna, even when she lost control and would unify whole restaurants in disapproval of her. It was her money, after all, and a great fortune; so he tended the garden of Donna's whims and made not even the faintest attempt to do anything else.

"What a beauty! What a beauty!" Dudley said, sitting down rather heavily and removing his large felt fedora. "Now, where's the little chappie? Oh, I see."

"Step in place, one-two-three. Now hold in place, one-two-three."

"Is the car outside?" said Donna.

"If it is, would you take us home?" I asked.

Donna made a face, and just then Josie came up to where we were all sitting.

"There's something on my neck."

"Hold on there. Let me take a look," said Dudley. "It's bleeding a bit."

"Bleeding!" said Josie, whose face crumpled and grew almost ugly, as it does when she is going to cry. "Bleeding!"

"Hold on there. Steady. It's a bit of a tick, I think."

"A tick?!" Josie shrieked.

I saw the entire class pause, the patent leather shoes stopped mid-merengue, and swivel to where we were sitting, the little mouths dropped open, the white gloved hands dropped from their partner's shoulders.

"Can I help? I'm a doctor," said a woman in the row behind us.

"Get it off! Get it off!" Josie screamed.

"I have a tweezer," said Donna. "It has to be smaller than a pencil lead to be a deer tick."

"Let me do it," said the doctor. "Does anyone have an envelope? You must save it to send to the bureau."

"It hurts," Josie said.

"All those of you with birthdays in February raise your hands," said Mr. Marshall. "The others leave the floor."

Eleven months of birthdays now stood around Josie, who was hopping on one pump as the pianist played "Moonlight in Vermont."

"Got it!" said Dudley. "It's just a wee little bugger."

"That means it's a deer tick."

"Don't get too close, Trevor!" Donna screamed.

"It's not catching," I said furiously, but then I remembered Donna had once abandoned the yacht she had rented, causing everyone else to leave too, in the beginning of the AIDS epidemic because the sailors did not stare at her enough and she thought they were gay and could be touching her food.

"I suggest you get that washed off and put some alcohol on it," the doctor said as we shot for the door, all thoughts of Donna and her car abandoned as we rushed through the older children who had been lining up for the next class.

I commandeered a cab as it disgorged two Havershams and a baby-sitter. "You'll be sorry," the woman said in a soft Caribbean voice.

"Eighty-seventh Street off Fifth—and fast!" I said to the driver, Abdullah Said Mohammed, over the loud Arabic music.

"What's your hurry? You think there's going to be a war?" *"Aieyahhhhhhh balahhhhh,"* said the music so all I could hear were fragments of his speech. "Satan in the White House . . . devils in Is-ra-el." It was going to be one of those rides. Josie put her head on my shoulder. She seemed flushed. Abdullah's speed mounted. I wrote down his name and number.

A bicyclist was weaving in and out, and Abdullah cut him off. It was very close. "Fucking idiot!" said the rider, who drew up alongside in the now motionless traffic to where he could see the driver. "Fucking wog!"

"What are you writing?" Abdullah said.

"I have a sick child here. I wish you'd slow down."

"What do you think I am—your *slave?* You don't like the way I drive, you get out," he said, slamming to a stop on Park

Avenue and Sixty-ninth Street. I imagined carrying Josie, her feet dragging on the pavement, for a whole mile. It was now five, the beginning of rush hour, and I knew "Younghandsome Dr. Cronje," as we always called him, usually left around six-thirty.

"Ten dollars if you turn off the radio, slow down, and don't talk till we get there, Abdullah. Otherwise it's the TLC"—always use initials—"for you."

Josie was slumping. I held the tick in an envelope that said "Colonial Dames of America" which I rather wished I could keep.

I glanced into Dr. Cronje's waiting room, which was crammed, burbling with very young children.

"I think he should see her *right away,*" I said to the nurse, Jane. "She's had a tick on her neck," and as I reached for the evidence, it was gone. I ran back outside, but the envelope wasn't in the gutter. Abdullah had the tick, but I had his name and number.

In the waiting room I sat back and studied the high-gloss peach walls, crudely painted over blobs of unsmoothed plaster patches. Two little boys were banging on all the toys, pushing carts into the wall. A little girl was wiping her nose with her hand as she looked at a book. A four-year-old pushed beads around a wire contraption until his sister interrupted; then there was a howl which woke the sleeping baby-sitter; and the boy, who had been eating a biscuit, came and rested his wet fingers on my knee. From the examining rooms came a series of long, curdling child shrieks, followed by a steady wail, then enraged howls. What kind of a person could work in this atmosphere, amid the constant cries of fear and pain? In front of me a new little girl, who had just come in, began to bang on a xylophone while her sister pulled a wagging wooden dog over to the four-year-old boy, who kept pulling toys from the infected plastic basket and flinging them across the green carpet, sneezing, and diving back in for the next.

"Stop it, Byron," said the mother, fondly, and she went to the tiny wooden table in the center of the room and put him in one of the red plastic chairs and opened a book. The baby-sitter sat with her eyes closed under the bulletin board with a sign that said "No Honey the First Year" and notices for other baby-sitters and child photographers. Her mouth hung open on a cavern of gold. Next to her a Hasidic woman wearing a wig pulled a bottle from a stroller piled with coats, causing it to tip over—another shriek. I tried to read to Josie. The room was a cocoon of germs. I could feel the particles of bacteria being sneezed into the air, the cyclones of sputum and effluvia rising, gummed on the rims of the magazines (one of which had the Pimpernel on the cover on "The New Glamour").

Dr. Cronje passed, looked quickly into the room, then was gone. I could feel my anger rising. I tried to count, but each time I swept my hand over Josie's hot brow, I felt it seeping up, boiling higher. That morning I had read an article on the destructive and life-shortening capacity of anger. Three nurses on rubber feet criss-crossed the pastel rooms, passing from the lavender to the baby blue room carrying charts. I got up.

"We've been here an hour. She had a tick on her neck." The nurses were eating pizza. Josie was lying with her head back, her mouth open, pale and asleep. "She's very sick. It could be Lyme disease."

The Russian looked up, the corners of her mouth wet with red and yellow grease. I hated her. I hated her face, her voice, the way she held the chart. I thought of spraying the nurses' area with bullets. I walked over to the large poster of seagulls floating lazily over a brooding sea and stared at them all as they ate. I imagined them choking, vomiting pizza all over the desk, slumping to the floor, white legs up in the air twitching, Younghandsome Dr. Cronje running out, the figure of my wild night dreams.

Whole sentences of the anger article came back to me, for I had read it many times. "During anger the sympathetic nervous system raises the blood pressure and heart rate. In the chronically hostile the parasympathetic system fails to restore them to normal."

"It's now been an hour and fifteen minutes."

The Russian got up and went around the partition, motioning to the baby-sitter with the two little girls. I felt a jolt.

"She came in after me. Are they sick?" I said to the baby-sitter, sticking my head into the lavender room, where she was undressing them.

"Just here for a checkup," she said.

"Well, don't undress them. We're next."

"She came in *after* me, and those children are *well*. That is unacceptable."

"But she had an appointment," the Russian said, walking to the chart pinned to the refrigerator, where Dr. Albumen, Cronje's partner, kept her Nutrifast shakes and the vaccines and serums. The Russian smiled. I felt the destructive fight-or-flight hormones coursing through me in thick, harmful streams, torrents of them shortening my life, bubbling and boiling like the Snake River. "Underactive cool-down response . . . anger, whether stifled or released in tantrums . . ." We were standing now in the central hall, yet another shade of pink, before the definitely inaccurate plastic height chart.

"She got sick at dancing class. I couldn't call. She had a tick on her neck. Look at her. Those children are well."

"If you would just let me speak, Mrs. Alexander," and she kept pointing to the list and something written there in green ink as I felt the rush of what in me was always close to the surface, for I was one of those people the article described who always jab angrily at the "Close" button in elevators and count the number of items of the person ahead in the express checkout lane.

"I don't give a *fuck* what it says on your list! I want her in a room and I want her in *now* or else I'm leaving for good." I thought of where I would go, with Josie sick, in the night. "If he sees those children ahead of her, that's it."

By now a row of toddlers had lined up to look at the madwoman with the pumping hormones in the baby-blue room. Josie had gotten up. She came over and tucked her head under my arm. She was used to Mama's fits.

"Put her in the green room," said Jane, and I was glad I had given her two bottles of perfume from the Revlon gift hamper every Christmas since Josie was born, for she had been with the doctor before Cronje and Albumen took over the practice.

"But look here," said the Russian, pointing to the chart, and then she and Jane started to argue in whispers as the babies stood there tugging at their diapers. I heard Jane say, "... Pimpernel in the *Herald*."

"It might make an interesting column to write about a Fifth Avenue pediatrician's office out of control," I said loudly, but Jane was already moving, beckoning us into the Nile-green room, which Dr. Cronje never used but was Dr. Albumen's favorite. "I'll just pop you in here."

"Things are out of control in this office," I said to Dr. Cronje, who had kept us waiting another eight minutes.

"They are out of control in this city—in the world," he said, and paused for me to appreciate.

"I had to wait an hour and a half and she had a tick on her neck."

"Next time you have to yell at someone, yell at me, not at my staff."

"I did not yell. I did say 'fuck,' but I said it in a *very low voice*."

"My stahf"! I glared at him—rather, I glared at his ass, for he had turned his back, raised Josie's hair, and was studying her neck. His shoulders were broad and thin. He had this most annoying way of dressing, his shirts always open to show his chest hairs, bad shoes, slickster shiny pants, never a white coat. I think he was trying hard to be American.

"Did you save the tick?"

"I did, but I left it in the taxi. We were rushing, but I took the driver's number. I'll get it back."

He came over very close. "How long was it embedded? And how did you get it out?"

"There was a doctor there and she pulled it out with a tweezer."

"Do you have a dog, Josie?"

"Yes, we have Sade—we have a dog."

"It's not 'dawg,' it's 'dahg,' " he said, as I studied the chart of Mickey Mouse through the ages from 1929, when he was a cute, ratty little dude with pointed snout, to 1950 and beyond, when Disney pumped him full of collagen.

"Let's hear you say it," he said, poking his otoscope into her ear and bending over. His ass was thrust out, and I had an urge to touch it. I leaned back against the box of B-D syringes.

"Dahg. *Dahg.* My dahg is in the dahghouse. Ouch!"

"Let me feel your stomach."

She stretched out on the table and crossed her thin little arms behind her head and smiled. Whenever she did this I wondered just what Dr. Cronje might think of me. I stared at the hollows of her armpits.

"Mrs. Steinberg's on three," said the Russian. He picked up the phone. I was sitting on the stool, and he stood next to me very close so that I was looking right into the front of his shiny gray pants with their Morse code of black threads. As he spoke, he reached out and, almost in the way he might pick up a chart or a prescription pad, he picked up my hand and held it. I could not move. His hand was still slightly moist from having washed it, and his skin was very warm. It was the most quietly shocking thing, and he did it so absently, almost as though it were a mistake; but then he slowly moved his fingers over my hand, grazing in between my fingers. He knew just what he was doing, and I felt my face flushing. I was scared at the surge of feeling, as strong as my anger had been and very close to it. I studied the blood-pressure cuff on the opposite wall.

"I'll be here late," he said into the phone. "If there's no change, but I'm sure there will be, you can bring him in. I'll be here until eleven," he said, and I felt him looking down right at me then for the first time; but I could not look back, so I studied the Tempra and Junior Tylenol samples next to the box of Baby Wipes, and very slowly I raised my head to Josie, who was putting on her undershirt and obviously had not seen anything. For a moment I thought I heard her voice—like all children's sounding just like Mickey Mouse—as clearly as if she had spoken: "Why is Dr. Cronje holding your hand, Mommy?" as just then he lowered it, slowly, as though he had been taking a pulse. I could not look at him.

"When are we getting out of here?" Josie asked, and suddenly I was very happy. For the first time my fantasies had actually matched someone else's, and at the same time. I had to be calm. I had to make sure I understood.

"You'll be here until eleven? If I can get the tick from the driver tonight, I may bring it by."

"Actually I'll be staying a little later than that," he said, looking right at me, so damn young. "Dr. Albumen and I have our new mothers' breast-feeding and counseling group, but they should all be done by then, and I won't be seeing anyone else."

"I hope I'm understanding this correctly."

"I hope you are too."

"What? Am I going to get a *shot?*"

"I hate Dr. Cronje," Josie said when we were out on the street. "He's so snobby."

"You mean 'snotty.' That's just his personality. We have to find that tick, and we have to wait six weeks, and then you have to have a blood test."

"Why was he taking your pulse?" she said, and I wondered how Nathaniel Hawthorne had come so close to Josie in Pearl of *The Scarlet Letter.* I decided not to write about the Haversham Classes for the Pimpernel. Instead, I would do the city on the verge of the Gulf War, make a few calls, use Donna with her Mountain Valley water. All this was a way of not thinking about the tick and Dr. Cronje—now "Charles." I wondered if I had lied about my age on Josie's first forms and decided that of course I had.

"Let's get to the drugstore," I said, but I was planning: black pants, black cashmere sweater, red suede boots, or the blue dress; underwear or not. None. This was a very complicated situation, and I remembered Dr. Albumen asking once if I knew a girl for Dr. Charles. Suddenly I thought of my eyes, which he would notice.

We passed vendors selling chestnuts and salt pretzels, trays of polished fruits, nuts, cooked peanuts wrapped in pimples of sugar, Chipwichs, hot dogs, souvlaki. There were men with racks of scarves, wool headbands, trays of sunglasses and rip-off Chanel earrings, gloves and umbrellas, fake Bottega Veneta bags and belts and shirts, Russian dolls, Philippine boxes made from twigs, Peruvian sweaters, all transplanted here.

We walked quickly, not looking into the faces we passed. Already Josie had learned to empty her face of expression, for the only people who walked the streets alone and smiling, however they were dressed, were instantly taken for lunatics, or at best the simpleminded.

"Look," I said, showing Josie the cardboard hut that had been turned into a newsstand. The top was filled with slightly out-of-date magazines, meticulously arranged. On one side a small swinging window had been carved from the cardboard just big enough for a pair of eyes. I bought a *Pan* for two dollars, dropping the bills into the cup, and instantly a dirty hand slid from the window and removed them.

"God bless you," said the man.

"What if they are angels?" I said to Josie. "And every time they call out to you it is a test? Let's say God has sent them down and made them look and smell bad to see if you will help. Like the lepers."

She was looking at me now.

"Christ would have washed their feet, bathed them with his tears, and dried them with his hair."

"Oh, Mom," she said, but a little uncertainly. Last Halloween the homeless had been the top costume at the private schools.

We walked past two Senegalese men selling copies of expensive watches. One had a leather attaché case open on a stand; the other had unrolled a piece of felt on top of a carton. As we passed, a breeze of fear swept through them. One folded up the attaché case and the other rolled up the felt blanket, and both strode quickly past us to stand around the corner. Each carried his bundle but left the packing cases on the street. I explained to Josie that they could feel a cop's presence, however he was disguised, and how whenever one of them did, he would signal down the line. There must have been someone behind us. It was like beating the drums in the jungle. Cronje was a Boer descendant. I thought of the cheeks of his buttocks in a flapping loincloth, that nasty superior voice lecturing me, mocking the random bits of medical knowledge I had learned in my first marriage.

I scanned Park Avenue for intimations of war and thought of people to call. Meanwhile I Fed-Exed a request for my tick to Abdullah in Staten Island so that it could be sent to the lab. Josie's fever had gone down, though there was a raised red lump on her neck, which in some way I blamed on Charles.

He came right to the door instead of buzzing me in. The sleeves of his blue shirt were rolled up and I saw the thick fair hair on his forearms, but I was afraid to look up at his face.

"I've been waiting since ten," he said.

" 'Now that you have found me, how long will you stay?' 'Till the end of time.' *The Thief of Baghdad,* one of my favorite movies."

"I would have given you till eleven," he said. Now I saw that when he was tired, his accent was stronger, a beautiful voice.

He came right over to me then and half nudged me into Dr. Albumen's office, which was dark, and there, against the door, he began to kiss me. It was a strange kiss, half biting, half sucking, almost painful, and I drew back, but he continued a long time, nibbling, probing, hurting my lips.

"I know it's different for you," he said. "Try to trust me."

"But I don't like pain."

"Are you sure?" and he began biting at my lip again until I

tasted the salt in my mouth. I felt a mad and crazed desire, almost a swooning, beating in the blood, and he began to pinch at my nipples until they too were sore and he was panting and I was too. He put his hand down between my legs and moved it back and forth, the palm rigid like he was sawing, and that too hurt—and then I began to feel it, and all the months without sex, the anger of the day, the frightening tension, the risk, mounted and I could not stop. I twisted and turned against the door as over and over again it happened, maybe eight times, maybe ten, until I slumped down and he pulled me up by the hair but I scarcely felt it. Then he let me fall and went to a drawer, from which he took a set of keys.

"Come with me," he said, and when he saw I could not move he waited. "I have to shut up the office." He began pulling the blinds as behind him a shaft of neon light glared on in the childish pastel rooms, which added to the wicked mood.

"I should have asked if you minded staying here. Would you get some of the lights?" and we walked through the rooms with the wastebaskets overflowing and the instruments waiting to be autoclaved so that I wondered just who was going to clean up and when.

"Come in here," he said, and it was a room I had never seen, way in the back off the pink entry and obviously his private office.

I have always, at least since my first marriage, believed that most doctors have had severe childhood illnesses or injuries, something to have brought them into long contact with hospitals and doctors. Also that the specialties they choose are no accident, and that the art in doctors' offices always looks like their specialty. Charles had nothing on the walls but six ugly warped tin sculptures looking rather like tumors hung in very neat rows.

"They're Tibetan. They make the blood pressure go down twenty points just from looking at them. We tested."

His office was painted white. He unlocked a cabinet and stood in front of it almost as though he was shielding it before he opened the door. It was full of riding crops and slender switches and thongs and cords, kind of like the crop corner at Kauffman's, but not quite. I almost laughed.

"I assume this makes the blood pressure go up. Way up."

"It's a good thing you start so low."

"How do you know?"

"Because I took your pulse before. I keep these here because I'm rarely home. I live in New Jersey."

And then I wondered if he had two sets of these.

"Let me show you," he said, and he had the grace to look embarrassed, and I could see he was very excited, also very large inside those gray pants. He had shaved since the late afternoon, and he wore his shirt open. In my high boots I reached just to the triangle at the base of his throat. I rested my head there for what seemed like a long time. I put out my tongue and licked the spot where I knew I could kill him, until he lifted my face.

I saw a few small rings attached to the ceiling up by the large white air ducts and wondered for a moment about all those lactating moms who had been sitting in Dr. Albumen's office next door discussing feeding schedules and formulas a few hours ago.

Certainly, if I was eighteen, I would have run from there, but I decided to stay and learn. Since the age of nineteen, I have been a very good student.

XIV

Bunkers

Libby, hold it. Can you take off the shades? One more. With Angelo. Have him be showing you something in one of the booths."

"I just bought a little green apple box," Angelo said, pretending to point to a Chippendale mahogany side chair from the Parrish family which was outside the first booth. "Whose suit is that? It's terrific." He put his hand on my shoulder where Charles had just switched me with the red fly switch. What could be my explanation for all this, even to myself, except that Charles was attractive and people fall into things despite all common sense?

"Another, honeychile," said Don Stock, bobbing up and down as he saw the others closing in. I knew they must be desperate if they were photographing me.

"You've got good color today," Angelo said as we went past stone urns filled with ten-foot branches of quince and pear and curly willow to the receiving line.

"Have you been reading Lightfoot's journal? I've been saving them all. They say he's going to live."

Blanca Dell had halted for the photographers, leaning on Philip, her eyes cast down because of the war. She was dressed in dark clothes and she had a yellow ribbon tied around her wrist.

I was glad she had come. I hoped the others would too. The Winter Antique Show was one of those unquenchable events, one of my annual standards, like the ABT or the flower show, the old library and museum dinners used to be, a ritual massing, as everyone strolled up and down the aisles at the Seventh Regiment Armory, now cleared of tanks and filled with antiques. It always gave me a column—sometimes two, if I wrote about the benefactors' tea and the patrons' reception weeks before. Still I was worried. Who would be here at four p.m., the children's hour, in the middle of a war in the age of repentance?

"Go see what Tack Gordon did with the artisans," Angelo said, moving me down the receiving line, which immediately caused Nancy Noyes, who had seen me, to step back. Up ahead I saw the dark blue bulk of Sandy Fisher, who also was not speaking to me.

Now I entered the corridor of tableaux vivants. On both sides were artisans working away—a finial carver pretending to whittle and chisel, a book binder pretending to tool some leather, an upholsterer stitching. Two tassel and trim makers were braiding colored silken cords as the two masters of the faux finish sat with demonstration chunks of faux shagreen, ivory, burled wood. A man bent over a shattered Imari bowl, pretending to glue it. There were gilders, French polishers, cushion and pillow makers, and I was sorry for them all, for they were so out of fashion now. It was like a museum of the last decade, an archive of all these unnecessary crafts.

"It sort of seems wrong now," said Philip behind me. "I've been watching the war all day."

"Me too," and I thought of all the men in camouflage in front of maps, counting sorties, talking their own language of sweeping and capping and egressing there up high in the air war. Blanca, who was studying the faux shagreen, put it down quickly.

The first aisle was alarmingly empty; the few who were there were sunken, spiritless, scared to be seen by me. Of course, there were always those who would go two hours later and pay two hundred and fifty instead of five hundred dollars, and those who would come when the photographers had left because they didn't want to be caught in one of those pictures laughing, carrying off the little wing chair covered in old chintz in wartime. I was very nervous as I imagined my people tucked in their houses in small groups still hooting it up, showing their new treasures to each other, things they had bought secretly on the phone. Their displays continued, but without me. I was shut out.

"These are intriguing," said a woman poised before some candlesticks. She was still wearing her gray hair in pairs of combs as she had in college, and she looked like one of the ladies from the settlement house, who usually go two days later and then only to look at the flowers.

"A beautiful pair, because they are so tall and very little has been done to them," said the old boy who ran the booth in a voice full of love, rippling his long fingers in the air alongside them.

"I can do the whole show in ten minutes," Hilary Reed said to me, her coat floating out as she sped past. A waiter dipped to offer me a tea sandwich. Every year the food for the expensive ticket got cheaper. Over his shoulder, in a booth filled with Empire furniture and paintings of Napoleon, I saw George Solomon's sphinxes and stopped suddenly.

"May I help you?" said the booth master, hopping forward.

"I've seen those before. They belonged to friends of mine. They look much smaller here."

"How sad," said Gayle Pope, coming up to me and the sphinxes. I nodded to Bill and wondered if they got a bodyguard discount or if guards were like social ciphers and came in free, and made a note to ask.

"Lee bought them here, now they've come back. You look wonderful tonight. Isn't that Danny Gates over there?"

He was studying an English sand painting but really seemed

to be scanning up the aisle, as though he were expecting someone. He looked displeased when he saw us, and tried not to
frown. The Popes had backed off. He leaned over and squeezed
my shoulder.

"Did I hurt you?"

"No, it wasn't you," and I felt my face grow very red as I had
a picture of myself swinging from one of the rings in Charles's
office, bound by a tourniquet, staring out into Mickey Mouse
1953, the rise and fall of the switch, his coming up behind me.
I shivered. How had I gotten into this?

"You look good. Really good. What's different?"

"What are you doing here? I thought you always sent Andy
and your scouts."

"I'm looking for Veronica. She's been away at the new house
in the country for a week, and I thought . . . well. Have they
come back yet?" I did not know.

Over the last weeks there had been calls from Gates and
Veronica, those jubilant voices wanting me to know but not to
tell. I heard their voices full of laughter—the least little thing
would amuse Gates. And what he was saying was, "Thank you
for making this possible, and what may I do for you, old dog, for
helping me along? What can I buy for her? What can I buy for
you?" Finally they exhausted me. I turned from my own bad
deed. I wrote nothing, of course, though I had nothing else to
write about.

"Nobody's on to anything, are they?" Veronica would say,
waiting for it to be discovered, as though only by its being
written about could it be confirmed in her own mind. I found
that she was telling friends and letting it be known. I began
getting calls from the usual town criers.

"It's almost out. I think Diana must have it. What can I do?"
I said.

"Please do nothing. I can take care of Diana. We have Veritas, and after that I can sit down with you and we'll make a
decision."

I waited, and a day or two later Diana did run a blind item, which was lost in the war and the astounding reaction to what had become known as "the Lightfoot Diaries," now running in the *News*. At first Lightfoot was going to die; then live; then he was precarious again. But even in his feverish state, when the editors of the *News* came to him for permission to run excerpts from his notebook, he had agreed. They were full-page descriptions of walks and parties, low and high characters he had met, all the night crawlers. They were daring; they were original. The *News* blacked out the names, which made the diaries even more visually arresting, and it became a game to figure them out. Some names were changed, as though the diaries were meant to be published, but anyone could figure them out. Still, the war and the diaries hardly existed for Veronica, who set off on a wild chase to find out who had "betrayed" her as she reread the few sentences for clues. She was frequently on the phone with new suspects, tracking leaks. She insisted Jack had not read it yet, but we both knew it would be sent to him from many directions. "He only reads the Diaries now. He's had them all put in the computer," she had said.

We had left the booth with the sphinxes and now were standing in front of the torsos of Eros and Psyche, half draped, with their arms around each other. Gates turned the stand slowly; the spotlight aimed from the top of the booth shone on his face, the dark glasses.

"Do you know their story? Psyche lost him because she could not trust him," I said. "Her sisters told her he was a monster instead of a god, and he came to her only at night. He'd been pricked by his own arrow and had fallen in love. One night she decided she had to see his face and leaned over him as he slept. The candle wax dripped on his skin and he woke up. Then he had to leave. 'First century A.D. Roman,' " I read from the card. " 'His left hand would have cradled the back of her head, and he was holding her right hand to his lips.' "

Gates was making that nervous snicking sound deep in his throat. The dealer was closing in, obviously pleased with my story.

"The gods were always coming around to mess up mortals. But they needed our worship and we needed their meddling. It worked very well, after all."

"I think I'm in very bad trouble all around," Gates said suddenly. "Let's walk. Hey, I need something. Should I buy the statues? I like the story. She loses him because she doesn't trust him. She listens to others. She has to see his face to know if he's a monster or a god." He smiled his beckoning smile then, admitting the dealer, who had not dared interrupt, and they went off into a corner of the booth, where the woman wrote out a bill.

I saw Donna and Dudley with Athena and stepped back so they would not see us. Gates had none of my interest in people, was not at all curious about their lives, and uncomfortable in groups. Occasionally I caught him looking at the way they were dressed or the assorted acts they put on, but it was as though he were forcing himself to care. For him each encounter was an assault. I think, like the true actor, he was shy, and thus he went along the aisles, half ducking as though battered by light blows, dodging into booths, not so much to look, as for respite from the flow. Though he did not have much to say, he also had no chitchat.

"I just bought myself a present," Danny said. "Now that I have no money, what else should I buy?"

"Why don't you ask *him?*" I said, pointing to Jean-Pierre, who was passing with Holly Whitney.

I was surprised and almost disappointed to see her. I knew she wrote to the troops. I knew her moral core. I knew she set standards for others. But now it seemed she was too much around. To be at the Solomon auction and here were contradictions in the rest of her long life. She slightly inclined the tower of her sable hat towards the wall where Jean-Pierre was pointing.

"Would you show Mrs. Whitney"—here his voice rose with a pride he could not control, and the dealer looked up sharply at the name—"that Madame de Pompadour letter?" he said.

The old man went to take it from the wall and held it out in its gold-beaded lavender frame, and they were all bent over it when we came up and stood there, very close but not yet perceived, for they were studying the signature.

"Jeanne-Antoinette Poisson, Marquise de Pompadour. Fancy that! Her name meant 'fish,'" said Holly.

Then I introduced Gates, who was still distracted as we went around the booth looking at the letter from Marcel Proust from the Grand Hotel in Cabourg; at Madame Du Barry's tiny signature; and Freud's letter to another professor, with its large slashes slanting up to the right and many crossouts and notes in the margin. "He lacks decision," Holly said.

Machiavelli apologized to his nephew for not writing, and Elizabeth I presented her list for the Order of the Garter, including her lover and the King of Spain. Gates was still far away, his eyes on the aisle, making that sound in his throat.

"'Never put off till tomorrow what can be put off till the day after tomorrow just as well,'" I read from Mark Twain's postcard.

Gates had stepped from the booth and was standing there looking back at the entrance. He asked the time.

"Maybe they are not back yet," he said, and brought Jean-Pierre and Mrs. Whitney round the partition to show them his new statue.

"Sandy Fisher said they were tearing all the land apart. They're doing a lot of work," I said. "Making whole new lakes, moving hills."

"I know—I've seen. I went up and sat on the road and watched the bulldozers. I thought she might come out by herself, but she didn't. The phone in the car was broken."

I was frightened by the thought of him on the road like a boy waiting, clutching the fence at a girls' school. He was acting against his nature, pulled from the old patterns of his life by a force I no longer understood. He told me how he had sat there most of the day and then had to return for a meeting with his bankers.

"A lot of new trouble there, Libby, but don't ask me about it yet," he said, and pulled me along. I saw Dr. March deep in the back of an all-black booth filled with weapons and armor. We went in, past blunderbusses inlaid with ivory and Japanese helmets. There were no Japanese here tonight; they too, rebuked by the war, seemed to have vanished. There were pistols and ritual daggers, shields, powder horns, and armor, which Gates went over to study. Dr. March was bent over a French eighteenth-century hunting sword. He and Dr. Goldin, his young, polo-playing assistant, were holding it tenderly. Behind him in the case were some of the old brass microscopes that I knew he collected, for I had seen them on his bookshelves. I thought I saw Dr. March's hand shaking.

"Can I answer any questions for you?" the dealer said to Gates, who ignored him.

"Finally she did come out," he said to me. "She said she would come here tonight, if she could." But there was something else he was not saying. I could see Dr. March pretending not to know me but looking at Gates as though to memorize the features of his face.

"I think that's her," Gates said, almost running back up the aisle, but midway he stopped and sat down heavily in a tufted leather wing chair, crushing the card that was on it. "No, it's not her. Everything she says to me is a lie. There's always uncertainty. I must get out of here—she's obviously not coming."

It was still early, but I knew that those with the five-hundred-dollar tickets were always on time so as not to get themselves confused with the later crowd. This made the Winter Antique Show the only event of the season for which people were always prompt.

"You cannot sit there, sir," said one of the booth fellows, and he stood over Gates until he rose. Blanca was passing with Philip, obviously on their second walk round. He had gotten a New York suit, was settling in, but was still sockless—no, tan socks. They looked like they were about to come over, but they saw Donna and veered to talk to her.

"Let's walk," Gates said, and he picked up my hand. Suddenly, I was very proud to be with him. Don Stock rushed up to take a photograph as we walked. Napoleons looked out at us; an Audubon whooping crane stood poised on one leg before a doomed lizard, next to old maps of extinct places. I wanted nothing. With the recaptured Renoir, I had lost all desire for possessions. I was shocked at my behavior with Charles and hugged my arms to my wounded back. Rebuked by the normal flow of society, the watchful eye of ancient beauty and its delicate guardians, I vowed not to participate any more in his madness.

Sally Adams was barreling down the aisle, tilted way forward, as though in the armory drafts she was fighting a strong rear wind. She was scowling, her eyes forward, but of course seeing all with her famous peripheral vision, which could, without change of expression, pluck a Mennecy figurine from a table of trash. Her chin was up, all her loose skin shaking with the palsy of her perpetual indignation, her white hair bursting out and quivering in the armory lights. Her anger at the new prices and the new people, even though there were few around tonight, had long ago beamed outward into an anger at possessions, and I knew she took all the beautiful unpossessed things she saw on both sides of her as some sort of rebuke. Her old friends had left or been driven from the show. Once she and Evelyn de Young had ruled here; now there were dealers who didn't even know who she was. She scowled at me in reluctant recognition. She certainly did not know Gates, nor would she want to, and he did not know her; yet he looked over at her, then looked again, drawn by the force of her presence. I saw her pass and ignore Hugo, who came up and whispered to me that Athena Rossos was coming and wanted to find me to tell me something. I gave him a message to deliver if he saw her. He went off pleased, wagging with the triumph of his tidbit, bearing his message as carefully as I had seen him carrying his little shopping bags along Park Avenue on mornings after a dinner party, gifts for his hostess of the night before and unnecessary insurance he would be invited again.

Had we already been down this aisle? We were not sure, for there were all these dead ends and partitions within the booths. They were shallower this year, but there were still so many places to hide, so many screens. Though laid out in rows, a few booths cut across to join a new aisle, in a new direction with further turnings. Some booths led through and some stopped at a wall, and there was no way of knowing which till you were deep inside. To this confusion Gates added his own—that half-painful, half-joyous feeling of waiting, which is always the hard part of love. He was all stirred up. We had turned up the second aisle, but I saw Hugo and Chica and so we swiveled around and hid from them in a booth guarded by two stone garden lions. At one point Gates thought he saw Veronica again, just the trail of a jacket he recognized, a twist of other fiery hair floating back-wards till it was out of sight. We were caught and pulled by the crowd, and Gates had to stop and talk to some man who had something to do with his advertising and a magazine editor who had just asked me to fly to an island with Sting.

Where were my people? I looked around. There were so many missing, so many I had seen just last year before the big revulsion, entering these same aisles, preening in the Chippen-dale mirrors, picking up and turning over objects that the dealers called "smalls," in animated discussion with the dealers, pulled towards each other across the aisles. Now there were only these abandoned objects, the shells. These creatures had shed their old hides, their possessions, for the scavengers to find and buy.

I closed my eyes and imagined the old crippled dinosaurs heaving themselves around the forests, dragging their heavy plated tails, the immense burden of their cold bodies. A massive object from outer space had smashed into the earth. There was a rain of glass and acid and then the chill from the cloud. A storm of dust covered the world and blocked the sunlight, temperatures fell, and more than half the world's species died 65 million years ago when the dinosaurs of the Cretaceous period disappeared and the mammals of the Tertiary period appeared.

In the freezing climate they died and disappeared into the earth to become oil. I saw them, the big old ghosts with their warm, rotten alcohol breaths, lifting their large heads with the tiny brains with a decided effort. They were freezing, trapped in the rain of glass, as their quick prey skittered past to survive.

Now we found ourselves at the center aisle caravanserai, filled with mossed obelisks and urns and topiary twists trimmed with nuts and pieces of barklike growths and fungi, eight-foot branches of curly willow, pots of ivy, and, posed among them, a cast-iron buck from Hirschl and Adler's folk department. Gates sat down on one of the white benches and pulled his hand through his hair in a rather theatrical gesture. If this was the center of the maze, as it seemed it was, it was the place for the mythical encounter with the beast, the place to fight, but there was no one here to fight, only the staring iron stag.

"And you put on the ticket 'one leg replaced,' " said a man with a pair of tortoiseshell glasses looped through the buttonhole of his tweed overcoat.

"No, no," laughed the other dealer, in a chesterfield, whose long brown hair was striped with gray.

"What can I do? All the arrangements . . ." said Gates, and he was up, pretending to study a giant painting of the Turkish forces battling the Venetians hung against a black chintz curtain at Randall Hobbs.

"That would be perfect for the war room," said a woman to her friend.

"Or that," said the other, stopping before a red figure kylix of Theseus dragging the Minotaur out through a doorway, his hand buried in the tuft of fleece between the beast's horns.

"What arrangements?" I said.

"C-c-c-could you fax to me in London? Lovely. Thank you, I've got to shoot. I'll send you the Lightfoot clips," said an Englishman into a phone behind an extraordinary huge bureau cabinet that looked like a mahogany house with pillars, pediments, arches, and secret doors.

"Could you tell me something about this?" Gates said to the guardian, who resembled both the genie and the younger son of this large dark house.

"Yah, sure," he said in the way English have of talking to Americans. He wore his Prince of Wales suit with a green paisley tie and the silk pocket square folded, not stuffed. He had one of those young crinkled faces that look far unhealthier than they are and light cherub curls. He was very thin, drifting among the big brown pieces as though one of the armory winds might blow him out and off into the night on the next gust. His long white hands with prominent blue-green veins pulled out the drawers and tapped around to show us the secret compartments and hidden partitions.

"It's English, of course, about 1750—Cuban mahogany with oak linings, architectural forms, lots of pigeonholes. I'm sorry, but we don't know where it comes from," he shrugged, with the wonderful new kindness all the dealers were showing in these hard times, so that I almost wished I could do him a favor and buy the piece. It was not necessary for this booth to provide typed cards of explanation with a presence of such shy charm.

We moved left, over to the marble busts of Sappho and someone called the Immolator, who was in charge of ritual sacrifice and whose tight, frowning lips reminded me of Charles.

"Now I *do* see her," said Gates suddenly. "But why would she be with that decorator, if she really is going?"

"What do you mean?"

"We're leaving tonight from here. I have to get her away from him. I have Julio's plane. He's meeting us," and we left the young man with his hand trapped in a secret compartment.

"Chica, over here," Hugo Salm whined, as we cut deeper and deeper into the maze, chasing now after a flash of dark suit, some bright hair, and the tiny, strict form of Jean-Pierre. The center garden radiated into spokes, and Gates went one way while I went another. We turned corners and went round and round, but they had disappeared, lost in the turnings and partitions. The show had been built on the plans of Angelo, who studied mazes and labyrinths and had once explained to me that in a maze the way to get to the center is to go away from it. One had to follow the marked route, the laid-out path, or get lost. Soon I found myself back at the moss gardens, as did Gates, who was still alone.

"Daniel," said a heavy voice, and we stopped, for it was the former secretary of state. He was with Tony Kronheiser, the investment banker, who had just been let out of jail, having received a light sentence for cooperation with the government. Tony had been allowed to take over the garbage recycling plant in Fairfield as part of his community service. It was kind and brave of the ex-secretary to be seen with him.

"Don't you think the Democratic position is an unreal one?" he said. I could not imagine why he would be saying this to Gates, the least political of men, but then he introduced him to Tony, for whom he obviously wanted a favor. "It's been quite clear all along that you are dealing with a person who will not be brought to heel by any sort of embargo or anything but the direction we have taken. . . ." I looked at the quilts in the booth behind me. "It saddens me that we are so out of touch with reality and the sentiments of our constituents and events. I feel a terrible sadness that the Democrats have misread Saddam Hussein and the feelings of the public—it's almost as though they are hoping things will go wrong. But the President is doing what he has to do."

"There you are!" said Andy, rushing up before she quite saw who was with Gates. "Oh, sorry—I—uh—just wanted to tell you I bought some really great stuff," she said, backing off.

I saw Julio Ruminoz-Caetano heading down the aisle, looking at the watch he wore strapped over his cuff. He saw Gates and made flapping motions with his arms like wings. Gates saw him and shrugged. Once, after a party in Bahia, I had gone to Julio's house on the side of a cliff. His wife at the time had cut off the bottoms of all his suits from the knee down and burnt half the living room floor to charcoal. Upstairs in his study he kept a large Kodak camera box filled with cocaine. He told me how after the fire he and his wife had lain in the dark for days making love.

"Oh, Leeby," he said, picking up my hand, which was none too clean, and rubbing his nose in the air above it. He drew me aside for a drink as the ex-secretary continued. All the time Gates was nodding but looking over his shoulder at the flow of people, which now included the omnipresent Barnetts, those music people, who tonight wore matching sweaters with American flags. "My pilot will wait," Julio mouthed back at him.

Don Stock and Sal went rushing past, followed by the others. I moved off to the side and saw, in the center of an enormous corolla of strobes, the heads of Jimmy Dell and his new girlfriend. She was laughing. I looked for Blanca and stepped away from Julio and Gates. It was hard to know which drama to follow. Angelo rushed past. Then I thought I actually saw George Solomon's head, and excused myself and ran, my heels clicking over the armory floorboards where the Knickerbocker Grays and the reservists drilled.

I came to a bunched-up crowd and paused on the fringe. Two movers were carrying out a chair over their heads, and Sal was photographing. A man in a down jacket was reading from a list, gesturing and pointing as a marshall hoisted a stool. Another marshal was bent over, packing a Staffordshire lion into a box. The owner of the booth, in black tie, was huddled with a woman in a purple blouse with a hard, disappointed face. I asked what was going on.

"They're stripping the booth. They have the sheriffs and a court order. He's bankrupt. He owes him money."

"He owes *me* money, too," said a woman behind us. "He's completely broke."

Now the movers were lifting a large gilt mirror from the back of the booth. The crowd parted respectfully. They were very silent. The three men staggered as they raised it, and the dealer turned as they carried it past the figures of a shepherd and shepherdess, who each held a stone apple out to the departing mirror.

"That's his lawyer," said someone. "Bobby always goes to the auctions and bids things up. A real dirty player."

"Not *that,* Bobby! You're already over the limit," said the dealer, but the man in the down jacket was waving his hands and stamping his sneakers, and the sheriffs themselves picked up a brass tureen by the handles.

"Poor fellow," said Gates, coming up behind me. "They may be doing this to me soon."

"I found her," Julio said, rushing up, and I saw Veronica two booths away. No sign of Jean-Pierre.

"Go away, Libby. Right now—please," Gates said, almost shouting, as he rushed forward into a strange-looking booth.

I could not see how Angelo's committee could possibly have accepted Sybil Antiques, for it looked as though the whole shabby affair and its owner had been plucked up and set down here from one of those craft shows on the pier. It was set up like a tent, hung with gorgeous old textiles and cloths, all pulled and shredded, in obviously bad repair, whereas everything else at the show was repaired and French-polished to a dreadful glow. A large, fat crone sat at the entrance like a gypsy guarding her tent, and everything about her discouraged entrance. She, too, did not belong among the smiling ladies with their good shoes and gold earrings and their low, educated voices, so eager to help out, as were the old boys in their ties with their dim smiles in front of their monomanias on display. She was wearing an old peasant dress with a scarf knotted on her head, and she was knitting and wheezing.

I could see Gates and Veronica, half hidden, talking alongside a glass case with a tree inside, its branches filled with stuffed hummingbirds. Veronica was shaking her head. There in the center of this womb of old textiles they stood, very close together. Veronica was thinner than I had ever seen her and actually almost disheveled, like the booth itself, her hair hanging down in strands, her eyes shadowed but obviously staring at Gates. Her face had lost all its color; her clothes were black. She kept clutching and unclutching a pair of black leather gloves.

For a while they were hidden by the sheets and stacks of faded crumbly fabrics, the clothes hung from wires. I stepped forward, but everything about the strange old woman and her booth said "Stay back," as though she, the guardian, were protecting them, wrapping them in one of the lacy shawls, her web of safety. She was very big and looked almost too heavy to have moved herself creaking across the wooden floors to this booth.

I looked away as the sheriffs passed, carrying out another mirror from the raided booth. The silver from the booth across the way reflected in it, blinding me, and when I looked again, Veronica and Gates were gone.

I could not stand there any longer. I saw Hugo approaching with that gliding walk like a Hovercraft and went back to head him off. "I remember now that Canada thing with Veronica Kahn. It was all in the papers about the affair. It came out right before some benefit the wife was heading. Everyone thought Veronica had told."

Just then Sandy passed, pretending to look into the silver booth as a way of averting his head. I ate three rolled tea sandwiches.

"What *are* you doing? That suit is tight enough," said Hugo, "and much too short, but your makeup is good tonight," and he raised his chin, which hung from his face like a dropped drawer, and studied me. "I've just been with Lightfoot. They think he's going to be all right. Kunkel was there—he's his agent now. You can't imagine the offers."

"Where are the two people who were just here?" I asked the old woman, and she waved her full sleeves up the aisle. I saw them now. I saw people pulling at Veronica and claiming her and Gates withdrawing as she was clutched at and taken then by the whirl. I followed them. She could not leave, she could not say goodnight; she was a social creature, given over to the pack that was the enemy of Gates.

"What's going on, Julio?" I asked, but then he, too, having reappeared, backed into the crowds.

"Oh, *mama mia,* you have to *tell* me!" Angelo moaned, rushing by me to the raided booth with the auction columnist from the *Herald* and Jean-Pierre, who asked where Veronica had gone.

"I want her to see the Adam and Eve and the apple tree at Ariadne. Don't let her leave without going over." In his pocket was a small package wrapped in tissue with a thin yellow ribbon. Ahead of me I saw Sandy, swinging the attaché case that contained his phone, and I paused to let him stay far ahead.

Now I was near the entrance. I could see beyond the glass doors the next crowd, who were still barred from entering, and there, in front of them, about to leave, were the figures of Gates and Veronica, twisting and turning slowly, pinioned by the strobes.

They must have gone off then leaving both their cars behind, for an hour later when I went out for air, I saw Peter leaning against Gates's car, as well as Veronica's driver far down the line. I said nothing. I did not know how far they had gotten or whether they had reached Julio's plane at Teterboro, for he, too, had vanished. I went back into the armory, where I followed other threads.

I saw Jimmy Dell and his girl turn a corner and come face to face with Blanca and Philip Ives, who were going the wrong way in the flow. Each pair had its own media swarm, and the two swarms met and merged into one huge ball of light. Philip nodded to the girl, but none of them said anything. Blanca and Jimmy looked only at each other and totally disregarded the other's friend, about whom they might normally have been very curious. Then Jimmy walked off, his cashmere coat flapping open, and the girl stumbled after, scarcely able to keep up in her tight dress, which Hugo looked at angrily. What a song this would make for Philip, pounding a white piano in some darkened lounge months later, after Blanca had dumped him as around him the drinkers drank and the couples talked and no one cared anymore as he jammed his shoes soundlessly on the pedals.

In the big rush of the third crowd I lost all hopes of finding the figure I thought might be George Solomon. Of course he would have left, especially at the sight of the marshals.

The next morning I looked at the photographs in the *Herald*. Sal had taken a strange picture: all those faces pressed to the glass, looking in, and Veronica and Gates, not quite identifiable, obviously wanting to escape. He had his hand on her elbow, and she was whirling so that her hair fanned out. It was so different from the usual frontal society shots, all smiling teeth and self-awareness as two people gripped and grinned at those they liked and those they feared and those they envied with the same bright expressions. Here they were visibly unhappy with the process, and I was surprised the *Herald* had run it. But after all, it was Gates. They never got Gates, and now twice in the same half-year he had been taken. The picture said they were lovers. You could cut off the heads and isolate almost any body part—the hand on the elbow, the twist of the forms—and it would say the same thing as had the statue of Eros and Psyche.

I looked out the window to where a man was selling roses and American flags from car to car. The first yellow ribbons had appeared on the awning posts of the apartment buildings in differing styles. Young men in helmets with their wills made out practiced crawling the silent sands on their stomachs on this moonless night. The oil had just been spilled into the Gulf, and black-necked grebes floated on the poisoned seas, stuck motionless, and staring. Doomed cormorants were being lifted from the beaches and washed off in tubs. I kept my television on and stared at the limp creatures.

"The thing that bothered me the most in combat was the noise," said the general with the face of a doorman, and one white cowlick from the center of his part trembled in the television lights as he talked of "attackin'," Scuds and Patriots, sorties, things being optimized. I came to know his voice from the others. Meanwhile, no one was calling, not even Hugo. The war had given the Peabrains something to do. It allowed them to watch television all day without excuse.

XV

Surrenders

It was just after two in the afternoon, the hour when writers all over my neighborhood burst from their cells like the undead from their coffins as the first streaks of moonbeam arced onto their red-veined lids. I would usually go out then to buy the new magazines and stand flipping the pages, tense with jealousy. I would walk down Park Avenue, which was not distracting, or through Central Park, thinking of what I should have written and stopping to phone in changes when it was possible. Often I saw Joe Daley, who was finishing the second volume of his history of New York, coming out of the Society Library; sometimes I saw Hugh Bendor, always holding a folder and underdressed for the weather, though he also made a point of striding through Central Park at eight to prove he could still, after a little Kahlua in his coffee, get up in the mornings. I always saw the man in the red wool stocking cap who wrote in his notepad as he walked, and the dog walker with eleven golden retrievers on her afternoon shift. Sometimes, too, I would see my old schoolmate the now almost best-selling (*Loins and Lions*) Helen Kasmanian with her book bags, encircled by her own dark cyclone of fury, frowning and murmuring to herself, outraged about something or other. Her slightly torn pockets bulged with clippings and letters from midwestern academics who had attacked her. When she talked to me she always whipped one out, much creased from being much produced. She would read it to me, her rapid voice rising over the sounds of the street corner, seeking some kind of seconding opinion, though I knew she disapproved of everything I had become. She would always stare at my shoes as though the heels were too high, and then her eyes would travel up and she would shudder at the whole and brush back a wisp of her soft, graying hair and squint into the palm of her hand which screened her from the weak sun. I knew the next time I saw Helen, I would have to bring up the lecture and Veronica.

Today I skipped the newsstand but walked down to Sixty-fourth Street and Lexington, then turned up the block, passing the house where a single flowering bush was chained to a railing so it would not be stolen. I headed up Park, the canyon where the rich stared into the windows of the other rich across an island of green, happy they had bypassed Fifth, where each bench now held another history of mental collapse. I walked west to the building where Charles had his office. I imagined him inside, his stethoscope pressed to some tiny chest, the child's heart quickened with fear, his large moist hand holding the thin arm, his face close. I thought of him holding and pinning me, biting open the knots of the tourniquets.

I thought, too, of Sandy, of how we might heal things. Where was he? He would not return my calls. How little I had chosen to know of his life. I had permitted our friendship to remain focused only on me and his attendance on the Pimpernel. In twenty years, I had never been inside his apartment, which I assumed was small and poor, though he kept buying all these antiques. In the country he lived with his lover, perhaps mistreated, but in great luxury and full indulgence of the taste he had brought to Gates and drawn from him. I would have to apologize, though that would change the character of the friendship, which depended on his perpetual courtship.

I crunched through some slivers of smoky light-bulb glass on the pavement. Overhead the one bulb that had not been caged was smashed and the filament hung down. Ahead of me a man pushed the shopping cart that contained his life in supermarket plastic bags gone limp with age. A hair dryer was tied around his waist and hung down like a tail. It was best never to look too closely.

I thought of the Lightfoot diary excerpts, the last of which had run today. A large minor talent, and so young. The way the journals had grabbed the city was the way Dickens had grabbed his London. Lightfoot was quoted. Excerpts were read aloud. A Saturday-morning television show full of coughing panelists had analyzed the diaries' appeal. In coffee shops, papers were left folded to the excerpts. I saw a homeless guy fish one out of the garbage, but he threw it back.

At home there was a short message on my fax, and I could see from the number it was from Sandy, who must have been thinking of me just as I had been thinking of him and sent me the message by mistake. It was a transmission for Jack Kahn, telling him that Veronica and Gates had left the armory together. "Julio was with them. I don't think I'm cut out for spying, I'm just too large."

I called Sandy and told him he had sent me the message for Jack and perhaps he should forgive me since I scarcely remembered what it was about—a lie, because it is always about his friend. I asked him why he was spying on Veronica and told him how dangerous it was. Susceptible to any attention, he had secretly become Jack's boy.

"Gates only wants faraway locations now, and he's gotten other people for that. He even got himself an explorer. He threw out all my last Polaroids, Oliver told me, and I didn't get paid. Of course, the store's empty with the war. Everyone wants cheap clothes and bargains."

"But didn't you work something out with Veronica?"

"It has never quite taken place—all these details about

money. I got a warning letter from Gieves & Hawkes, and they never send warnings. I have to pay them. Anyhow, I'm not the type to hide in the bushes. He hates her now."

I knew what Sandy cared about most was being at the center, doing his small damage, telling his stories. As he talked on, describing all the war events I had missed while swinging from the rafters in Charles's office, I opened the afternoon paper carefully with one finger, inching past the war news up to the nasty surprises Diana McBride's column always contained, but before I could get to it, I saw a picture of George Solomon with Howard Goldenson whispering into his ear at the courthouse on Foley Square. Lee was not with him. Sal had taken the picture—an almost perfect example of crouching and looming behavior. I turned back to the front page. I hadn't even noticed the headline: SLAMMER FOR SOLLY.

"Get the *Post* and call me back. George surrendered. I knew I saw him at the armory. It could have been my story, and instead I went running after Gates."

After he called back and read me the *Post*'s story I was so nervous that I had to go out again. I saw Helen Kasmanian returning to the Society Library with a fresh box of computer paper, which meant she must finally have gotten her own carrel there. It was not the time to stop her, and besides, she turned her head and pretended not to see me. Still, I waved, though not in such a way that she would pause, and as I did that, I remembered that I had Lee Solomon's most recent private number and that I had always been very kind to Lee before she dropped me. I knew she would not talk, but I called as soon as I got home.

"Your number cannot be completed as dialed," barked the man, and even that recorded voice of the city was crude and full of triumphant hostility.

Just then Veronica called me.

"I thought you might be on Julio's island. Where did you go? What happened?" I asked.

"How could I go anyplace with the Veritas thing coming up and we haven't gotten Helen Kasmanian or sent out the invitations? If you're going to do this for me, it must be now." I could not understand, though I knew she was careless, rushing away, abandoning messes for others to clean up after her departures— but still, who runs away in his heart and stays to chair a benefit?

I told her to meet me at the Society Library in twenty minutes. "Don't dress down for Helen. She loves the high life. She loves big displays. She'll like the idea of the lecture. Until a few months ago, she was really pent up. Now she's exploding all over the place. Everyone's listening to her for the first time in forty years, and for money. Helen always loved money."

"Well, that's easy."

I was still a member of the library, so we walked up the white marble stairs, Veronica's heels clicking, her eyes flicking over the portraits of the Clarkson family, her rump-hugger red suit climbing her legs. Instinctively, she had known to show a bit of tit: she wore no blouse under the jacket and had left the top buttons undone. The librarians were still watching our ascent, the unfamiliar intrusion of beauty.

"Ames Reed inherited an ownership share here," I whispered. "Don't worry, it's impossible for Helen to refuse."

I was still out of breath as we pulled open the heavy carved doors of the reading room. Helen had taken over the whole of one of the leather-topped tables, which were really meant to be shared, like partners' desks. She had her colored note cards spread out in rubber-banded stacks that took up the surface, anchored by three pairs of black-rimmed glasses, one with a safety pin in the frame. Her fierce expression discouraged any challenge of her space. She was hunched over, her shoes off, and I could see a hole in one of her black socks. Strands of hair hung into her face, and she was blowing out her cheeks as though she were hyperventilating. She had not seen us.

A woman looked up from one of the two prized window desks and shook her head but did not stop staring. She looked familiar.

We stood in front of the desk, Veronica such a bright figure that it was impossible not to look up. Helen didn't. Now every other head was raised—the magazine poachers, the blocked playwright, the professor's son, all of whom I had left here in pretty much their same places ten years ago. Helen frowned down at her note cards. Veronica and I shifted, letting Helen get down that last thought. She put one hand on the card she was working on as though shielding it from us, but I saw that it was written in her almost microscopic hand, impossible to decipher anyway—those shocking thoughts in that tiny, cramped hand. Then, when she saw that this red form and shadow, these distractions, were not going away, she looked up, enraged, but instantly fascinated by Veronica's beauty. Her mouth hung open a bit as though she could not put me together with Veronica, though she knew this was exactly my world. Usually my people did not go into a library, though if they had to, they went there—rustling about, startling everyone and enlivening their calm days. It was all in Veronica's favor now.

"I feel the sand slip beneath my feet in Virgin Gorda." That line, written by one of Josie's classmates, came into my head. Then I realized no one had spoken.

"Helen, could you come out in the hall for one second?" I whispered.

She looked from her cards to Veronica, hesitating; then she took three books from under the table and covered all the exposed sections of her cards, searched with her black socks under the table for her black sneakers, gave up, stood, and began to walk out. "I think I'll just take this with me," she said, holding her yellow card and looking across to the woman by the window, who pretended to look down at her book. Now I recognized her as Marianna Klein, another member of the class of 1971.

"Is that Marianna?"

Helen did not answer. I introduced her to Veronica, who began—very smoothly, I thought—to explain to her about Veritas and the lecture. Of course the accent helped.

"It's five hundred people—a thousand dollars a seat for most of the seats. They'd give you seventy-five hundred—unless you want to donate your fee," I said.

"Everyone in the city is going to be there," said Veronica. "There will be a lot of press too, because it's really the big event of the spring. I'm the chairman."

"Veronica loved your book."

"Really? Which one?" said Helen, and she began cleaning one of her very short nails with the note card.

"Lions and Loins," said Veronica, and Helen looked at me, verified and triumphant at the mistake. "I loved that chapter on male-female rebonding. You're much younger than I thought. We're all just about the same age," she said kindly.

"What's the date?" said Helen.

"April twelfth. The lecture would begin at six, and then we're doing a dinner, or perhaps a series of little dinners. Me, Boots Simpson, Chica Starck, maybe Gayle Pope."

"The bitch whose picture is in the papers all the time?"

"Well, yes, she *is* a bitch," Veronica said happily.

"You write about all those bitches, Libby—rightamIright-huh?"

"All of them. I'll do the lecture, too."

"I never thought I'd make the Pimpernel. Yah, well, why not. Okay. Why the fuck not. But I think I want more money."

"Would this be all right?" Veronica said, writing a number on the corner of her *Harper's,* which was not a subscription copy and looked recently purchased.

"Okay, okay. Yah. I've got a black suit, yeah, and a lot of blouses. I like bright colors. Okay, okay," she said, her eyes beaming into Veronica. "Part of my plumage," and I could see her revving up.

"That's super—I'm so happy!" Veronica slipped her arm around Helen's waist and kissed her cheek, which immediately darkened.

Someone opened the reading room door, and I could see Marianna now hovering near the stacks of magazines up front, flipping the corner of an *Omnium* which contained my article on "The Neo-Blacks" (clothes, not people). Helen saw her too.

"So happy. I'm going to give you my card. Call anytime, and on the twelfth, don't hold back. You can say anything you want. Where can I reach you?"

"I don't have a phone. But I have an agent," Helen said, giving her the number. "There's something different about you, Libby," she said, studying my face, "something with the eyes."

"I had them straightened."

"But they look like you are staring. Can you close them?"

"Athena Rossos asked me the same thing." That silenced her, for she and Athena went way back to a bad plagiarism case; Helen walked back to her desk, where Marianna was waiting.

"What a scary little person! I hope she's going to be good. She doesn't seem to have much to say," Veronica said as we passed the iron ladies. "Maybe we should get someone else on with her. Someone with another point of view about men and women, like maybe Athena—or something totally different, like Freddy Gresham on his house."

"Helen would never go on with Athena—I think they're still suing each other. But Freddy . . ." The more I thought about it, the more I liked it.

"And he's a Sir. And he'll be here if the money's right. I know him from my Greek friend. I know him well."

I went home so tired all I could do was to click on the TV and stare. Again and again the same figures came stumbling over the rise, sinking into the desert, their faces striped with sand and tears and dirt, their sad bellies exposed as they raised their hands over their heads, falling to their knees. One grabbed at an arm to kiss an American boy's hand, salaaming to kiss his feet. "You're okay. You're okay. Don't do that. Don't have to do that," the marine kept saying, nice as American pie and cool, pushing him back. It was the emotional blood East, those dark sun people, bent down before Nordic America. The East, hidden under the sands, emerging but with secrets, always more secrets. As I watched this scene replayed again and again, it reminded me of Helen pulled from her desk by Veronica in her hot red suit with her arm around Helen's black sweater and Helen's dirty toe poking through the hole in the black sock, squirming on the floor in the capture that was like a deliverance.

XVI

Home Safe

Because of his position and the fabulous way he was known to live, Gates often saw people at his home. Over the years, these visits had become so ritualized they never varied. There was always the lightly trained girl to open the door and lead the visitor upstairs to the distant sight of Gates at the end of the hall, connected to his phone and usually not fully dressed. He was like those movie people I used to interview, summoned to their suites to wait while they did business that was meant to be overheard, business that ended as soon as I got tired of studying the room and took out my notebook. When I re-entered Danny Gates's life, I became another one of the people who would sit on his velvet sofas and listen and wait for him to get off the phone. These days he was home more often than at the store, where, even in his office, he felt exposed, unable to shout. He had been forced into having people fired and was hiding from scenes. Contact with smiles was difficult enough for him; when the faces were sad or accusing, it was impossible. Like his father, who would hide in a bathroom and run the water whenever a bill collector called, he had surrounded himself with his screens to ward off trouble; but they were being pulled away, his protection was toppling. Now often his voice was raised, and there were lawyers coming in and out with their accordion files and big, sincere shoes. There were trips to investment bankers that I knew were difficult for Gates. Sometimes, though, he got them to come round, and then the House of Morgan or Dillon Read would visit the house of Gates.

This morning one of those changing proprietary voices who would answer his phone as though she had just moved in forever had summoned me here to watch this familiar play.

Gates lived in the East Sixties in the house he had bought and rebuilt when he returned to the city. Over the years, he had added to it and pulled from it everything he could. The wives passed through it as good guests, never leaving their finger-prints. Everyone who knew Gates doubted he would ever move out. By this time, the rooms had achieved an extreme luxury that would be difficult to repeat anywhere else, even for him. They were crowded with things: past collections that had lost their interest, antique magnifying glasses, bronze cowboys slumped in their saddles—things with no particular coherence except that once they all had meant something to him and would be packed up and carried along wherever he went until finally he left them behind. Then the things would go on out into the world—the better ones to the auction houses, the lesser to thrift shops—and someone else would become attached to the things and consider them his own. Gates never looked at them much after he got them but would know and be disturbed if something was missing in his landscape.

Downstairs he had put in a large tiled pool, and the whole house was full of its heat and the sound of the moving, steaming water. Guests were always aware of the water lapping, even when they could not quite hear it. This was his shell, a series of conspiracies meant to seduce almost all who entered as they sank into the sofas in front of the perpetual fire. No woman who had ever been there had been able to separate Gates from these black and dramatic rooms, and one woman I knew had even married the rooms, not knowing that wherever Gates was he transported the same environment and could conjure anything and make the climate exciting.

I remember once hearing a story about how Gates had flown out to the beach wearing only a vest over his bare chest and tight black pants, and when he got off, two model girls whom no one remembered getting on were with him, attached to his arm, as though he had produced them mid-flight from the small leather bag he always carried. He stood in that airport of baby planes among the men with their ties loosened and their blazers strung across one shoulder as they scanned the horizon and jabbed quarters into the pay phone to summon their wives and looked over at Gates with the girls. That story was famous around the beach one whole summer, until Chica's husband was seen nuzzling a girl in Fins 'n' Claws, which gave everyone something else to talk about.

"The exits are closing, Libby," Gates said, looking up. "I get up in the morning, only it's not morning, and I look at the ceiling with my eyes like this and I start to worry. I start to figure it out—how I can get out, what I can sell—and it's never enough. They may take this," he said, and looked around the rooms.

"How far would you go with me, Libby? If I gave you a business story, would you be able to get it to the right financial writer at the paper and have it run exactly as I tell it? Would you be able to control it through?"

"No one decent is going to agree to that."

"They don't have to be decent. But it has to be exact. Howard has told me that. He'll dictate it for me. He has his own guy at the *Herald,* but I thought . . ."

"I think I can trust Dave Spero, but I can't promise. What's the story? You better tell me first."

With Kesselman's other businesses failing, Castle Industries was "bleeding"—that was Kesselman's word—and he had let Gates know that some time soon he could break it all up and sell Gates. This could be good, Gates said, if he could raise the money, he could buy back his business.

"No," he said, motioning to a girl at the door, who was holding up a phone. "Tell him ten minutes." "What?" he said into another phone, holding it away from his tan face, which grew paler with his anger. "The numbers won't work," and he went into a long conversation. I waited, half caught and half annoyed—the mood of so many others here before me—as I studied the pictures of Gates alone and Gates with the beautiful women next to him looking over into his face, which never once looked either ugly or happy. There were no pictures of him significantly younger than he was now, none from *The Angelfish Club,* for he had wiped out those days. He walked around scowling into the phone, aware that he was being watched and enjoyed, as he bit the rim of the glasses hanging from his mouth. I wanted to get up and walk through the rooms, but I was afraid to open any door, afraid that any sight here, like a bed with a napping girl, might be trouble. Occasionally Gates looked over at me, but I knew that since Veronica, I had fallen into that category of woman-with-child that held no interest for him, whereas for me he was still the movie star in the white sweater, stared at by the room as he threw his arm over the banquette at the Polo Lounge, asking me to stay. And even as I thought of this, I now wondered if he had not said "another day" instead of "another week" and if, after all, it really had been the Polo Lounge and not Trader Vic's. I began to hear those words coming from one of those high rattan thrones, and now that I had this new image I could not lose it. My story was ruined. Now I saw him handing five dollars to the Trader Vic's parking wallyo who, of course, thanked him by name.

"I have to take this—Jimmy Dell," he said, cupping the phone. "Jim, I want to have a conversation that never took place. . . . George *did?* No, I didn't hear. . . . No, of course. Let me know if I can help.

"Carol, did you place the calls to Howard and Bill Pope?"

"I didn't know you talked to Pope," I said. "You always kept away from that group."

"Sometimes I have to pay for not bothering with people. And

now it's business. Work on that guy for me. If you need something to trade, you can tell him Solomon just turned in Jimmy Dell, but tell him right now. I'll talk to you later," and he turned back into his phone world, as the girl appeared and my audience ended. Things had turned bad for him; that they had turned bad for others was no consolation.

"I'm going to Veronica's. To write about the dinner after the lecture."

Gates nodded, but he did not seem to hear me, and I saw him from the end of the hall bent over the phone looking into one of his photographs and stroking the arm of his chair the way I had seen him stroke flesh, as he savored his luxury in misery.

Hylas, whose talent with orchid obelisks had been given little exercise since the last decade, met me at the door, clutching a bouquet of gold quills. He wore a splendid striped shirt and snakeskin suspenders, which he snapped as he slid toward me. All the Veritas dinners had now fused into one to be held after the lecture in the Hammerman University Library.

"She's in the dining room," he said, waving the quill. "This is the mock-up of a table. Trust me, everything's cheap cheap, and we're doing it all ourselves."

The table, in its scarlet taffeta underskirt and "glazed chintz overskirt in jewel tones," as Hylas explained for quotation, was set with black and gold quills, marbleized balls, with little neo-classical "scholarly" objects culled from a desperate Lexington Avenue massed in the center along with a goldfish in a small bowl, "to watch something alive."

"Can't wait for that boy tonight," Hylas said, for Blanca Dell had invited the whole Veritas committee to hear Philip sing at Garters.

"I hope he's funny," said Veronica, coming in, wiping her hands on her tights.

"I think you're getting into trouble here with this stuff," I

said. "Veritas is about putting minority kids in private schools—
it's not this."

Veronica circled the table, her sneakers squeaking on the
marble. Quite predictably, she wore a man's shirt with her
fourteen-millimeter pearls and no bra, from which the small
targets of her nipples stuck out. From the terrace, the door to
which was open despite the cold, I could hear the ball bearings
in a Krylon paint can being shaken as one of the staff sprayed
the turkey feathers gold and killed off another layer of the ozone.

"It's really too late," she said, waving into the dining room
filled with cartons full of imagined detritus of an Edwardian
schoolroom. There were even plaster busts from the Great
Thinkers series.

"We used shoe polish to muck them up a bit," said Veronica,
"and we broke their noses to give them character. That was
fun—even Jack took a few hits," she added, as the spraying of
the turkey quills continued, the gold paint rising in a fine,
poisonous mist. The committee had tried to be serious, but bits
of the wild fuss and extravagance of the last decade kept popping through like pinfeathers from a pillow. I started to ask
Veronica something when suddenly she looked up and ran to
the great curving staircase. Two old country people stood staring
at the disorder.

"Mum, Daddy, you got off at the wrong floor! Two hours
early! Why didn't you call? I was meeting you with Lazarus,"
and Veronica rushed the stairs and bent over them, stroking and
holding each close to her, patting and cooing to them, still
bundled in their coats and much older than I would have
thought. I tried to pull Veronica from their faces. She had her
father's eyes, her mother's square face.

"We're early," said the mother in a heavily Australian voice.

The father took off his cap as I told him about Veronica in
New York and who I was and how I had come to know her. I
told them what I did, for they did not know enough to be
cautious and would have told me anything I asked. I did some-

thing then that showed me I was no longer young and almost finished with this game, for I protected them and asked no questions.

"I'm glad you've all taken Ronnie in, if that's what she wants, but I hope you don't mess her up with all this fanciness down here," her father told me in a scolding voice, looking at Hylas and the table. "I've been reading that Lightfoot fellow. We get him in the Sydney papers."

"Oh, Dad, it's all what *he* wants," Veronica said, looking up towards Jack's rooms. "Let's get your coats off and we'll have something to eat."

She had forgotten the famous Hylas, who stared at all of us as he raked and twisted his golden quill. She buzzed happily around, taking their bundles and handling their coats as if they were treasures, and that moment was when I began to like her.

"You don't have to worry. They'll all ask you about their children," I told Charles as the cab rocketed through the park to Garters.

"These people . . ." I began—but how could I explain them? Boots, Hugo, Donna? Their carelessness, their fears and joys and a certain foolish bravery as they went out into the night to laugh at themselves and each other? Philip Ives had written new songs, and they were all about us. I knew, anyway, that Charles had enough doctor arrogance to carry him through any situation.

Charles, who usually dressed like he was about to run over the rooftops of Bed-Stuy and slam some doper into a wall, was wearing a pale gray Norfolk suit and one of those little-boy down jackets that I knew would give the Peabrains much enjoyment on their next walk around the reservoir. We were late, and by the time we were seated at one of Blanca's large round tables with Donna and Dudley and Ames and Hilary Reed, Philip was already on.

His dinner jacket was open, his fingers seesawing off the keys. He sat on a kitchen stool, his legs spread wide apart, his feet in second position. Whenever his voice rose, his shoulders rose and his left heel rose from his shoe, revealing the circle worn in his polka-dot sock.

> *Let's go and dance with George and Lee*
> *Fly their plane and drink their wine*

I saw Donna and Blanca studying Charles, who was oblivious, but what surprised me was the attentiveness of Hylas. He was like a little dog perched on his hind legs to beg, all quivering and aware, totally focused on his treat, which appeared to be Charles.

"Who are George and Lee?" said Charles.

"What a beauty! What a beauty!" said Dudley into the air, vaguely in our direction, his charm more frantic now than ever, as though it might all be taken away—which, knowing Donna, was not impossible.

"Sebastian, over here!" someone called, and waved to a young blond man. Upstairs at Garters was one of those dark places with potted palms shivering in the beveled mirrors and sofas against the walls filled with artistically slumped young men, their dark velvet jackets open over their jeans and white shirts, where everything, even when it wasn't, seemed maroon. Behind Philip a worn Oriental rug hung against the wall, covering the bricks.

> *Going broke, it's no joke—*
> *Had to sell the largest boat*
> *Planes all gone, copter too,*
> *Maintenance is overdue*—woops!
> *But the babies need their shoes,*

Charles passed me a note on his prescription pad, but I could not read his impossible doctor hand.

"What?"

"I *hate* him," said Charles out loud. A few people, like Chica, heard. Philip glanced out at him from behind three carefully chosen prop books next to his very dark Scotch.

" 'So it's Charles Jourdan and'—*woops!*" Philip stumbled

again and looked desperately around, eating the air. " '—and Maud—' "

"Frizon!" prompted Blanca.

"He wears Bennis and Edwards in prison."

Just then Charles's beeper went off, and, as he left the table to call in, I saw Angelo studying the belted back of his jacket as if it might answer just who he was. With his eye, Angelo would come close but never guess, for in Charles, as in Veronica, the elements did not combine.

"Who is he?" Blanca whispered.

"Very attractive. He looks familiar," said Blanca's friend Wendy from the other table.

"He's my daughter's doctor," I said, deciding to end this. "He likes—"

"Music?" said Donna, and they all laughed, Dudley loudest.

"—places like this," I said, looking around the darkness through the flames pinpointing the faces and shadowing them with the corruption of the night. They were all talking now as Philip sat wrapped in the orange spot, his head metronoming from side to side. He wore his dinner jacket without a shirt, and stretch evening pants with thongs under his pumps, and the whole thing of black and bare white skin worked very well on a man. Charles returned, and I saw Hugo get up from his table. Even in the dark I could tell his eyes too were on the Norfolk jacket like a beacon and he was smiling. But, as Veronica started toward us from another direction, Hugo reversed and withdrew to his table, where he lifted Wendy's thick red hair and weighed it in his hand.

"This is my romantic song," Philip said to Blanca, as a young man with a haze of beard seated at a table of six men kept eating. He was cutting his meat, his left hand wrapped around his fork, protecting his food with his right like a prisoner. He never stopped, never looked up. Philip Ives was just a free dinner to him, but now he finished and began studying Veronica, wiping his hand in circles on his black T-shirt.

" 'Who Dun It'—my stock market song," said Philip, and took a deep gulp of his drink.

On what desert isle did they entertain
Serving their—er—coconuts in the wet rain . . .

" 'Wet rain'? And why does he keep forgetting the words?" said Charles furiously. Loud talking had begun in the rear of the room, where the young models were tired of waiting and wanted to dance. A few of the men and some in our group turned back to frown and hush them, but soon they, too, had to give up.

" '. . . No place to cry like L.A.,' " sang Philip.

"I'm going to have to punish you for this," Charles said, smiling.

"Who's this?" said Veronica, bending over us so that her long hair fell between us like a thin burning rope. She had left her parents at home.

"My husband's a doctor, too," she said to Charles. "Or, at least, he was."

"Oh, Jack Kahn," said Charles, sighing elegantly over the "ahn" to show off his accent, but just then Count Farnaut came in with a large band of Europeans, one of the last around, and as they swept past, their old eyes glittering in their young faces, Charles was distracted by all the beautiful girls combing their hair with their long fingers. Their tiny Lycra rumps nudged his shoulder as they passed.

" 'Buy me a com-pan-y . . .' " sang Philip, turning the pages of his large loose-leaf.

The Europeans moved from cushion to cushion, and, as their group parted, opening and closing like a night flower, I saw George Solomon in the center. The girls were all over him, hanging like butterflies. I knew he had heard the song. I had to go over. I had to leave Veronica with Charles. As I was getting up, I was almost washed from the room by a wave of Japanese men, ready to dance.

"Woops!" said Philip.

XVII

The Fool on the Hill

Ha o ma sow."

"Excuse me?"

"Ha o ma sow."

I stood there with Josie, trying to figure it out.

"Ha or ma sow? Ha or ma *sow?*" It was a question. She was getting angry.

"I'm sorry, but I cannot understand what you are saying," I said to the woman, and I thought of Charles and his endless pronunciation corrections.

She slapped Josie's fajitas into a bag and held up a little bucket of sauce. "Ha o ma sow?"

"Hot or mild? Oh, no sauce at all."

"But I want sow," Josie said.

"Mild sauce."

"He ot tay owt."

"I think we'll take them." I was weakened by this encounter, as though it was my failure.

"Mine has a hair," Josie said on the street outside McDonald's. "Some dinner." But then her mouth dropped. We had stumbled into a knot of men, about ten of them, waiting to cross Lexington Avenue in the early evening. They were chained together at their wrists and had shackles on their ankles, and their quiet was dreadful as they went across Lexington to an empty city bus that was parked for them.

"Are they slaves?"

"No, they're prisoners. But I can't think what they are doing here."

"Perhaps there's a clinic nearby," said Mrs. Lazarheit, coming up to us, for I was meeting Josie's sitter here on my way to the Veritas lecture.

"I'm sorry—Lourdes is gone," I said, handing her three fajitas, ashamed I had failed to provide dinner. Lourdes (with two syllables) had left, supposedly to return to her native country, in which a live volcano was erupting. Working for me seemed to have made the Third World look good to many of my recent employees, who were driven back to their native lands, however distant and troubled.

I looked at the chain gang disappearing into the bus and walked slowly up to Hammerman Auditorium, still thinking of the silent men.

From the dark rear of the hall I watched as Veronica checked the roped-off seats, tested the mikes and the pointer light, and even shook out the curtain behind the stage. She had not seen me yet, and, as she worked, she seemed to be trying to remember something that was not on the list she kept looking at. Hylas and his team must have been next door in the library, where the dinner was being given. She trailed her hand over the backs of the seats and then sat down in a middle row, studying the hall.

The names of the Giants of the Earth according to Samuel Hammerman were etched overhead in a golden procession—Moses, David, Isaiah, Jefferson, Washington, Shakespeare—and ceiling mikes hung from the cantilevered roof of the stage. The table, draped with a green cloth with a Hammerman University crest (Hammerman was the result of a gift so large it had replaced the name of the city itself), was flanked by the Veritas and American flags and held the usual sweating water pitchers in the midst of a grove of Veronica's bonsai.

Veronica went up the wooden steps and saw me.

"I'm glad you're always early. How does it look? We're putting most of the Hammerman kids upstairs. We had to save them a hundred seats."

As she went into the library to check on the tables, I leaned back. I had been to lectures here before. I thought of the room filling with the patient middle-aged, tentatively creeping in on their rubber soles. They would sit here waiting, their space shoes coiled, while someone fiddled with the tray of slides on the stand with the expandable legs. They'd stare into the blank silvery screen until the dark came and words of wisdom about "The Past of . . ." or "The Future of. . . ." It was never the present, a time that made them uncomfortable. I saw them, glasses gleaming, bags sagged at their feet, all looking more or less like John Chancellor. And I could almost hear their sighs interrupting the polite hush when the lights went out and the picture of a castle garden went on and they were transported. Perpetual students, learning and learning, waiting for words to write down, then forget when the lights came up. This was the time of many minds nodding in the same direction, of stored dreams and often a particular kind of New York anger waiting to spill.

"We're here to save you!" a voice called out from the rear, and in came Chica, Barbara, and Boots Simpson in their bright silk suits, looking totally unlike any three creatures who had ever been in Hammerman Auditorium.

"Where should we sit?" said Boots, whose glasses had grown ever larger and blacker since her Tibet evening.

"I want to go next door and see the goldfish," said Barbara. "Oh, look—Libby's taking notes already."

"I still haven't read Helen's book," said Chica.

"Neither have I, but I'm sure *they* have," said Barbara, pointing to the students who had now begun to fill the roped-off section. Few had bothered to change clothes or wash their hair, and those who had, had let it dry in the air. As always, the least attractive people were the most natural.

"I hope we get all the husbands," Veronica said, watching

Hugo, who held Chessie Bell's cast and was scrutinizing the rows, trying to pick out the best seats.

"As long as we get Lightfoot," Barbara said. "It's his first appearance. They say he is still fragile."

There was movement among the students as Helen entered from the rear, placed Marianna in one of the front rows, and mounted the stage with that same male waddle I remembered from school. Immediately, a few of them went up to talk to her, and she hunkered down on her heels at the very edge of the stage, gesturing and studying the filling audience.

Lee Solomon stood uncertainly in the back of the room. Her brown curls were pulled back to show her cheekbones, and her eyes darted for traps. She had once been too grand for Veritas, but now she needed redemption. And even just standing there, dressed quietly, people turned to look. Blanca and Philip Ives held her on either side like sleek blond bookends. A few photographers had pushed in behind her. If she posed, they would leave, but the others would be drawn—and how could she be photographed smiling with George out on bail? And how could she not, for it was a denial that anything was wrong. Instinctively Blanca and Philip, neither ever reluctant, leaned over her until there was just a sliver of Lee when the photographing started. Chip Streeter danced down the aisle with a girl I hoped but doubted, was his daughter. Soon the familiar bobbings and signs of recognition began, with all of them behaving as though it had been about a year since they last saw each other, when I knew it had been exactly four days.

Veronica leaned against the edge of the table waiting for all their joy at rediscovery to subside, tossing her hair forward as if she might hide behind it as she studied the note cards which Helen was reading over her shoulder. As far as I could see, Jack Kahn was missing. I watched a few students rising to get a better look at the freshly accused Jimmy Dell, the only one who interested them at all aside from Helen. He stood as long as possible, waving and cocking his finger at former close friends in the audience. A few nights ago on the news I had seen him being lowered into a Plymouth. The detective's hand was cradling his head so he wouldn't bump it as he got into the car. He was handcuffed and trying to shield his face with his shoulder as the swarm fell upon the car.

Veronica shaded her eyes and peered into the crowd as Freddy Gresham came down the aisle with Athena Rossos and Jack. When she saw them, she nodded to Gray Miller from Veritas, who introduced Veronica as "an admirable art collector and horticulturalist."

Gresham slid into the seat next to Helen. She flinched aside and seemed unable to stop staring at the large wen on the tip of his nose, which looked like a drop was about to fall. She made wiping gestures, as people always did when they saw Gresham, much in the way people meeting me now unconsciously stroke their left eyelid, or if I have a pimple, will touch the same place on their chin as though checking themselves in the mirror of my face.

A Veritas woman bent over Olivia and John Pinza, who had swept in like jibs on the big sails of the Popes. She seemed to be discussing tickets or payment with them, for she kept pointing to her clipboard.

Sir Alfred Gresham, introduced as "a baronet of Great Britain," moved out from the table and stood at the podium, tie slightly crooked, taking command.

"I'm very touched you could come. It's rather a selfish talk, this. We only just arrived yesterday, and Holly Whitney gave us the most thrilling party," he said, bowing his narrow body and his pleasingly decayed face in the direction of Holly and looking quite misplaced here in Hammerman Auditorium, standing under the golden "Isaiah." He should have been descending on the Grolier Club from his own cloud of wet lawn shavings, old dog hairs, and furniture polish to lecture on orangeries or the preservation of Trust houses. His voice was low and hesitant, as though he were trying to control a stammer. It was half bemused, half apologetic—that tone of the upper-class English with their permanent modesty and slight embarrassment over having been called out into real life. Like the Queen and Prince Charles. He had none of that wet mouth affected by Dudley. His suit, like a country house itself, was the accumulation of years worth of accretions and deletions in tailoring.

"I'm always asked what a baronet is." Helen's natural eyebrows rose. "It's an ancient title—the baronets sort of accompanied the king into battle, and King James . . . I thought he hit on a splendid way . . . we write 'B.T.' or 'Bart.' at the end of our name . . . a rush by the great landed families. . . . My family did rather well in the china trade, moved into the silk trade, and all married German princesses," he said, rushing to apologize by lowering the great dome of his forehead.

I looked around for Donna, all of whose English dreams had been thrusting towards this, and thought of Caroline Streeter, now Lady Redding, who had run away with her carpenter-lord—all for the spell the aristocrat weaves on the American, the old lure of the title, the attraction of the strange rich man in the big house on the hill for the staring, fearful townspeople.

". . . and became members of Parliament for the next hundred years—and went steadily downhill, har! har!" The audience laughed. The spell! Helen's feet were twisting under the table. She hooked her heels on the rungs of the chairs and began jiggling madly.

"Just fox hunting more or less . . . grand tour of the Ottoman empire and became the lover of the Vizier's wife. He had a passion for clubs. The Gnomes, for men of short stature. The Divan Club, which was only open to people who had been to the Ottoman empire. The ladies were called Sultanas—"

Hissing rose from the student seats, like someone had poked a snake pit.

"—and were always painted with one bare breast." More hissing. Helen smiled. Veronica peered out into the dark. I began to feel guilty.

"The Inferno Club met in a secret old tomb, had a tethered goat dressed as the devil—"

"Get to the point!" a young voice called out. Boots turned

around and frowned. And, as though on cue, the lights were dimmed and Gresham picked up his pointer to trace through the greenery to the positions of the Greek temples and follies on his property as the thousand-dollar audience sat enthralled, hoping for country-house tips. There was none of the usual shaking of sneakers and jiggling tassels of the Hammerman audience. Boots was taking notes with a small gold pen. Gresham spoke even more hesitantly now, as though it was too much to presume to take their time.

"At the Pembarton shoot beating the bushes with his artificial limb . . . grape stompings at the temple of Bacchus . . . Temple of Venus—everything has to do with a lady's abdomen."

"Boo!" said a young female voice.

"We all had to wear fig leaves and grapevines. We all get stuffed in this mausoleum . . . one has to choose one's urn. Hello! Sorry, I think this is the end of this section."

"Give us a break!" said the same young voice.

"Go stuff yourself!" said another.

"Problem with ghosts . . . Reverend Gherkin went around sprinkling holy water from the Duchess's Schiaparelli bottle," said Freddy.

Helen was kind of bobbing in her chair now, and it was like one of those movie storms with the dark clouds rolling over the sky and gathering to a black mass on her forehead. She even put her head down in her hands and leaned way forward, almost as though her head might crash onto the table. She started taking furious notes, as if this were a debate with points to refute. Across the aisle I saw Chica yawn.

"Face it, Freddy bombed. We lost a quarter of the audience," Chica whispered to me at intermission. "It was the slides."

"I don't think so. They'll come back. It was just some kids."

"I told you we should have gotten the Dalai Lama," said Boots. "Or Lightfoot."

I saw Charles moving through the crowd, looking very young,

and I felt like an evil shepherdess drawing him into this. He slid past Sandy, who turned aside, but Charles greeted him, and as he did, Sandy and I looked at each other, and I would have started forward.

"What's that?" Boots said.

A group of girls wearing red leather jackets surrounded Helen, who was again crouched on the stage talking to them.

" 'Go Girls'—what's that?"

"Look, they're chained together. Through their ears."

"No! Let's go closer."

"Come on up here, sisters," said one of the women, who was very beautiful. She took Chica gently by the arm.

"This is a dyke, and this is a dyke, and this is . . ." she said, introducing Chica to the Go Girls. Boots moved forward as if mesmerized, but the rest of us held back.

"Go, girl!" said one of the women as slowly, on reluctant feet, the thousand-dollar ticket holders returned, staring hopefully at the Go Girls around Chica.

". . . author of *Loins and Lions,* her third book, which has just been awarded the Benjamin T. Marshall prize," said Veronica in a tiny voice, interrupted by stamping and cheers from the Go Girls and the free seats. I saw Boots raise her fist—only half a fist, actually, since her nails were too long for her hand to close.

"Who are they?" Hugo whined. Then Helen stood up and rolled her shoulders.

"I can hardly breathe. The Waspiness hangs heavy like a miasma over this auditorium," she said by way of a beginning.

"Oh, God," I groaned, but low, and it was absorbed by the utter silence.

"Lord Gresham—Bart.—Bartman to me—with his Greek temples and his sultanas with the bare boobs.

"Imeanit'salljustalotofJacktomeThewholeideaofaninherited-aristocracyisfalseabsurdOkayokayIamstandinghereunderthese deadwhitemalesisn'titcrashinglyobvious . . . whoneedstheseso-cietyleftistswiththeirtrustfundsandtheirsmashedliberalismthose whothinktheyhavetheanswerIjustfoundoutwhatVeritasisTHE

WHITEMAN'SBURDENthewhiteblonditophallicgodsshoulder
ing their Asian and African American brothers and giving them a leg
up the educational ladder so just maybe I will return my fee but first..."

It was like fireballs lammed from the stage. Helen's finger was
out and jabbing. Olivia had stopped polishing the pair of glasses
on her sleeve. Holly Whitney's pen remained in the air, but
Lightfoot, who was next to her, kept writing.

"In my book *Loins and Lions* I'm exposing them I have like twenty
minutes and you better cut me off I'm like a feminist and a fighter I
punch and kick I'm just about the sixties a guerilla fighter from the sixties That's what I'm doing right now with my book trying to stir things
up Yeah that's my agenda Academics are completely out of it boring
and terrible."

"Who is this person? She is very disturbed," Charles said. I
looked around. Hugo was sitting up very straight, with his head
tilted up into his total disapproval pose, from which there was
no redemption. Chica's little bow mouth, slick with gloss, hung
open. Veronica seemed to be pressing her temples together. I
felt a terrible headache beginning.

"People hate dogma of all kinds I'm a libertarian Okay. There are
certain formulas we have to memorize. I had a disastrous literary
career," she said, slowing, "but because I have not risen through
the ranks there are no encumbrances on me and I have the
position of the independent commentator."

"I,I,I," said a thousand-dollar voice behind me. "She's an-
tagonizing this entire audience. Why didn't she prepare?"

But I recognized the act. Helen the brat, the bad clown, who
would say anything, however senseless, just to provoke. It was
an old trick to handle a formal subject in street language. The
cork had been pulled, she was released after years of captivity,
and the earth would be scorched. But why now? And why
hadn't I remembered that, even in school, Helen had loved to
be booed—or had I?

Behind me a man was muttering in anger; the woman with
him was skating her feet on the floor and twisting unhappily in

her seat. I turned to see who they were. Gayle Pope tried to smile, but her mouth disobeyed.

"She's full of shit," Bill said.

"Trash," said a woman near him. "Can't understand a word she says."

"I'mexposingthemthesebackscratchingasskissing—"

"What a nerve!" Athena said, rising and trying to lift Mrs. Whitney along with her, but Holly sat back down.

Gayle Pope started to hiss. From the back of the hall came a loud sound like a wail, followed by a roar of fury from up front.

". . . sponsored by this rich person, this Wanda Kent, who probably never read a real book," said Helen.

"Wanda underwrote the dinner tonight with Jack," I explained to Charles in the horrible rustling that swept through the thousand-dollar seats. Now the room was full of threat.

"Here here," Dudley called out, protesting as cheers rolled from the free seats. Boots immediately raised her half-fist, the sleeves of her black St. Laurent bat coat falling back.

"HeadlockedsocialitesOkayokayTheirhubristurnsmystomach withtheirmilliondollarapartments—"

"We wish," said Dudley.

"—andtheircountryhouseswiththe—"

"What a little bore!" Hugo said loudly, getting up. "I don't know why anyone would stay." He put out his hand for Chessie Bell, who didn't move.

"Ninny," said Helen, who was boiling over the lectern now, as though her lifetime of knowing more and not succeeding had been stored for this moment.

Baron Gray was walking up the side aisle with Sally Kirk. Good. Veronica had turned and was looking at the departures.

"Goodgoaheadandleave," said Helen as the exodus continued.

"Why don't we go too? I rented *Hard to Kill*," said Charles. He loved Steven Seagal movies. Often I found him in my den laughing as Seagal cracked some tiny illegal alien's back over his knee or sent another body arcing into the air.

I saw a few people turning around. Danny Gates was in the back of the auditorium scanning the seats. He began to walk down the center aisle. One of the Veritas girls stepped forward to take his ticket, but then she backed away. He saw me but kept on going, and I could almost feel the outdoor air following him.

"There are two Greek-American dominatrixes," said Helen. "Athena Rossos is one and I am the other, and she is totally wrong. She was positioned to play this role, but what is she doing? Marrying some rich boob. Her new book is a snooze. I go into a coma reading it."

Veronica, who had returned to the audience after the intermission, had her head down when Danny found her and stood in the aisle by her seat. "This is unnecessary," he said—or at least this is what I was told he said, much later. I saw him put out his hand.

"What are you doing here?" Jack is supposed to have said, and there was some sort of scuffle, which I could not quite see because others were standing, but which many people were eager to describe to me afterwards. I know that even Helen paused for a moment at the commotion, and Freddy Gresham rose as though he were about to leave the stage and intervene, and Dudley protested "Here, here-uh," and then, in the next moment, they were walking quickly up the aisle. It was all so fast, like a wedding couple escaping, she half-crying and laughing at her deliverance, Gates looking pleased with himself for having succeeded and shocked that he had. And I knew for them both, there was the sense it had finally happened, that the night of the armory, long stalled, had taken place. Like the couple who have the typical and often prophetic fight and parting before they marry, they were resolved, and had this been the wedding, we would have followed them out, some reflection of their expressions on our faces. It was not supposed to go this far, and now that it was too late I didn't want it to happen. I found it all unbearable, but then, after all, what creator can bear the face of his own creation? Gresham had his hand out as if to stay them.

Kahn's shoulders were motionless, as though he were strapped in; Helen continued on wildly, her reckless words dimmed by their real action. Only the students knew nothing, and, when she finished, filed forward to the microphones in the aisles, ready to ask their stored questions.

"When I was working with minority children in the 1970s . . ." said a woman, beginning a long chronicle.

"What's the question?" said a voice, ready to turn on the rage.

"Get to the question!"

But the night was over. The cultural critic from the *Herald* had rushed up the aisle.

"The dinner! We must get them next door," said Chica.

"Is she coming back?" said Olivia.

"She's gone. And I mean *finished*. We all, at least, must carry on. Someone has to apologize to Wanda Kent and get rid of that Helen," Gayle said, and she looked at me.

"I'll see what I can do, but I have to write," I said.

As I rushed for the doors, I passed a small redheaded woman who looked lost between the two audiences, who had formed angry clusters and were arguing with each other.

"Am I too late—is it all over?" She pulled at my sleeve. "That's my daughter," she said, pointing up to Helen.

"I'm Helen's friend from school. She was great. Maybe you want to stay for the dinner we're giving in her honor," I said, pressing the card with my table assignment into her hand. I knew I had been seated next to Freddy Gresham.

"Why did you do that? I wanted a good dinner," said Charles, who was thinking of the striped three-caviar pie.

"I'll make you some pasta and you can see *Hard to Kill* while I work."

"What was that all about? Why did your friend run away?"

I was about to explain when Athena came loping down the aisle, large and determined against the departing flow. Up on stage Helen drew back at the sight of her, but Athena stopped and bent over Jack, anxious to be the first to reach him. Already the waiters were lined up in the halls, toes out in balletic positions, and someone was walking the injured Lightfoot in.

None of the audience questions ever were answered that night, and many who were not on the committee escaped, looking over their shoulders as they climbed into their cars, still revved by the night. It was only on the way home that their excitement would harden into anger at Veronica for abandoning her own event, at Helen for insulting them, and at Freddy Gresham for somehow letting them down by being way above it all.

Boots, trapped in a paralyzing garden conversation between Freddy and Helen's mother, had gone downstairs to the bathroom with a bottle of brandy. She had intended to return, but it was so comfortable there, with a sofa and everything that used to make up a powder room, that she had fallen asleep. When she awoke, the kitchen staff were upending the fishbowl centerpieces into the trash. She had rushed to the dumpster, where the goldfish were dying a quick and bitter death, stifled by fish-egg pie. Boots had tried to stop them, but the task was too enormous, and she was very tired. She did get them to leave about thirty fishbowls till she could rescue them the next morning. Boots slept late, however, and by the time she had gotten to Piscatorium and bought their most expensive aquarium and had the man follow her home to set it up, she was tired again. She sent her maid to Hammerman, but the fish were gone. She went back to Piscatorium herself then and spent another three hundred dollars on tropical fish. She had spent over twelve hundred dollars and saved none of the goldfish, but she told me that, somehow, she felt much better.

XVIII

Bad Press

 I am watching Ames Reed vanish. He is almost here in Howard Goldenson's twenty-sixth-floor conference room, trying to pay attention as Gray Miller babbles on about the Veritas lecture. Howard drums his manicured finger pods on the fitted granite table, but Ames is fading out, as though some invisibility potion is working inside him: first the wonderful old blazer with the Knickerbocker Club buttons goes, then the dandyish shirt, and finally the face with the little nose. A spectral Ames is rising up, polished loafers dangling as he flies through the walls out into the Park Avenue evening, home to his beautiful, civilized apartment with the peeling ceilings, and on to other causes now that the Veritas that he knew is irretrievably gone. That, too, Ames; that, too.

"Do I hear a motion?"

Howard is drawing Christmas trees and triangles to the right of the puppet head of the board, trying to look like he is not in charge, though this is his room, his water pitchers, his fruit pyramids and cookies and selected Wall Street buddies; but the minute he clears his throat and looks up, the men with two chins lean forward and stop shuffling through their paper mountains. We sit here in this haze of criminality. The closer the Veritas trustees come to personal scandal, the better they look, so I inspect them monthly for that sudden polish that presages a fall.

Here comes the motion introducing the amendment in the bylaws that will take care of all such future mistakes as the Hammerman lecture, which has somehow come to be blamed on me. Helen Kasmanian is referred to—eyes averted—as "your friend" and "that gal" when all she did was tell the unspeakable truth. The unbearable fact that we, fat white faces and hanging two chins, are here to give a white solution, a white-whitey life to these smart dark children. We have removed them from their schools, taught them to think white and write white, and made them zombies in their own neighborhood, gray beings neither here nor there. Well meant, but a shocking responsibility.

"I'll go," says Ames, offering to make the apology visit to Wanda Kent, and he looks across the hard, glowing table at the tan wool walls with the downtown art under the neon grid hiding the soundproof waffle. We both always think of how it used to be when we were panting up those five floors at St. John's with Gray and the Radcliffe girls before we were discovered by investment bankers and venture capitalists who had to write off their blood money, which they called "giving back" in my column, and even that was stolen. No, impossible to see them, with their pocket squares and their squash racquets and their heavy English cases that I hear opening with a chorus of snaps and thunks at the start of every meeting, anywhere but in these offices with all the security checks.

Once I sat next to Ames Reed at a small party given for Gigi Farnaut. The count, a depressive, was in one of his down moods and sat under the ceiling of dangling pink balloons in the deepest of funks. He winced as the violinist played in his ear, looked mournfully at his hostess as if to say, "Captured, but not all here." She tried hard with her toast, which merely wound up a catalogue of how long she had known everyone there—one of those toasts when how long you've suffered each other becomes the passport to all virtue. And then Ames rose.

"Well, I only know *two* people here—Boots and Gigi. One

summer in Switzerland he lent me his Facel Vega. I was going to some costume party in Clarens dressed as a Japanese whore, with some mini-*jupe* thing on, and I wrecked the car, totaled it. They took me to jail and I called Gigi and told him and all he said was, 'How is it there? Who's there? Is it amusing?' "

Count Farnaut had smiled slightly for the first and only time that night.

A man named Wildstein leaned over from the next table then and ruined it. "Hey, do you still have the windshield? I have five Facel Vegas, and I could use a windshield."

"Well, who are you? Ralph Lauren?" said Ames, and everyone laughed.

Wildstein had leaned forward, ready to talk cars, but Ames and Count Farnaut pulled back and retreated into their whole gentleman thing of what one says and what one does not, and left the guy hanging over his chair, alone with fifty rare old cars that did him absolutely no good here.

Of course Ames is rotating off the Veritas board the moment he can, but he will serve out his time and do the trips that no one else wants to do and take his table in the rear of the Veritas dinner and quietly fill it with Mellons and Rockefellers who through marriage have different last names, so that no one doing the seating knows who they are and puts them in the back, these nameless people who could buy Howard and his four floors tomorrow, while Howard and the big boys he has brought in sit and expand in the golden circles of their fifteen-thousand-dollar tables. Ames says nothing, makes no fuss, but mentally leaves the room right now. I will miss Ames with his elegant heart and the impression he gives that there is always time enough to be kind.

"Do you have the final figures yet?" someone says, and I feel the eyes on me as though this disaster was my fault.

Now Howard is on to concentric circles on his pad, his body straining for release inside his dark suit. Howard has a round face that people expect to see smile, though he is really most often cranky and restless. He is even more trimmed and groomed than usual, with the light on his silvery part descending to waves around the ear and crashing in a symphony of shines to the black shoes planted alongside forty-four others on the pale tan carpet. I always picture Howard unloading his Mercedes station wagon in front of some enormous Tudor castle on the dunes as his couple scurries out: the crunch of the white gravel, Laurie Holt still in tears from the brutal drive, and, inside the house, the phone ringing with the next ruined man. Howard, with his big, swollen girl lips, takes the call, takes the case, his flesh spilling over the sliver of gold mesh on his wrist, over his belt, over his tight, gleaming shoes that look like they have never been walked on, over his blue collar holding up his two chins like one of Boots's Buddhas. Buddha with the red face, red face, red face—Buddha with the red face on.

I don't realize I am humming out loud until Lionel Frankenberg nudges me.

"Eight hundred and seventy-four thousand dollars," says John Pinza as we all turn the pages of his handout. I see the Popes have given ten thousand, the Dells nothing but Blanca's two seats, which does not surprise me. Chica, seventy-five hundred. Jack Kahn, two fifteen-thousand-dollar tables, plus half the underwriting with Wanda Kent. The Gates Foundation, ten thousand. I was put on the Veritas board simply because they knew everyone I wrote about would give. I was put on in the old days when we used to examine the provenance of our major donations, when people with "dirty" money were rejected by the Nominating Committee. Jimmy Dell had been rejected in that go-round. The Pimpernel brings them perhaps eighty thousand dollars a year, and so it doesn't matter that I haven't said a word in two years, not since they all attacked me when I suggested making Gigi Farnaut the honoree.

I draw Gates's profile on the legal pad they now give us at each meeting and lean back in the black leather chair. Some emergency meeting! We hop from secured board room to board room these days, but most meetings are here at Goldenson, Warburg, and Simpson, which is so big I sometimes go early to the wrong conference room on the wrong Goldenson floor and sit alone at an identical granite table under the hiss of cool air until I realize my mistake.

". . . for next year's honoree," one of the new women is saying. They too have attaché cases and snap them open and look around fully prepared.

"He's leaving the firm," someone says, proposing another name I haven't heard of.

"Not him. He's up to his ears in alligators."

Another name.

"Great trouble there. Under investigation. Where are we with the Barbara Snyder nomination?" says Howard. "She's very dynamic."

"I think you're forgetting Tony's feud with her husband," says Lionel. "I know he would be opposed to having the wife around."

"I don't think I can serve on any board, any *charitable* board, that gives in to that kind of pressure," says Howard, shoving back from the table as though he is going to get up that minute, and suddenly it is very silent.

"We need someone with executive ability, who has run something and has some taste," the woman says, glaring at me, but I look across to the secretary who is taping and taking notes, a leftover from St. John's who adored Veronica.

"Do I have a motion to adjourn?"

"Are you covering the lecture in the Pimpernel?" Howard says, coming up to me after the meeting with his late-afternoon old man's breath.

"I'm not."

"Have you seen this?"

It's Diana's column, titled "The Runaways," entirely devoted to Veronica and Gates and their flight before dinner. Helen's few remarks, quoted, sound even worse, though fortunately Diana missed the entire "white man's burden" theme.

"This is not going to help us next year."

"Listen, Howard—you wanted the kids to sing. That was your idea. These kids are heading for Harvard, not some gospel

choir." Howard had been thrown out of Harvard his sopho-
more year and never readmitted. "And 'Climb Every Mountain'!"

"It's Laurie's favorite song. Helen Kasmanian was *your* idea.
That gal is your friend. Veronica, too. Those Go Girls." He
actually shudders. "They surrounded Laurie."

"We had to have the Hammerman students—that was the
deal." I do not tell him I heard Laurie whispering to one of the
Go Girls like she was an old and intimate friend. She wins who
waits. "And no one could predict the Veritas kid."

" 'We feel like the only raisins in a bowl of milk.' Very cute."

A young man comes into the room through a side door
hidden behind the mirror next to the buffet. Howard sees him
and immediately excuses himself to pick up the phone the man
holds. I am only half watching, but I read the word "Gates" on
his lips.

As the young man puts down his folder and goes for the
cookies, so do I. I look at the folder as I pass, but it is blank.

"Wishful thinking," says Howard as Ames leaves the room,
followed by a few men eager to get home to their second families. I've been on the board with them for years but still do not
quite know their names. Then the door behind the mirror opens
further and I see in to what must be Howard's or a very senior
partner's office and the back of a head that is Danny Gates's.

I want to go right to him. I cannot stand having him in the
same building without being near him. Last night I dreamed
about Gates in one of those dreams that make me vulnerable to
the dream subject as the first waking happiness, that false anticipation, carries through the day. I am the victim of my dream
and, until I shed it, left with this disembodied feeling of love.

Gates turns, and I see a sliver of the early moon over his
shoulder as he looks full into the room, startled that it has these
leftover men and surprised that I am among them. The moon
cuts into the hollows under his cheeks, marks the cleft in his
chin, and the small dimple under his nose and ages him. Even
here, dressed for business, he looks like a relic from a French

movie of the sixties, with his eyes masked by the smoky glasses and his long hair. It would make a wonderful photograph for one of those ads where no one can figure out what is going on: Gates, the men, the half-opened mirrored door, and the moon.

The door is shut then by someone else inside, and the young man takes his cookies folded into a napkin and goes. I have no further excuse to stay, and yet I linger, again waiting for him, and it is then Howard says into the phone, "He's here right now. We can rough out the whole thing . . . letter of agreement." Howard glares at me and I have to go. I cannot understand quite what this means, but the fact that Howard is so intense means there is money in this.

"Not yet, Jack," he says, and I fiddle with my papers until he leaves the room and the girl comes in to clear up and lock the door.

Much later I will find that this scene of Gates with the moon over his shoulder and the frozen men, this moment that Howard was about to join and rule, was the beginning of the real trouble for Danny Gates. Of course Howard, looking down at the stacked triangles mounting to the top of his page, would have presented it as a "new chapter" for Gates, played it happily as a way of helping Kesselman and himself. "Who is the buyer?" Gates had said and Howard had described them as a consortium. "They're gold" he said. I knew Howard, and I wondered who was here to protect Gates. Since the beginning there were rumors about Gates and the mob, though I never believed any of them. It was easier to say "mob" than to try to understand his success. Gates had gone to Hollywood from Florida with certain assurances, but I felt those who watched over him were benign. Gates never vigorously discouraged any of the talk; it was just an extra thing about him, complicating the picture, making it more difficult to get to him, which was just what he wanted. He felt safer surrounded by the aura of a bad boy.

It would be a sale. Howard, the broker, acting for both Gates and for the consortium, already a conflict, which Howard assured Gates would not matter. Thus it was roughed out. Gates wrote down the figures—what he would get. He would be "relieved" of much of his designing duties, consulted only for concepts, though Howard presented this part hidden in such legal language that no one could have understood it. He made the deal sound great, and because he was such a salesman when he saw a fee like this, Howard banished his usual irritation and became charming. That mood change alone often was enough to sell people. "I talk to you as a friend," he would say, in the way doctors tell you this is what they would do for someone in their own family. But Gates was no fool. Since they were both somewhat depressed men, they knew exactly how to work on each other.

As this was going on I left the building and went into the blue dusk of Park Avenue. I leaned in the window of the Wagoneer, where Peter was reading Diana's column. Immediately he tucked it away and looked up with his bland face, ready to be of service to anyone in the orbit of Gates.

"How's it going at the house? I saw Mr. Gates upstairs."

"They didn't come out all weekend, disconnected the phones. A few of your guys were down on the street all Saturday, hanging around. I had some job. I had to get her clothes from the store. The papers were piled at the door. It's a good thing it was a weekend and there weren't any stories till now. But they would not have noticed."

I saw Peter downstairs in the guard's chair by the front door, looking out through the grillwork at the press stakeout, long ago convinced of Gates's dimension. I saw Veronica at the foot of Gates's bed, presenting herself damp from the bath only to find herself pulled back down into white Montana sheets; Gates in his robe with his bare leg stuck out the door to push the papers aside, as he drew in the clothes from the store and I hated this image and made it go blank.

"You have a headache? Wish I could drive you back, but . . ." Peter shrugged. "He sent the girls away and we really need them. The house is already collapsing. At least he's gone out now, but I haven't seen Mrs. Kahn since I drove them home. Didn't know she had a kid," he said, gesturing to the paper.

I had been away from Josie too long. I began to walk inside the crowds racing home. It was one of those midtown nights when there would never be a cab except by accident and it would take longer to call my dial cab than to get on with it. I began to compose my letter of resignation to Howard and the board, something I did after every meeting of Veritas. And then I thought of that little boy and his "only raisin" speech. He was getting a far better education than Josie. People passed me carrying transparent plastic bags, and I could see sagging through them the containers of prepared foods and lonely oranges they would have for their dinners.

I was up in the Seventies on Park now, and I saw the usual lineup of dark cars that told me something was going on. I knew the cars and bodies even a block away in silhouette. I saw Barbara and Donna and then Chessie Bell and, with her, the limping Lightfoot. Then Athena and Jack Kahn, which suggested he was not the "Jack" on the phone with Goldenson, though I could not be sure. Even from a distance he looked sleeker, as though abandonment became him. Whose party was this? I would have to look up the address in my reverse phone directory.

I was getting very annoyed as I hid in a doorway.

"Give me all your money." It was a high voice. A girl?

I turned slowly and saw a boy about my height. He had a tiny rusty penknife—the kind that would have had the Empire State Building or the Statue of Liberty washing in liquid, trapped in plastic on the side in the 1950s. It could not possibly have reached a vital organ, however it was used. Still, I took out my wallet.

"Do you want the change?"

"Don't move. Don't turn around. I'll cut your face." He threw down my wallet.

I did not move. A mini-mugging, but I was plenty scared. I

was watching as the car doors were opened, and I saw the ankles of the guests emerge. My knees were crashing together and I began to shake. He was gone—maybe. I tried to get the Valium from my pocket. Instead of rushing forward into the light under the canopy, I turned and crossed the street, ready to hide again, as if it were my fault. I was still shaking very badly. I heard a laugh and turned back to it to see Hugo, and then, suddenly, I did not care. I thought only of that tiny knife and that squeaky voice and home. My home, with my painting in my living room, the color of bone and blood, decorated with a kind of permanent impermanence which baffled Charles. He did not see it as a final dwelling place for him.

I stepped into the street for a cab though I lived just three blocks away. I needed alcohol, and I felt like I would never be safe again. I kept looking over my shoulder.

Josie, who had never quite adjusted to the new placement of her doctor at the head of our table, had retreated behind a door full of hostile, misspelled signs.

"I've just been robbed. You must be very careful," I said, sitting down heavily on her Angelo chintz and watching as she looked up from her screen, where she was planning a simulated urban paradise. She was frightened.

I told her the whole thing, making light. Actually, the boy had been underarmed in a city where six-year-olds go to school with semiautomatics and a few rounds in their pockets. Josie had never walked alone on the street, had never been more than an arm's length from an adult. She had never roller bladed around a corner without an adult in pursuit, had never bought a candy bar without a "guard." At nine, in terms of functional independence, she was age two.

She told me the phone had rung a lot and there were messages on the machine, but we went through the calm routine of her dinner without the remote withdrawn creature referred to as "Dr. Charles" who sat at our table like a beeping guest. Imelda came out of the kitchen carrying a stack of his freshly ironed undershirts and tennis clothes, leaving a wake of fire in her footsteps.

"Two hours work, then I'll read to you. I'm going to quit Veritas—it takes too much time."

I went inside to look up the address to see whose party I had missed. The two names I knew there were unlikely to draw the crowd I had seen, so I called a broker, who told me George and Lee Solomon had just moved in.

"How is that possible?"

Charles walked in and began to empty his pockets on the dresser he had taken over, stacking his change, straightening the sized stacks. One dour look before he went in to take his forty-minute shower.

"Because he still has cash and the board can't be so choosy," the woman said.

When Charles came out I told him about the robbery, but I could see he was more interested in his dinner. Like many doctors, he had an involvement with his food that was almost unnatural.

"Did you see that rat article? I have it right here. They now outnumber us. Listen—'The rodents can grow as big as cats, have lion-sized appetites and the agility of leopards.' They call them track rabbits. They're social creatures." Charles often came to dinner with his terror clippings. He was collecting evidence that he had landed in the very worst city on earth. Josie usually pretended to laugh; but how could she not be haunted by dinners with the Cadaver Cabbie, who "found bodies where most people found old sneakers," including a box with six heads, or with peregrine falcons dive-bombing off skyscraper ledges to eat the pigeons?

"I need some more Valium," I said, to provoke the argument that would end my presence at the table.

I had to write a column about some private Caribbean island that a friend of mine was renting out. From the air the island was shaped like half a dog. It had its own helicopter and hopping servants. She had Fed-Exed me some pictures from her house in Telluride. " 'Her Island in the Sun,' " I typed, and soon after fell asleep at my desk. Charles returned to the hospital, the dog peed in the living room, and Josie read herself to sleep as the tireless blue men bounced all night on her screen and took care of their enemies.

XIX

Afterlife

I lay still, studying Diana Vreeland's chandelier in the powdery lavender light of the midnight
sky as I plotted my escape from New York. Charles's arm was
outstretched, forcing me into a small well where the bed met the
wall. In the rumbling and screeches of the city night I imagined
the doomsday rock hurtling through space. The odds of it hitting the planet were greater than those of a plane accident. We
were trapped here, as in the iron lung dreams of my childhood:
poor pale bodies pressed forever inside a giant wheezing can that
breathed for them, and if ever the body got outside, it would be
squeezed to death by the awful pressures of the universe—
crushed, unable to breathe for itself. There was no escape. The
Rock was coming, and all the private planes and private pilots
on standby, all the drivers and bodyguards would not help.
There was no getting out of the city—the five-hundred-dollar-
a-month garages would be taken over, people ripped from their
cars, pulled onto the sidewalk, and left splayed like greasy turtles
plucked from their shells, like the poor pale bodies flipped
gasping from the iron lungs. All the country houses, the escape
holes with their antique baskets and hooked rugs and quilts,
would not matter, for no one was getting over the bridges or

through the tunnels. The rock was coming right through that hole in the ozone layer over Antarctica, my new worry. So what did daily dangers mean? A boy with a penknife, the crossfire of bullets, rabid taxis mounting the sidewalks, rats as big as cats, race wars, turf wars, school shootings, and all the minor assaults that kept my dog at a constant quiver. Crushed to death in a crowd, squashed, their chests caved in. Pushed onto a subway track. I had begun to feel the bodies tossed into the air, the falcons diving down on the pigeons, the poisoned seals gasping on the beach, and the avenging cleansing Rock coming straight through the hole like the taxi that had ripped through Lampwick, driven all the way through, right to the kitchen.

Charles was outraged when I walked the dog into Central Park at night. Sometimes he brought me to the edge, but he would never allow himself past the entrance. From the darkness, alive with green things and Norwegian rats, with the rustling and panting breaths of people setting up their blanket pyramids by the benches, I would look out and see the specter of Charles and his beeper and wonder just how far he would go in to protect me. Often I felt safer in the fraternity of these lost souls than I did with Charles, frowning into the neon circle of light.

I could not sleep. This was yet another night when I would get up and search for a biblical epic or tour the shopping channels, the land of lost stars, where people like Frankie Avalon hawked Twilite Tan and Zero Pain and Angie Dickinson sold her cat jewelry. In the living room I picked up *Home* and watched my hands tremble. Simple white sailcloth now covered the sofas and chairs, as if to atone for the bobbles and fringe; floors were bare. I started to read about a decorator matching floor planks by taking down old barns, and something about it made me turn back to see the name of the writer. Lightfoot. This must have been before the attack. He was everywhere now— event dinners in department stores, the fashion shows—photographed with his new red plaid blazer and his cane. He went downtown, hitting the clubs at all hours in his bandages, encircled by models and stars and night creatures. He called my group "Mr. and Mrs." and seemed to take them seriously, which they loved. He also copied me, but he was fresh, green as the times, and a victim. I kept seeing him at parties, always moving, always smiling, his face still half bandaged, that damn plaid jacket, the shirt cuffs open, not so much for effect as because he didn't have any cufflinks. I'd see him across the room from where I was sitting still as a stone, waiting for them to come to me, and I'd watch him going round to them.

Hugo had given a party for Jason Braeborn, the television pioneer, who had retired and disappeared years ago but had just published a book of photographs. Braeborn had obviously just had some face work. His thinning hair was painted a deep purplish orange, and his tight, waxy cheeks shone with the surgical tan color of scars. It had been years since he had been in the city; his screen had gone off a long time ago and he was unplugged, all the animation gone from his voice and body, as if twenty years of a professional good mood had been more than he could take. Hugo brought him over to me.

"It's so good to finally meet you," I said. "I learned what talk is on your program," I said and then tried to think of something else to say.

He looked at me, blinking, his head swiveling through the whirling alien crush. He had never heard of me, but for one second he really looked. "What is the point of this? Who are these people? I don't know anyone," he said in his famous voice.

But I could not answer the old star, and Hugo led him on into the crowd, very few of whom remembered.

I went inside to eat, but soon Hugo came hopping back. "You're missing everything. What's the matter with you? Gayle Pope just arrived."

"I'd like to have some dinner. I'm starving. I know everyone. I've got your list."

"But you should get back in there."

I knew I should, but I could not move. I looked out at them draped over Lightfoot. They were wayward and deceptive, my creations, disappointing in every way. I felt like the angry Old

Testament God picking his way among the ancient misbehaving Israelites, looking for one just man before he smote them all. And still, after the flood had wiped all the life from the earth, after Sodom and Gomorrah, after forty years in the wilderness and all the warnings, they misbehaved.

"Be careful of Lightfoot," Sally Kirk had called to tell me when she announced her retirement. "He's the only one who could be as good as you," and then she asked about Veronica.

"You're still digging. You should forget all this nonsense up in Camden," I said and did not ask who was going to take over her column. There were rumors.

"I'm still going to keep reading you, honey," she had said, and quickly hung up. I feared for her on the icy country roads and was glad Baron would stay with her part of this winter. I had heard about the tag sale in her Central Park West apartment, filled with evening clothes and her fabulous Christmas bribes. A tray of vodka bottles with lipstick marks on the rims rested on her unframed Christian Bérard drawings. She had sold everything, and now she had enough money to escape. She had won. She was off to live my Eddie Bauer catalogue fantasy. She could get fat and have gray hair, wear relaxed-fit jeans, and carry her cocktails to the fire to study her gardening books and read English mysteries in large type all day. This year I had begun to read wilderness catalogues, stare at pictures of open roads, and dream of crossing over the border, trunk loaded with survival gear. I would be the first one driving on the newly built road with its clean yellow broken line stretching into the mountains.

Spring was just the time to get out. Doormen were cracking open car trunks on radio cabs, loading the duffles and hard cases. Little private-school children dressed for the islands, waited inside the cars, their new white shoes crossed in anticipation, for they were flying to faraway cays, places that required transferring to very small planes flying low over periwinkle waters. Doormen also were loading the bundles of those crossing over the bridges to the weekend life that sustained them. The city was torn between the rich desperate to get out and the poor desperate to get in, pressed against doors that would not open until their chests exploded.

It had been several weeks since Veronica and Gates rushed out of Hammerman Auditorium. A batch of articles had appeared examining the escape as though two people had never run off together. Those who had seats on the aisles were tracked down. I saw Hugo's hand in this, getting revenge on Veronica, and Sandy Fisher acting against Gates, who had dropped him as part of his corporate cuts. I heard their voices in the blind quotes and sniffed their revenge. Two magazines asked me to write about them. Blanca called to tell me Philip had written a song about them, and she seemed relieved to have been pushed from the glare.

"This may be the last time I talk to you," Jack had said, blaming me for everything. "I infer contextually other misrepresentations."

"Are you calling me a liar?"

"All I know is that I have a crashed marriage over this silliness. Veronica pulls people into her paranoid fear. She fractionates information and it loops back. I found a book that describes her borderline condition—pathologic narcissism. When I read these descriptions I go a little cranky."

Now he no longer called, having replaced me with Athena and others more attentive and less judgmental. Obviously, a new life had begun for Gates and Veronica, and finally the city seemed to have forgotten them, as though not to be photographed or regularly mentioned were not really to exist. I heard they were here; I heard they were away; and then I heard nothing. It was common to disappear for a decent interval. Of course, there were those like Caroline Streeter who were never seen again, and those like the Dells who reappeared, repaired, as soon as possible. Disgrace was okay. Brazen it out, as everyone did. The only sins were to lose your money or to get caught being stupid. Honor was nothing; self-esteem and being hot were all that mattered, holding oneself high whatever happened, like Cigarette.

That very weekend, I did see Gates and Veronica walking on Madison Avenue. They were both wearing jeans and Gates blazers, and they so fulfilled my earlier vision of them that I wanted to duck into a store and vanish. It was a Saturday, one of those optimistic spring afternoons when the streets, emptied of those who had fled to the country, belonged to the innocent. I knew they had seen me, and we had one of those embarrassing approaches, waiting to wave until we were closer, but seeing all of the other. From a distance they looked younger, as all the rich do until they give up and sink back into their flesh and the younger arms that propel them around, waiting for the money. This meeting was all it took. We were back.

"We've been hiding," Veronica said. "All those West Side cellar restaurants. One night Danny forgot and got up from the table like he always does, and the waiter chased us all the way into the street."

"I'm spending all my time with the lawyers. I may have a big story for you," Gates said.

He looked up as a pair of girls with long streaked hair passed by. They were both dressed in long, tight jackets and black stirrup pants with fourteen-hundred-dollar Chanel bags on their shoulders, sunglasses as headbands, and gold oyster watches on their right wrists, and their bare dirty heels poked from the holes where the stirrups met their shoes.

"He's been waiting for a call from Kesselman for a week. He keeps picking up the phone and dropping it," said Veronica. "Kesselman wants to break him, to break his toy."

"She's got me going to the gym at six-thirty. We're still hiding. Peter screens the calls, and we cross the street when we have to."

Veronica said she loved this city-within-the-city, but I knew Gates had always lived that privately.

"Libby, would you telephone Aurora? My calls are so rationed. Would you do that and report?"

"I'll call as soon as I get home. Where will you be?"

"Where we usually are," Gates had said, and they both laughed, and I decided not to call Aurora. But just then I saw Helen Kasmanian crossing the street, and Gates and Veronica drew back into the crowd so swiftly they might not have been there.

"You know Lightfoot. He's doing a piece on me for *Omnium*," Helen said, and she gestured to a young man without bandages. His face had changed completely. His heavy jaw was gone, and his nose was carved into a new shape.

"Were you talking to Danny Gates just now?" he said, and even his voice had changed. It was, if anything, more western, to go with his new cowboy boots.

"You look wonderful," I said. "I'm so glad about the book, Helen."

"It was Veritas that did it. Nothing like a scandal, and I was part of the whole Gates thing."

Lightfoot scribbled this down, though I couldn't think why. A few people squirmed past us on the sidewalk. One seemed to recognize Helen and paused to stare.

"It happens all the time now because of the television. I've got a camera crew with me tomorrow for 'Profile.' "

"Can I take you to lunch at the Four Seasons? *Omnium* has given me quite a deal. I'll give you a call," Lightfoot said, and as I was about to give him my number, they were carried off in the flow. Lightfoot shouted back, however, giving my most private line to the crowd. How had he gotten it?

"Was that Lightfoot?" someone said.

"No idea," I answered.

There was a message from the paper that Carter wanted to see me on Monday, but instead of calling back, I called Aurora.

"Mommy's plants burned up. Lazarus threw them out. Athena gets a sunburn in the greenhouse. She's naked. I'm going to be her flower girl."

"How is school?"

"I'm going to Spencer next year."

"You will love Spence. Is your father home?" But if he was there, Jack would not come to the phone. I immediately called Veronica, who invited Charles and me for dinner. Gates had seen the store again on the way home, and he was furious.

"Charles is scarcely the person to cheer anyone up," I said, but I promised we'd come, and Veronica told me she had forgotten Aurora would be there.

"I don't see why I have to cheer up your billionaire friends and I'm not having dinner with a five-year-old," Charles said as I buffed and swung and snapped my shoe rag on the shoes he had left by the front door. This was my own fault, since I could not bring myself to ask Imelda and was too cheap to pay three dollars. I knew this infuriated Charles, but not quite enough for him to do it himself.

The house was very dark when we arrived, and strangely messy, as though they had quite forgotten about us. Even the fire seemed more subdued, and from its too-artificial, even burning, I knew he was using those Duraflame logs. Veronica complained to Charles about Aurora, who was lying in one of the back bedrooms, very hot and cross, and I deliberately avoided his pale and terrible eye as he went in to look at her. This left me alone with Gates, who chose to stare into the chemical flames. There was a fine misting of powder on the table that he made no effort to remove.

"She has a terrible temper," he said. "Don't tell her about the trees. Kesselman is dealing with Jack Kahn. They want me out. Can you imagine Gates without me? I wonder sometimes if I had found Nadia . . . she'd know what to do." He licked the powder from his finger and scoured his gums. He could not see that the name and the idea of "Gates" had gone way beyond him, that it could function now without him, that his name was bigger than even his original vision. He faced the unbearable prospect of having others successful under his name.

Veronica rushed in and sat down and then immediately stood, as though she had done something wrong. They both looked thin and nervous, slightly less beautiful, as though the sex and the coke and being shut up in all those rooms without sun had drained them. The neglect made Gates seedy—an image that would not have pleased his corporate people. It was strange, too, to see a vain woman with her nails ragged, wearing a pair of stretch pants that now hung on her. She seemed to have lost all her sun. She had come to him even emptier than his previous women. All her totems, her crystals, her beads, her magic and protection had been abandoned, and these new things—Gates's things—meant nothing and were no defense. She was a stranger to them all and wanted to sweep them away, clear the surfaces, and make room for herself—either that or run away with him to their own new things.

"Aurora has chicken pox. Charles is bringing her home with me, but you stay, Libby. We'll be back in a minute," she said, as Peter handed Gates the phone.

"No, Oliver. No more desert. I want the jungle and bodies. Rain forest. Rima, the bird girl. . . . No, it's a book, *Green Mansions,* have them get it. Waterfalls. Forget Kesselman's guy. Spend what you need. Big, wet green leaves, clothes falling off. You have to resist them. We're still the talent."

When Charles and Veronica returned, she was carrying four tiny trees, dead in their ceramic dishes. She stood in the doorway looking as wild as I have ever seen her, and we had to ask about Aurora before she told us. Jack had tried to keep her from the greenhouse, but she had gone there anyway. "Look," she said, and held out the trees and shook one, and the tiny leaves fell off and made dots all over the table.

She told us how she had stood at the greenhouse door for a long time before she could go in. Jack had walked away. The little trees were flaking and falling, their earth hard and parched. It was the ruin of all her small worlds. She had seen right away that some could be brought back, but others, some of the oldest and rarest—trees grown on rock and trained to cascade, trees started by others before she was born—were gone forever, and she had sat down on the small step and could not move.

"I told him he made no effort to save them. He could have

had Nordis or Lazarus water them or gotten in someone from my bonsai club like we do when I go away. I would have had them brought over. He knew what they meant. And now I'll never go back."

"Of course you won't," said Danny, looking surprised. "Why did you say that?"

"He made sure of that. It was a vicious thing to do. I'm going to take the ones I can save. I've marked them all and I can go back there tomorrow."

By now we were all exhausted. Veronica rang a small hostess bell and Peter came in with the fusilli as we began discussing when we all had chicken pox and if you could catch it again. Veronica kept talking about the island I had described, asking me all sorts of questions and whether she might call the friend who owned it. She was ready to run again.

"We can't go. Not now," Gates said.

"But what if it's just a few days? They have a fax and everything."

"I have to look at their faces when they talk to me," he said.

But I knew Gates would never go there no matter what. He always had to go back to the same rooms on the same islands and repeat the few places he had been. He still went back to the same club in Palm Springs with the pictures of Charlie Farrell and Marilyn Monroe turning yellow and cracking under their glass on the wall alongside Gates in *The Angelfish Club,* trapped in his happiness. He went back even though the club was on the wrong side of town, loyal to people who were no longer even there and loyal to his own memories. He kept looking for what he called "magic," which was really nothing more than his memory of his past. He still went to gamble in Las Vegas and even Atlantic City, losing himself in the seamless, timeless stretch of marble and beveled mirrors under the giant chandeliers he did not see. Nor did he see the people around him, so they couldn't offend him. He was so far in someone else's taste that it didn't matter, as long as the vision was unified and thus not disturbing. He stayed down there in the Baccarat pit for hours, not seeing the faces in the halo of light over the green table, fingering his stacks, peeling off hundreds for more chips, as some girl bobbed down drinks in front of him, smiling each time though Gates never looked up. That was his rest; but Veronica had to run further, and so the island became a promise for later.

"I think you should re-emerge," I said to her. "Blanca is having her spring lunch, and you could go with me."

She knew she didn't look well, though she pretended not to care. She needed that world of her women judging her or she would fall too deeply into this hole. The social creature in her still felt the pull to be around, back in the world of groups, though this sexual love was the enemy of any group. I urged her back, knowing I was jealous of the way she was shut up with Gates, for I had never surrendered to anything like this and felt I must draw her out.

"This has been the worst year of my life," Gates said suddenly. "They are removing me." There was silence all around the table, where suddenly no one knew where to look or place his hands. Only Veronica was calm—unnaturally so, as though his pain was a story she had heard him tell too many times before. It was a very married attitude.

"How is that possible?" I asked, for I was shocked despite the rumors muttered into my phone that morning.

"I don't really own my business anymore. They can do whatever they want with me."

I looked furiously at Charles, who was still poking up his pasta, scooping and twirling it, digging in as though every bite was a small victory for life and health and a rebuke to death. I could understand why Gates had never told any of this, because the worst crime here is to be thought stupid enough to make a bad deal. It was not accidental that the dyslexia industry flourished among the private schools. Gates could never have sued to get his name back, because he was afraid of what might come out.

It was a relief when Charles's beeper went off and he had to leave for the hospital and I went with him. I studied his back as he walked down the stairs. Those shoulders, his voice, and his devotion to the sickest of his children were the best things about him. I thought of him as a good man with a monster tucked inside.

In the next few weeks, the hair and makeup people came bouncing in with their kits and chatter. They petted and clucked over the small ruin of Veronica's beauty and tried to look into the other rooms for Gates. He had fled, for all this reminded him of his shows and the shoots for his ads, and he now felt distant from that in a guilty way. He knew Jack and Kesselman were going ahead with the buyout, but he had postponed thinking about it, knowing he was almost powerless to raise money in this climate.

One of the first repairmen was Ronaldo, one of the current hair gods, who was always booked through June, whatever the season. "This hair is so strange," he said, picking up a piece and letting it drip through his fingers as though it were something odd and dirty. His four assistants all wore black and stood around worshiping, with their hands folded behind their backs. "Who did this to you? Well, it must go darker and it must have shape, like hers," he said, pointing to me. "It's so vulgar and sad. It pulls down your face. We can't do anything here. We bring you in," and the acolytes nodded solemnly and began packing up and unplugging their hot rollers.

I went home, but I heard that Ronaldo had made her up himself and told her about Dr. Albion, the lip man, who filled all the supermodels' lips with collagen until they had all plump sausage mouths that looked like they had been bitten on and swelled. There had to be color on the mouth to go with the color on the eyes and the hair, and slowly all that was indefinite and free in the portrait of Veronica was made distinct. She got Chica's new trainer to go out running with her, and he would walk by, carrying his weights, looking into the rooms where Danny sat half-dressed and unamused. Veronica worked at it until she had hard legs and those string-bean arms with a tiny muscle popping up and the darkened hair and the big new mouth. While she was perhaps more beautiful, she looked older and more definite.

I was not there, but I know that Gates lost what he had first seen and always remembered. He could not control himself; it was like the duster and the Windex in the window of his store that night of the explosion. His picture was ruined. This was not his vision, and it must have been then that his love started to fall away.

With his gambler's heart, how could he not believe she was part of his run of bad luck? And what could end it? The player moves to another table; he changes the shoe, the dealer, the color of his socks. He gets a new girl to hang over him, resting her elbows on his shoulder as the game continues. Once, Gates had told me about his fear of places with the "whammy." He would never buy a house where there had been a fire or a crime or any history of bad luck, which kept him away from all the great houses. They were all filled with the whammy—bodies floating in pools, shots and screams in the night. He went away from Veronica then as surely as if he had gone out the door. She had the whammy. She had let in the bad things.

After that crew, the magazines were back on the phone, even though they knew she would refuse. All I told Blanca was that I was bringing a guest who liked her, and she accepted that for she was too distracted to care. Her spring lunch had grown to seventy "top women," as she put it, and she had been forced to move it since the taxi had driven through Lampwick.

At first Veronica hung back, hugging the entrance in that pain-of-fame way, as I had seen Lee Solomon do at the Veritas lecture. She waited by the door for her presence to register as the heads turned from their groups of three and four. All the women had something to say—how good she looked, how "different," meaning how much the same as they looked, with that layer of polished desperation. They were so busy with her they forgot to flatter me as they usually did. Blanca, at the door in a red dress, was almost crying with the double emotions of having her own importance confirmed and drawing out the invisible

Veronica for her first public appearance. It had taken a year and one scandal for Veronica to go from an unknown to the focus of this room. She moved forward. Gayle Pope and Chica bounded over while Boots Simpson frowned into her group and raised her shoulder pads. Boots had gone back to school and was doing her thesis on solid waste disposal and why corruption in the city made it impossible to recycle more than newspapers.

I took notes, because I wanted this right. I had not liked Carter's voice on the telephone when I again postponed our meeting. I watched Athena's moving away and Barbara's following her. The waiters passed trays of wine and the talk continued and I found myself claimed elsewhere in the deep rose room. I kept following Blanca's red dress and Veronica as she was absorbed by different groups. I watched all their movements as though this were choreography and they the principal dancers. Their words were not as important as the way they grouped themselves. At the same time I wondered, not for the first time, who outside this room would care at all about these women when two thousand people lined up in the middle of the night to get forty jobs—rows and rows of them hunched over filling out applications, biting their pencils, worrying about their spelling and handwriting and all their deficiencies, unable to read the questions, cold, hungry, and furious, the hopeless and those who were still, irrationally, full of hope. Perhaps this was their circus: Blanca Dell in a red dress in a rose room, yet again the fascination of the townspeople for the bloodsucker in evening clothes in the castle on the hill. Those howls in the night, the strange scratching at the windowpane, the figure rising from the bed, the curtains blowing in with a snap.

I was wondering this when a large group of parochial-school girls came in, single-file, in their plaid jumpers and navy shoes, and arranged themselves in neat rows on one side of the room. Blanca, highly regal now, her voice grown fainter and more ladylike with divorce, stepped forward, introduced them as the St. Anne's Chorus, and said they were going to sing some songs about friendship for us. Everyone grew very silent as the women lined themselves up facing the girls and holding their hands like swings in front of them. They tilted up their chins, laid their glasses of white wine and bags at their feet, trying to arrange their legs so their knees would look all right. I studied this lineup. I could have written a two-page history on most of them there, and still I could not guess all the cruel towns left behind, the early marriages and divorces, abortions, cancer scares, the recoveries from their addictions (though this was a disciplined group), rejections, heartbreak, the loss of real loves—all the things too painful to think about—that crossed their faces quick as a grimace when the songs were sad. They were studies in self-preservation and learning to live with compromise. I thought of all the corrections of physical nature it took to get them here, polished and hung with gold, staring into the faces of these young girls bused in on a school day.

Their throats were open as they sang about friendship in this room of easy betrayal, these girls who had yet to consider this world a ladder or a competition. All the women were thinner than all the girls, who were really not the most attractive lot— kind of doughy and spotty, with their nuns in the back keying them on. One had to guess which ones were smart or athletic or lazy; but I knew that none of these women, most of whom had traded even the illusion of happiness for their position in this room, would change places with one of these girls and have to go through all *that* again.

They continued, the girls' faces getting a bit red with the effort of singing for the rich women. I was sorry for what I had done; horrified that anyone could look on these women as important or glamorous. I could consider my life truly wasted, the whole thing an exercise in the diminution of interest. My childhood had placed me beyond awe; close observation had led me beyond contempt to a kind of affectionate tolerance, but now that was gone. Why quote, why scrutinize and name what no longer interested me? The lazy habits of my mind had stranded me here in this room; only energy would enable me to escape, and I had little energy left. I was as trapped in my job as any laborer, who at least might go home, get drunk and forget, at the time I was just going out the door.

The singing was so loud, the faces so false in their response. I felt a hand on my elbow—Sally Kirk come round for a last look. The room was peeling away, the makeup falling off the tired faces, the poor bodies posed with pots of flesh at the stomach, like starving children. I forced myself to stay for lunch. Blanca had given me a baby table off to the side, thinking that wherever I sat, I made it a good table.

I looked over to where Blanca sat with Donna and Gayle Pope, as Barbara, who had been drinking a lot, got up to toast her.

"What a girl! Blanca Dell will rise again! We all know it. She doesn't need Jimmy—she is famous herself. She stayed with me and my girls in Aspen over Christmas and she was followed on the slopes. Everyone loves her. She walks down the streets and everyone says, 'Blanca's so beautiful—she's even more beautiful than her photographs!' All the young girls, like my Stella, think so, and so do their boyfriends. At first they were embarrassed, but then they came up for autographs—and the husbands too," and with this she shifted a little and sagged, and Olivia helped her sit down.

There was a silence, broken by applause, half for Barbara and half for Lightfoot, who had been leaning against the door and had just come into the room carrying a bunch of those four-foot woody roses. Well, it was just luck that Lightfoot, who was taking over for Sally Kirk after all, had such a debut and got to write it all a day ahead of me; just luck that Blanca allowed him to stay and be the only man at lunch; just luck that he had such a precise memory.

XX

Little Birds

Carter's black hair coated his forehead. As usual, his office looked like it had just been professionally searched by people who didn't like him at all. On his glass table, I noticed tear sheets of my last dozen columns fanned on top of the bulging mess, but Carter seemed to ignore them as he scooped up some papers. The sight of those pieces made me very alert. It was strange that I could not remember any of them as I leaned forward, trying to hear him.

"I have to talk to you, but I just found out I'm having the Turkish ambassador tonight. I'm cooking dinner. Of course you could ride downtown with me. Is the car here, Emily?" he asked in his whispery voice. I had to lean way forward to catch the lost mumbled syllables as he looked somewhere to the left of my shoulder, hissing. Carter and I had had a brief dance years ago, and occasionally I would see a moist remembering come into his eyes. Not today. The door that shut him off from the newsroom was closed, as it was only when someone was getting fired.

The last papers went into his schoolboy case and we left, Emily following us for final instructions. Carter went cruising along the desks, eyes ahead, determined not to catch sight of anything on the screens. All his clothes sagged off him, leaving the impression of exhausted tweeds and corduroy and lending him a boyishness well into his early old age. He kept himself messy as a sign that his intelligence was so demanding it excused his neglect and as a false signal of approachability. He slouched and slithered and shambled his way out as the entire newsroom tucked their heads into their phones like sleeping parakeets.

"What have you been working on?" I said, knowing that he always had one safely obscure project as his pet.

"Have you been reading the Inquisition series?" he asked, knowing I had not. And then, as we rode down the elevator and got into the car and traveled down Seventh Avenue, he told me all about the chronicles and why their discovery interested him, all the while mumbling and studying the rubber mats of the car, his lap, the pictures of the driver's children in Easter clothes. Then Carter rocked into silence and was alone, having exhausted the Inquisition mysteries and not ready to begin the next topic, which was me. He was perfectly happy here in the realms of the obscure, which always protected him, for Carter read things nobody else could ever read without his head crashing onto a desk. Carter read not only to gain a few pathetic intellectual points, not only to hold dinner tables in thrall, but because he really liked to wallow in the unimportant, and nothing was too arcane for his notice. It was part of his antistance that made people back from him at parties despite his power. For the last few years, our conversation had been restricted to Carter's saying "Where is it?" I began mentally shuffling through those Pimpernels on his desk, trying to remember. But I couldn't even fish up Monday's.

"The Inquisition is beginning to seem like fun to me compared to this," I said.

"What?"

"Sitting here in this Telecar with you and your not getting to the point."

"Maybe you want to stay for dinner," he said. Carter had been left by some of the best women in New York. I had especially liked Sabrina, the huntress. In those days, dinner at home was always something hard and rather raw that she had shot, and when she moved out, instead of finding bobby pins, Carter had found bullets in all the drawers.

"I can't. I have to go out, for work."

"That's what I wanted to talk to you about," he said, his head lowered, staring between his shoes. Then he rocked into silence and was alone.

"No energy," he said finally. "Did you read Lightfoot? Even in a coma, he's stolen your jock." This mixture of the arcane and profane was another affectation of Carter's, not unlike Helen Kasmanian's high thoughts in low language. I thought of the driver hearing my life as we pulled up to Dean & Deluca's, leaving our papers in the waiting car.

A woman in an army jacket, her face wrapped in a scarf, approached. "My bathtub. I miss my bathtub. And I had a separate dressing area—*a separate dressing area!*" she shouted at me.

We burst into the light and color and smells of the fruits and vegetables. Carter picked up a little wire basket and made eye contact with the produce on the right, his dark eyes touring the Mineolas, and murcotts, the Rome Beauties, and berries and fastening on the lemon grass as if on salvation. He picked up a bunch of that curly Italian frisé lettuce and something called Trevisano and then got on line.

"How are the chanterelles?" he said to the man at the register.

"Very good."

"Give me a few, and the portobellos and the cremini. Is the marjoram fresh? I'll take a bunch. Any chives?"

Meantime a long line had formed behind us, all these evening people with their breads tucked under their arms, cradling their cheeses, all these people who had left the produce section for last. But Carter was reaching for the jalapeños, the Japanese eggplant, something called tomatillo. The man, with whom he obviously had some kind of a nightly history of discussing produce, was helping him.

"I'll take a bunch of the chervil. How is the broccoli rabe?"

"Do you think this is fair?" said the woman next on line and her voice quivered and I loved her for this, and now there was a lot of shoulder shifting in the ranks and lip sounds and muttering. People had been killed for less, and I knew Carter would have to give up being waited on. But of course he was enjoying the anger and spite collecting behind him. I shrugged to absolve myself.

He lifted his shoulders, threw some ginger and baby artichokes into the basket. "Can you believe this town?" he said finally, fastening on me to take it out on. "The last six months, one very tired Pimpernel."

There was so much now to look at, and he took full advantage. This was the hour after six when all those desperate for cute foods and impossible vegetables appeared—stuff no one had ever heard of before they got to New York and developed taste. This food was supposed to convince you that you really were living in an international mecca where you could get Sharon fruit and that therefore would excuse all the abuses. Carter loved his food. He loved to cook. He was nice and round inside his peacoat. Here he was like a little plump pasha, all nods and smiles, his eyes racing from the baby coho salmon to the countermen, his padded hands stretching out to little blue bottles of water from who knows what mountain peak, all these treats rewarding a day of servitude. This food said how much all these people wanted to love themselves. It said life was a design that they had mastered, because none of this, except perhaps the cheese, was the stuff anyone would put on a plate at midnight when he was blue. This food was the stuff of social interaction and impression, and it did not interest me.

What did interest me was the peculiar guilty hunch of Carter's fleshy shoulders as we left the produce and passed down the aisle of cakes and tarts and muffins and lemon bars near the stacks of foreign (*quel* metropolis!) newspapers. I had lost my appetite by the time we came back to the waters, but Carter made a sharp detour left to the jars of shriveled pears and peaches. I stared into the glistening eye of a dead red snapper that seemed to know how I felt as we approached one of the meat counters, full of pink meats and Lugano and Tuscano sausages, past the boxes of Arabian pilaf.

"Do you have my Cornish hens?" Carter said, as though this butcher knew that Carter H. Clarkson himself stood before him.

"All right, then I'd like three Cornish hens—split and pounded flat," and he turned to take the fact that the man did not know him out on me. "What about the Solomon story? You did not get that. No, leave the skin on, but scrape it. And Blanca Dell's lunch? Lightfoot beat your ass on that. And there's a whole new set of people—that Pack group—the Jameses and the young Hammermans and those music people—"

"Patty and Tim Barnett—they've been here forever."

"And that designer."

"Gates—I know Gates."

"No—what's-his-name and his wife, the model?"

"The long-ex-model," I said.

"They're all together and you don't cover them. No one wants to read about the Dells or that drunk Pope. Your people are too old."

"They're around forty. Same as those others. They've just been rich longer and they're not as bisexual."

"They give the impression of youth. They're new. They hang around with those musicians. That's why we've just hired Lightfoot away from the *News.*"

The butcher's mallet struck the cornish hens and pounded their little bones flat as Carter outlined his plans for me to write only once a week.

"Lightfoot! I admit I'm bored, but I won't go to once a week."

"I've given him The Pimpernel."

"I invented The Pimpernel! That's *me!* Twenty years, Carter. That whole stance—that attitude. It isn't Lightfoot. He's a victim."

"We own The Pimpernel."

"What can you possibly mean? *I* own it legally—ask Kunkel. I invented it. You can keep the money. I have no intention of giving that little fuck my life! . . . I won't calm down. I'm going right to Kunkel and the *News*. It's not my fault if no one is going out anymore. It's not my fault if everyone is afraid to invite me. It must be this paper. And the space I get, and the crappy old pictures. You can pay out my contract. I'm not going to sit home!"

And suddenly I focused on his two bulging baskets. I wanted to see those murcotts flying. I wanted to stomp those mushrooms into black grime on the sawdust. The butcher took another whack at the stunted chickens. It reminded me how my father had accidentally stepped on a tiny dyed-green Easter duckling I had won in Palm Beach. Was it really an accident, or didn't he want to bring a live green duck home to Park Avenue?

"I want you to go to the car and open my case and read your last few columns."

"But they were on your table," I said ridiculously.

"Sit down, turn on the light in the car, and read them. I know you're a pro. Then I want you to come back and find me at the cheeses, or maybe the breads."

I don't know why I obeyed. I walked out past the plates and the wine racks, the cookbooks and four thousand kinds of beans, the dishes of celery remoulade, the cornichons and colored olives in white ceramic crocks, past the pâtés and fresh pastas and the hams with gynecological metal racks jammed into their innards, the cheeses, shrunken and wrapped in grape leaves stuck with pink peppercorns, the breads—what a wealth, and how nauseated I was!—past the honeys and Provençal pears in pear eau-de-vie. My tears plopped onto the sawdust on the floor. A very fat woman, one of those food dependents who go on "Phil Donahue" weeping about how food was "always there" for them until they learned to love themselves, was reaching for some black pasta. I was the only one without a wire basket or cradling a cheese like a baby's head.

The sidewalk was seething with food victims. The woman with the army jacket was still there, furious about her lost bathtub, as I got into the car, opened Carter's case, and found another set of copies of the Pimpernel. I looked down at my lead from last Wednesday. It occurred to me that all this had been planned. I was following Carter's script. I read, though I could scarcely bear seeing my column in type, its deficiencies by then irrevocable. I could accept his offer—I'd still have my money for two years, and I could start a whole new life—move to the country, wear Tevas. But fired, after twenty years! Replaced by a professional victim with a degree in me. The Unitarian church in my neighborhood had just advertised a sermon on "Victims and Survivors." That seemed to be the only choice. I thought of how many times I had quit the paper and stormed from Carter's office, only to be followed by him pounding down the stairs, panting and heavier each time, closer to heart attack, till the last time (how long ago?), he had finally let me go, knowing I would call. Lightfoot could have the Pimpernel's space, but he could never have the name, the persona. The Pimpernel was mine—and Leslie Howard's. I was not afraid to share with the dead.

I looked out at the woman. There was nothing I could give her. She wanted her lost bathtub and her separate dressing area. She wanted her old life back. I knew I would have to go back inside and face Carter, who was now lingering by the desserts. I could see his round silhouette by the front counter as he looked at the foreign newspapers. I knew he expected me to be gone when he emerged with his pounded birds and fragrant parcels.

Charles, who said he had slept in New Jersey the last two nights, stood in the doorway, his face covered with hideous pustules, two large black Hefty bags bulging at his feet.

"Chicken pox from the Kahn child," he said. "It's rare to have a documented recurrence. I must have been misdiagnosed. Either that or I may have to write myself up."

"But how could you have caught it now?"

He shrugged his bony shoulders. "I'm going home for a while. Freddie Albumen is going to take care of me."

I went closer. The pustules were all reddened, popping and pullulating down his face—some freshly blistered, some scratched and already crusted.

"You shouldn't have picked them. Anyway, there is no need for you to go. I can take care of you."

The Hefty trash bags worried me. He had moved in with them, since his trunks were in storage.

"Actually, I'm leaving. I need some time to be alone."

"But you are alone here."

I went close and touched his arm and he winced.

"Freddie knows what to do. She has a well-run house and serves a proper dinner. She keeps her help, and"—he struck a very effeminate hipshot pose, rendered ineffective by his leprous scabs—"she knows how to comb the back of her hair."

"What?"

"Don't you ever look in the mirror? It's always bothered me."

"What! When you hang me up in the air on a meat hook, the back of my hair bothers you?! Am I hearing this? I've just been fired, and now a sadist with chicken pox is complaining to me about combing the back of my hair and keeping help! I hope you've packed your crops. I hope Dr. Albumen appreciates a little light whipping with her Nutrifast."

He began dragging the bags down the hall, and I thought for no particular reason of Santa Claus.

XXI

Nothing Is Lost . . .

The deposed Gates and the deposed Pimpernel both existed for about a week in that wonderful period of grace and private disgrace before the calls and the looks when it becomes known and is written about.

Gates spent it in a kind of lethargy, a paralysis of the body and failure of nerve that made it impossible for him to act to save himself. The forces of Howard and Jack and Kesselman marched upon him, co-opting first Martin, then Andy and the others, then pulling in the little designers and convincing them that Gates Industries could and would exist without Danny. To his gambler's mind it all seemed part of his luck's turning. Perhaps his guilt over having been almost happy with Veronica had made him feel he owed Jack. In any case, I could see the fight draining from him even as he threatened to launch it.

First, Gates stopped going out even to walk; then he stopped taking calls and getting dressed; finally he narrowed the number of rooms he would visit. He would get up and sink back down, start to do something and become distracted. The skimmer was turned off in the pool, because he said the sound of the lapping disturbed him now, and already a film of algae had formed over the top. The television stayed on, an extra light in all the rooms;

movies were brought to the door. He watched a lot of sports; whenever Veronica passed by the set there was always someone running, jumping, swinging or kicking at some ball as he sat there among his slumping bronze figures. Veronica found herself an irritant, unable to stir him from his slumber. She tried to find him an independent lawyer, but he refused anyone from her group, and since they were the best fighters in the city outside the mob defenders, Gates was left with a choice of second-raters. Kesselman had betrayed him, and his disgust at ever trusting him made Danny turn and blame himself. Now he could not work; he could not even direct Oliver for the ads. Oliver was forbidden to take his calls but at least was loyal enough in this most talkative business to keep Gates's secret. About the only thing Gates could do was to get out of his chair and pack and find another part of the world to wait in until his purdah was finished. For this he had always used the desert or some casino.

Veronica told me how he paced and sat at the window seat for hours, and when she or Peter would come in with the phone, he would wave them away as though he had scarcely energy enough to raise his arm. I always believed this is the mood, the physical climate that breeds disease and allows the entrance of a cancer, because while the body is idle, the mind is never free of grief and that intolerable sense of what is almost lost.

A few times that week Gates and Veronica hid in the movies, Gates in the back row, entering at the last minute when the theater was dark and the opening credits had already begun, though it didn't really matter. They became part of the world of daytime movies, joining the lost souls of Third Avenue—the old and the maimed, the purposeless and the truly depressed. One day Gates even called me to join him, for I was one of the very few he had allowed to remain in his narrowed world.

We met in front of the theater. Gates stood behind one of the columns, pretending to study the posters as a bottomless trash bag circled the sky like a dark flying donut. It is a bad sign when someone who is always late is waiting for someone who is always so early that I usually have to circle the block and buy unnecessary shampoos so I won't stand alone. He was wearing very expensive mirrored sunglasses and a dark brown leather jacket, and people who had no idea who he was were looking at him because he was so astonishingly unlike the usual dim and dismal afternoon crowd.

I had never done something this ordinary with Gates, something this far from his controlled environment, and that made it strange and wonderful. The ordinary world did not diminish him to me but, rather, showed how unusual he was—the only attractive person in the crowd, lit by his nervous animation. The daylight ruin of his beauty made it more effective. When he raised his glasses, the pale blue circles under his eyes, the carving under the cheekbones where the flesh had just begun to sink etched his face with a beauty stronger and more appealing than youth.

"How's the chicken pox patient?" he asked.

"I'm afraid he's passed forever into the orbit of his partner. They're taking care of each other, as far as I know."

"He never impressed me. All that jargon and that use of his accent—very stagy. But I did like the way he dressed. That boy had his own style. I'll take one of everything," he said to the woman at the concession stand, lavishing a bit of extra charm, to which she responded with a slack mouth. "All the candy. I don't know which I'll like."

But she still didn't get it, and the line behind us was impatient. To expose him to real life was like exposing an endangered tribe to the strong white bodies that could poison them. "Don't touch him," I wanted to say to them. "Don't draw his eye. Don't get too close." This was my afternoon, borrowed from Veronica, and I was possessive of his attention for the time I had it.

"I'm glad you're in such a good mood. It makes you very handsome."

We watched the audience. They came in singly, not caring at all what they looked like, only that they were warm, alive, and not in too much pain. A few looked like they needed keepers; others looked like they might erupt into violence and sudden shouting. Many were not all there. All around me I felt the danger of the city, where random evil crops up in the dark and being famous or beautiful is no shield and often just a provocation.

"Do you ever think rats will run over your feet in a movie theater?"

"All the time," he said, looking down.

"Don't die before I have you," I thought, and for the moment, surrounded by all the horrible snuffling sounds, the cracklings of sandwiches and pungent cheeses being unwrapped, the heavy, inappropriate breaths, I loved him.

The screen was now showing one of those message boards full of guess-who facts about the city and quotes, mostly from Ralph Waldo Emerson.

" 'Nothing is lost until you start looking for it,' " Gates read from the screen. "What do you make of that?"

But the lights had gone off, and we were in the middle of a burning jungle, tearing open the candy boxes and digging into the popcorn just as though both our hearts had been broken. I did not quite watch as the stars swung on steel cables through the wet trees, high above the steaming forest, for I was shifting through strategies for revenge on Carter and Charles.

"I give this whole press thing a few days more before it breaks," said Gates afterwards, gloomily scanning the late paper. "Where's the fucking car? I'll take you home."

I hoped that Pedro was still on the door, because I wanted him to see Gates's new car. My stock in the building had fallen since Charles left, dragging the Hefty bags. Our tiny staff counted on me for their entertainment. They read The Pimpernel, and my recent, now-infrequent columns (I had kept a reduced Pimpernel—Lightfoot used his own famous name) had been dull. The sight of Gates, even if Pedro didn't quite know who he was, would restore some respect.

"I'll be right down," Gates said to Peter, and I was sad because I wanted him to stay. He leaned on the buzzer. No Pedro and no elevator. We kept pushing the button and Gates kept looking at the door until finally we heard a loud squeaking from one of the upper floors.

"I guess you don't go into buildings like this much."

Gates didn't answer, but studied the falling numbers of the floors, for I had lost his attention. The heavy brass door opened as slowly as usual, and there, taking up almost the whole interior, so that it had to be wedged in sideways, was a coffin. It was supported on a collapsible platform with wheels and held on both sides by two big men. A third, sour man in a black raincoat sort of escorted the whole affair out. Gates jumped back and almost knocked me over—we both had been standing too close to the door. They wheeled the body out, and one of the men said, "Excuse me."

"We have a back elevator. I can't think why they used the front," I said, and then I started to laugh above the squeaking wheels, because it reminded me of that day on the *Angelfish* set when we had seen those wounded soldiers and began collecting death images all day.

"Always when I am with *you*," Gates said, upstairs. "Neither of us needed that." And he was laughing, too; but he turned right around to go and backed down the hall as I watched tiny versions of myself waving into his mirrored glasses.

CHANGING OF THE GUARD AT GATES, it said on the first page of the *Herald*'s business section. If Gates had to go down, it was good to go down on the front page. "It is doubtless his stamp on the clothes and the store, and Gates has guided it to its present eminence. Under his leadership, Gates Industries grew from a small business started by an actor to a global empire with tentacles extending even into the Far East. . . . He has resigned with his reputation, but some important questions remain unanswered." The *Journal,* not so kind, referred to his dismissal with a "tin handshake." GATES STUMBLES, said another; GATES, BE-SIEGED, QUITS AMID MOUNTING CRITICISM. The worst was the profile accompanying the *Herald* story, with charges of his extravagant spending habits, the "lavish redecoration" of the offices, the cars and flowers and gifts, how he overspent opening the store, his sponsorship of the Gates Classic. The profile showed Gates withdrawn in his house, trapped by details at the time of his perfume launch, obsessed by the quality of the cardboard in the box, the thickness of the cellophane wrapping, the anatomical shape of the bottle. It showed him spinning.

Always here it is not so much what really happens as how it is perceived. Horrible failures have been crafted overnight into brilliant success, and the reverse. Gates was a man who believed his own press, especially since he created most of it, including the lack of it when he wanted. As much as he hid, he still had wanted to read about himself in hiding in the last few years, and he opened his doors to those reporters he knew he could control in those magazines his ads helped support. Gates, always so expert at news management, had let Kesselman pre-empt him, and while we were watching our movie, Kesselman had activated all the stories he had been planting for weeks. The company was sold to Jack Kahn; Gates was out.

Peter had driven Gates from my house right to the country; they hadn't returned until late that night. Back home he found the messages, but when he tried to call, the reporters were gone and he was left giving quotes to the copy desk. He had fired his public relations firm, which existed to keep him mentioned but unavailable, months ago.

A few days later, the newsweeklies came out. One had him stumbling down the runway at his last show. Another credited the little designers and his staff with his ideas, and that, because it was not true, made Gates angriest of all. How could he fight it? And of course it was the one story everyone who did not know him believed. It was ten in the morning on the day it came out, and he could hear in the voices of all who called and did not mention it that they had seen it. Gates knew that it had already been faxed around to those cannibals who were out of town but always ready to feed on the bones. In between calls, he was rereading every line for his lawyers, but he had almost no defense. He was a public figure, a name inside countless collars and waistbands and shoes. Some who called and got through told him to lay low and not answer, that his response would make it more of a story. He kept studying the name of the writer—one he did not know—as though the name itself might, after a time, explain something, but it didn't.

Jimmy Dell called immediately and told Gates he wanted to read him something about being "hurt but not slain," bleeding and rising to fight again. He told Gates that he believed him, but "that's what happens when you keep yourself private." Gates wrote all this down and repeated it to me with a perfect mimicry of Jimmy's southern accent.

George Solomon, though he was still emeshed with Howard Goldenson, called the next day and offered Gates his house in Southampton. He, too, like all the injured men, had a quote for Gates—this from Richard Nixon, about how only when you've been in the depths can you appreciate the heights. "Did the magazine try to contact you? If not, it shows 'reckless disregard' and you might have a real case," he said. For a while, Gates felt almost good again, because they understood, and it didn't sound as though they thought he had been stupid. Gates made his joke about being the man without the name living across from the name without the man.

I could see he liked the way the big guys stuck together and could pick up the phone and call the owners of the papers and magazines. And yet, however hard he tried not to, he felt himself believing these things because they were written. He read each word many times, thinking it would not be so bad without this or that sentence. Phrases came into his head as he was eating or just walking around, and they made him sick. He told me that a few times a day he would feel his heart thumping. According to his doctor, there were times when it was missing every sixth beat. He had a new gesture of pressing his fingers to his neck and taking his pulse. Veronica left with her trainer earlier each day and worked out with a violent new energy.

XXII

Connection

If I were looking down, I would see this lost person in an evening coat standing in a crowd of other satin coats and men in black tie waiting to get into Carnegie Hall for the rain forest benefit on a Sunday night. Everyone is pressed together, rubbing frictions, without affection.

I have already observed two reactions to my fall. "Jesus, Libby, you've been taking it easy!" says Howard Goldenson, who has been away. He hits my back. Howard, who is trying to move into entertainment law, has underwritten the Samba and Supper portion of tonight. Laurie Holt is twitching away, trying to signal Howard, "Keep away. She's dead. Don't waste a minute of your two-thousand-dollar billable hour," and twisting her new face, finally shooting out her heel and getting him in the calf, so that Howard winces and kind of hops across the Carnegie stone floor, restored with his money, and then she whispers, and I get the new look, a kind of shock mixed with an appraising pity, because Howard has saved brown pelicans and loggerhead turtles and Veritas students and the Carnegie Hall floor, so why not one declining social scribe?

Barbara skitters away behind them, eyes averted, waving at a wall ahead, and I know she has not yet planned what to say.

"You look great, Libby," says Ames Reed, chipper as drink will allow. "It's quite a crowd, isn't it? I don't know where to look."

Behind him there is a surge of photographers, because the Pack has entered, and this is their event, and we are pushed and knocked about on their riptide, and Ames scoops under my elbow and bobs me up, and I see his pale eyes on them and a quick, wordless moment of judgment.

We old self-destructives are uncomfortable with these re-formed self-destructives. This is their cause. Once so devoted to self-eradication, now all cured, they are the natural leaders to fight the destruction of the planet. They understand what it is to crawl out of a club at dawn, gagging on the morning air, wincing as the first uncertain shaft of red sun pierces through the buildings like white beams through ancient wet trees, a big fireball of chemicals inside the head they lean against the building. They are all black and glittery, their faces ranging from the usual bored to sour, moving all together like a high school crowd who sit at one table and put sweaters down on empty seats to save them for each other, as though anyone would dare penetrate their cool, dark circle. The light of the photographers' strobes falls down on them now; they are in the beam of envy, and in their center, their new pet, Helen Kasmanian, more petulant than ever with fame, and restyled. She's lost the silver jewelry, plucks her eyebrows, and now wears Armani.

"Aren't you glad it's my turn to write tonight?" Lightfoot says, peeling out from the group, which immediately locks in its circle like a disturbed amoeba, his kindness much worse than neglect, his eyes already on his fast-moving, recombinant group.

Ames cuts over to Athena, who's staring at the movie star in white tie (they always get it wrong) carrying two Filofaxes. He's trying to wave at the social wife of a rock star in the middle of the flow of designers and their hired socialites and *tout* white New York lurching in one misguided dressed-up body of survivors and victims to help the endangered.

If I hadn't already half packed it in, the sight of Boots sweeping by me leading Chief Rani, who has a dessert-sized clay plate in his lower lip, would finish me. I am alone, ready to sit down on a filthy curb and weep, and the only comfort I can take is the thought of Charles in his slimy gray Aveena bath, trying to keep his hands off his itching scabs, and all those flakes of scummy oatmeal, those opaque bubbles of scum swirling around him. This gets me down the aisle and through all the seated, tentative greetings, the uncertain smiles until the light goes down and Shandy comes out.

It's a different Shandy, stripped of jewels and leather, a minimalist, subdued Shandy in white tie and pumps, the tightest pants, hung with an old-fart watch fob, he has a black straw cap and one gold earring. He's almost unrecognizable to the audience that has paid $250 to $2500 a ticket. They aren't quite sure it is Shandy and hesitate before raising all those precious digits to applaud a nobody.

"In this materialistic world, he does care about something other than his career and his family," says a woman, introducing him. "He does care about things in this world. He cares. Here is Shandy."

" 'There is somebody I'm longing to see. I hope that she will turn out to be/Someone to watch over me,' " he croons, with no movement, not even a sway or a tap of the patent leather pump. His backup group is in black tie, even the one with the blue string in his dreadlocks. Shandy is playing bass, and all around me people are nodding solemn rhythmic agreement, like in those extinct Village basement clubs. He's the perfect Irish school lad who has taken his music lessons and practiced. I remember Shandy from the days when there was shrieking and keening and little girls sobbing with balked lust; I remember when he used to slither and leap all over the stage, snaking his microphone, with his milky-white girl's arms, smutty rimmed eyes, and the back of his pants cut out to show his buns.

Shandy's woman comes out on stage, the crests of her breasts bobbing from this Versace jeweled bustier, one of those thirteen-thousand-dollar ones in the shape of a heart. She is carrying him a glass of tea; the plumes of smoke rise up into the blue spots that follow her black leggings. Kind of an unserious look—except that Versace, along with Howard Goldenson, has underwritten the dinner, and that makes it all right.

"The reason I first went to the rain forest is that she made me go. We are a partnership of concern," Shandy says, introducing a video of trees and waterfalls and the complex ecosystem of birds and turtles and two-thirds of the plant and animal species of the world. There's a close-up of a fungus on a tree. "The cure for cancer and AIDS could be growing here. Every second, we lose an area the size of a football field. An area the size of Pennsylvania is destroyed in less than fifty years. We are losing people, too." There is a picture of Shandy himself hopping in the waters with the Indians. Among the upturned faces, I see Jack Kahn, a medical man after all, and, two rows behind him, Veronica, who seems to be with Sandy Fisher. Jack is looking at her, only her. "All things are connected—the Indians, the forest, the planet."

Yes, we are all connected: Shandy and Chief Rani with the clay plate in his lip. The Pimpernel. Chica Starck, the Native Americans, Sylvester Stallone, Boots Simpson, Jimmy Dell, Jack, Veronica, Olivia, Danny Gates, Veritas, all in the same rotting ecosphere. The beluga whales, the Eastern spinner dolphins caught in the plastic filament of the tuna drift nets, the vanished socialites, the weeping statues, the omnipresent and the endangered, the photographers and the photographed, the bison, the great horned owl, the grizzly bear and the yellow spotted salamander, the head of Tribeq Records, Gianni Versace, Howard Goldenson, Senator Graber, Count Farnaut. All in this together, all people who live with the idea that the fires are getting closer.

And where do I now fit in the food chain of concern? I am adrift, a bird on its back with feet up in the air twitching, a spaceman bobbing somewhere in the deep black on the thinnest of lifelines, looking down, seeing the mysterious water coming from the eyes of the plaster saints, trying to understand the manifestations, the bleeding priests.

Shandy bows off for an intermission as a picture of the smoking forest stays on the screen.

"It's so low-key," someone says.

"It's so relaxed."

Now we are all pushed aside for the large train carrying the movie star, with two guards in front and two guards behind him, one uniformed guard flanking each side. The star is fairly young, but his face has the rough, red, boiled quality of drink, and his cheeks look like they have been pressed to the pavement all night. His hair hangs in dreadlocks of grease, and his eyes are wild and red. His overcoat, which he keeps on all evening, flaps apart as he moves through the crowd with a violence to his walk, determined to see nothing but merely to pass through, receive his stares, and punish us for looking at him. He has the new model from the Roots campaign with him, and she defies his messiness with her perfection.

She sees three of her supermodel friends towering over the crowd, talking to each other, and she reaches out to wave to them, but the star will not let her break from his circle. The three form their own league, giant girl creatures from elsewhere, and they look only into the frightening beauty of each other's velvet faces. They are all over six feet, and the black leather pants the blonde wears rather touchingly fall three inches above her ankle. All the nasties who dress and undress these doll girls and arrange them in poses and curl their hair and paint on their faces are hovering nearby as the girls stand trapped by their height and distracting beauty from being anything but what they are. The movie stars, because their beauty is of a different order and so mixed in with fame and pursuit, try hard to look as scruffy and disappointing as they do, and thus need their bodyguards around them to be noticed.

Chica and Blanca and Veronica and all the great New York beauties pretend to ignore these girls, all young enough to be their daughters, and the models ignore them as well, unimpressed by their clothes and jewels and husbands. They are taken, however, with Chief Rani, which causes the greatest photographs of the night.

Jack has been stalking Veronica, placing himself in her sight lines and staring, and I see that he is affecting her and she swivels in the crush so that she does not see him. She moves away and tries to hide inside the crowd.

When we return, there's a new lineup silently staring out at the audience: one rain forest Indian with a headdress of yellow quills, with one red feather in the center quivering in the blue spot, his lower lip stretched over a red clay dessert plate; one American Sioux chief, costar of a recent movie; and one Jewish composer with a flute and love beads over his jacket who plays as the Sioux chief reads a two-hundred-year-old letter that later is exposed as a hoax.

"The white man is a stranger who comes from the night. I am a savage and I do not understand. I have seen a thousand rotting buffaloes shot from a train. What is man without the beasts? All things are connected. Where is the eagle? Gone." The musician stops playing the flute and shakes a tin canister-like instrument.

Chief Rani talks, answering the question of many in the audience. It's a long speech in Portuguese uttered around the plate. The audience is at first completely silent. The plate—no one can stop watching it. How did it get there? How does it stay? How does he sleep? I must ask Boots. We are all connected. The blonde with the dribbling hair in the rump hugger and black boots; the burning world; Athena, who woke up this morning and felt it was going to be one of her hot days; the gasping fish; turtles without sand for their eggs; the chief of Bear Stearns; Veronica's team on the terrace spraying the feathers with criminal hairspray. Aboriginal Australians, northern Inuits, African Dogons. Lancadone Mayans. Greenpeace volunteers placing themselves between the whales and the explosive harpoons, out on the ice floes to protect the whitecoat harp seal pups from the bloody clubs of the seal hunters. And, hey, Jambo friends, what about the Eastern Arc Rain Forest at the Yale Club? No one is translating Chief Rani, and on he goes.

"Keep it short, Chief!" says a voice from the audience, finally, but it has been six minutes and they're mostly still silent, proving that repentant New York, in the grip of its new seriousness, will listen to anything. Only so long, however. Applause starts. A woman comes and taps the chief, but he goes on. More applause to stop him, but what can he think?

"He has said, 'Leave the forests alone. Leave the Indians alone,'" the woman translates, kind of tugging him off. Then come the old Brazilian samba stars and the swaying girls with their angel voices—the other Brazil of bossa nova and those Rio women in Paris couture gliding round the room, of roués in nightclubs and girls in thongs walking Ipanema to the sea when it was still safe.

This light music puts everyone in a good mood for dinner, which is exploding in many rooms of the Tavern on the Green.

"I feel very bad for you, Libby," Veronica says, scooping up my hands. "What can we do to help? And thank you for getting Danny to the movies—but, of course, nothing could get him *here.*"

Sandy has walked on ahead and is hovering, pretending to study the Tavern souvenirs and artifacts. Behind him surges the Pack—the Jameses, the young Hammermans, the Barnetts, the other music people, the studio head, and Helen are all trying to get through the narrow mirrored hall without separating or becoming struck motionless by their own reflections. They keep collapsing their circle, their raccoon eyes, permanently dark with the remains of previous substance abuse, looking back for each other, now swallowing the model and the senator but managing to exclude his aide.

As usual, they are trying to find their way to a private room, a little niche set apart and roped off to preserve their specialness. Wherever they are, they always steer themselves to an upstairs room with unmarked doors and large guards where they can isolate themselves with each other. All of this is an unconscious movement back to their days in the basement at Studio 54. They are trying so hard to get back into that lost room of their youth.

The Pack is truly of this new age, being so private and insecure they are invisible. They are addicts of hidden luxury, reveling in the secret ostentation of their white houses. They are always in motion, always packing up and boarding their G-4's. They give the impression of activity, movement from vacation to vacation, snow to sun, collecting younger, thinner, more famous people on the way. Not young themselves, they are merely childless, rich, and sexually experimental enough to move carefreely. Through the grinding of the Jeep's gears as it climbs the corniches of St. Bart's come their shrieks of private hilarity.

They shoot down the hall, dangling little cameras so they can catch each other looking good. There is a tension between the two groups as the Pack passes through the others in the narrow hall. The Pack bobs through, unseeing, carefully mussed, their lower halves defiant, the men in jeans and cowboy boots with their dinner jackets, the women with motorcycle jackets over dresses on their thin, trained bodies, and the others fall back against the walls, feeling overdressed and ridiculous with their jewelry and big dresses. As they pass us, Helen reaches out and scoops up Veronica, whispering to her.

How could I not have seen it? The Pack has taken her. She has found her set. She has been ready for them all along, with her green, her Shakti Gawain, her obsessive concern for what she puts into her body, her need to wander in luxury. Perhaps she has always belonged, but hasn't found her way to them till now. She never looked convincing in any of her new clothes with her bright hair and her spirit way up in the air—the wild bird that flew into the room.

"You've been talking to Jimmy," Blanca says, putting herself in front of me, huffing up her shoulders. I look behind her and follow the progress of Chief Rani's yellow and red feathers trembling through the crowd, walking through that lit-up glass box with all the colors and the electricity in the trees overhead. Chief Rani, from the forest to the Crystal Room, where the sky is falling, the world is burning.

"How do you think he eats with the plate in his mouth?" says Blanca, pausing for a moment to stare at the feathers and bits of bone in Chief Rani's ears. "I'm telling you, Jimmy is dangerous. What room are you in?"

Since we are both in the Crystal Room, the best room, we walk in together following Jack Kahn. The favors are wooden rain sticks, which the Indians have made with tribal decorations on the sides and filled with little seeds. You turn them over and they make the tinkly sound of water in the rain forest. All over the room guests are playing with them, but the gentle water sounds are lost in the clinks of forks and glasses. All the women also have burlap sacks of Roots, the new cosmetic line made without animal testing. A little piece of paper falls out of my pouch, saying, "One touch of nature makes the whole world kin."

"We—my former company—did some of the research for this," Jack says, stopping behind my chair as I study the tube of cream with no animal-derived ingredients. His heavy hands are on my shoulder, which means he wants something.

"I've missed our talks. It seems you're always on the wrong side of these things," he says, sitting down next to Blanca.

"Yes, she talks to Jimmy all the time. She believes *him*," and then Blanca whispers my recent fate to Jack.

"Really," he says, and looks at me again. "Those are beautiful earrings, Blanca. Would you sell them to me?"

"We have so much in common with these tribes from the forest," Athena is saying, smoothing the front of her white suit hung with chains not dissimilar to Rani's bead bandolier and sitting down. "Yes, half-naked and hung with jewelry. And the face painting, the smoking and drinking, and the desire to protect our indigenous territories."

"Well, you're the anthropologist," someone says to Athena, as I notice that Veronica has been placed directly behind Jack.

Shandy walks by Veronica and suddenly stops, looks hard, and then falls to his knees and begins whispering to her and everyone watches, finally astonished. He picks her up and hugs her.

"I knew her from the Canyon, when she was Sunshine," he says to the table. "Making our garden, writing those little books in her own runic language. Right, Sunshine? Come sit with me later. No one knows where you went."

"She has to wear Armani. She works for Armani," a voice says. "Did you bring the Xanax?"

"I can dig it," Helen is saying, "S&M Music Factory," as Blanca dives under the table and begins patting the floor with her hands. She comes up, her eyes wildly circling and so flushed I think she may be having some sort of choking or panic attack and I half rise to help. A piece of hair has fallen from her professionally tousled tower and swung forward on her cheek, and then I see she is wearing only one of her famous earrings, the huge ruby pansies with the moveable petals.

"My earrink! What is the earrink?" She looks at Jack. "I showed you my earrink!" forgetting her new whispery voice.

"I do not have your earring, Blanca."

She stands up, and I know she is looking for Philip Ives or Bill Pope, who she must have forgotten has finally gone to Hazelden. She looks ready to scream.

"I tell you I do not have her goddamn earring! Does anyone want to search me?"

Chica has twisted around from another table. The Barnetts are also staring at him.

"It's all right, Jack," Athena says, and I watch Veronica, knowing from the tilt of her head she hears his name.

"Oh my God! Oh my God! What can I do? You son of a bitch! Where's Philip?"

There is such a silence pooling around our table that I can actually hear the rain sticks and the sound of Patty Barnett popping the lids off the plastic containers of food that her chef has packed for her. The rest of the Pack turns as one. "How cheesy! Why have jewelry if you can't afford to lose it? Why the fuss?" their dead eyes say.

"Where did she get them? Van Cleef's?" someone says.

"No, JAR made them for her in Paris. I think they're his best work."

Now everyone dives under the table and begins ostentatiously patting themselves down. Blanca does not move, but glares at Jack.

"You shit!" she whispers in one of those displays that makes people either look away or stare because they know they will spend half the next day describing the scene on the phone and they must get it right.

"What would I do with one of your earrings?" Jack says to Blanca.

"You'd have it copied for . . . for . . ." and she looks around and settles on Athena, who wipes her forehead and shakes her heavy hair.

"This is unfair," Veronica says, suddenly standing over Blanca. "Let's go back to the entrance and then we'll go to the bathroom and you can take everything off, Blanca. That's only right." Her voice is so low that Blanca stands up almost in a trance and the two great beauties walk from the room with their arms around each other, their dresses trailing and their eyes down, studying the patterned carpet.

Jack is turning over his rain stick, his face very white, watching Veronica leave as though he has never seen her before.

"How are things going for her? She looks so different."

"Gates is not in a very good mood. She has no one to talk to and he won't let her go away. Maybe you should not have bought his company and thrown him out."

"Aurora is suffering, and I am too. Do you think this has played itself out? Could I do anything for her? I am very tired of all this," he says, looking around. "How can anyone act like that woman?"

"I haven't stopped seeing you at all these places. You're just another rich guy saying to himself 'What am I doing here?' but afraid you'd be missing something if you don't go," I say, looking out to the hallway, where Blanca has paused to adjust the strap of one of her evening sandals, that eternal feminine gesture old as the Maenads. Veronica stands beside her, and then both of them dive for the floor and come running back.

"We found it. It was down my chest. I didn't even feel it. Veronica saw it drop out," Blanca says, and everyone is thinking that that's what happens when you have fake titties—you can't feel a thing.

Jack does not answer but stands up and goes around to Veronica's table, and I see him bending over her. "At least talk," he says. But her head is down and the lights dim, for Shandy's woman has more to say. Blanca is playing with her recovered pansy, and when I look back for Veronica, she is standing with Jack in the hall as Shandy passes by them and almost stops, but Jack has picked up her hand and is separating the pale fingers, and I know he is making his deal.

XXIII

Earth Movers

On the brick wall in the office of the landscape architect the project was labeled "The Kahn Residence," and those waiting for the slow loft elevator to mount eleven floors had a lot of time to study its grandeur and scope. I looked at the drawings, as Sandy insisted. Behind us, twenty or so young men sat outlining little trees and bushes on long sheets of paper. It was completely silent in the loft, and I got the sense they were waiting for us to leave before some secret explosion of fun would begin.

Sandy, now my friend again, felt responsible for the project, as if he had begun it himself. He had been there when the large earth movers lifted sections of inferior hills and dug up the unacceptable trees. The road was rutted, and the only neighbor, far distant, had been disturbed to the point of a lawsuit. He was there for the daily procession of trucks carrying better, imported rocks and trees with giant burlap sacks around their root balls. He watched when the rocks were placed and the hills were raked because it disturbed Jack to look up a slope filled with seasons of dead leaves. Jack had prepared this place for Veronica's return even before she had left.

Next to the rendering of the house and grounds was a second

long diagram, this of an immense glass pyramid, and a third showed it in relation to the house. It was an ominous-looking structure, as is any pyramid, and its size taunted the smaller house.

Shelby, the architect, came up to us. "We pruned all the mature trees and fertilized them," he said, pointing to a painted grove. "If something short-lived was adjacent to an oak, which goes on hundreds of years, we'd just remove it in deference to the oak. That's why England looks the way it does—years and years and years of relentless pruning."

"It can go on forever," I whispered, looking at his face. He was very tan but not well.

"Yes, it takes the rest of your life and an open pocketbook, which Jack Kahn has. It's the best work I've ever done," he said, and as the elevator door shut, I saw him rest his sun-bitten face on the wall.

"Shelby's very excited about this, especially the pyramid," Sandy said. "I don't think it's ever been done before for a greenhouse. He always wanted to do a big one since he fell for Doris Duke's."

He had double-parked as usual and tore up the ticket on his windshield. We had to stop by my house for the suitcases, for we were going up to the "residence," as I now would think of it, for the weekend, and he had gone downtown only to give Shelby some notes. He belonged to the lady Veronica now and was no longer quite at ease with me. He was held in residence there, in that limbo between friend and servant, a semipermanent guest, shambling around in his linen suits and straw hats, loping over the hills in his tan buck shoes. He was the substitute body to talk to when one of them was in town. He invited their guests, met trains, sat under an umbrella at the pool stoking the conversation, and formed a large buffer zone at the dinner table, which was often joined by Helen Kasmanian. After her hastily issued *Collected Lectures* had flopped, she had been abandoned by the Pack and now treated Kahn's house as her own private Yaddo, sometimes even feeling comfortable enough to bring

Marianna along. Then, the two large people sat at the table, lapping over their chairs in a configuration Aurora already understood. Marianna and Sandy had developed an immediate antipathy. They were both going to be there this weekend.

Sandy asked me how I felt now that I had fully regained the Pimpernel. Indeed, many things had changed so quickly. When Lightfoot's diaries were finally published in hardcover, they too had not sold well. People felt they had read them before, and here it is always the ability to seem new. Lightfoot left for Hollywood to do the screenplay for real money, and Carter had asked if the Pimpernel would again appear three times a week. I had finally gone to a modest syndication.

Boots was working on the draft of her garbage thesis, getting ready for her orals, going from a sludge facility in the Bronx to dinner at Holly Whitney's. She did manage to have one party. Less than a year after the Gulf War, she had given a dinner for the Syrian ambassador. Everyone stood and raised their glasses. "It is a time to heal," Boots had said. Chica had left Veritas and was working for pro-choice groups. Jimmy Dell was in court vindicating himself. Veritas, more Wall Street than ever, was very hot and had decided to honor Gigi Farnaut after all. The Boys' Club Settlement Showhouse this year was in the mansion of a man who had to leave town because his newspaper business had failed and the contractor had taken over the house. My neighborhood bookstore had also failed, and they packed up their leftover books in shopping bags from the music store next door, which had gone out of business.

The Pack, the no longer quite so new order, had retreated to East Hampton and were riding their Harleys and being waited on in their bare white mansions with nutritionists in the kitchen, the live-in tennis pro at the breakfast table, and the personal trainer unpacking his weights with a clunk on the white gravel of the driveway. The Solomons had gone to Eastern Europe. Hugo Salm had finally slowed down somewhat and had begun to wear a small hearing aid. Lampwick had never reopened. The scaffolding had disappeared from around my house, but in the bare light my dog shook even more wildly.

I asked Sandy if the Kahn place had been named yet, but he made me wait until we came to the entrance, for now there were large wrought-iron gates and a gatehouse and a plaque that said "Pyramid House."

"At least North America rewards some of its scientists," he said, and I was glad we had started to think the same thoughts again.

Everything was beautiful, since all nature's mistakes had been pried up and raked away. All the planting was clipped and symmetrical and matching. If on one side of the long road stood a huge rhododendron bush, it was the same on the other, and all the vistas were mirror images of each other. Shelby had taken a giant scissors to the whole property and clipped away to make his own final little England. It was almost shocking—even to Sandy, who had watched it all happen, who had gotten them Shelby and, I'm sure, a cut of Shelby's commission. A dark Mercedes passed us, driven by Kahn's driver, and I saw Aurora sitting in the backseat, alone and perfectly centered.

Jack and Veronica were standing in front of the house, having been buzzed by the guard at the gate. They were standing so close, without a sliver of air between them, that they seemed never to have been separate. Veronica rested her head on Jack's shoulder as he turned toward her and cradled her in the arc of his arm. We were looking at a statue of the way they wanted to be perceived, and behind them rose the huge point of the pyramid, for which no scale map could have prepared me. It seemed to pierce the first low cloud and glinted in the sun bouncing from its facets. The trees around it had been pruned into perfect topiary trees, all in obedience to this other kind of beauty that forgives neither flaws nor trees that do not live forever. It was a very lonely sight, like the child lined up in the center of the seat in the navy car.

Even in the country, Veronica had kept her new look, as

though a remote tropical bird had flown into eastern Connecticut for a brief season. Her clothes made no concession to the
state. Behind Veronica a chill streamed from the open door of
the white marble house, in contrast to the glare from the facets
of the pyramid. Though both sustained life, the two structures
were tombs, the pyramid a gesture large enough to call down the
evil eye. It was beyond anything Fisher had described, and I
knew I would not have the words when we got out of the car.

They were ready for the tour that people with recent money
feel impelled to inflict, assuming that every detail of their taste
must be laid immediately before the guests. But this was
Veronica's way of getting me alone as we walked, and I duti-
fully marveled my way through her arbor on the way to the
greenhouse.

"I've heard about the collaboration," she said.

"Then you must be talking to Danny, because nobody else
knows—not Sandy, not my agent or his lawyer—and we haven't
even begun yet."

"He has such a story to tell—but then, we all do—even you,
Libby, I'll bet."

"Even now, I don't quite know your story," I said, thinking
of Shandy and his "Sunshine" but no longer much caring. We
were in the greenhouse, and Veronica, showing off, pressed a
button that dropped enormous shades of parachute silk to shelter the plants from the full intensity of the noon sun. I saw a
small plaque hung by the switch at the doors and went over to
read it. A calligrapher had copied out a quote from Truman
Capote, and it was framed by an expensive gold frame such as
one might use for a painting.

"Jack's present," she said, reading it out. " 'It is instructive to
watch the mistress of the manor wandering around their misty
subtropical interiors adjusting a hyacinth here, straightening an
orchid there; she seems so exotic; and, I can't say why, a bit
sinister. . . . Perhaps the atmosphere of hothouses, the quivering
green light, the verdant haze scarcely rippled by slowly turning

fans, makes everyone look like that.' Jack found that in one of my books in the middle of the night and was so excited he ran in to show it to me. He likes the 'sinister' part, of course, but he has forgiven me." She turned and dared me to doubt her, but I kept thinking of how her new puffed up lips had barely been able to get around all those words.

As we moved along the rows, I could feel the moisture sliding down my nape and trickling along the sides of my body and I felt almost faint with the green and the colors and the odors of the soil and leaned against one of the cold frames. Despite the size of the place, the atmosphere was dense and moist, all that light and heat captured and blown back down on us by the fans so that the lowest six feet were now the warmest. It was a mature environment of things grown elsewhere, in other nurseries and hothouses, and brought in for this weekend's show. Veronica, comfortable in the heat, was picking at the camellias, tending them as though she had grown them here from seedlings, quite deliberately acting out the woman of the quotation in the heavy air.

"No bonsai at all. My bonsai professor was heartbroken. I'm out of the club. I resigned Veritas, too."

"When are the others coming?"

"Not till after lunch—we have plenty of time." I looked outside to where Jack was leading Sandy around, gesturing to the bushes, until they both disappeared over a reshaped hill. Jack was not a man who belonged in jeans or cowboy boots, and Fisher was not a fellow at his best in shorts. As I looked at them walking up, I had a terrible sense of burning lava already sliding over the rim of the hill.

"Sandy's been very useful to us. I sent him home to talk to Danny that night of the rain forest and he was thrilled. I don't think he ever got that close in all those years. He had to explain why I was leaving him." I said nothing about leaving those who have already left us.

"I kept all the things you wrote about us, about that time.

Someday I'll show it all to Aurora to help her understand. I think it died because of the press—he's so private, you know," she said.

How could I speak, remembering how excited she was to be, as Chica called it, "in the publicity," how she had said "It was written very nicely" and if she was going to be in the columns, why not like that?

"And now, a whole new old life," I said, waving my arm as far as it would go and still failing the dimensions of the place. We were walking to the white house, which, as she explained, they had tried hard to make theirs, as though every reunion of two souls required its own new mansion to celebrate. The house had been brought back, the marble polishers stirring up clouds of the poisonous dust, the window men fitting the new panes; and Jean-Pierre had covered everything in white until it was just another monochrome interior with small, bright Oriental rugs on the floors like postage stamps. It was not a country house in the country.

Jack had come back from his walk with Sandy, the two of them breathing hard and sweating, and for the first time I saw Jack's forgiveness was complete. Gates was something that had not happened, the story of an old California night that had never been played to its end, the accidental bumping of the wrong stranger.

Donna and Dudley arrived, driving Blanca, who was alone and had been pardoned by Jack for the earring incident. Then Olivia and John came with Helen and Marianna stuffed in the back, and Marianna frowned at Sandy. Gigi Farnaut's driver carried in his luggage and carried it out when he found he was not in the main house. He was supposed to have been with the Barnetts, that couple from the Pack, but they had canceled at the last moment. I guessed they had called the rest of their group and found that none of the others would be there, and were too rich and insecure to chance it. Jack made them uneasy. He was both hopeless and smart enough to have figured them out and rejected them already. He couldn't play. He sat with the Pack one night, the spiritual grandfather of the table, about as far from rock and roll as anyone can get. How could they read a man whose eyes would rise for neither a pretty girl nor boy, a man you could never put in the first row at a fashion show, however he was dressed and even if he owned the house? When Veronica returned to him, they didn't get it; but then, none of them believed in history.

Peter Crothers, one of those political movie stars, arrived last, and everyone tensed up and began to perform. Jeeps were crunching up the gravel, taking guests to the other three houses on the property, for Kahn's house was too small for them all.

I was there as the Pimpernel, and Veronica had obviously explained it to everyone, for the smiles were the old ones, comfortable with success, innocent of suspicion. With each arrival there was a new procession into the greenhouse, though most of them, unlike the English and the born rich, found gardens boring. Plants took too long and didn't return enough. They didn't understand them unless they had been brought in blooming on a truck, and some of them ripped up their annuals the minute they died and replaced them with others so that theirs were gardens of the constant conquest of death. I saw Chica rolling her eyes above Veronica in the greenhouse as she was naming the plants. "Who did this place?" Chica said finally.

"Shelby."

"Oh, I thought he was dead. I heard he was dead."

"Your pikake is mislabeled," said Gigi Farnaut.

It was going to be one of those nervous weekends where there was always the sense that something better was going on in another place, that round the corner or down by the pool the group was more amusing. The star made it that way. These weekends required sets of clothes and moods, like a beauty pageant with its costume changes, and many eyes were always watching your backside as you walked away from the constant activity and constant talk. Only the star and Helen did not bother to participate, but sat hunched over each other. "I think I was in this movie," I heard Crothers say. "Someone always gets murdered at one of these."

I went back to my room to change. Someone had been busy making it perfect, and I wondered what was left to do when the last white piqué tissue holder and set of electric rollers and fruit basket had been inserted in the last guest suite. I looked at the books by the bed, which of course included the Lightfoot diaries and Helen's collection.

We were having drinks in the pyramid, the front of which looked down the hill. A tornado of gravel dust spiraled up from the gates and we followed the white plumes as they curled up the hill. Someone was driving very fast through the shimmering bands of heat.

I turned to ask Jack who else he was expecting, but he had gone to call the guardhouse. A black Ferrari pulled up right in front of the house. Danny Gates, wearing a deep blue silk shirt and very tight tan pants, threw one leg over the side of the car and jumped out. He shook back his hair as he stared into the faces lined up inside the pyramid and sheltered his eyes, trying to sort them out. He walked into the pyramid, and as they recognized him, one by one they stood up in half unconscious tribute to fame, ruin, and beauty.

"Hope I'm not too late for a drink?" Danny said at the door. "What's a house party without the unwanted guest!"

He still had the timing of the actor he had been, I thought, as I watched him walk in. He did not look at Veronica or me.

"What has happened to him?" Chica said. Jack—who had, after all, entered New York rimmed with guards—was nervous with any intrusion but had actually paled at the sight of Gates.

"No one knew he was coming," I said to clear myself.

I knew how to be a step ahead and walked past where Kahn, facing Gates, was now talking in the glass hall that joined the pyramid to the house. I went into the library, where I knew they would go next, and was pouring myself a drink when they walked in. There had been no tour.

"I thought you didn't drink," Gates said.

"Oh, sometimes," I said.

Gates did not look too good up close. There were flecks of dandruff on his dark blue shirt, and he was very thin. He looked at me as though I should leave, but I did not move.

"I want my business back. I've raised the money," he said, throwing himself into a puffy white chair and dangling his feet over the side. He was wearing driving shoes without socks, and he swung them back and forth in Jack's face. Jack could not stop watching the shoes. I felt a rustling in the house, as though everyone was making a sudden movement for this room to hurl themselves at the keyhole. But I was there. As I had learned from my one political campaign, placement is everything.

"Howard says he should handle this, but I wanted to speak first. I guess this isn't a very good time for you."

Jack was still watching the dangling shoes, examining them, and then Gates began to pace, a soft, pantherish pace, and poured himself a drink, and Kahn watched him toss it down. Jack put his hand down on the edge of the bar, but it slipped off.

Gates was sweating. He had managed to make himself look very unwell.

"Are you all right?" Jack said. Suddenly he had no voice, as though he had not yet stolen the right words, and the formal way he spoke could not answer Gates. Gates was like a wounded animal let into the room, and Jack could only observe, afraid to stretch out a hand or protect himself in the wrong way.

"I guess it's not a very good time. But I do have the money. And now things are important." Gates had lowered his voice to that croon he once must have used on the middle-aged buyers when he sat across a table from them and picked up their hands and pressed them back into the banquette with his eyes. What a good actor he was after all. What a good salesman—to leave the threat unsaid but somehow there when he left.

"I heard you were here. Rescue me!" said Peter Crothers, bursting in, but then, seeing Jack, he backed out. We heard the sound of a helicopter overhead. Outside the new grass flattened as it set down.

"That must be Howard," said Gates. "He has my whole offer—I hope you can put him and Laurie up here. Looks like you're pretty full. I guess it's not a very good time for you. That's a hell of a pyramid. Mind if I let Libby take me around?"

We ran out to the helicopter. "That was quite a performance," I said into the roar.

"Are you sure?" Gates said, but I was sure.

XXIV

"That She Did Pity Them"

We had long ago decided that I
would be the one to write the story of Gates's return. I was the
only one to "get the excitement of it," he said—the same thing
Jimmy Dell had once said to me. I had been there for some of
it, and I went back to "out there." We both knew it would be
a good story, because as much as everyone enjoyed a fall, they
also liked those who crawled up from their holes and took back
their territories. The city was now filled with collapsed stars,
walking bankrupts, a whole new class of the broke and the
ruined but still out and about. They needed manuals for their
comebacks.

There were parts of this, like the end with Jack, that could
never be told quite as they happened. I was to tell Gates's life
but make it like one of his window fantasies—full of infinite
promise, suggesting good things and gentle, forgiving worlds. I
would be creative with facts like the source of Gates's fresh new
money, the restructuring of his company's debt. It was the
Japanese, seduced by his image and a few long nights at his
home, who had bailed him out just before Japan itself collapsed.
"Anyhow, this is not a business book," he kept saying. I could
not quite understand why he now wanted to "tell himself."

Perhaps he wanted to be understood and to understand it all himself in the telling. Our contract said he would have to do television, and he practiced by watching the afternoon shows, thinking how he would answer the questions, staring into the faces of the innocent and angry audiences he could not believe existed.

I was being very well paid for the book, and it pleased me to inform Carter I would be taking the rest of the summer off. I had been in too many crowded rooms, bumping through that same wall of eyes and teeth. My creatures had gone off to their good deeds and private sins, and now that I had lost them or they had left me, I was free. No more "Joy to the World" in the Temple of Torment. I might never go back, and it gave me great pleasure to toss out those invitations for the American Hospital in Paris and for the Foundation for the Art of the Painted Finish.

Danny had bought back his name. When he walked into the store with his new desert tan the young blond girls had raised up on their tasseled toes and actually started clapping, and the people from out of town, who only dimly recognized him, had instinctively moved towards the commotion to be closer to him.

We started our work upstairs at the store, but even though he had given me an office, there were too many interruptions. Other voices appeared on the tapes, indecipherable whisperings and laughter. There were calls that could not be held and constant papers, some pinned with swatches of fabric, being put in front of him. Eventually we switched to his house. Though it was risky, I had brought my painting over, and it hung behind me on a wall he had cleared. I would turn around to it from the bulletin board stuck with note cards of dates and names, people who had vanished from Gates's life, leaving only their photographs behind. I flattened out the folded sheets of paper that he had saved from his pockets—smoothed them out and tried to understand just as though they and he were important as we shared our worship of his life.

Then I would turn around into the tiny landscape and enter the house. The "Gates" I had created would be waiting and I could say everything I had forbidden myself to say outside in the fire of the dead sun. Another door was here, invisible from the outside. I could walk out, but I was not ready. I put my hand out and felt the bones of his back. I had touched him only once and never would again.

L'Arbre d'Or had hung in the vanished apartment on a bent nail covering the three holes around it. It was somewhere near the peach silk curtains and the old wooden game with the marbles. In the summer the furniture around it was slipcovered in white linen. It shone there alone and abandoned, for we were off with the magicians of my summer birthdays. Then, wrapped in a towel, it was carried to the smaller apartment from which it was taken away, disgraced and probably fake, but not to me.

Gates and I planned to spend a week at his country house for the final stages of the book, but for now we were staying in town. Josie had gone to her camp in Maine. Gates tore through his rooms, going through his files. Girls flitted all over the house in light clothes, some his "assistants," others waiting with their model portfolios, leaning against the halls or down by the pool. They tossed their hair and kept their portable phones pressed to their impossible faces as they balanced appointment books on knees brushed by the last summer sun. They would kick off one shoe and rub the bare foot on the other tan leg and wait.

Some mornings, Gates walked out of the bedroom, with his arm around the girl from the night before. She'd go searching for pieces of underwear drowned in the sofa, while yawning and looking me over suspiciously. At least they still did that. Sometimes Danny would forget what he was saying as one of them passed in front of us, posing, sucking on her Glacier water, and he'd get up and take her by the elbow and whisper and I'd know he was asking her to come back that night. Those were the girls I really looked at, the ones for future arrangements.

Sometimes we sat in the garden and argued over everything. We disagreed on the title, how and where we would begin. His facts were usually wrong, and he had no comprehension of time or dates, before or after. He had never kept a journal, but he did have appointment books—all bound in luxurious maroon leather and filled with names he had forgotten. He was more interested in his pictures, and he had thousands. He began calling them his archives. He had files, scrapbooks, large parts of his life documented as though he had always been planning to come back to them, but there were gaps. The time with Nadia was blank, and we still could not find her. He now refused to discuss his family, and he had left a big hole in his boyhood. Many mornings he would give me notes he had written the night before, and I realized that this man who had built and regained his empire was almost illiterate.

"You've made yourself an orphan who drops on earth in Hollywood at twenty-five," I'd say. "That won't do."

"Why not? It's all anyone cares about."

Sometimes I would storm out, tired of trying to find other people's voices, telling other people's stories. He wanted the book to have "magic" and all his dreams. "What's wrong with reality?" I'd say, but he was still looking for Nadia and the night with Veronica in California, to get them back, to be young.

I had to get him to remember, and he remembered only when he wanted. Then he acted out various scenes, becoming Kesselman getting his toenails clipped at a meeting or the casino boss shaking his head or the fashion editor who had leaped in the air with her bangs flying when she saw his first things. I had made a brief effort to check some of the stories, and so many were lies or improvements that I had given up. I never tired, however, of hearing his voice or watching his face. I guess that's what beauty is all about. It can be endlessly watched. It can be broken down into its components—eyes, nose, hair—and survive. To me, he was always as he had been when I first knew him, when he gripped my elbow as we hurried through the sound lots and he turned to me and really wanted me to like him.

He was very optimistic these days, no longer afraid of failure. He was launching Green Rain and looking everywhere for his Rima. He knew the face he wanted to see peering through the leaves but had not found it yet.

We were almost at the Veronica chapter and we both knew it.

"I couldn't look at her anymore," he said one day, and when we got to that California night, I asked him what he had been reviving.

"She was in a bad situation. She needed my help," he said.

Then he told me, now that it no longer mattered. They had been outside with his dying roses falling over the fence and his dark blue pool, heated to a fever, the petals falling and that sound of the water circulating. She had bent down to pat Peter's dog, which he had just taken from the pound, but she had been too sudden and the animal had lunged and bitten her above the lip. Gates was always ready to run from any emergency, but Peter was out, so she had bled in his kitchen among the ruins of the party (Gates always sent his rented staff away at night, whatever the mess). He fished for ice among the rows of melted buckets and had driven her to the emergency room, trying to go fast, though he had never quite learned how. Above his monogram on the towel her pale eyes had studied him, but she was shaken with the pain and crying, and even with all his pharmaceutical knowledge (until now devoted to preparations for amusing himself), he could see she was going into shock. He kept talking and talking and not allowing her to lower the towel to look at her lip. A friend of his passed them on Sunset and thought he had beaten her up, and the towel was getting redder and her eyes were getting larger, her lashes matted with tears into the points of stars. The triage desk was, of course, very busy and hot, and there were lots of people ahead, moaning and pressing various bloody towels to their bodies, and young guys slumped over holding their bellies, and people trying to be brave until their painkillers took effect. There were pretty people full of California cocktails mixed in heated spoons. There was a waiter who had been stabbed in the hand by the cook in his restaurant when he tried to reach for the spaghetti pot. The bartender, a young woman in a blue shirt, had brought him in, and she was telling it all to a young actor, who had recognized Gates and whose fiancée had an ulcer.

It was the perfect way to begin to love someone without making any effort, which is what Gates liked, a medical situation that reduces one to real names and mumbled dates. Veronica had to give her date of birth, address, and occupation, and each question both reduced and intensified her mystery. They found themselves alone in that other dimension, both for once powerless, deprived of their courts. He was a stranger, and yet he knew her data, had seen her dependent—bleeding on him, leaning on him, her thin shoulders shaking and her long gold legs sticking out from the metal chair. Around them in the bright light was pain and a roomful of stories and the whole charged atmosphere of medical drama. Palm trees smacked against the windows. They had half watched a horror movie with Piper Laurie, and always after that Gates had smiled whenever his friend Piper came on the screen, because she too was part of that night. The movie made no sense at all, but heightened everything with its scenes of severed heads and eyeballs floating in jars. (By this time in his narration Gates was up and almost dancing.)

They had begun to look at each other—she hurting above the bloody towel, he more than aware that his young face could withstand the lights, both of them for once blessing their beauty and ready to fall on each other, drawn by tenderness but held back by the room and the fact that, at that time, they each belonged to someone else. All the better. He began to perform, using only his eyes. She had widened and narrowed her eyes in brighter lights than these. That's how they spoke for two hours, until her case was deemed sufficiently serious for the plastic surgeon to come in from his date, by which time she was very faint and he was slightly in love. Then some man named Gregory came for her and she was gone, and a few weeks later Gates had, not entirely accidentally, run over the dog in his driveway.

"No, you didn't!" I said.

"It makes the story better," he said.

Gates never spoke to Sandy Fisher again, though I tried to get him to take Sandy back. He talked all the time with Jimmy Dell, who wanted to be written about too, and I could have had a whole industry writing the stories of ruined men.

All I wanted to do was to be one of those girls to get Gates to drink enough one night so we would go upstairs, but in all this time—whatever I wore, whatever I did, however much we argued or laughed—I never again saw any interest. Still, I worked very hard, for that was my only way with him. I had some money now, and after we had finished working for the day I would try to spend it, but I was very lonely any place but in that house, and I shook if he ever put his arm on me and would move slightly away and pick up my notebook and look down. I tried to concentrate, to listen for the water lapping in the pool. I tried to feel its rhythms to stop my drowning heart beating its way against the currents to the safety of the side and the cool of the tiles.

Sometimes, as I was waiting for him, I would go into the kitchen to talk to Peter, who had been with Gates since California and had a much better memory. He remembered Veronica from that night only because the bed had not been slept in, and he told me how he had found two deck chairs piled with blankets pushed together the next morning and blood on the tiles. I could have found out her life, too, if I had wanted.

I heard that Jack and Veronica were separating. Pyramid House was on the market. It was considered unsalable until the pyramid was torn down. It was hard to sell such a big piece of property, and now that everything was fixed, it had to be expensively maintained. Veronica still had a world of rich men and undiscovered islands to explore, though it would get harder each year to find them. Her trust from Jack was enough to stay at Blakes or take the Concorde, as though she had something important to hurry to. It was enough to cruise the Turkish coast and see the Pyramids before they closed, enough to last till she became the lady with the big house on some island where white-faced monkeys hurled mangoes from the trees, greeting the natives by name, someone attractive behind her to carry her parcels and put them on the boat. The captains who handed her on board would be younger each year, until she became spiritually evolved enough to be alone, and then one night she might see that rare island phenomenon known as the "green flash." The sun would sink into the horizon, and all the red and blue rays would be absorbed until there was only a bright instant of green that meant she would have something else to wait for in her life.

Sometimes Fisher helped show Pyramid House. He had nothing much to do now—no one to serve. I still saw him walking along Madison, searching for his lost Veronica, scouting locations he would never use. Once or twice a year, I knew, Veronica would call on him, her rough voice crackling through space from some conveyance, asking him to join her. She would wire him a ticket and off he'd go. I think he lived from trip to trip and tried to think of things to please her in the meantime. I missed him, but we both knew we could never go back to the times when we stood in a corner pointing to some hostess, abusing her room and questioning her origins.

I still saw the Pack cruising through restaurants, and whenever I was with Danny, they stopped and hung around the table, no longer quite as convincing in their leather jackets as their drivers waited outside in their Fords. I noticed they could no longer stifle their yawns when it got to be eleven thirty and were all wearing transdermal "No Smoking" patches. There was an even newer group now, a fraternity of the supermodels, their photographers and courts—all the slaves of beauty. No one could get near them except to stare, and even that was an intrusion. During one notorious incident they took over the only elevator going to a party and held it captive. They brought in bottles of champagne and trays of hors d'oeuvres, and whenever the doors would open they'd be sitting on the floor laughing and hurling out breadballs at the waiting crowds, all of whom were furious but secretly enchanted by their gorgeous childishness.

On visitors' weekend, I brought Danny up to Josie's camp. No Ferrari, I told Peter—bring in the Wagoneer. Gates had never been to Maine, though he had been trying to capture its look for years. He was very concerned about how to dress, and asked me several times. He pulled up in the Ferrari and I saw that, after my whole lecture about fitting in, he had chosen white flannel pants and a black sea-isle shirt with a peach cashmere sweater knotted over his shoulders, thus managing to look exactly like one of those Wall Street bandits on line for the East Hampton Cineplex. He stared unhappily at my clothes and my green rubber gardening shoes, as though I had let him and his wonderful car down.

The little girls were already lined up on the road in their camp uniforms, each searching only for her parents but smiling at the others because that's how they were raised. We passed through their lines, and some of them looked at Gates because they had noticed the car and others, the older ones, because his face and his clothes were so different from those of the fathers panting along with their coolers and tote bags, their bellies hung with cameras. At the end of the path, we still had not found Josie and were faced with fields of straw and mud before we could get to the tents. Gates stood and stared at the scene—the big red wooden bunkhouse, the white tents spread across the fields, the streams of young girls running over the grass. The camp had been planned and maintained to look as it had in the 1930s and thus to suggest to the parents of these private-school girls that life was still that young, comprehensible thing of healthy values and safe journeys with loons popping out of the dark waters at night. In fact it looked like one of Gates's dreamscapes, except for all the fat parents. It was a whole universe, out of his fantasy, created and existing in innocence, not dressed up and recreated by his teams. He looked extremely pleased, as though the scene had captured him, and he set out across the field, his trousers already cuffed with mud, sinking slightly with each step into the puddles.

We found Josie in her tent, which was filled with girlish welcome signs and pictures taped to the walls. On the pole above Josie's bed was a small picture of me in evening clothes and six photographs of her father, from two of which I had been cut. She looked at Danny and scratched a scab on her leg so that it bled. Gates had brought shirts and caps for the whole tent, and the girls all tried them on right away.

There was, of course, a program to follow. Gates liked the horse show with the Irish riding instructress in her tight britches and the little girls bobbing up and down, their legs wrapped around the steaming horses as the dust rose. Their boots dug into the horses' wet sides; their rumps were raised as they cleared the hurdles. Sometimes a hoof would strike the post with a particular hollow pocking sound. The drill team appeared with their pinnies and criss-crossed each other, the horses' bobbed manes bouncing. Gates loved it all and immediately called this his new Gates Classic.

We walked over an old wooden dock that wobbled on its barrel drums to watch Josie in the synchronized swim.

"I heard you, Reed," an older woman said behind us.

I tried to pick Josie out from the other bobbing white caps and tiny arms flashing from the water as the girls formed and collapsed their water flowers. We missed the tennis, but Josie had changed for the gymnastics exhibition on the front lawn. One woman sat on a shooting stick, cradling her Nantucket bag, and looked displeased as her husband, who wore a needlepoint belt with flags, videotaped girls who were not his daughter. All the slenderest girls were lined up in their bathing suits with the parents in a circle around the mats, and the record was started.

> I *was beat,*
> *incomplete,*
> *I'd been had,*
> *I was sad and blue*

Madonna sang.

"My God!" Danny whispered. In their one gesture to capture something of the modern world, the camp elders had let the younger counselors choose the music.

Like a virgin
Touched for the very first time

One by one, the little girls took off across the mats, their thin young legs, slightly muscled, stretching up into the sunlight in practiced slow cartwheels.

Like a vi-i-i-ir-gin
When your heart beats
Next to mine . . .

Now they were ending the cartwheels in splits, rolling across the mats all curled over, going into backbends, these arches of girlflesh in the moist part of the full noon.

Can't you hear my heart
Beat for the very first time,

Madonna sang.

Some girls were up on the bar, now balancing, dancing, and doing all sorts of contortions as the record repeated. Josie's group was still tumbling, their little bud bodies, some on the verge of development, some with tiny sharp breasts, flashed across the mats, hurrying a bit. The parents stood there flesh-bound, mouths slightly dropped, for how could they fail to hear the words, played so loud right into the sunny day? A few of the fathers were swabbing their foreheads, but all pretending that nothing was wrong, it was just another song, no one even daring to look at each other or smile except for Danny, who had to excuse himself and walk up the path a bit.

The girls jumped over the leather horse, danced wobbling on the bar. Now they imitated cats pawing the air, stretching, licking themselves, innocent of provocation. They slithered over the rubber mats, stopping to pull their suits down over their rears or up over the tiny bosoms.

Gates came hurrying back, and I saw him staring into a group of older girls, the junior counselors, who stood over by the main house, talking. Of course it was the dark-haired one, so much taller than the rest and so thin I saw her bathing suit was safety-pinned under her arms. Her hair was pulled back tight from her face. Large, dark eyes slanted up, and she laughed with the other girls and stroked a cheekbone. She stood like a dancer.

"There's Rima," he said, and I let him go forward, out over the muddied field, sinking into the ruts and puddles, his arms wrapped around his body because now he was cold. I watched him heading out toward his next adventure or magic or whatever he would call it. I saw him enter the group. He was talking to her and writing down something she told him, and then he wrote something for her, and all the girls were bending over the paper, examining it, not him. He looked back at me, but I let him go away, and I finally gave up and held Josie close and felt her heart, still pounding from her exertion, through the thin fabric of her swimsuit.

A Note on the Type

The text of this book was set in Simoncini Garamond, a modern version by Francesco Simoncini of the type attributed to the famous Parisian type cutter Claude Garamond (ca. 1490–1561). Garamond was a pupil of Geoffroy Tory and is believed to have based his letters on the Venetian models, although he introduced a number of important differences, and it is to him we owe the letter that we know as old-style. He gave to his letters a certain elegance and a feeling of movement that won for their creator an immediate reputation and the patronage of Francis I of France.

Composed by ComCom, a division of Haddon Craftsmen, Allentown, Pennsylvania. Printed and bound by The Haddon Craftsmen, Scranton, Pennsylvania.